GAT

Matt Drabble

ISBN-13: 978-1481221955
ISBN-10: 1481221957

CONTENTS

CHAPTER ONE

They ran in the dark; the tree branches whipping viciously at their faces. Mother Nature apparently choosing sides. They stumbled and slipped in the mud as the moonlight barely permeated the hanging foliage cover, making their escape all the more difficult and unlikely. They grasped hands in desperation, their palms sweaty with exertion and cold with terror. The man dragged the woman painfully in fear as she lagged dangerously; her breath hitched and struggled as she panted. Panic rose and scaled the fences, rendering her conscious mind useless; all thoughts now were primal and frantic.

The woodland was heavy and unforgiving away from the established paths. The trees were thick and lush, stretching as far as the eye could see, dominating the horizon. The man cared little for what lay in front of them, only for what they were running from. The ground became uneven as they thrashed and crashed through the greenery. The slope became more pronounced as they staggered downwards. The man's feet fought for purchase, and he let go of her hand as he cart-wheeled spinning arms in the air for balance. Suddenly she slipped behind him, her stability lost. He felt her slender weight as it landed, driving both of them forward. He grabbed frantically for a branch to catch them, his hands slapped against barked wood but missed, and gravity had her way. Suddenly they were airborne as the ground gave way. The slope was steep and unforgiving and they fell and rolled as one. Arms were interlocked as they crashed through the trees and shrubs, the wet mud lubricating their mad descent. The man winced more at the noise they were creating than the pain they were causing. The fall seemed eternal, their heads spun as they crashed ever downwards, spinning out of control.

Abruptly the wild ride ended, the man crawled around in the darkness looking for her. His hands scrambled hysterically, looking for her softness amidst the sweet smelling pine. His face was black with mud and filth, his clothes were ripped and torn and a cursory check to his face found sticky wetness from several head wounds. He hoped and prayed that head wounds, although notoriously bloody, were not always serious. He pulled himself along the muddy ground looking for his wife - the silence was deafening- and there were no soft moans or struggling pants. He dragged himself around the meager search area; his left leg hung loose and useless behind him as he crawled. The broken bone shards rubbed agonizingly together and he gritted his teeth against the pain. His hands suddenly snagged on her, several feet away from his starting point. Her cardigan was shredded by the fall; the caressing fabric felt familiar through his fingers. The top had been a birthday present two weeks ago, and what felt like a hundred lifetimes ago. He pulled himself towards her, leaving bloody trails in the wet mud. He heaved himself up and felt for her face in the dark. His fingers traced lovingly over the face that he had kissed a million times before. He found her throat and checked with a trembling hand for a pulse, but it was silent. Her head rolled grotesquely loose on her neck; the break was obvious and fatal. Off in the distance he heard them coming. They were not subtle or stealthy and they charged through the woodland like a herd of rampaging elephants. Their desperation had abandoned all sense of reason; the search party was badly organised and running purely on adrenaline.

Powerful flashlights suddenly pierced the gloom above him to the top of the slope as the first pursuers reached his fall from grace. Loud shouts of excitement mingled with relief rang out to whoops and hollers as they celebrated the successful hunt. He dragged himself to her; he gently pulled her hand over his shoulder in one last embrace and could do nothing but wait.

CHAPTER TWO

Michael Torrance fought to keep his eyes on the road; the dominating skyline was simply breathtaking and was demanding of his attention. The rental car swerved worryingly as his vision drifted again and he glanced over nervously at his sleeping wife. Emily slept on undisturbed, and he sighed with relief. As much as he loved her, the last thing that he wanted was a screaming argument fuelled by exhaustion. She had suggested that they spend the night at the airport motel after the long flight over from England, but he had been desperate to start their new life in the US as soon as possible. It was one of the few arguments that he had won successfully. The tiring travel seemingly robbing her temporarily of her argumentative powers.

The desert stretched out before him as they travelled west; the sloping canyons and sweeping mountains framed the horizon as far as he could see. Michael was thirty four and his wife twenty nine. They had been married for five years with four and a half of them happy. He was English born and raised and had only ever travelled as far as Europe for holidaying purposes. The sheer size and scale of the tiny slice of America that he had witnessed so far was startling. It was one thing to look at images online and imagine, but quite another to see it firsthand. Back in the UK there were rolling hills and green plains, but you would never see a horizon that was completely uninhabited. As he drove, the space just seemed endless as the deserted highway stretched for an eternity and beyond. He had not seen a single car for over two hours now and he luxuriated into the quiet.

Michael was a solitary man by nature and by profession; he was a moderately successful writer of horror fiction. He wasn't about to give Stephen King's agent sleepless nights, but he made a living in a vocation; one that he would have happily maintained as a hobby, even if nobody wished to read his work. He was a quiet man of means and tastes, and often mistaken as a little aloof and distant, but his wife carried the sociable torch in the family. Emily was a teacher and shaper of young minds; she was light and airy where he could be dark and sullen. Emily was outgoing and gregarious; a free spirit, always eager to talk and meet strangers. Their union had baffled many of their independent friends, but they both felt that they filled a missing piece in the other. Emily taught the equivalent of second grade, relishing the enthusiastic and open minds of children as yet unsullied by the world around.

They had met at a party some seven years ago. Michael had been dragged there by his literary agent determined to haul him away from a dark home office and a flickering computer screen. Michael had gone-not quite kicking and screaming-but it had been close. The party was loud and boisterous and Michael had quickly faded into the background. At one point in the evening he had been having a discussion that had rapidly turned into an argument and was threatening to escalate into a brawl. A drunken guest had started in on the disproportionate sentences being handed down to the participants of the previous year's rioting in the capital. Michael was far from considering himself some right wing extremist, but the terrifying loss of order and control had necessitated an extreme response. The drunk had been shouting loudly about the civil rights of the arrested when Michael had lost it.

"What about victims' rights?" He had raged, "Where are the civil liberties groups when it comes to victims? Where are the campaigns for helping them?"

"I suppose that you are part of the hang 'em and flog 'em brigade are you?" The drunk had sneered; his expensive Chardonnay spilling. "You have no idea just what those rioters go through on a daily basis. The sheer desperation of their lives. They were looting just to survive."

"Survive?" Michael had exclaimed incredulously. "I could believe that, and come to understand it if they were carrying out diapers and baby food, but they were taking gaming consoles, televisions, and trainers you dozy prick."

"Oh, I wouldn't expect the likes of you to understand," the drunk had replied condescendingly.

"Well the likes of me are going to give you a slap," Michael had replied taking a menacing step towards the drunkard.

Suddenly a hand at his elbow stopped him mid-step; the drunk's date had appeared and looked up at him with gentle eyes. He was abruptly embarrassed by his behavior. He looked around and saw that he was the outsider here; the judgmental eyes were all condemning him. He had been seconds away from decking the annoying drunk and fulfilling his brutish stereotype in front of the middle class audience. He was born of a working class background but he was abundantly capable of handling an argument without resorting to violence.

"Don't I know you?" The woman asked him distractedly, ignoring her peers.

"I don't think so," he responded, suddenly desperate to leave the party and these people. He'd turned to leave the disapproving stares when he really saw her for the first time. She was around five feet six, slender and petite; she had thick, dark hair that hung in loose waves and the darkest eyes that he had ever seen. He fell deep into those beautiful black pits and was lost forever; they had left the party together and had never looked back.

The hot sun beat down as he drove. He wore camouflage combat shorts and a light cotton shirt, but the heat was still merciless. The sky overhead was the bluest of blue, and wisps of white cloud floated slowly on the limited breeze. The U-Haul trailer behind the rental car rattled along carrying their essentials. The road stretched ahead, holding their future and their new beginnings in fragile hands. Michael felt the sudden pressure in his bladder and pulled the car over to the hard shoulder. Rest stops appeared to be few and very far between on their journey so he figured that no-one would mind if he took a leak out in the open. Emily's head bounced once as they stopped, but then was still again. He greatly envied her ability to sleep regardless of circumstance.

He exited the car and stretched, relishing the release as his spine cracked and neck popped. The narrow highway was still unsurprisingly deserted as he walked to the metallic crash barrier that lined the road and peered carefully over. The canyon fell away sharply; the bottom only just visible. Gravel slipped over the edge as he moved too close and it echoed downwards on descent. He relieved himself over the edge and turned his face upwards to the warming sun; his eyes closed, and a smile on his face. *A new beginning*, he thought.

Their courtship had been smooth and pleasant. Within weeks they'd already felt comfortable and content. There were no great movie style theatrics and histrionics, no professions of love in the rain, no last gasp dashes to the airport. They were in love from the start, and the bond only grew stronger over time. They had dated for only around four months before she moved into his apartment. They soon found that marriage was a logical and inevitable next step. Michael discovered that the marriage had come quickly and relatively painlessly. Unlike a lot of women he discovered that like him, Emily was more interested about being married than getting married. Four years into the marriage, Emily had discovered that she was pregnant; both had accepted the news with happiness and no real surprise. They had never sat down and planned their life together, but both simply knew that these were all things that were meant to be. Michael's career grew steadily; his readers were loyal and decent in number, Emily loved her work and all was as it should be. Perhaps if they'd suffered during their time together, then maybe they would have coped better with the first and only black cloud that fell.

Emily was six months pregnant and waddling pretty well; the night outside was black and the weather was foul. The English winter was in full swing with an icy choke hold, and the sleeting rain fell heavily, making the roads treacherous. Michael was working away furiously, desperate to make his latest deadline when she had come to him requesting that he took a supply run. She had come into his office several times over the space of a couple of hours, each time receiving only a cursory glance, and a distracted promise that he would "go in a minute". Eventually and with only minimal frustration she had snatched up her coat and headed out into the cold, wet night.

Michael was only brought back into the real world when the pounding on his door grew to unavoidable levels; he'd opened the apartment door to a stone faced policeman.

CHAPTER THREE

Emily returned slowly to the world; her sleep drained away back into the darkness and she left the black thoughts behind, where they belonged. She shielded her eyes from the clear sky and blinding sun. The day was hot and the warmth filtered through the windscreen. She checked her watch which read 3.30pm, but her internal clock told her that it was still mid-morning. She marveled at the time travel element of international flights.

She suddenly realised that the car was not only still, but also empty. She looked around with panic. She had seen enough "Innocent travelers fall foul of desert cannibals" movies to be worried when waking sleepily in an empty car. She spun around in her seat, fast enough to crick her neck; her heart skipped a beat until she saw Michael standing over the crash barrier. Her pretty nose crinkled with disgust when she realised that he was happily peeing over the side. She looked away and noticed their surroundings for the first time. She got out of the car, and her breath literally felt taken from her. The sheer scope and natural raw beauty stretched as far as she could see, and she felt dwarfed by the mountains and endless road. She was immediately reminded of the opening scene to Kubrick's Shining movie. She was not a fan of horror in general, but had relented to Michael's assertion that she read the novel. She had been impressed by the abilities of the author and ashamed by her instant dismissal of the novel based solely on the genre. She'd enjoyed the book more so than the film; the idea of a haunted man rather than a haunted hotel was a fascinating deconstruction of the human mind and spirit.

She glanced back over at her husband, her man, as he urinated oblivious to the world; a small smile crept across her face as he raised his arms out in a Titanic pose. For a moment he did look like the king of the world.

"Put that thing away, unless you're going to use it properly," she shouted laughing.

He turned to her with an adorable shy grin. She loved him then. It was complete and absolute, a simple fact of life that he was just going to have to try and accept again. She knew that he carried a crippling heavy burden, one that he refused to unload from his shoulders, no matter what she said. There had been times at the beginning when she had held resentment and anger deep in her chest, but the blackness had never been directed at him. She realised now that he had taken her fury to be aimed at him, and she had been in no state to tell him otherwise at the time.

She had grown infuriated with him on that cold, wet night just under a year ago now. He was lost in his work and dead to the world. She had rung his doorbell and pounded on his metaphorical door, only to have him fail to look up from his book. There were times when he was writing that she felt jealous of the work. The worlds in which he created became his sole purpose, and there were simply no outsiders permitted inside the castle walls. He guarded his writing passionately and aggressively, he never shared his ideas or thoughts, and never sought out hers. She had learnt at a very early stage in their relationship not to trespass into this area of his life. The gates were up and they were electrified. She was heavy with their child and uncomfortable with their joined bulk. She knew that Michael was always worrying about her going out at night, and always insisted on going himself. On the night in question, however, he had been lost in his world of monsters, traversing his hero's path and ignoring her requests for a supply run. In truth, she had desperately wanted to take a relieving stroll out in the cold night air, regardless of the weather. Her back ached from sitting down so much under Michael's loving but smothering care. Eventually she had wrapped herself up warm and dry and left the apartment convinced that he had not even witnessed her leaving. The local shops were only a ten minute walk and the fresh air had felt blissful against her pale skin. The throng of homeward bound travelers on the roads drove noisily and eagerly, their impatience exacerbated by the slow moving traffic. The night was black and the clouds gleefully emptied an ice and slushy mixture of rain and snow, making the roads and pavements treacherous under foot and tire. She never saw the car skid and mount the pavement behind her; she was only dimly aware of screaming people and brakes, and then her world turned black.

She watched him now as he came to her. His six foot frame was leaning toward the soft side; a combination of a sedentary occupation and a lack of life weighed on him. She shook dark thoughts from her mind and ran towards him, knowing that even here, amidst the deserted wasteland, his cheeks would flush beetroot. She leapt into his arms and kissed him passionately; her lips mashed against his and her tongue flicked deliciously into his reticent mouth. After a brief pause he kissed her back, matching her enthusiasm. His body pressed into hers with a familiarity that is the way of lovers of long standing. She broke the kiss and took his hand. Giggling, she pulled him back into the rental car, amused as his face registered confusion when she opened the rear doors instead of the front. She scrambled with her clothing, watching as his eagerness grew to match her own. As he slipped delightfully into her, joining them as one, she whispered professions of love softly into his ear.

They lay sleepily entwined afterwards as always, his head upon her chest as she stroked his hair; this was a time of peace and tranquility between them. The sex they shared had always been warm and tender and she hoped that the frequency could increase in their new life. It was time to truly put the past in the rear view mirror and step full throttle on the gas. There had been far too few smiles and laughter for far too long.

"Come on sleepy head," she roused him gently. "We're supposed to have been there by now," she tapped her watch to illustrate. "Want me to drive?"

"No chance m'lady," he laughed, "Just how would that look to our kind new hosts, first impressions and all that?"

"New beginnings," she said lightly, but her hand gripped his seriously.

"New beginnings," he agreed solemnly.

CHAPTER FOUR

They both gasped aloud when they came around the bend. The world went from a beautiful but desolate wasteland to just simply beautiful. Michael pulled the car over to the side of the road as they took in the vision. The town lay out before them at the bottom of the valley like a stunning painting. White buildings peeked up through perfect greenery. They could see the length and breadth of the town; a town centre square was manicured and lushly green. A steeple chapel stood tall and proud gleaming in the sun. Large, full trees lined perfect streets and the houses stood to attention, spotless and polished. The thick woodlands hemmed in the town from behind as the foliage stretched to the horizon.

"Wow," was all Emily could muster.

"Holy shit," was how Michael more succinctly put it.

"It's like a dream, it's just so, so..." she whispered.

"So perfect," he finished, squeezing her hand tightly before raising it to her hand and kissing it gently.

He put the car into gear and they headed down the steep incline towards a new life. The closer they got to the town's provenance, the more cared for and sculpted the surroundings became. The hedgerows growing supposedly wild were suddenly trimmed and sculpted into perfect shapes and contours. The fields were farmed and neatly structured, with perfect lines of freshly dug earth open and ready for insertion.

They approached the welcoming front gates; the building was stone and glass, landscaped rockeries were plush and brimming with a rainbow of flowers. A large stone sign was carved into the centerpiece of the display; it read "Eden Gardens". The rocks were pristine, dimpled stones of perfect grey encasing the flora and the grass was lush and green, even in the heat. The security booth seemed warm and non-threatening. The sun bounced off the immaculate windows as the glass sparkled and shone. There were two lanes, one either side of the booth, and both protected by a barrier arm on a counter balance. Michael was so distracted by the undeniable beauty that he forgot which country he was in and approached on the wrong side of the road. Two security guards exploded from the booth in a flash. Both were large and burly, wearing matching deep blue uniforms that fitted snugly to their muscular frames. Emily jumped in terror as both men drew large handguns from holsters and raised them menacingly. Michael slammed on the brakes and lifted his hands off the steering wheel in a submissive gesture.

"Sorry, sorry," he shouted through the driver's window.

"Keep your hands where I can see them," the first guard barked with an authoritative tone that refused debate.

"It's ok," Michael called, "We're moving in today, here I've got some ID," he reached towards the glove compartment.

"FREEZE!" Both guards roared in unison.

The echo of the guns cocking chilled Emily to the bone and she reached out and desperately grabbed Michael's arm before he leant forward. He turned to her in puzzled bewilderment, unaware of the immediate danger that they were both in.

Suddenly the second guard appeared cautiously at the driver's window, "Step out of the car slowly sir," he instructed.

Michael eased himself out of the rental car and for the first time felt the electric tension crackling in the air. "Easy, easy," he stuttered nervously, his hands outstretched in front of him in surrender. "We're the Torrance's. We're expected, my ID's in the glove compartment," he pointed, stepping back.

"Ma'am," the guard instructed never taking his watchful eyes off of Michael, "Put your hands on the dashboard and keep them there." He reached into the glove compartment and pulled out Michael's ID. With a nod, he turned to his partner and the tension fell from his face and the situation. "I'm terribly sorry Mr. Torrance, Mrs. Torrance, when you rushed the barrier we didn't know what was happening." His face was polite and courteous. "It's ok Jerry," he called to his partner, "They're expected."

Emily turned to the second guard, Jerry, and saw a flash of anger across his face, before his features cracked into a stony smile that never quite touched his eyes. She turned back to Michael to see him engaged with the first guard, his name badge read James, and across the top it said, "Welcome to Eden". Some welcome she thought.

Michael was talking eagerly to the security guard, his fear soon replaced by interest, "Is everyone armed over here?" He asked excitedly having never even seen a gun before.

"Oh that's right," James replied, "You guys are from England, right? Your cops aren't even armed, man that's just too weird."

"Can I hold it?"

"Michael!" Emily scolded from the car, "Don't you dare."

He turned to her sheepishly, half embarrassed and half angry at her tone in front of strangers, his eyes returning a scolding of their own.

"Don't you worry Mrs. Torrance," James said amiably, "It's against policy." He turned back to Michael and said softly, "There's a gun range in town, they'll set you up with a weapon on the range, let you squeeze off a few rounds," he chuckled conspiratorially. "Just don't tell the missus." He led Michael back to the driver's door and escorted him safely inside. Jerry appeared at his shoulder and handed him a clipboard. "Here you go folks." He passed Michael a window sticker. "That's your entry and parking pass, make sure that it's in the car at all times."

"Oh this is just a rental," Michael replied, "It's getting picked up later today, some college kid should be coming on the bus to drive it back. We were going to pick up a vehicle here hopefully."

"Ah, you'll be visiting Eddie Halloran's place then. Tell him that I said not to rip you off," he laughed.

"Is he not trustworthy then?" Emily asked.

James looked shocked, "Oh hey, I was just joking Mrs. Torrance, this here is Eden, heaven on earth and twice as nice."

Michael laughed, only to realise that he was the only one doing so. He turned it quickly into a coughing fit to cover the awkward silence.

"You'll need to head straight down this road," James continued. "About three miles down the way you'll find the Welcome Office on the right, Mr. Christian will meet you there."

Michael gave thanks and drove through the now raised barrier, Emily looked over to him nervously, her face still a little white with stress.

"Hey, hey," Michael spoke softly, "It's ok, they just do things differently here."

"Those men were pretty scary," she said shakily, "with scary guns."

"That's kind of the idea don't you think, they're out there stopping people from getting in."

Or getting out, Emily's distracted mind couldn't help but think.

CHAPTER FIVE

Eden Gardens – *Heaven on Earth and Twice as Nice,* the website banner had loudly proclaimed to Michael, who had been flicking idly around the internet. The word document containing the work on his latest novel lay minimized on the bottom tab staring up at him forlorn and abandoned. He ignored the book as best he could despite her pricking around the corners of his mind; his resentment and guilt were still fresh and raw wounds. Emily was sleeping in the apartment bedroom; she slept a lot since she had returned from the hospital he had found.

The car that had ploughed into her on the icy pavement had left them both scarred with injuries that would never fully heal. She had suffered a broken leg, three cracked ribs, a concussion, and most hurtfully, the loss of their baby. Whenever he had tried to talk to her about the accident she would clam up tight and profess to being tired. He knew that she blamed him, and not without good reason.

His eighth novel was now a ludicrous tale of vampires taking over organised crime. As much as he knew she blamed him, he blamed the unfinished book. His agent, Simon Day, had already begun lightly pestering him for updates on the novel, even though it had barely been three months since his and Emily's lives had been devastated. Simon was a heavy set man who seemed to be perpetually sweating whatever the temperature. He was shaggy haired and bearded, short and rotund. He had been a decent agent, always working for Michael with loyalty born of the twenty percent share. The phone messages and emails had begun a little over a week ago; at first they were consoling and cajoling, but now their tone was growing ever more impatient and concerned. Michael knew that his audience was loyal to a point; he shifted decent enough numbers to write full time and provide a respectable standard of living. He was born of working class stock and with most of his ilk, the only thing worse than not having money was to gain it and then lose it. The bulk of his earnings over the last eight years were safely tucked away. The lump sum of just over 1.1 million provided an annual interest income of around 50,000 a year, which was more than enough. Michael had a vast imagination when it came to creative writing, but when it came to creative spending, he was an amateur.

"Eden Gardens", the screen flashed again. The picture was a photograph that Michael felt must surely be doctored. The sweeping woodlands surrounding a picture perfect town of immaculate white buildings gleaming in the faultless sunshine. He had always felt an affinity for America; he had grown tired of the UK's downbeat, negative attitudes and softness towards crime. He knew that he came across to others as reticent and sullen, but he had increasingly felt that perhaps it was his surroundings that were dragging him down. They lived in an apartment block containing sixteen other dwellings, and yet they knew only two of their neighbors. In the UK if you tapped on a door across the hallway, you were unlikely to have the door opened, and even if it was, then you were met with suspicious glares. Perhaps a little sunshine and a little infusion of sunnier dispositions was just what they needed. He scrolled down through the advert and began reading. About two hours later two things happened; a hand tapped on his shoulder, and he was in love.

CHAPTER SIX

The long, narrow road was lined with stunning sycamore trees; each was perfect in size and shape, the trunks were long and the heads were lush and healthy. Michael felt like he was in a dream and did not want to wake up anytime soon. He looked to Emily, whose face was glowing and happier after their scare at the security booth. He had been a little shaken by the armed aggression at the gates but figured that they would both have plenty to get used to before even the first day was over.

They soon came to the Welcome Office; it was a smart single storey building. As all of the buildings that he had seen so far, it was a perfect gleaming white. The tarmac parking area outside was a deep black that looked new and was not faded by the hot sun's rays. The lines dividing spaces were crisp and symmetrical, and a new looking Chevrolet Captiva sat aligned in one space. Michael pulled the rental car in beside it, the U-Haul trailer shuddered to halt behind them. Michael jumped; since they had hitched it he had often forgotten it was there.

The office front door swung open and a tall man stepped out into the hot day. Despite the roaring temperature he glided gracefully down the handful of wooden steps in a full three piece suit and tie. He looked around sixty, but hale and healthy. He was about six feet four, slender and lean; his hair was white and full and swept back in well groomed waves. His suit was a light grey pinstripe and his waistcoat held a glinting gold pocket watch on a chain. He strode towards the rental car, his face beamed with enthusiasm and welcome; his arms opened wide with eagerness.

Michael was barely out of the car before his hand was grasped and pumped with gusto.

"Mr. Torrance," the man pumped furiously, "It's so wonderful to meet you, I'm Casper Christian, we spoke many times over the phone."

"Yes, yes." Michael managed amused, his arm already aching. Since their landing in the country he had been overwhelmed by the friendliness and vociferousness of the greetings by complete strangers. Their English accents had been met with more and more squeals of delight the further west they travelled.

"Mrs. Torrance," Casper stepped around the car to greet Emily as she exited to join the party. "It's a delight my dear."

Casper stooped as he spoke and formally took her hand; he bowed and kissed her hand with a soft feather touch. Emily blushed at the older man's ceremony, "Please, it's Emily and Michael, Mr. Christian," she fought the urge to curtsey.

"Then it's Casper my dear, Casper to you both, and you are both very, very welcome," he added seriously.

"So where do we start?" Michael asked, feeding on the upbeat vibe.

"A quick tour around Eden to show off our wonderful town, and then I will show to your new and last ever home."

He spoke in a pleasant and buoyant tone, but Emily still felt a stab of concern over his choice of words. She looked over to Michael who was glowing along with the town manager. She knew that this move had been Michael's original suggestion, but she had gone along willingly. His work and their finances meant that they could afford the move, and the immigration papers had welcomed a financially wealthy couple who would spend rather more than they would take. She had a marketable skill as a teacher, and the town council had arranged for her to take a recent vacant position at the local school. It would be her first foray back into work and she was more than a little apprehensive about working with children again so soon after their loss.

"Shall we?" Casper's voice startled her back to the present.

She smiled pleasantly at Casper in acknowledgement and looked over to Michael who was viewing her worriedly; she flashed him a reassuring look. She knew that he would continue to be concerned over both her well being and the imagined blame that he felt she held for him. Her reassurances seemed to matter little to him, she had told him over and over again that she did not blame him but he would not swallow it.

She thumped her chest lightly with a clenched fist twice; it was their secret sign and it drew a real smile from him. Michael had played rugby to a decent level in his youth and had been an active amateur when they had first started dating. When she had watched his first game and he had scored a try, he'd looked to her on the sidelines and thumped his chest twice with a clenched fist. After the game he had explained to her that it meant every time his heart beat, it would now beat twice; once for him and once for her.

They loaded up into Casper's SUV; the interior was large and roomy like most American vehicles that they had come across so far. The seats were plush and comfortable, and the air conditioning was most welcome. Emily found herself drifting off as Casper's timbre tones regaled them.

"You are arriving at the perfect time of year; we are only a few months away from our Woodland Festival, the crowning celebration of the year. Eden Gardens, although most folks just refer to it as Eden, was founded a little over two hundred years ago. I know that might not seem impressive to you folks across the pond, but for us, that's decidedly old indeed. It was founded back in 1808 by the Christian family, I'm proud and humbled to say. They were a logging family heading west looking for new forest areas to process. They found that the vast woodland offered extremely high quality timber, which was naturally renewable at an astoundingly fast rate. The town grew up around the Christian family and those of the workers and soon there was a town developing around the loggers and the mill. Normally you would expect an area of such natural resources to be mined dry, but my forefathers were blessed with foresight and only took what could be renewed. As a result, the town thrived and grew; our industry still exists today and would appear to be recession proof. Here in Eden we are currently at a population of 3,208."

"That seems a rather precise number of occupants," Michael interjected surprised.

"Oh we know every one of our town's folk Michael; it's what makes us special. We have a school, a movie theatre, a downtown shopping area including many national franchise stores, a hospital, and many other amenities. We are a self contained town and we have a zero crime tolerance approach."

"Really?" Asked Emily stirring from her drifting, "Zero?"

"Yes my dear," Casper answered proudly, "This is the safest place that you will ever live in."

Michael watched the town approach as Casper spoke. As much as he might wish to embrace the open nature of his American cousins, he was still English and the sense of skepticism was hard to shake. He could tell that Casper spoke with great pride of his ancestors and of Eden, but surely nowhere could be this perfect.

They slowed as they reached what appeared to be the town square. A large expanse of beautifully manicured lawn and shady trees held dozens of picnickers bathing under the hot sun. The stores that lined the square were a multitude of categories; there were restaurants, delis, clothing outlets and antiques. All were immaculately groomed and maintained, and all had matching awnings. The colours and logos were all different, but the size and shapes were all the same. The pavements were clean with a fresh scrubbed glow and neither Michael nor Emily could spot a piece of litter anywhere, even the trash bins were buffed and shiny.

They cruised around the square slowly. Michael watched as people walked easily amongst each other, there was no pushing and no hurrying. The faces were happy and smiling, nods and warm greetings were common place and everyone met each other's gaze. Back home, he corrected himself, back in his old home, people walked with heads bowed and visions averted. Eye contact was viewed as aggression and met with such.

Casper pulled the SUV over to a parking space outside of a bright and cheery store that read "Candy Pops" on the awning. Emily stared in fascination at the vibrantly decorated display in the large front window. The shop held every type of old fashioned candy in large, clear glass jars standing to attention along the shelves.

"Fancy stretching your legs a little?" Casper asked, unbuckling his seatbelt. "I know that just about everyone is dying to meet you."

"Sure," Michael replied positively, jumping out of the vehicle.

Emily felt tired and overwhelmed, but she did not want to distract Michael from what felt like his first happy mood in months. "Let's go," she enthused.

Michael slipped his hand into Emily's as they walked along the sidewalk; he felt a reassurance as she squeezed warmly. Casper was regaling them with the history of the square; another area that owed its creation to his distant family, but Michael's mind was already wandering. The whole scene was perfect; the square was spotlessly clean, the faces were happy, the grass was green, and the sky was blue.

When he'd first started the application process to Eden Gardens, it had been nothing more than a distracting idle fantasy to take his mind off of the black cloud that hung heavily over their marriage. His agent had been aghast at the very idea of his relocation, terrified that he would soon be out of sight and out of mind. Michael had assured him that he had no intention of leaving the agency. As far as Michael was concerned you always left the dance with the date that you brought. Simon Day had helped build and shape his career, and he owed a debt to the man, regardless of where he lived in the world. It was only when he had been having long drawn out discussions that bordered on arguments with Simon that he realised just how much he wanted the move. Emily had been distant since the accident. He knew that she had desperately wanted the child that she carried, and the loss was crippling. He felt the same sense of loss - but he was a man after all - he felt that he was born with a vault where all men lock away their secrets to fester in the darkness. Whilst Emily had her friends and a younger sister to talk through her pain, Michael merely crushed his under a vice and locked it away from sight and thought. He knew that their leaving would be seen by many as running from the problem, but as far as he was concerned there was nothing wrong with a little running every now and then.

"CC," a loud voice boomed, startling them all. "Are these the newcomers?"

The large man stepped from a butcher's shop next to the candy store; he was all bushy faced and rosy red cheeks. He was around five feet five and wore a red check shirt, blue trousers, and a huge white apron that somehow remained immaculate despite his profession.

"Good afternoon Justin." Casper greeted him. "May I introduce?"

It was as far as he got before the butcher brushed past Casper ignoring him and gripped Michael in an almighty bear hug, "Michael," he exclaimed as though meeting a long lost relative, "Emily," he shouted turning his attention and his hugging to her.

"Really Justin," Casper spluttered, "This really is most inappropriate."

Emily giggled as she was heaved off the ground in the rotund man's embrace and Michael couldn't help but smile along.

"Oh shush CC, we need to welcome the new blood you fusty old man," Justin exclaimed, he cast a wink at Michael. "We can't have these poor folks thinking that we're all old codgers like you," he laughed, his voice deep and rolling.

Over the next twenty minutes, Michael and Emily were bombarded with hearty welcomes and shrieks of excitement as the residents swarmed out of the local stores to greet them. By the time that Casper had managed to slowly extricate them from the masses, both their heads were spinning from the attention. Coming from the UK, their senses were simply not used to such direct and uncensored human interaction. Michael was starting to feel like a performing monkey as people demanded that he repeat their sentences in his unusual accent. Emily was exhausted from the incessant questions that came from a hundred angles at once, but both of them had never felt so welcomed.

"I can't apologies enough for that debacle," Casper professed as they sat back in the car. "Whatever must you think of us?"

"It was lovely, really," Emily soothed, "Just a little overwhelming."

"I just don't think that we were expecting to meet the whole town all at once," Michael exclaimed. "You'll have to remember that we're English Casper, stiff upper lips and all that," he laughed.

"Well, let me take you home," Casper said.

"Home," Emily and Michael said together, it sounded good.

CHAPTER SEVEN
Interlude: A Brief Town History Part One

Eden was indeed formed and grown on the back of Casper Christian's ancestor, Tolan Christian's broad shoulders. He was a pious man of strength and breadth that set God and his perceived Will above all others.

Tolan was born in 1761 to Jacob and Chastity Christian; they were a family of loggers from an age back. The Christians were most at home within the confines of the forest, the green foliage was their shelter. The sturdy trunks offered protection and the woodlands provided sustenance. Tolan lived his life in his father's shadow. Jacob was a large man with a ruddy weathered face and a hulking strength born of a lifetime of manual labor. Despite the surname, Jacob had little tolerance for the word of God and suffered no intrusion into his daily life. He was a hard working, hard drinking man with a quick temper and a shorter fuse. He ruled his own house with an iron fist and endured no questioning of his authority. As Tolan grew into an inquisitive child, he grew a long streak of natural curiosity about the outside world, but his father bore little interest in whatever lay beyond the boundaries of the forest. Tolan's inquisitiveness bordered on mutiny as far as his father was concerned, and his frustration grew the more that he was unable to beat it out of his boy.

Tolan's other great love - along with his dreams of travel - was the bible. He was indulged by his mother at an early age as she taught him how to read. This was achieved beyond the sight of Jacob, who would have beaten them both had he known.

Chastity Christian was a strong woman; she had to be to endure her husband, but she had made the commitment and would see it through to the final days. Her husband had been a man of charm and grace when they had first begun courting. Her father had identified Jacob as a sound provider for his daughter's future. Jacob had indeed been an adequate provider at first, but he could be cruel and domineering. Even the birth of Tolan hadn't seen fit to mellow his ire. She doted on her son and wished for him to see the world as she had never been able to. She taught him how to read so that they could share the bible together, and so that he would know God's words and love. When Tolan was finally able to shake off the shackles of his father and venture out into the world, he would do so under God's protection. The bible would be his strength and his guide; it would also ensure that he would never walk the dark path alone.

Jacob began to sense that his iron fist grip was slipping as Tolan started to cower before him less and less. Soon Tolan's face would grimace mockingly and he would tremble behind a hidden snigger. Jacob's wrath swelled as he pictured his wayward son and wife laughing behind his back. Every time that he left their small house in the forest he could feel them plotting and planning. He could hear their contemptuous mutterings in his head when he was alone in the woods. He knew that they knelt before their God, scheming Jacob's downfall, and under his own roof no less. Jacob would spend his evenings downing the product of the local distillery, more often than not staggering home barely able to stand, his head and his senses buzzing. He would crash through the door of their small home, clattering around noisily and daring any challenge to his authority, ready with a swift, violent response if he met one. Soon he was less and less able to work as the drink took hold and his moods grew blacker and more aggressive. Soon he was hearing and seeing disrespect at every turn. He caught sight of every slight in his wife's eye and every smirk of his young son's mouth. Retribution for the imagined insolence was swift and vicious.

Chastity endured as she always did, stretching their meager and dwindling resources further and further. She endured the violence with a prayer in her heart, for she did not dare to recite one aloud for fear of driving Jacob even wilder. She endured the drunken and raw assertions of his marital rights, as he took her roughly and painfully; more it seemed for the pain he caused than any sexual satisfaction. She endured-as a good and loyal wife should-according to her bible. It was only when he turned his full attention to Tolan did she snap. Tolan had come in from the forest early one evening after a day with his father. She had been unwilling at first to let Jacob take her son for the day, but he had been so convincing and sober. He'd promised faithfully that he would change. He would return the family finances to their former, healthier state, and he spoke of moving away, to see some of the world. To her eternal shame she had fallen for his devious nature; she had no way of knowing just how far Jacobs's mental state had fallen. The pure alcohol from the distillery was never meant to be consumed in such volumes as her husband was managing. The more that he drank, the more he left them alone and so she left him to his own devices.

Unbeknownst to her, Jacob was now circling the drain of a full blown psychological breakdown as his mind was fracturing and providing him with random thoughts and voices. The tainted but potent alcohol was causing a cunning and deceptive animal to emerge. He knew his family were plotting against him at God's behest, and his hatred grew towards them all. He knew that he had to strike back at Chastity's religious beliefs; he had to shake her of those and draw her away from God's reach. He had promised her everything that she had wished to hear and had charmed her with a snake's grace. Every word that he sung with allure was forced through a grinning smile until he felt that the poison he was spewing would twist his guts and kill him. Eventually her fears relented and he won the battle. He knew deep in his now black heart that she wanted nothing more than to believe him. It was her own desperation that colored and clouded her vision.

He had taken the boy off into the woods with him early one morning, his wife believing that they were going to off to work followed by a little fishing. The perfect day, the perfect opportunity for a little father and son bonding time, fences to mend and futures to plan. She had waved them off on a bright and clear morning, a father and son, hand in hand. The picture of happiness and hope as they disappeared into the dark forest.

Tolan was eight years when his father took him into the woods, and the day would be forever lost to him. The memories of just what his father did to him that day would be buried so deep that mercifully only glimpses of the abuse would float around the corners of his mind during the deepest of sleeps.

Chastity had stood on the steps eagerly awaiting the return of her men. The night was falling and she had repeatedly chased away the doubts from her mind as the shadows lengthened.

Tolan had emerged alone from the dark trees; a small, tender boy, with a distant look in his eyes and a mind sent far away. His face was sallow, his skin dirty and his clothes torn. She had run to him and scooped him up into her arms fearing that he had been attacked by some animal; in a way, she was right.

She had stripped him of his clothes as he sucked on his thumb mercilessly, the look on his face faraway. He was silent and her demands and pleading elicited no response. Jacob was nowhere to be seen, she could only think that a bear, or perhaps a predatory large cat had taken her husband and ravaged her son. As she took off his shirt, she could see that his puny frame was racked with cuts and grazes; the blood dribbled in places and was congealed in others. Surely this had to be the work of some wild animal, but as she looked closer there were no claw marks and the wounds didn't look like any fangs, if anything they looked like teeth. She chased the thoughts away before they took hold and became tangible. She took down his trousers as he trembled, and she gasped and cried to see that his underwear was filled with blood.

It was past midnight when Jacob had finally staggered home, his head seemed clearer despite the heavy alcohol fog that engulfed him. In his heart, he felt that he had achieved greatness today. He had chased the demon God from his house, and saved his family in the process. He lurched up the two steps to his log built home and held onto the door for purchase to steady his frame. Inside was pitch black as it should be at this hour. His wife and son would be safely tucked up in bed sleeping the sleep of the righteous. He was a little aggrieved not to receive a grateful welcome from his wife over his sacrifice. No matter the morn would dawn soon enough, and he would soon bask in his reward.

He sat down heavily in his favourite chair, a piece that he had carved over twenty years ago, and still stood as a testament to his prowess. Suddenly he was aware of another presence in the room.

Chastity moved out of the darkness and stood before him. Her face was a granite mask, passive and still. She hefted the sharpened axe and swung it silently, fuelled with the power of a mother's love and guilt.

The blade simply shattered his face, cleaving it in two. Blood pumped and sprayed the walls and grey matter trickled out of the gap between the two sides of his head. His legs thumped and jerked loudly, pounding on the wooden floor. The noise echoed around the cabin in a death mask dance of the most macabre variety. Chastity attempted to pull the axe from her husband's split head to no avail. The blade was embedded by the hand of God, and the power that had flowed up her arm had surely been heaven sent.

She packed some meager belongings and supplies that night, determining that her son would not spend another second in his father's company. She spilt oil from the lamps around the wooden cabins floors and walls. She held Tolan outside as they watched the house burn. She secretly hoped that Jacob could still feel the flames as they roasted the flesh from his bones, and she prayed that his pain would last an eternity. She took her son and they headed west.

CHAPTER EIGHT

Colin Murray twisted in his seat again as the bus moved smoothly through the countryside. Since they had left the rather un-bustling metropolis of Hanton and headed further west, the more uncomfortable he had become. The looks from his fellow passengers were beginning to tell him in no uncertain terms that he was an outsider here. There was nothing controversial about the way he looked or dressed; he was twenty and clean cut. He was smart and presentable, and yet he felt like he was gate-crashing a church baptism by urinating in the font. The bus had slowly dwindled in occupants until all that was left were those heading for Eden Gardens.

Colin was a Sociology major, and looking to earn his passage back home for the holidays by retrieving rental cars and trailers along the way. The advert for the job had given him several choices for pickups, and he had been able to carefully plot his course across the country towards home. The retrieval at Eden Gardens was his last job before finally heading home and all he wanted now was to get the last job over with.

The idea had been pregnant with promise, sitting in his college dorm room when he'd first come up with the plan. He'd had visions of long, sunny journeys, driving along picturesque back roads, taking his time and seeing his country. The reality, however, had been full of flea bitten mattress motels and chronic diarrhea from roadside diners. His back ached and his stomach was still tender and raw, protesting at its treatment every now and then by releasing spiteful gas bombs.

The Arrowhead bus was clean and well air-conditioned. His fellow riders were quiet and watchful and they all appeared well-dressed and heeled. There were no extravagant hairdos, no inappropriate piercings or tattoos on show. The woman seemed to favor longer dresses and skirts than the weather dictated, and the men tended to wear smart suits, or shirts and ties, despite the heat of the day.

He looked down at his watch, pleased that he would be on time; his pleasant nods and smiles lay barren in the air, unreturned by his compatriots. He was no longer able to pass the time by finding fascination out of the window. The flashing greenery had long since lost its charm on him, and he longed for the concrete jungle once more.

The bus began to slow, and he leaned out into the centre aisle to seek a view out of the bus's front window. He could just make out that they seemed to be approaching a security entrance of some kind. He knew that Eden Gardens was a gated community, but the closer he got, the more it seemed that Eden was in fact a gated town.

The bus slowed to a smooth stop and a broad-shouldered security guard emerged and walked to the bus entrance. The doors opened with a hissing whoosh and the guard strode on board. He greeted the driver in a friendly manner and began to speak before the driver ushered him in close. Their conversation was whispers and the guard suddenly whipped his head up and his stern gaze fired down the aisle. Colin couldn't help but inexplicably duck back into his seat. He knew that it was paranoia, but he couldn't shake the feeling that they talking about him. The guard disembarked, and the bus eased through the raised barrier and into the town's borders.

As a Sociology major, Colin was fascinated by a whole town that existed within its own boundaries; he wondered what restrictions and limits were placed on the citizens. Did they have their own system of government, social structure, law, class, or religion?

The bus had only gone a couple of miles when it pulled up to a small building that read "Welcome Office".

"Your stop son," the driver called towards him pleasantly enough.

Colin grabbed his backpack from the overhead compartment and walked forward through suspicious glares. He did not know how the driver knew that he was supposed to get off here, but he did not care. He was just eager to be away from the creepy and hostile atmosphere.

"Thanks," he muttered to the driver.

"I understand that the car you're picking up is waiting here for you," the driver replied, "But I wouldn't hang about if I were you," he whispered low. Before Colin could ask him just what he meant by that the door was closed, and the bus was pulling away on the ominous tone.

Colin swung his bag over his shoulder and walked across the tarmac parking bays towards the office. The rental car and trailer were there, parked neatly and looking as though they had just been washed. He stopped to peer in the car window; there were no visible leftovers from the previous occupants. When he had first taken the job with the rental company they had told him to always check for maps and sunglasses etc, as renters would often demand that the company post back any left behinds. His instructor had told him that a man had once demanded that the rental company post back a half eaten candy bar that he had left rotting on a dashboard. He gave the trailer a hearty shove. It was obviously still fully loaded, to his annoyance.

Colin headed into the office, the door swung open with a soft bell jingle that hung above. The interior was blissfully cool, the doorway opened into a small waiting area behind a high backed wooden counter that was fragranced with perfumed polish. It appeared deserted beyond the high desktop and Colin looked around for occupants or a means of attracting some. There were two matching desk tables inside, high metal filing cabinets lined the rear wall, and neatly kept shelves were full of paperwork stuffing. "Hello?" Colin called out, his voice echoed lost and lonely. After his journey and the creepy bus ride, he was eager to be on his way out of this sterile test tube. "HELLO?" He shouted loudly, his voice infused with impatience and irritation. He leaned over the counter, trying to hopefully spot the rental car keys. A large manila envelope lay just in sight on one of the desks. The envelope had the name Torrance printed neatly across the front and Colin knew that this name belonged to the rental client.

The counter had a hinged middle that swung up allowing entry to the inner office. *Screw it* he thought and lifted the hatch. He quickly crossed the distance to the desk and picked up the envelope. The hefted weight rewarded his initiative with a metallic jangle. He emptied the contents and the keys slid neatly out onto the desk along with some papers. He took the keys and tucked them into his pocket. He was pushing the A4 paper sheets back into the envelope, when his eyes processed enough of the words to make him stop dead in his tracks, and then his world exploded in pain and darkness.

CHAPTER NINE

The drive to the new house was both too quick and too slow. Both of them knew that photographs on a computer screen could only tell you so much. Michael watched the neighborhoods that they drove through intently. They were heading for an area known as Fairfax. The photographic images online had looked wonderful, but he would never fully trust anything other than his own two eyes. The houses were huge stately homes compared with their compact apartment back in England, where space was at a premium and you paid expensively for every inch. The surroundings here looked like a movie set; the houses were enormous fronted mansions with long winding driveways that snaked invitingly towards the road. The homes were two and three stories with stone fronts decorated with intricate brickwork and pillars. Michael felt Emily's tension; he knew that this whole move had been primarily powered by him, and it would stand or fall largely on their new home.

Michael suddenly noticed a group of industrious individuals washing the side of a house with gusto, under their soapy hands he could just see watery green paint running in streaks.

"Hey Casper, what's going on over there?" He asked.

Casper visibly bristled in the driver's seat, "Just a little graffiti," he almost growled.

"I thought that there was a zero tolerance policy on crime?" Michael said a little teasingly.

"After we catch them, you'll see how little tolerance we have for the criminal element." Casper's voice was thick with menace.

Michael and Emily shared a nervous look over Casper's intensity.

As the houses passed, Michael was struck by the American design of having open fronted properties. Back in England houses were fenced and hedged in. You drew your possession lines around your home and barricaded yourself against the outside world. Here, all of the houses, despite their obvious luxury and value, did not separate themselves from their neighbors. You could walk across the whole street of front lawns from one end of the road to the other. *It be must indicative of the psychological differences between our cultures,* he thought, *one more thing to get used to.* In truth, Michael was looking forward to living a more rounded life. The idea of having friends and neighbors who were positive and open was appealing to the self confirmed "miserable git".

Emily also watched the properties that they drove through. She worried that they were heading out of the affluent area and that the other side would drop to a more realistic tone. Surely only the fabulously rich and famous lived in such opulence. She knew that she and Michael lived relatively comfortably, their income was steady, and they had no mortgage to worry about. Michael's money was tucked away safely, and treated with respect. She knew that Michael had concerns about their finances, and he seemed to live in perpetual worry that it would all disappear at some point. She had grown up in an upper middle class family, with decent and loving parents. Money had never been a worry to her growing up, nor a real interest either. She'd gained a good education and had emerged with her teaching degree and without the burden of the heavy debts of her classmates. Her parents had let her live rent free in one of the properties that they owned around London, and her income from her teaching job was more than sufficient. She wished that Michael would take more enjoyment from his success and financial rewards, but he held on to the money that he earned grimly and with white knuckles.

The SUV slowed down and stopped outside of one of the larger houses on the street; both Emily and Michael assumed that they must be pausing for some secondary purpose.

"Here we are folks," Casper said. "Home sweet home," he added sincerely.

Michael looked at Emily speechless; this couldn't be theirs, could it? They both slid out of the car on shaky legs.

"Michael?" Emily asked in a soft whisper, "This can't be ours, can it?"

Michael could only stare up at the house; it seemed to dwarf their puny frames as they stood before it and stared up to the heavens. The house seemed to Michael to be all sloping, pointed roofs. English houses tended to be rectangular boxes with a single level pitched roof. The mansion before them was more than they could have ever dreamed of; a vast weight slid from his shoulders when he looked at Emily's eyes as they filled with tired emotion.

"It's so beautiful," she whispered, in a hushed and awed tone.

The winding driveway was a deep red brick color; beyond the sides were immaculate lawns of the deepest richest green, and conifer trees stood pruned and pretty in the grounds. *Grounds*, thought Michael, *that's what we have now, not a garden, but grounds*. The front of the house was covered in light stone cladding that glistened brightly in the sunshine. The deep, rich slate roof was spotless and the house windows gleamed proudly. Small bulb lamps stood to attention down the driveway, ready to light their way home after dark.

"It's actually nicer on the inside," Casper's amused voice interrupted their collective thoughts.

Michael and Emily linked arms as much for physical support as love, and they walked on unsteady legs up the driveway. The front door was massive at over eight feet tall and around five feet wide, it was built of sturdy oak and it pushed open easily as Emily twisted the handle.

"It's not locked?" She exclaimed worriedly.

"This is Eden, my dear," Casper smiled as if that explained all.

"Heaven on earth and twice as nice," Michael said approvingly.

"Quite right Michael, shall we?" Casper invited with an urbane sweep of his right arm.

If the outside was impressive, the inside was majestic. The entrance opened onto a large airy atrium. A sweeping staircase dominated the space as it wound its way to the top. The ceiling immediately over them reached all the way to the roof, sending natural light cascading down.

For the next hour, the large home echoed with squeals of delight and shouts of amazement as they regressed to children on a Christmas morning. Every corner of the house revealed more and more secrets as it opened itself up to the new owners, teasing and tantalizing. Eventually they both near collapsed into breakfast bar stools in the large open kitchen as the light shone through the patio doors that framed the rear gardens. Michael could see the exquisite landscaping towards the outdoor pool, but wisely decided that neither of them could handle any more delights without having a sit down first.

Emily found the electricity was on and working. She discovered a kettle on the gas hob and proceeded to christen the house with tea, as is the English way.

“So what do you think?” Asked Casper as they sat.

“Well, I was hoping for a big house,” Emily teased.

“Oh I assure you Mrs. Torrance, this is one of the nicest properties on the market. Fairfax is one of our premier areas,” Casper blustered, not picking up on the English sense of humor.

“She was joking Casper,” soothed Michael. “It's perfect, beyond our wildest dreams, I promise you.”

A car horn blasted from outside, “Oh that’ll be your things,” Casper said, “I had them brought over from the office, apparently the rental car and trailer were picked up earlier.”

“That was very thoughtful of you Casper,” Emily answered, “All I want do now is sleep for about a week.”

“Well then, let’s hustle up a little help, and get you both settled in,” Casper said

Michael and Emily followed him wearily back to the front door and onto the driveway. A 4x4 truck towing a trailer similar to the U-Haul one that they’d rented sat on the road. It was all gleaming chrome and blue metallic paint, with a logo that read “Darnell’s” on the side.

“That’s Kevin Darnell, local handyman and fixit merchant; he handles all of the maintenance for the lease houses,” Casper informed them. “I hope that you won’t have a need to see much of him,” he joked.

A couple of faces poked out of the large house next door to them, and Casper immediately waved them over. “Let me introduce,” he said as they approached, “Chris and Janet Beaumont, your new neighbors and good friends I’m sure.”

Michael surveyed the approaching couple; Chris was around six feet tall, and he was lean and toned with the healthy glow of an outdoor enthusiast. His hair was cropped neatly short and peppery silver. Michael put his age at around mid forties; he wore a fitted polo shirt and ironed cargo shorts. His wife looked a little younger, and held the air of a woman whose profession was to grace her husband's arm. She was about five foot six; her hair was a skillfully shaded blonde. She wore a short fitted polo shirt, and her long brown legs swished seductively under a short tennis skirt. Michael was admiring the approaching legs when a swift elbowed dig in his ribs told him that his admiration had not gone unnoticed. He grinned back sheepishly towards Emily's scowl. He soon found his hand being pumped enthusiastically once again as Chris' iron golf grip took hold.

"We're so pleased to meet you," Chris drawled eagerly, his face stretched into a genuine smile.

"Seconded," Janet said as she smacked his cheek with a hearty smacked kiss, before hugging Emily with gusto.

"You need anything, anything at all, just hop on over," Chris said warmly.

"Thank you," Michael answered.

"Oooh, I just love that accent," Janet squealed. "Say something else."

"Now, now Janet," Casper warned, "Let's give these nice folks a little breathing space, before we smoother them to death."

"Quite right Casper," Chris said. "First things first, how can we help?"

"We've got a trailer full of belongings that need to get from outside to in." Casper pointed to the trailer behind Darnell's truck.

Over the next hour they were moved into their new home with barely lifting a finger. Every time that Emily tried to help, she was shooed away with hospitality and kindness.

They had obviously only been able to bring a limited amount of items from across the pond, and what they brought was mainly personal. There were clothes, some books, and files, some of Michaels harder to find DVD collection and sports memorabilia. The only piece of furniture that she had managed to bring was an old oak writing desk that had been handed down to her by her Grandmother. Michael had fought hard against her, as the extra weight was a significant expense, but she could not bear to part with it.

The new house was furnished, and part of the agreement had been that they were only able to lease the house for a twelve month period. It had seemed a very sensible option on both sides. They would not be tied to house in a new country if they discovered that they wished to leave, and the real estate company would not have to find a new buyer if they did. After the twelve months were up, they would have the option to purchase the property outright. Looking at their mansion, she could not ever see herself wanting to live anywhere else.

Michael was sweating after he and Chris had lugged the heavy writing desk up the main staircase to the second floor, and into what Emily had decided would be her den. The desk was a major pain in the ass, and he would have happily set the damn thing on fire. In their small apartment, it had consistently managed to catch him in the shins as he walked past and he'd always viewed the desk with suspicion and malice.

"Go for a cold one Mike?" Chris asked, shaking him from his wandering thoughts.

"Cold what?" He asked genuinely.

"Beer my friend, it'd just about hit the spot about now?"

"Sounds good," he said thinking that they hadn't even thought about shopping for groceries yet.

"Here you go fellas," Janet's voice surprised him from behind as she entered the room carrying a couple of heavenly moisture dripping cans.

"Babe you read my mind," Chris greeted her.

"It ain't hard sugar," she purred, winking at Michael.

The cold beer was bliss. The taste was sweeter and weaker than what he was used to, but not being much of a drinker it tasted just fine.

"I can't thank you guys enough," Michael said, "Everyone has just been so welcoming and friendly, it's a little..." he paused.

"Overwhelming?" Offered Chris.

"Yeah," Michael said embarrassed.

"Hey look buddy, I'm a kind of a quiet kind of guy myself, and when we first moved here I thought that it would drive me nuts you know, so I can only imagine what a couple of Brits must make of all this."

"Pretty bonkers to be honest."

"Bonkers!" Janet squealed in delight, "What's bonkers?" She quizzed, running her tongue around the strange word.

"Uh, a little mad," Michael translated.

"Bonkers," Janet repeated committing the word to memory.

"We'll grab Casper and get out of your hair," Chris said tugging his petite wife out of the room and down the stairs. "We'll get together this week. How about a BBQ at our place tomorrow? Nothing formal, just a couple of steaks and a few beers."

"Sounds great," Michael agreed and waved as they left. The weariness was overtaking him at a rate of knots now, all of the travelling and the stress of moving half way around the world was starting to hit him hard.

Emily was staring out of the kitchen patio doors, her tired mind drifting on the warm breeze.

"I wondered if I could trouble you for just a moment Emily?" Casper surprised her from behind.

She turned, too tired to jump, "Of course Casper, what can I do for you?" She asked jadedly.

"I just needed a signature on a lease document," he said as he walked to the kitchen counter producing a stapled sheet of papers as he marched. "I'm afraid that the originals were misplaced in our office, nothing to worry about," he raised a comforting hand to her worried face. "These are copies of the originals that you signed over in the UK. If you could just give us a quick signature then I'll grab Michael's and get out of your hair."

Emily took the offered pen and looked at the contract; she remembered the originals and the first couple of pages that she leafed through looked identical. Her eyes blurred with tiredness and she yawned loudly, giving up the ghost. She flipped to the last page and scrawled a weary signature.

"That's wonderful my dear," Casper said as the contract vanished from sight into his inner jacket pocket with a magicians sweep. "I shall leave you in peace."

With that, he was gone. Emily wandered up the staircase looking for Michael. Suddenly left alone, the house felt cavernous. She found Michael curled up on a sofa in what was to be her den, the writing desk sitting happily ensconced under a large bay window. She curled up beside Michael on the sofa, he absently wrapped his arm around her, and they snuggled.

"Bloody desk," he muttered softly under his breath and with that, they both slept a first night in their new home.

CHAPTER TEN

The next two weeks flew by in a succession of delights and surprises, as slowly Michael and Emily began to get familiar with their surroundings. Gradually the house lost its intimidating air and started to feel like a comfortable home, one in which they filled the vast space rather than merely occupied it. Michael soon claimed ownership over the kitchen, as the member of the partnership that had always worked from home; he had always assumed responsibility for the cooking. Spotless sides and counters began to fill with personal touches; a photo frame here, a book there and little pieces of their personalities wormed their way into the mansion. The biggest addition to the house was their love. Their relationship had blossomed and bloomed, perfuming the home with beautiful fragrances. Never before in their marriage had they spent so much intense time together. Emily had feared- unnecessarily as it turned out- that they would soon tire of such close quarters. She had been wishing the days would pass until she started work at the town's elementary school, but she now found that she was somewhat dreading the time when she would have to leave for the day shift.

Their evenings had slipped into a comfortable routine spent with the Beaumont's next door. Michael and Chris would often share a beer in the warm night air, alternating between back gardens as they bonded quickly over their shared love of sport. Chris was attempting to explain the finer points of American football and baseball, whilst Michael was endeavoring to interest Chris in real football and rugby. Their good natured bantering was a welcome change to Michael, who was more used to the spiteful tribal rivalries that permeated British sport back in the UK. Chris was apparently excited by the prospect of this year's "Woodland Festival"; it was apparently the event of the summer, and one not to be missed.

Emily had shared her own bonding sessions with Janet, finding her neighbor to be far more open and less guarded than some of her friends back home. They often spoke of their hopes and fears for the future, of life and happiness, and Emily had been surprised to find herself speaking candidly of the accident, and of the miscarriage.

The days were hot and perpetually sunny. The sky was so perfectly blue that Emily often found herself wondering if it was real at all, or just a painted canvas hanging over their heads before they woke every morning. They began to feel familiar with Eden, and spent most days wandering around the downtown area, window shopping in the never ending stretch of cute stores and boutiques. Emily had even managed to persuade Michael to loosen some of his legendary iron-fisted control of their finances, and they had purchased several delightful antique pieces from one of the stores.

Today was Sunday, and it was the last day before Emily started work. They strolled through their neighborhood, both wearing shorts and short sleeves under the baking sun. Several people were in their front gardens as they passed; everyone waved and wished them a good morning. Every face was friendly and welcoming, and both of them had never felt such warmth as they walked hand in hand. Emily had noticed that they held hands now whenever they were out. Normally Michael had held such a typically English aversion to displays of public affection, but he had relaxed into his new surroundings almost subconsciously.

They reached the bottom of their hill on foot, it had been the plan to purchase a car as soon as they had moved into Eden, but they had soon found that the public transport system was such that they now rethinking this. Tram lines crisscrossed the town and the trams were spotlessly clean and always on time. The drivers were characteristically friendly, and the fares were free.

Emily always enjoyed the tram rides around the town, and had spent several afternoons on her own exploring Eden via the transport. It seemed that wherever you needed to go, a tram would take you there. She had already taken a journey out to the school early one morning to test the times for when she started work. There was a stop right outside the school, and she had watched the children during recess. She had suddenly found herself sobbing uncontrollably as the little legs pumped and ran, and shouts and squeals of delight lit the air. She wept for her lost child, and the life that she and Michael had forgone. She also wept for the life that they had found, and the hope for their future. Here, they truly could start again. It would be a new marriage, a new beginning, and they would create a new life here. For the first time she felt like they could start trying for a baby again. The thought shocked her, as she had truly believed that a baby was not meant to be for them, but here, away from the tragedy that had befallen them, it felt right.

The tram rattled along towards them happily, its ornate gold and red colouring was adorned with golden trim and shining windows.

"Morning Eddie," they both greeted the driver.

"Good morning Torrance's," Eddie beamed back.

They moved to the rear of the carriage, nods and smiles guiding their way down the aisles.

Michael watched the town move slowly past them as they headed downtown to the square, his hand holding his wife's as they travelled. He stole glances at her every now and then when she wasn't looking, his mind was settled and calm, and he felt at peace. It had been a lifetime ago since he had been so loved, and in love. The move here had exceeded all of his wildest hopes and dreams. They were like teenagers here; they spent every night wrapped in each other's embrace, the expensive air conditioning competing with their sweating bodies in the spicy night air. They held hands out in public, often sharing cuddles and sitting in the parks giggling like love struck teenagers. It was all totally unlike him, and yet totally natural. He knew that Emily started her new job tomorrow, which also meant that he had to start work again as well. His latest novel was slow in progressing; since their arrival he could not have felt less like writing a horror story. The days were warm and sunny, and the cloudless sky refused to be darkened by his imagination. Every scenario of death and misery seemed like a tasteless perversion of their new home. He had set up a writing studio in one of the upper rooms, the view out of the large patio door windows was spectacular, and the cooling breeze was a necessity. He had commandeered a large oak desk for his laptop, but so far he had sat in his high backed leather chair staring out of the window. Michael knew that he had always been a writer reliant on his imagination being a fluid process. He always started a book roughly knowing the beginning and the ending, but the journey between the two was always an evolving progression. He more often than not was surprised and entertained as he wrote and the story unfolded and revealed itself. He knew that to look too deeply into his method could possibly be detrimental. Now, however, he found himself questioning where his thoughts and ideas came from, he was disengaged from the motivation for his work. They had enough money to live on, as long as they were careful, and their home and new life were perfect. Emily was going to love her new job he was sure, so where did that leave him if he was done writing? Could he try a different genre perhaps? The thought of producing a cookbook for stay at home husbands made him smile, and the thought of just what his agent would say to the suggestion made him cringe. He had slowly started to tickle around the edges of an idea based on the town. He had not been seduced totally to the point of ignoring its obvious "Stepford" connotations. He had played with the idea of writing about a similar town, where behind every door and every smile lay an evil intent. He had suggested the proposal to Emily, who had been horrified at the very thought.

"You can't make our neighbors out to be monsters!" She had exclaimed late one night as they'd lain satisfied and content.

"It's just a book you know, it wouldn't be real."

"I wouldn't be able to look Janet in the eye if she read such a thing."

"Well, maybe..."

"No," she stated sternly. "No maybes, no what ifs, you're not writing something horrible about Eden."

He'd pulled her onto him at that point, excited by her stern tone and demeanor, but even as their panting mixed and her soft groans exuded, the idea still lingered.

The tram pulled in downtown, and everyone stood slowly. Emily had noticed that when trying to get off the trams, the whole process was lengthened by an "after you" policy. Eventually they were off, and headed straight for the deli. "Tasty Bites" had been their destination for many marvelous lunches since its discovery. Emily had found that when back in England and you entered a deli, then the attitude of the customer always had to be "What have you got?" Here, however, the attitude of the store was always a more shocked, "What do you want?" Reply to the question.

"Well now, fond greetings to my colonial cousins," Morgan welcomed them. He was a tall rotund man whose products were of obvious delight to paying customers and himself alike. He stood at well over six feet; he had broad shoulders and large hands that seemed as though they would be more at home on a farm than a deli. He, like everyone else that they had met in town, was warm and friendly from the very start. He was always eager to listen to their day and his interest never felt feigned.

The store itself was always filled with the most appealing of aromas; the hot fillings were always sizzling away in the background making mouths water and stomachs rumble. The display cases were long and dominating; meats, cheeses and a million other foods sat tempting amongst the clear glass. The chilled cabinets hummed their quiet motor song along the back wall showcasing cold cuts and meats, salads and wraps, as well as drink bottles and cans. Michael and Emily had eaten takeout from the diner for almost every lunch for the last two weeks, and they had yet to eat the same meal twice.

"What's good today Morgy?" Michael asked.

"Roast Beef," Morgan answered. "I've got some that's wafer thin and just delicious, I keep it out of sight for special customers only," he winked conspiratorially. "A few slices with fresh tomato, lettuce, mayo and a little grated tasty cheddar."

"Sounds good," Emily drooled. "Wrap us up two to go."

Back out onto the street again they walked slowly along the row of shops, they had managed by now to adjust their pace to that of the town. There was no hurrying here, no pushing and shoving, every gaze was met and welcomed and heads were nodded in silent, warm greetings. They waved into several of the store windows at faces that were already growing in familiarity. Justin the butcher waved enthusiastically at them both through the large fronted glass window of his shop. There was also Mrs. Tomkins, who owned the "Golden Times" antique store where Emily had made several purchases. She was a small woman of primness and reserve enough to make Emily feel back in the UK. There was the "Bits & Bobs" arts and craft store. Emily had been meaning to try that one as she felt a nesting urge to knit or sew something. There was also the "Crowning Glory" hair salon, Emily had been particularly concerned at finding a new hair salon, but Janet had sworn by the place. Despite knowing her for only a few weeks, Emily knew that Janet was to be trusted when it came to hair and beauty recommendations. Janet was always immaculate regardless of the activity and Emily found herself for the first time being slightly conscious of her own appearance. She had never been much of a clothes horse or a frilly girlie-girl, but she was beginning to wonder if she would like to make more of an effort. Michael had always referred to her as natural beauty, and had never expressed any sort of unhappiness as to her appearance. But she was starting to think that maybe she would like to make more of an effort for herself as much as him. The town appeared to be completely self-contained and every store that you could wish for was here. There were several banks, a hospital, a courthouse, a town Sheriff and jail house, even though she had been assured by almost everyone that they had met that there was no crime in Eden. She had come to realise that back in the UK you would tend to order a product online and have it delivered. Neither of them had ever found much enjoyment in slogging through busy shops, elbow deep in competitors fighting for the front. The US however, was so vast and Eden was so far away from the nearest town, that having anything delivered would have taken days if not weeks. The local stores were also so welcoming and friendly that shopping was a delight and a great way to meet the locals.

They crossed the quiet road and walked onto the town common. The large expanse of perfect green lawns was always busy. Couples strolled and families played; the many trees offered light shade against the heat and picnics were always the order of the day. Blankets were dotted around the ground away from the organised tables; playgrounds were filled with swing sets, slides, and jungle gyms. All were usually full of happy children running and playing happily. Emily felt a tear spring to her eye and she tried to bite down on the sorrow that ached low in her guts. Michael placed an arm around her shoulder and squeezed her gently.

"You think that we're ready to try again?" he asked softly.

"Yes," she whispered through bleary vision, "Yes".

Casper Christian watched the couple from across the square, his face a picture of quiet contemplation. He felt the presence behind him without turning around, "Good afternoon Sheriff."

"You know it always spooks me when you do that Casper," the Sheriff replied. Gerry Quinn was a bear of a man; tall and broad with the shoulders of a linebacker that were still firm and square. He was around six feet five and close on three hundred pounds of what had once been entirely muscle. He moved slowly and steadily as though he felt as that he didn't have to move quickly for anyone. His bulk had softened somewhat over time due to a degenerative knee injury that stemmed from his college playing days. The damage had been severe enough to end his dreams of a pro career, and despite the constant dry heat it would often ache miserably making Cardio exercise near impossible. He could still bench press around 350lbs when motivated, and being Sheriff of Eden gave him plenty of frustrated time to waste. He had been Sheriff in Eden for over twenty years; his post was an elected one and his coronation a mere formality every four years. His uniform shirt strained across his powerful chest for all the right reasons, and strained across his stomach for all the wrong ones. He wore brown slacks with a bright yellow trim line; his shirt was light beige with brown cuffs and collar. The star badge pinned to his chest was heavily polished with pride and sparkled in the bright sun. "So what do you think?" He asked.

"Oh, I think that they will be just fine Gerry."

"Well, I certainly hope so Casper, as I don't need to remind you that they were your choice," Gerry said smugly.

Casper spun around with lightening speed, despite Gerry blocking the town manager like an eclipse of the sun; he stepped back with a subconscious, almost primal fear of the smaller man.

"Perhaps it's you who needs a little reminding Sheriff," Casper spoke low and menacingly.

Quinn was aware of several people nearby turning in their direction, and stone faces of disapproval glared his way. "No, not at all Casper," he said appealingly, "My apologies."

Casper looked at him a moment longer to emphasize his superiority in this and all situations concerning the town. He turned back away from the Sheriff, dismissing him without a word, his attention focused back across the common. The Torrance's were watching the children run and play, he could feel as their loss and sorrow being slowly replaced by hope. That was good; things were progressing nicely and as planned. After all, he should know better than anyone that hope really did spring eternal.

CHAPTER ELEVEN

Emily woke bright and early; her stomach churned with a mix of nerves and excitement. Monday morning had arrived as promised. She checked the bedside clock, it read 6.15am, and Monday the 23rd. There had been no last minute reprieve. Apparently the Gods of time and space had not seemed fit to delay the start of her first day at work.

She swung her feet out of the large wooden bed, her feet touched the warm wood flooring and she paused on the edge of the bed bathed in the sunlight. She considered for a moment "accidently" waking Michael from his lucky sound slumber, but decided to be above such pettiness. The door to the bathroom did somehow mysteriously manage to bang loudly as she closed it. She cursed the drafting winds that must have blown it shut as she heard Michael grumpily stirring. She showered with a smile, relaxing into her new routine, and beginning to relish the day. She dressed quickly and quietly before heading downstairs, managing to bump the bed with her hips and a grin as she passed.

The day outside was sunny and blue as always. She made tea in the kitchen and took a fresh fruit salad out of the fridge. She carried both through the patio doors and out onto the garden furniture, where she sat enjoying the peace.

"Big day neighbor."

She jumped in surprise as Janet walked around the side of the house, "Shit Janet," she exclaimed coughing up chunks of melon.

"Oh I'm so sorry," Janet laughed. "I didn't mean to scare you; I just didn't want to make any noise this early."

"Well congratulations on that," Emily said, "You were like a damned ninja," she laughed regaining her composure. "What are you doing here this early?"

"I just wanted to wish you good luck on your first day," Janet said seriously. "Here," she offered out her hand with a rosy red apple, "For luck."

The tram rattled round the corner and pulled up on time as usual, Emily climbed on board with a skip. She wore a light summer dress of yellow, flat open sandals and she carried an old satchel bag over her shoulder, it was one that she had used ever since her first day at her first school.

"Morning teach, looking forward to the festival?" Eddie greeted her happily.

"And a good morning to you Edward," she replied primly in her best teacher's voice, "The festival isn't for months yet is it?

"Never too early to plan for the festival," Eddie winked.

She moved to the back of the tram as always, the many now familiar faces all wishing her luck for her first day. As the tram rattled its merry way along, Emily watched the pleasant town pass by out of the window. The houses were pristine and the lawns manicured. The sun bounced its hot rays off of the roofs, and smiling happy faces lined the streets bustling about their business. Emily noticed that there was a group of several people scrubbing away at green paint on the post office building as they passed by slowly, intent expressions, and sweating foreheads worked furiously.

"Isn't it just awful?" a woman said as she leant across her looking out the window. "The Sheriff needs to get a hold of these criminals, lock them up and throw the key away."

"I'd flog them in the town square, in front of God and everyone," a man spoke from across the aisle with gusto.

Emily was taken aback by the normally pleasant regular tram faces that were now contorted with murderous venom, "It's just a little paint," she offered in a small voice.

"That's where it starts," an elderly man said from a few seats down. "It starts with a little paint, then a little stealing and dealing, and the next thing you know it's Sodom and Gomorrah," he spat.

By the time the tram had reached the schools stop, her head was spinning with well wishers, and advice as to the best way with which to deal with minor criminal acts. It had been a relief to stand alone on the sidewalk.

The school building was neither large nor imposing, as many of the British buildings tended to be. Centuries of history and sternness were often embedded into the very bricks and mortars of the schools that she had previously taught in. Eden Elementary was quite the contrast; the school looked newly built, the walls were low, and the façade was light and welcoming. A low white picket fence prettily decorated the front lawn that looked designed for aesthetic reasons rather than security. Overall it looked like a large, friendly house rather than an austere school of disciplined learning.

She crossed the road nervously; so many first days are starting the same all around the world, she told herself. The hands on a clock always moved forward no matter what, and time always passes. She barely managed to open the gate before the front door exploded and about a dozen children barreled forward and out, leaving a laughing woman behind them. Emily was suddenly engulfed in the throng of squealing voices all chiming at once and a thousand tiny hands all tugging at her dress for attention.

"I'm sorry," the woman at the back shouted over the high pitched din, "They couldn't wait," she laughed.

Michael prepared himself for the long, arduous wait; the installers were due this morning to fit the house with the high speed DSL line that he required for work. The broadband connection would be his link to the outside world. He was only thirty eight, but he could still remember having to research everything by hand. He had spent so many lost hours in libraries suffocating under piles of dusty text books, trawling for obscure references and information. As a writer he was always in need of instant and accurate data. He would prepare his requirement lists as best he could, jotting down great swaths of questions to which he required answers to. The only problem was that when he was writing, things would more often than not occur to him as the prose flowed, making his previous requirements suddenly obsolete. His story would often make savage turns without notice, taking him down roads as yet untraveled, and his painstaking research would become useless. The internet had been a Godsend to him; suddenly he had the entire world at his fingertips. Whether it was common names of the 1700's, information about dissociative disorders, or just recipes for Yorkshire puddings - everything was in reach.

The operator had promised faithfully that the installers would be with him promptly at 9am, but he wasn't holding his breath. He was used to a system back in the UK where you were allocated a morning or afternoon slot that consisted of a six hour window, and the van would usually pull up sometime after that.

His ears suddenly pricked as a low diesel engine drew up outside, he stood puzzled and walked to the window. Outside was indeed a Nissan e-NV200 panel van with a DSL Direct logo on the side. Michael checked his watch, it was 8.59am, and the doorbell rang its merry tune as the numbers tumbled over to 9.00am.

He opened the door to a pleasant and smiling face. The man stood before him wore dark brown cargo pants and a dark brown canvas, with a short sleeved shirt and the company logo embroidered on his left chest pocket, and the name Dale on his right.

"Good morning Mr. Torrance."

"9am?" Michael answered surprised.

"Of course sir," the installer viewed him nervously, "9am, that was the time wasn't it?" His tone had become worried.

"Yes, of course, I'm sorry; I just wasn't expecting you to be so prompt, I guess."

"We do everything here on time sir; I mean what is the point of giving a customer a time, only for us not to show up. I'm sure that you have got much better things to do than wait around for us all day."

"Come in, come in," Michael said remembering his manners and feeling embarrassed. "What do you need from me?"

"Oh, nothing to trouble yourself about sir," the installer said, his cheerful demeanor returning with a vengeance. "My name's Dale and I'll be out of your hair lickety-split, just point me to where your computer is, and I'll do the rest."

Michael showed Dale upstairs to his writing room. He steeled himself for the inevitable long and drawn out cheery conversation that seemed to be the staple of his new townsfolk. Dale however appeared to notice his quiet demeanor, and he was thankful for that. Whenever people discovered his occupation they all seemed to have a million questions about writing, and they all seemed to be the same ones.

"You just carry on with your day Mr. Torrance, and I'll be as quick as I can."

Michael left the installer to his business and wandered downstairs, amused that he actually found himself disappointed that Dale was not looking to talk. The house was still enormous to him, and he feared that he would rattle around in the home, lost and lonely after Emily had left for work. It was only about twenty minutes later when Dale returned back down the stairs. Michael was drifting around the ground floor level aimlessly, unable to settle or commit to any activity.

"All done Mr. Torrance," Dale said.

"Already?" Michael asked surprised.

"Yes sir, you are now back on the grid, the world is your oyster once again."

With that Dale was out of the door. Michael watched as the works' van fired up and drove away. The efficiency was mind blowing, in, out and done inside twenty five minutes, without a coffee or an uncomfortable chat. Michael positively ran back up the stairs to his office and switched on the computer. He scanned the room whilst the system booted up and was pleased to see that Dale had made no mess, you wouldn't even know that he'd been in this room.

Six hours later Emily finally sat in the small teacher's lounge and drew breath. A steaming cup of coffee was slowly starting to lift her flagging energy. The day had been a whirlwind, and in the months that she had been off of work she had grown educationally flaccid. Her system had grown fat and lazy to the demands of teaching. A couple of short hours with a class full of seven year old children had worn her to the bone.

"You look exhausted," a voice startled her from behind.

Sarah-Jane Mears was one of three employees at the school including herself and the headmistress. Sarah-Jane was twenty seven, and just about the bubbliest woman that Emily had ever met. Sarah-Jane positively bounced rather than walked, she was a touch on the cuddly side, Rubenesque of build, but with a boundless energy that her frame seemed impossible to contain. She was an attractive woman, with natural blond hair that Janet would have killed for, and a cute face that beamed innocence. It was Sarah-Jane that had shown her around the school and introduced her to the other member of staff, the Headmistress. Despite the friendly surroundings, Emily was still expecting to meet a more formidable educator.

Mrs. Olivia Thirlby was a widow of around fifty, her hair was streaked with silver and redundant of vanity. She was a tall, lean woman, healthy and hearty and she had welcomed Emily in a friendly, if somewhat more formal manner than her staff and pupils had. Emily's head was spinning from the enclosed space and rushed introductions, everyone including the staff were fascinated by her accent, and where she had come from. Some of the children had viewed her with awe when she had read them a story after lunch, her English accent sparking their imaginations like never before. Her class was small and easily manageable; back in the UK classes ran to over thirty children, making any sort of intimacy impossible. Her class here numbered exactly eleven children, and she had already memorised all of their names. She had felt an instant rapport with the class and her new colleagues, who were following in the Eden tradition of smothering with kindness. Sarah-Jane was a constant buzz at her elbow, always desperate to help in any way, looking terrified that Emily's first day might not be perfect.

"I said you look exhausted," Sarah-Jane repeated.

"Does it show?" Emily laughed, "I can't believe that I'm so out of shape."

"It'll all come back soon enough, like riding a bike."

"I keep falling off bikes," Emily said not entirely joking.

"Well I can't tell you how glad we are to have you here; the children have been so excited like you wouldn't believe."

"Oh man, they were just wonderful, I never realised just how much I missed teaching."

"I must say as well," Sarah-Jane whispered, leaning in close, "It's great for the staff as well, ever since Jessica left, we've been desperate for another teacher. Mrs. Thirlby point blank refused to employ another teacher until she found you."

"Who was Jessica?"

"She was the teacher here before you, I thought that you knew all about her, didn't you just move into her old house?"

"Ms Mears," a loud voice boomed from behind startling them both. "I do believe that it's your turn for crossing duty."

"Oops, sorry Mrs. Thirlby." Sarah-Jane was up and gone with a smile and a wink towards Emily.

"So how was your first day dear?" Mrs. Thirlby asked officially.

"It was lovely Mrs. Thirlby, I can't thank everyone enough."

"Well, that's nice to hear my dear."

Emily watched as the headmistress turned to leave, her back ramrod straight, her shoulders back and hands clasped in front of her. "Oh Mrs. Thirlby, what happened to the woman who was here before me?"

"I'm afraid that she left, it turned out that she just wasn't Eden material after all."

For just a split second Emily thought that she saw a crack in the iron mask that Mrs. Thirlby wore, her neutral expression rippled as a flash of desperate sadness flickered through. Then it and she were gone, leaving Emily to pick up her bag and head for home, for a dip in the cool pool and a kiss from her hot man, and not necessarily in that order.

CHAPTER TWELVE

Michael stared out at the window view. Not for the first time he felt that he had made a mistake by putting his office in front of such a distraction. His right elbow nagged achingly, a steady dull pain radiated throughout his lower arm caused from repetitive strain at the keyboard. He had worked since he was twelve years old, from everything from a butcher's dogsbody to a graphic designer. He had never shied away from hard work and thanked his lucky stars every morning for his privileged position of being able to write for a living. He would only rise after Emily had left for work, so as to not get in her way whilst she showered and dressed. He would take a mug of tea out onto the patio much as Emily did before him. He would sit for a short while appreciating the weather and his home, before clocking in upstairs.

The new novel was progressing along nicely, but for the first time in his marriage he was lying to his wife. He had told her that he would not pursue the book idea of writing about their new town, but here he sat some 15,000 words into the novel. Normally when he wrote, he would start with a prepared beginning and finish with a prepared ending. In between everything else evolved organically. He would often be delighted and surprised as he wrote, he would read his own work as a reader would come to, and never knowing exactly what was around the corner. This new novel, however, seemed to be a different animal altogether; his path felt somehow predetermined, and the book was merely passing through him in long and undisturbed sections. He knew that Emily would not approve, but his agent was into the idea in a big way and this prevented him from turning the tanker around. He had found over the years that when an idea took hold, he was cursed to finish the book, no matter how it turned out. He had several files containing finished novels that would never see the light of day because they were simply not good enough.

He leant back in his chair and stretched. The clock on the wall told him that it was quitting time if he wanted. He always tried to discipline himself to at least 2000 words a day and the word count on screen was waving him off. He saved the day's takings on file and on a backup flash drive; he could not imagine trying to work using typewriters and paper when so much could go wrong.

They had been here now for over two months, and they had almost fully settled in. Slowly their uniqueness to their fellow townsfolk had faded, and they had become less of a circus attraction. For the first month at least, everyone had been fascinated by their accents, England, and their pronunciations. Pavement for sidewalk, lift for elevator and so on and so on. Gradually they had become more and more accepted as just a couple who lived in Eden, and it still felt tremendous. The magical Christmas morning element that had accompanied their arrival had faded back into a mere daily joy.

He turned his face upwards into the streaming sun, the light was warm on his face and he was utterly convinced that the perfect weather more than played its part in his good moods. Dragging himself out of bed on cold rainy days back in the UK - he never referred to the UK as back home anymore - was a depressing grind. The UK summers were spotty and inconsistent, and most times he would find himself depressed at the inability of the sun to find and warm England, even at the height of the season.

The long view from his writing window always fascinated him; the sweep of lush green fields stretched unbroken from the rear of his house out towards the banking forest that rose to the horizon in the distance. The distance looked to be quite a few miles between himself and the forest. He looked down at his expanding paunch that rolled over his belt in his sitting position. The food in Eden was fantastic, but the portions he had found were massive and he knew that Americans had a worldwide reputation for obesity. He had discovered that the food consumed was of a far better quality than back in England. Everything was fresh here, and additives and preservatives were conspicuously absent. The burgers and steaks that he purchased from Morgan at the "Tasty Bite" Deli for barbecuing were wonderfully unsullied, but they were huge. When he had eaten regularly at the "Munchies" Diner he had dived too many times head first into their version of the Philly cheese steak. His stomach rumbled and his mouth watered at the very thought. His pants - he must not think trousers - would strain at the waist as he waddled home. He had enjoyed cycling as a younger man, and suddenly the thought was totally appealing. The thought of skimming around the relatively flat town on a bike seemed like a great idea. He grabbed his wallet and keys, he could still not quite bring himself to leave his door unlocked, and headed out.

He crossed over the front lawn towards the Beaumont's in need of directions to a bike shop. Chris normally worked from home, but he was away for a couple of days. He was an architect and he had to commute to Dallas a few times a year. He had told Michael over beers one night that he hoped to cash in from his partnership at the firm in a year or two and retire. Michael still headed for the house as Janet might be home, as she was a slave to her exercise regime. Mondays were yoga, Tuesdays were swimming, Thursdays were tennis and Fridays golf. Today however, was Wednesday, and she could be home if she wasn't out refurbishing herself. Michael was lucky that Emily was such a natural beauty and didn't feel the need for primping and plucking.

He knocked on the door and waited, he knocked again louder, still no answer. He eased the unlocked door open, soft music played inside the house, so he knew that at least someone was home.

"Janet?" He called quietly, not wanting to shatter the silence.

He entered the hallway, ever since they had become neighbors, both Chris and Janet had insisted that they drop by whenever they wanted and should never feel the need for knocking. However, Michael and Emily were both still very British at heart, and could never envisage barging into someone else's home without first receiving engraved invitations.

"Janet?" He called slightly louder.

His voice echoed off of the long hallway. The floor was tiled in a Spanish style, the walls were terracotta orange, and some exquisite pieces of oak furniture that Emily loved lined the hall. The corridor opened into a large open kitchen, and the music seemed to be playing from there. Michael approached delicately feeling like an intruder.

He walked around the corner to find two writhing bodies sweating in time to the music on the kitchen counter. Still being very much English at heart, he couldn't help but think of the hygienic implications, and he took a shocked step backwards hoping to avoid detection. He was about to leave when he suddenly noticed that the pumping ass on top of Janet's lovely brown and toned legs was not Chris'. The man was Hispanic and going to town, Janet's perfectly manicured nails dug passionate grooves in his bare back as she writhed beneath him. Her legs were wrapped around his powerful torso; her pristine white tennis skirt was rucked up around her waist and her top was bare. Her eyes that had been closed in ecstasy suddenly snapped open and terror filled her face as she saw Michael for the first time.

"Oh God," she screamed.

The pounding man took this to be encouragement and doubled his efforts; Janet was suddenly squirming for different reasons as she tried to extricate herself from her elevated position. Michael stood transfixed to the spot, his embarrassment total and all consuming, his face burned and he looked away.

"Alvaro, ALVARO," she shouted, slapping her partner's face.

The man turned and saw Michael, his face drained and paled. He stumbled backwards, his pants around his ankles and he desperately pulled at his clothing to cover his nakedness. Alvaro clutched at his pants and Michael could not help but think that there is nothing more ridiculous than a man's erection, as it fought against its unwelcomed enclosure. Alvaro staggered out of the patio doors at the rear of the kitchen and out into the garden, buttoning his shirt as he lurched towards an ungainly escape.

"Michael, Michael," Janet panted as she hastily tried to rearrange her own clothing and Michael caught sight of a lot more than he wished to, as she pulled up her underwear.

For what seemed like an eternity they stared at each other, neither quite knowing what to say, both knowing that anything would be insufficient. When she finally spoke, it was the last thing that Michael expected,

"Please don't tell Casper," she begged.

Alvaro Hector Rodriguez, or more accurately, Brian Thompson, ran for his truck like his life depended on it. Clutching his unstable pants he just about managed to climb into the driver's seat without being seen. Brian had inherited his Hispanic looks from a grandparent on his mother's side. Growing up in a provincial neighborhood, he had found that when it came to the local ladies, there were certain benefits to standing out from the competition. He had worked through more than his own share of shitty jobs, and had been desperate to get his own business started. He had found that he loved working outdoors and had discovered a natural aptitude for gardening. He'd also soon discovered that Brian Thompson's gardening services were viewed with suspicion, whereas Alvaro Rodriguez seemed to fit the pigeonhole more acutely. During the six months or so that he had been operating his business, he'd also come to discover the delights of the suburban bored housewife.

He lived and worked out of Hanton some twenty four miles away from Eden. Normally he wouldn't have even considered taking on work so far away, but Eden was different. He greatly enjoyed the pleasant drive out to the gated community, the grass seemed greener, the air fresher and the sky bluer. He held the contract with Christian Casper, the town manager for several of the neighborhoods. Casper was a creepy dude at the best of times, and he had laid down the law to Brian before he'd even set foot in Eden. He had been warned extensively about his conduct in the town, and his behavior towards the residents. The money had been great and the work easy, with added benefit of the scenery. He'd been able to look and not touch the fabulous tanned legs of the beautiful housewives, until Janet. The woman had simply not taken no for an answer, and he was simply not able to resist for more than a couple of weeks. He'd started to schedule the Beaumont's work for the times when he knew that Mr. Beaumont would be home, reducing Janet to sulky pouts from a distance. Then, one day a couple of weeks ago, he'd walked into the kitchen via the rear patio doors to find Janet bent over the kitchen counter with her back to him. She wore black pumps with six inch silver spiked heels, her swishing short white tennis skirt was hiked up to her waist, and she was gloriously naked underneath.

"I think I need a little pruning," she purred seductively, and that was all it took.

For the last two weeks, Brian had been drained by the insatiable woman. It was getting to the point where the work that he was actually there to do was going dangerously unattended. He cursed himself for his stupidity. He'd had a fantastic deal going here, and he'd screwed it all up. Janet's neighbor had walked in and caught them and Casper was going to find out for sure, and he was going to lose the contract.

He slapped the steering wheel hard in frustration, it was not fair, and it was all her fault. When he'd tried to break it off, she'd threatened to accuse him of rape. She was just spiteful enough to do it. Janet was a woman desperately used to getting her own way in all matters.

He sped down to the main road narrowly missing the tram as it approached, annoyingly adhering to its timetable. Brian flipped the driver the bird as he passed, taking great delight in the friendly face's shock at the vulgarity. As attractive as Eden was, he was often struck by a feeling of smothering claustrophobia. He didn't know just how these people kept a perpetual smile twenty four seven. As far as Brian was concerned, a little piece of paradise went a long way.

He drove quickly through the downtown area, ignoring the curt looks and disapproving shakes as he passed, eager to be gone before Casper caught up to him. Let the freak fire him over the phone when he was safely back in Hanton. A face to face meeting with an angry town manager was the very last thing that he wanted.

He swung through Fairfax and Jubilee, taking the corner too quickly, his equipment in the back slid over and thumped angrily into the side of the truck. He saw one of Sheriff Quinn's deputies glare up furiously from his coffee cup as he sat parked on a bench outside a Starbucks. Sheriff Quinn was not a man to piss around with, so he had heard, and it was not a theory that he wished to put to the test. Quinn was a junkyard dog, big and mean, but he still had a master to pull his leash.

Casper had always exuded a natural magnetism. When Brian had first met him, he had witnessed the man turning the charm on full bore to a couple of executives from Dunkin' Donuts. The two men seemed reticent about placing a franchise so far out of the way, but Casper had turned the headlights on full beam and had turned them around in minutes. Brian's appointment had been immediately after, and he had watched the change in Casper as the two Dunkin' Donuts executives had left on a cloud. The temperature seemed to drop in the office as Brian entered, and when Casper swung his attention to him, he had wilted under the gaze. Casper had spoken with a religious fervor about the rules and expectations of his town, and he had laid out every do and don't for Brian with excruciating detail. As far as Brian could tell, his job was to provide an expert service and remain very firmly below the sightline of the residents. There would be no access to the town outside of his allotted hours, and he would never leave any kind of mess or equipment behind. He was not permitted to frequent the facilities downtown, and under no circumstances was he permitted to socialize with any residents. Brian had been preparing to tell the creepy dude just where he could stick his contract when Casper had presented him with the fee that was on offer. Brian felt his moral indignation slide away when he looked at all of those zeros; for that sort of money he could put up with some snobby stuck-ups. Casper's tone and rhetoric had been friendly enough, but there was a low rumble beneath his words, a roll of thunder on a hot summer day that said, *do not fuck around with me boy.* Brian had promised himself that he never would. He had a couple of steady girls back in Hanton who were only too pleased to please him on a regular basis. But those long tanned legs and pert ass bent over a counter top were drenched in forbidden lust, and they had overwhelmed both him and his senses.

He snatched a worried glance back the deputy and his stomach sank when he saw the burly man bark into the radio on his shoulder. He pushed the rickety truck faster, his unsecured valuable tools rolled around ominously behind him. His hands sweated on the leather steering wheel, and his knuckles whitened and cracked with tension.

He was through the housing and stores' development now. The land opened up and he could see the town outskirts. The great wooden tall walls beckoned him as he drove faster now that the road straightened. He drove desperately for his freedom as the town inexplicable bore down on him. The smothering claustrophobia was tangible, and the air crackled with menace. His skin felt clammy despite the dry heat and he pushed the accelerator to the floor. Suddenly he was desperate to be outside of Eden. He felt terrified, his primal instincts told him to get gone, to get out through the barrier and never come back. The truck's speedometer read seventy and the engine roared and spat in disapproval as the temperature gauge moved dangerously into the red, but he did not ease up. He was almost to the security gates and freedom when the flashing blue lights suddenly appeared behind and he knew that it was too late.

Michael sat on a plush leather sofa nursing a cold beer whilst facing Janet in a matching chair opposite, her face was drawn and heavy, adding years to her normally youthful appearance.

"Sometimes, I can't breathe here you know," she whispered through watering eyes. "Some mornings I cry just because I've woken up again and nothing's different."

"I thought that you and Chris were happy, you always seemed to be," Michael offered, uncomfortable with the intimate moment.

"This place just smothers everyone, it gets so that you can't even think for yourself anymore once you've signed that damned lease," she said bitterly.

Michael opened his mouth, hoping to find a secret relationship file to delve into, one that lurked around the hidden corners of his mind; he snapped it shut realizing that he had nothing useful to offer. He desperately wished that Emily was here. She was the people person and she would know what to say. "Why were you worried about what Casper would think?" Was all he could think of to ask.

"Huh?" She said looking up vacantly, her perfect makeup now smudged and blotched.

"Casper. You said don't tell Casper."

"I said Chris," she looked down at the floor as she spoke, "Please don't tell Chris Michael, it would ruin us. I still love him in spite of how all this mess looks."

Michael left her with promises of silence, despite her protestations he knew what he had heard. She had said Casper and not Chris. It had been the thought of Casper finding out that had terrified her and not her husband.

"She did what!" Emily exclaimed unable to take in the information as Michael shushed her, flapping worriedly as though their neighbors would hear through the walls. They were sitting in the large open plan lounge area after she got home from the school. She checked Michael's face again; at first she had assumed that he was joking in his weird offbeat way that she often didn't follow, but she could see that he was serious. "With the gardener?"

"Yep."

"In the kitchen?"

"Yep."

"On the counter, where we've had coffee?"

"Afraid so," Michael said with a grin as Emily's nose wrinkled.

"And she was worried about Casper, you're sure she didn't say Chris?"

"Yes, I'm sure, she said Casper at first and then changed it to Chris, but she was lying."

"You must have misheard," Emily said shaking her head firmly, "You're not always the best when it comes to paying attention you know."

"I know what I heard Em, it was too weird you know. This place, it's, it's alright isn't it?"

"How do mean?" She asked puzzled.

"Well, it is a little Stepford you know."

"Oh hey, it's just different from what we're used to," she answered in a considered tone. "You told me that yourself, all the attention and the friendliness, it's just not what we're used to. Back in the UK most people don't look you in the eye on the street when they walk past. How long did we live in that apartment without ever getting to know our neighbors?"

"Have you noticed anything weird?" He asked.

"Well, I took over from a woman called Jessica at the school, and she and her husband lived here before us, perhaps they disappeared," she waggled her fingers at him jokingly.

"What happened to her?" He asked seriously.

"Michael, calm down, I was just teasing," she laughed. "That imagination of yours may pay the bills, but sometimes it does run away with you."

"So what do we tell Chris when he gets back?"

"Oh hell, we are not touching that with a ten foot pole," she said seriously, "I genuinely liked Janet, or at least the woman that I thought was Janet, but after this, she's on her own."

"I didn't know that you were so cold," Michael said a little worried, "I hope that I never screw around on you."

"You'd better not," she said punching his arm not quite lightly, "Speaking of which, why don't we retire upstairs, I fancy an early night," she grasped his hand delicately.

He watched as she gently pulled him upstairs, her face a beautiful mix of innocence and seduction. Judging by what was happening next door, he felt blessed and lucky in equal measures.

CHAPTER THIRTEEN

Sheila's eyes drooped dangerously, the beaten and battered Chevy swerved worryingly across the road as she jerked awake again. The morning was hot and getting hotter, and she had been driving almost solidly for the past twenty four hours. Her laser mind had refused to allow her body to pause, even for a second.

Sheila Murray had been crossing the country for over a week now, following her son Colin's last route as he trekked across the wastelands, retrieving rental cars to cover his passage home for the holidays. Colin was a conscientious boy, a solid student and an intelligent young man. She had raised him well and single-handedly, and she took great pride from her dedication. She'd worked herself into the ground to provide for her child and given him the best possible shot at life.

Colin was a sociology major, who'd been raised with a strong work ethic both inside and outside of the classroom. She'd never been happy with his idea to pick up cars and trucks from strangers out in the middle of nowhere, as she'd feared for his safety, but in the end she'd had to respect his fierce independence. She'd offered to send him the money for a plane ticket to fly home, but he'd been raised too well to accept charity, even hers. He'd always called her after every drop off to let her know that he was safe and sound. Six calls like clockwork, and then nothing. His cell phone was dead. It did not ring and it was never answered, no matter how many times she called. She'd alerted the police on the first day that he'd missed his call, but the local police had been unwilling to even bother contacting the rental firm to start a trace. As far as they were concerned, he was an adult, and probably just taking a detour on his travels. As the days passed she grew more and more convinced that some tragedy had befallen him. Regardless of how far away he was, she could always feel him. But now there was only a deep, dark cavernous hole where her son had been, and she could feel him no longer.

The car swerved again as it drifted across two lanes, a loud horn blast startled her back from her thoughts and she yanked the steering wheel hard to the right. The Chevy lurched and spat gravel as she overcompensated and threatened to drive all the way off the road and down the embankment. She righted the car and ignored the angry looks and gestures of her fellow travelers as they swerved to avoid her. She knew that she should pull over and rest properly, but she was so close, so close.

She had managed to track her son's movements up until his last point of call in some town called Eden Gardens. She had followed the trail to a larger town called Hanton, where a bus terminal worker thought that he remembered Colin getting on a bus there. The rental company had confirmed that their car had been picked up from Eden and dropped off as scheduled. She had found the dealership where the car had been taken after Eden, and managed to convince a tired looking working mother to grant her access to some of the company's information. The woman had been reticent at first; point blank refusing to divulge any details, but Sheila was not for turning. She had followed the woman on her lunch break and battered her into submission with expert guilt prodding and tear teasing from one mother to another. Eventually the woman had agreed to help and had slipped Sheila into the office after closing when the building had been deserted. They had managed to track the rental car's pickup and delivery and she'd struck gold when the woman had informed her that the dealership had excellent CCTV coverage. Her heart caught in her mouth when she watched the car in question pull into the lot and a man exit the vehicle. Despite the man being covered with a heavy coat and a pulled down baseball cap, she could tell that it was not Colin, regardless of the similar body types, the man's movement were all wrong.

She'd tried the local police in Hanton, but had been met with dismissive skepticism. As far as the police were concerned Colin was old enough to make his own way home. He was over twenty one and not a child, common opinion was that he was most probably shacked up with some skirt that he'd met on the road. Sheila had been literally dragged out of the station kicking and screaming. She knew that her hysterics were detrimental to her cause, but sheer exhaustion had stolen her reason.

She now knew that Colin had headed for Eden on the Arrowhead bus to collect a rental car, but that someone else had driven the rental car away from the town. She would find her answers in the gated community.

Slowly the traffic thinned as she headed westwards until it disappeared completely. The road was long, straight, narrow and empty in front.

Suddenly from behind, a large black SUV appeared in her rear view mirror, the big car closed the gap fast and was soon right on her rear bumper. She could just make out that a large man was driving, and he filled the driver's seat and occupied the whole space with ease. He had large, broad shoulders and wore what looked like a tan colored uniform shirt of some description. He wore wraparound mirrored sunglasses and a blank expression. He sat behind her, matching her speed for a few miles.

Sheila gripped the steering wheel with worry, her eyes darting around desperately searching in vain for help, or witnesses. Just as the road began to curve and snake just ahead, the SUV abruptly accelerated and pulled up alongside her, presumably to overtake. She let out a soft sigh of relief, thinking that whatever the man's game had been, he'd tired of it. She slowed and braked gently into the sharp corner as the road swung to the right, she swore under her breath as the man maintained his course into the corner on the wrong side of the road. She looked over as they drew parallel with each other, time slowed as their eyes met and he smiled for the first time, it was not a pleasant smile and her bones chilled.

The ground beside her car slopped dangerously and steeply away down into a canyon that looked bottomless. The treacherous drop protected only by a tired and worn looking low metal barrier.

The man suddenly jerked his wheel to the right, and the large heavy vehicle smashed into her aging wheezing Chevy, it was no contest. The powerful SUV took only one dominant sideswipe to send her crashing with screaming twisted metal through the barrier, and tumbling ever downwards.

The large man pulled over to the side of the road, he plucked a set of binoculars from his vehicle and surveyed the damage at the bottom of the canyon below. The old Chevy lay in broken, ruined pieces. The mass of metal was beyond comprehension from the rolling fall, and life was hopeless.

He was pleased to spot a limp, bloody arm hanging out of what used to be a car. He watched for several minutes for any signs of miraculous movement. When he was convinced, he hoisted his bulk back into the SUV, carefully lifting his troublesome knee and then drove away, leaving the corpse to the emerging wildlife drawn out by the mouth watering scent of blood.

CHAPTER FOURTEEN

Michael skirted the garden with cat like stealth; it had been two weeks since he'd walked in on Janet's somewhat enthusiastic indiscretion. Chris and Janet had both been conspicuously absent since the incident. Emily thought that they would both be too embarrassed because of his unfortunate presence, but he was not so sure. Janet had never struck him as being anything other than full steam ahead regardless of the situation. No matter what the reason, Michael was still firmly English, and was borderline terrified of getting dragged into someone else's domestic troubles.

He kept his head down below the rear fence line as he ran back from the bird feeders that Emily had lined the garden with. She had been nagging him for days to refill them, but he had been too scared about catching either Chris or Janet in the garden. He felt emotionally inadequately equipped to deal with either of them. Would Chris want a shoulder to cry on, would Janet want a priest to confess to?

"Michael?"

His face clenched and he cursed his luck for being caught under the spotlight, he cursed the damn birds and Emily too.

"Michael, is that you?" The soft, feminine voice called out.

"Oh, hi Janet," he straightened and answered as casually as he could.

It was a little after lunch and Emily wouldn't be home for a while yet; he'd finished writing for the day and had been looking forward to a cold beer beneath the sun. The book was progressing nicely. The story was unraveling before him, as the characters spoke with natural ease and flow. Luckily for him, Emily had little interest in his writing; she was always supportive of his work and respected the effort and talent that it took, but the genre was never to her taste. He knew however that her thoughts were clear on the subject of him taking inspiration from Eden for his new novel. She objected to him distorting their new found home, to twisting the actions and thoughts of their new neighbors, from welcoming to sinister. Michael was very much a "crossing the bridge when he came to it" sort of man. He would write the book and worry about Emily's anger later. One of the main reasons that he was unwilling to give up on the novel was that it was actually very good. The protagonist couple were sympathetic and charming, and the townsfolk were suitably creepy and ominous.

He walked up to the wooden fence that partitioned the two houses. The barrier was about five feet high, just enough to duck under, but low enough for him to lean over. Janet stood on the other side, her hair was messy, and her face devoid of the perfect makeup mask that she normally wore. Her outfit was a mismatched tracksuit selected for expedience rather than fashion. The garden around her was overgrown and in need of attention. She obviously had not gotten around to replacing her gardener, and Michael hoped that it applied to all his duties, horticultural and otherwise.

"I thought that you were avoiding me," Janet said.

Michael felt shame at his antics; Janet's voice was laden with sadness and slightly slurred with alcohol, even at this hour. "How are things?" He asked, fearing the answer.

"Not great, but better than I deserve, I guess."

"How's Chris doing?"

"He's off in Dallas till the end of the week, he's going to come home with a decision," she choked off, her voice muffled with tears.

Michael stood awkwardly as she cried before him, the wooden fence stood between them preventing him from comforting her, even if he had felt able to.

"I'm sorry that you got stuck in the middle of this Michael," she said, her voice strengthening as she regained some of her composure. "It wasn't fair, Chris wanted to come and see you, to torture himself with all of the gory details I suppose."

"What do you think he's going to do?"

"I honestly don't know, I hope and pray that he gives me another chance. I told him to go and bang a million strippers if that's what it takes. I don't care, I just want him Michael," she sobbed as she ran back into her house. "I only want him," her voice faded away.

"I call this town council meeting to order," Casper spoke with a clear authority that would not be denied.

The town hall was a large wooden colonial style building that sat proudly upon the town square. Its perfect white slatted wooden walls were topped with powder blue window frames and shutters. The roof was pitched and layered, the lowest point was over the entrance and supported by four large white pillars. A turret extended out of the central roof, and there was a clock on each side facing out across the town informing everyone just what time it was in Eden. The interior was lined with a dark oak hardwood floor that was mirrored in color by the beams that ran the length of the ceiling. Small steps led up to a raised platform area at the end of the large open room, and a huge, long, and heavy antique table ran the width of the stage. The open floor was lined with comfortable chairs for the town's people to sit and listen during town meetings, with standing room behind for when the subject matter dictated a wider audience.

Today's meeting, however, was a private affair being held in a small private room at the back of the hall. The Woodland Festival was nearly upon them and nothing could be left to chance. The room was compact and concealed; this was where the true town matters were discussed, and this was a meeting of the inner circle. The windows were closed and shuttered against the outside world and prying eyes. The room was dark even with the side wall lights glowing. The furniture was sparse, save for the dark wooden table and chairs that sat in the centre of the room. Today all five seats were occupied.

Casper stood at the end of the table; his was the voice that chaired all such meetings, he set the agenda and his plans were always ratified as a matter of course.

"Today's first item," he spoke to the upturned faces around him, "Michael and Emily Torrance, I think that it's time we moved to stage two."

No-one disagreed.

Emily sat in the doctor's outer office; the waiting room was pleasant, it was sunny and light, with neutral colored walls and mellow artwork hanging to reassure. Another part of the town's benefits was the healthcare, being a relatively small community, they operated a private system. The contributions were low, but the structure and facilities were unlike anything that she or Michael had ever experienced back the UK. There, you could opt out of the overburdened National Health Service and take out your own private insurance. She was fortunate in that her own family had always had private health care, but one of the anomalies of the UK was that you found that private health care meant only that you jumped the queue. You would, on the whole, find yourself in the same hospital with the same doctors; you just wouldn't have to wait months for appointments. The staff as always were dedicated and committed, but the system was drowning under a sea of bureaucracy and red tape. Here in Eden, the monies collected went directly into the system. It was spent on doctors, nurses and facilities. The doctor's office looked plush and comfortable without being overly luxurious. She was beginning to get used to the overtly cleanliness of Eden and could not imagine having to get used to the untidiness of the outside world again.

The receptionist sat behind a large pine counter, her desk beyond was neat and tidy, and the computer screen was devoid of dust and gleamed in the sunlight. The woman looked around forty with a warm and friendly face, with a figure that was plump and short. She wore a mauve knitted woolen cardigan over a high collared crisp white shirt, her glasses hung loosely around her neck on a chain ready for action.

"It'll be just a minute Mrs. Torrance, I'm so sorry for the delay."

"It's really no problem," Emily responded happily. She checked her watch and found that her appointment was only running about three minutes behind schedule.

Today was her first check-up. She had been putting it off for a few weeks now, but the appointment now appeared unavoidable. She had been feeling under the weather for a couple of weeks, a little tired before the end of the working day and her energy levels seemed abnormally low. She had always eaten healthily and exercised, taking pride in her enviable figure, but now her waistbands all seemed a little tight and her stomach seemed bloated all the time. Most worrying were the headaches. She felt irritable most mornings and Michael was bearing the full brunt of it. It was he who had made several doctor's appointments for her and she knew that he was worried. They had entered into a repeating play, where he would make an appointment for her and she would agree, only to find a reason to cancel, and only for him to make another and round they went again. The clinic had now started calling every couple of days to reschedule. Even her colleague and growing friend at the school Sarah-Jane had been pressuring her to attend. She did not know why Sarah-Jane was so insistent, but she thought that perhaps her friend must have had a death in the family hanging over her head. Emily had never been overly scared of doctors, but she did have a healthy fear of clinics and tests. She was always pessimistic that a doctor would find some terrible impending sign of doom. To the outside world, she knew that she was considered to be ebullient and jovial. She knew that Michael was often intimidated by her exuberant manner with strangers, but she did have a dark side. A lot of times her over enthusiastic approach to life, was a cover for her secret fears and worries. Could she really ever be truly happy? Or would Michael leave if she ever grew too tired and old?

"Mrs. Torrance?"

The voice interrupted her thoughts, and she shook the darkness clear, this was a beautiful day and nothing could, or would spoil it. "Yes, sorry, I was miles away."

"Dr Creed will see you now," the receptionist informed her kindly.

Emily stood and headed for the private office. She wore thin and light white canvas trousers that were three quarters in length and a pink polo shirt; as usual the day was hot and sunny. She swung the door open and chastised her wandering mind's propensity for private worry, as it clawed around the edges with visions of disaster.

"Mrs. Torrance, so pleased to meet you," the doctor said as he walked around his desk to greet her.

She had seen enough television to expect the doctor of a small American town to fit a certain warm and cuddly, slightly elderly stereotype, but Dr Creed was not it. He was well over six feet tall and in his mid to late thirties. He was heavily built with long grey wavy hair that hung loosely around his face like a Woodstock hangover. His eyes were a piercing steel blue that peeked out from under the large mop of hair, and he wore a long goatee that matched his hair in color. His white lab jacket was stretched tightly over a red and black checked shirt and green tie. He wore stone colored cargo pants and timberland dusky boots that augmented his already impressive height.

He reached her and grasped her small, delicate hand in one of his large paws, he pumped her arm enthusiastically, and she couldn't help but smile back at his infectious grin.

"Please, it's Emily," she said, as she regained her slightly sore hand.

"And I'm Samuel," he responded. "Please sit, sit," he pointed to a plush leather chair.

The office was bright and airy, the walls were smothered in framed photographs, some were of famous landmarks, and some were of a more artistic variety. The office was delightfully messy; his wooden desk was large and covered in paperwork and files. The shelves that lined the walls were overflowing with books and manuals. A heavyset metallic filing cabinet stood with several drawers open off to the side, devoid of the paperwork that seemed to be covering his desk.

"I know, it's a mess, right," he said with a smile. "Blanche out there is always moaning at me, she says that she can never find a thing in here, but I can't help it."

"You make my husband look like a saint," she laughed.

"Ah Michael, I haven't seen him yet either, you must bring him in soon," he chided, "So what can I do for you today?"

Emily began to protest her medical innocence and apologies in a most British way for wasting his time, when she stopped. Something about his attitude, manner, or even the mess of his office made her want to speak openly. She listed her symptoms checking, them off one by one; he listened and didn't interrupt as she scratched around for accurate descriptions and articulations. Once she'd finished, she looked into his face expecting to see worry and concern, as though his internal medical mind had recognised a major illness in her symptoms.

His face was calm and friendly, he smiled at her worry, "Let's run a couple of tests and find out just what exactly is going on Emily."

About forty minutes later she looked at him stunned, "I'm sorry, what did you say?"

"Pregnant," Samuel said his face beaming, "You my dear, as they might say back home, are up the duff."

Emily sat back in the chair, grateful for the sturdy furniture preventing her from collapsing, "But how?"

"Well, I think it's a bit late for Sex-Ed," he grinned.

"Pregnant," she muttered to herself. She knew that she and Michael had been operating at a less than sedate pace since the move. He'd jokingly put it down to the open air, and good weather. Like rabbits, he'd laughed.

She closed her eyes and started to cry, weeping gently at first, then great, painful sobs of heartache wrenched from her chest, expelling the final refuges of grief from their first pregnancy loss.

"Oh, my dear," Samuel said suddenly distressed and concerned, "Am I to take it that this is not good news?"

Emily began to laugh through the tears as the poisonous misery at long last loosened its toxic grip, "Samuel it's the greatest news ever."

Michael was plotting when the front door breezed open; he was sitting in what had become his thinking position on a wooden steamer chair out on the rear decking. He would often sit here beneath the warm sunshine of a late afternoon. The red hot heat of the day had passed over to be replaced by a warmth that was bearable. He had a small table by his chair that matched the steamer - on it sat a cold beer can, a notepad and a pen. The condensation ran from the can, beading and pooling on the wooden surface. The stains were testament to his frequent musings; he would often lay back and close his eyes against the brightness. His mind would dance and pry around the edges of his book as he would trace mazes back and forth. From characters and scenarios, leading people up and down paths that sometimes worked, and sometimes didn't. He had found over the years that he could never plan his stories too far ahead; each had to build brick by slow brick until it reached the sky. Too much information, or too many ideas, would get in the way and block his creative path. Whenever he finished his day's work, he would retire to his spot and retrace his steps, poking for holes in the story, or gaps in character development. After he was satisfied with the day's work, he would sketch around the overall idea, jotting down copious notes that would often be illegible the following day. He was attempting to work around a roadblock that required two characters to be brought together, finding the right balance of suggestion, when Emily blocked his light.

"Michael?"

She stood before him, her expression was unlike any that he had ever seen her wear before. He sat up in apprehension, this was not a good look to be wearing after a doctor's appointment. "What's wrong, what did the doc say?" He demanded curtly, his worry overriding courtesy.

She handed him an envelope, he took it with a furrowed brow confused, and he opened the envelope. Inside was a Father's Day greeting card, the front read, "To the best Dad Ever" in jaunty printed writing. He opened the card, and the front message was printed again, but Emily had used a black marker pen to block out the "To" part of the message and written "You're going to be" in its place.

Slowly realisation dawned and Michael stood on shaky legs, "You're sure?" he whispered.

"Yes," she confirmed.

She sat beside him on the large steamer chair; they held each other and loved each other until after the sun set and the evening cooled. Words were not required and were unwelcome, as their minds aligned and adjusted to the bright new and perfect future.

It was three days later; Michael and Chris were standing over the charcoal grill in Michael's back garden, bathing in meaty odors whilst sharing beers and happy thoughts.

Chris had returned from Dallas, minus any STD's from his wife's "Stripperthon" suggestion. Michael and Emily had found various reasons to repeatedly wander past the front windows, waiting impatiently for any indications as to whether Chris would be staying or leaving. When dusk had turned into darkness, and there was still no sign of either Janet or Chris lugging luggage down the driveway, they had both relaxed. Emily's stance appeared to have softened a little, Michael thought. He knew that her father had been somewhat of a serial adulterer, aided by her mother's blind eye towards his indiscretions. It was a subject that she rarely discussed, and he had never pushed it. Emily had staunch morals when it came to fidelity, and somewhat repressed anger towards her mother's complicity.

The pregnancy was still in its infancy, both figuratively and literally, and they had not told any of their family or friends back in the UK. Michael instinctively knew that they were both afraid of shattering the beautiful illusion. Involving anyone from outside of Eden seemed to be tempting fate. For now, they would bask in their life as it existed in the here and now - a wonderful new home and life. Emily's job was perfect, his new novel was steaming along, and the pregnancy was the cherry on top.

Michael had been preparing the grill in the back garden when Chris had poked his head over the fence catching him off guard.

"Howdy neighbor," Chris called smiling at Michael's alarmed jump.

"Hey stranger," Michael replied, suddenly realizing with surprise that he had come to miss his friend. "How are things?" He asked softly.

"Better, much better than before in truth," Chris leaned on the fence partition and looked around checking that his wife was not close. "I think that things are going to be ok. We had a lot of problems that we weren't talking about you know, perhaps things will be better from now on."

"Hey man, I'm really glad to hear that," Michael said genuinely. He was never failed to be impressed by the typical American's optimism and positivity. He knew that if he was in the same boat, then he would crawl into a deep, dark hole and never come out again.

"That smells good, are those from Morgan's?" Chris asked, nodding towards the sizzling steaks on the grill.

"Yep, hey you want to come over?" Even as he spoke, Michael cringed thinking that it would be the last thing that his neighbors would want.

"You don't mind, you know after everything?" Chris asked awkwardly.

"If you've got the stomach for it, then so do I."

So two hours and a couple of bottles of wine later, the foursome were back in tandem again. Michael couldn't help but feel awkward around Janet to begin with; the image of her across the counter, and her subsequent revealing, but non-erotic redressing was hard to shake. But as the evening passed so did the awkwardness. He caught snatches of Emily's conversation and tone, as she spoke at length to Janet inside the kitchen. Emily's voice had been ice to start with, but she was slowly thawing.

"So when are you going to let me introduce you to the finer points of football?" He asked Chris.

Chris grimaced, "Soccer," he spoke as though dealing with a mouthful of spoiled steak.

"Not soccer," Michael bristled, "It's called football, you kick the ball with your foot, foot-ball," he emphasized.

"Yeah, but it's not real football," Chris teased knowingly.

Michael bit, "Ah man, American football is nothing but rugby with helmets, padding, two teams a side and endless pauses," he laughed. "Look, come over next Tuesday, around midnight and I'll sit you down and show you a real game, it's Liverpool vs. Man United. I'll show you what passion is all about."

"Passion tips from an Englishman, now I've heard everything," Chris laughed. "Anyway, can't make it next week, we're taking a trip."

"That sounds great," Michael said seriously, "Maybe some time away together is just what you guys need."

"Yeah, I certainly hope so, as long as we're back for the festival," Chris said looking back at the house and his wife's outline through the patio doors lovingly. "It's all going to be different Michael. I'm thinking that maybe Janet and I need to move away from here, to start somewhere new. I want Janet and me to be, just like you two."

Michael felt himself grow awkward with the praise, "Ah hey, we're nothing special."

"Yes you are my friend," Chris said as he held his gaze strongly, "You're going to be my new inspiration," he added lightly, not entirely joking.

The rest of the evening passed swimmingly. Michael felt himself on rare form, he was witty and happy. They ate outside in the warm night air as the buzzing insects were conspicuously absent as usual. They ate steaks, burgers, and salads, with chips and dips till they were all stuffed. The conversations were light and cheerful and the unpleasantness forgotten for now. It was gone 1am when Janet and Chris finally excused themselves. Michael was surprised when he saw the time, as he was usually growing itchy for people to leave after an hour or so.

When he and Emily finally turned in after clearing the kitchen, they both sank gratefully into the soft bed and drifted quickly.

"Did Janet tell you that they were taking a trip next week?" Michael asked as Emily's breathing grew deep and heavy.

"No," she slurred.

"Chris thinks that they're going to be ok."

"That's nice, good for him," she said a little tersely.

"You don't approve?"

"Hey, it's not my life or my spouse," she shrugged.

"Chris even suggested that they might move away altogether."

"That's a shame," she patted his leg absently.

Michael could tell from her rising shoulders that she was almost asleep and that further discussions were pointless at this time, as Emily was a heavy and deep sleeper once she went. He said his nightly silent prayers to the Gods that decided on his fate, that he wouldn't wake in the morning to find that his life had all been a dream. It was a common thought that he'd had ever since he had achieved any level of success - the idea that the whole thing was just a joke and one that was going to be whipped away at any second. As he slipped off to sleep, he curled one arm around his sleeping wife and baby and whispered in his mind, *one more day, just let me have one more day.*

Michael snapped awake suddenly, his stomach lurched in angst and his heart pounded hard against his chest. Instinctively he reached for Emily and breathed easier when she stirred next to him in the dark. The readout on Emily's alarm clock read 4:37am and his mind struggled to decipher just what was happening, when the flashing blue lights danced off of the bedroom walls.

He eased himself gently out of the bed, walked carefully to the window, and peered out to the street below through the thin net curtains. There was an Eden Gardens police car and ambulance parked outside Chris and Janet's house. The sirens were silent, but the lights on top of the vehicles rolled alertly.

Michael grabbed a pair of shorts and a hooded top off of the chair where he usually shucked off his clothes of an evening, much to Emily's displeasure. He struggled into them as he walked hastily down the stairs and out of the front door. His mind was racing, was their Eden to be shattered by the intrusion of the outside world's violent themes?

There were two deputies stopping the other emerging neighbors from getting in the way. Michael could see that their presence was pretty much redundant as the bedroom attired did not seem to wish to get too close. Chris and Janet's front door banged open noisily and two paramedics emerged pushing a gurney towards the ambulance. A prone figure was wrapped in what he could only assume was a body bag. The black plastic shone merrily beneath the artificial lights as the gurney came down the pathway, and Michael stepped forward to intercept it.

A firm meaty hand was suddenly planted in the centre of his chest punching the wind out of him and stopping him in his tracks.

"Some privacy sir," the hand's owner informed him in an authoritative tone.

Michael looked up into the eyes of the Sheriff, Michael had seen him around town, but had never had cause to speak to him directly. Gerry Quinn was a bear of a man, and Michael did not feel that the Sheriff was much for socialising. Emily had always expressed a slight fear of the man, but as far as Michael was concerned that only meant that he was doing his job properly.

"What happened?" Michael asked in a hushed voice.

"And you are?" The Sheriff replied, turning his full attention to Michael for the first time.

"Michael Torrance, I live next door," he answered refusing to be intimidated by the larger man's glare, "Chris and Janet are friends of mine."

"Well then sir I've got some distressing news for you, I'm afraid that Mrs. Beaumont took her own life tonight."

Michael was stunned, "That's not possible."

"Oh really?" The Sheriffs dismissive tone bordered on anger.

"They both had dinner with us earlier, she seemed fine then."

"Well I guess that we never really know what another person's thinking, do we sir?" The Sheriff's tone had returned to dismissive again "Strictly in confidence, Mrs. Beaumont was apparently unfaithful, and Mr. Beaumont left her. It would appear that she was overcome with remorse, and took her own life."

For some reason Michael paused, he knew about the affair, but he also knew that Chris had forgiven her and that they were actually planning a holiday away from here, and had even considering moving all together. For some reason, the Sheriff bothered him, his attitude felt wrong. His information disclosure was too concise to a member of the public. Michael had one answer, but a lot more questions. "Where's Chris?" He asked suddenly not seeing his friend anywhere.

"He's been taken to the hospital for sedation I understand, apparently when he informed Mrs. Beaumont that he was leaving her, that's when she committed suicide. I understand that he's terribly distraught."

The whole speech seemed too informative, especially to a virtual stranger on the street. Would a Sheriff really divulge such personal information? Michael didn't quite know why, but he decided to keep the personal information that he knew about Chris and Janet to himself. "I'd better get back to my wife."

"Of course sir," the Sheriff said warmly with a smile that never quite touched his eyes.

As Michael walked home his mind reeled, Janet was dead, suicide. Chris was telling him one minute that they were planning a trip and his hopes for the future, the next he was leaving Janet and she was dead. His writer's imagination whirled around in his head as the machine cranked into life, but he knew that he was often guilty of over stretching the truth in his own mind. Emily was always accusing him of reading too much into things, of seeing conspiracies and plots where there was only real life. As he entered his home, his thoughts turned to Emily, and he hoped that this wouldn't spoil everything for her. Apparently the Gods of fate that he prayed to every night, had only been half listening tonight.

CHAPTER FIFTEEN

The day dawned bright and sunny as was the want in Eden Gardens. The perfect weather was seemingly oblivious to the day's upcoming events.

Emily moved around the kitchen in a daze, the large station wall clock read 5.47am and Janet's funeral wasn't until 1pm, but the world outside was already in full swing. She nursed a cooling cup of coffee and watched as the small dainty birds in the garden swooped and challenged for the feeder's contents. Life hustled and bustled beyond her window. She'd slept fitfully ever since Michael had woken her four days ago to tell her the sad news. She knew that he was increasingly convinced that something was wrong with the whole picture. He was sure that Chris had spoken of second honeymoons or moving away, but Janet had mentioned nothing to her on that last night. Perhaps Michael had misunderstood, or perhaps Chris was planning a surprise. Either way, it seemed to matter little now. Janet was gone and she wasn't going anywhere anymore. Janet had seemed a little quiet on their last evening together, but Emily certainly didn't remember being scared for her well-being at any point. The evening had been pleasant and happy on the whole. They'd shared food and drinks with their neighbors, and for a brief instant it had been like old times again. They'd all been just friends laughing and talking in the warm evening air.

She heard movement from upstairs as Michael stirred. She hadn't wanted to wake him this early as he often had trouble sleeping. One of the drawbacks of his profession, she had always felt, was an overactive and over-worked mind, as his thoughts just never seemed to shut down and rest. She would often feel him rise in the middle of the night as she slept. He would ease out of their bed and head down to his den in the basement. The lower level was still under decorative construction, he had been making his own home cinema and games' room down under the house. Weekends were spent lugging large boxes of varying weights down the narrow stairs. The process was sound tracked by his shouts and curses as the boxes wouldn't fit easily. He'd installed an HD projector and screen, along with reclining seats. There were poster displaying frames lining the corridor and the staggered steps were currently being painstakingly fitted with tiny blue LED lights. She knew that the project had been a dream of his for several years. Back in their old apartment he'd spent many evenings scanning the internet and compiling endless images and plans for his vision. He was a man still very much haunted and scarred by his less than affluent upbringing. She would know him to take a larger candy bar than necessary, or even two, this being due to the nature of his childhood. His family were careful and frugal because of necessity; it was a hangover that had lasted throughout his adulthood. The little luxuries in life that he could now comfortably afford were always painfully dragged from his imagination and wallet.

She moved back into the kitchen and switched the kettle on again. Unlike her, Michael had no taste for coffee, and still stuck to the most English of morning rituals, a mug of tea to start the day. She made the pot and waited for his shuffling footsteps to enter. They had been here several months now, and she was still a little intimidated by the amount of space that they had at their disposal. She did not look back fondly on their cramped apartment back in England, and she didn't posses a pair of rose tinted glasses that allowed her to alter the past. There were no "Best of times" bullshit about their past life; their home was tiny and insufficient, commuting was a major chore, and they'd left no real friends behind when they'd emigrated. She'd already found more friends and acquaintances since the months following the move than she had in the years previous. Janet's suicide was the first negative experience that they'd suffered since their arrival, and she deeply promised herself that she would not allow it to affect them now.

She checked the clock again and decided to get showered and dressed. She passed Michael in the hallway as he entered the kitchen, "You look rough," she greeted him.

He grinned through bed-head hair that was getting long. She'd nagged him to get it cut, but he was persisting with what he described as an early mid-life rebellion.

"Thanks a lot," he yawned as he walked to the teapot brewing.

"And get a haircut you hippy," she called back to him smiling as she ascended to a steamy shower, one to help both wake, and steel her for the dark day ahead.

The churchyard was packed to bursting, and it seemed to Emily that pretty much everyone in town was here. She scanned the crowd noting the familiar faces; Justin Gaunt the butcher, Morgan from the deli, and Eddie the tram driver. Even the school had even closed for the day, and her fellow teacher Sarah-Jane - as well as the headmistress Olivia Thirlby - were all in attendance. Casper Christian was holding court with the handyman Kevin Darnell and the Sheriff, Gerry Quinn, who were both paying close attention to whatever it was he was saying.

Emily wore a full length black dress that had been packed away in the attic, unused and not needed due to the weather. It was a little fusty and she was glad this morning that she had somehow managed to avoid the dreaded morning sickness. She'd felt a brief stab of selfishness when having to pull on the heavy garment on such a warm day, but she pushed it aside quickly, appalled at her own thoughts. Michael stood beside her, squirming uncomfortably in a suit and tie. Despite his handsome appearance she knew that he hated to dress in such a manner. She flashed him a soothing smile that he reciprocated.

She watched the parade of townsfolk, heads bowed and faces blank, terrified of portraying life within death's setting. She had often thought that funerals should be tales of remembrance, happy stories sprung from memory's past and aired in public for smiles and laughter. Death was not always the end, she thought soulfully. Those that we love, live on and linger in our minds and prayers. She had not been raised with a particularly religious hand. Her family had attended church services as a matter of appearance within the small community in which they held sway. Her parents had never expressed their own beliefs as far as the existence of a God was concerned. Her own faith was limited at best, after the accident that had robbed them of a child, it was easy to believe that there was no-one looking over their shoulders and standing protectively with wide encompassing arms. It was often said that God moved in mysterious ways, but she was damned if she could figure that move out.

The service inside the church had been blissfully short as the interior was hot, humid and unfortunately not air-conditioned. The long wooden pews were jammed full of townsfolk paying their respects beneath high ceilings and tall windows. Emily noticed that the interior was simple and elegant, there were no expensive grand gestures aimed at praising an insecure God. The church was immaculately maintained and cleaned, a gentle apple blossom perfume hung in the air, and the wood gleamed with effort and polish. Michael had never been particularly religious, they had not attended a church back in England save for the occasional Christmas Eve service that seemed more magical than religion based. Both of them had been concerned about America's reputation for right wing religious fervor, but they had yet to experience any sign of it in Eden.

The church was near the outskirts of town and not on either of their regular routes, and before the funeral, they had yet to meet the local Deacon.

The grandly named Landon Sheldon-Wilkes was a thin, reedy man somewhere in his late sixties. He looked healthy and hearty with a friendly white bearded face and crystal blue eyes. Emily had thought that many a woman must have gotten lost in the eyes of a younger Landon. He had greeted her and Michael warmly with a firm handshake, and the other placed on their shoulders in a comforting gesture.

"Emily, Michael," he greeted them, "It's wonderful to meet you both, unfortunate that it's under such sad circumstances," he commiserated, "I'm Landon, Landon Sheldon-Wilkes if you please, but don't hold a silly name against me," he whispered.

"Did you know Janet well?" Emily asked.

"Not as well as I would have liked I'm afraid," he said unhappily, "Perhaps I would have been able to help the poor woman, so young and such a tragic waste."

"Have you seen Chris?" Michael suddenly interjected, looking around.

"From what I understand from Casper, he would appear to be too distraught to attend the service today," Landon replied.

"Casper told you that? Has he spoken to Chris? Because I haven't been able to contact him since..." Michael struggled to articulate, "Since that night," he concluded.

"Mr. Christian," the Deacon said formally, "tends to matters of the town, all kinds of matters," he added somewhat mysteriously, "You'll have to excuse me, I have my own matters to attend to, as I'm sure you understand."

Emily watched as Landon looked over Michael's shoulder and nervously exited the conversation. She turned to see what had spooked the Deacon, but all she could see was Casper standing serenely and showing sympathy with the townsfolk.

The service started soon after, and Emily sat as waves of comforting platitudes washed across the gathered congregation. Landon spoke clearly and concisely, his tones were pleasant and comforting. His rhetoric was soft and warm, nonjudgmental and gentle.

Before they were all too uncomfortable the service ended, and everyone trooped gratefully outside into the cooling breeze. Emily linked hands with Michael as they stood beyond the church's entrance. The townsfolk all began to slowly shuffle towards the rear of the grounds to where Janet would be laid to rest.

The church was a small, quaint, white wooden building, with a steeple top protruding through the roof. There was a porch jutting out of the front with an overhanging pitched roof and a pristine picket fence. The grounds were beautifully maintained as she'd come to expect with every inch of Eden. The grass was lush and a deep green, and not for the first time, she marveled at the horticultural skills involved in sustaining such greenery in such hot and dry weather. The graveyard was lined with immaculate white marble headstones, all standing to attention in perfect formation. She glanced at the engravings as they slow-walked from the church. Most of the dates covered extraordinarily long lives, 98yrs here, 102yrs there. Before they'd emigrated she'd morbidly looked up the average life expectancy in the US, and found that it was worryingly only around 78yrs. The people of Eden were beating those odds out of sight according to their headstones.

The burial was short and to the point, Emily did not know if any of Janet's family from outside of Eden was present. She knew many of the town's residents, but she could not possibly recognise everyone. As soon as the casket was lowered, people seemed to thin, as couples drifted away at the first opportunity. Emily and Michael shuffled with the crowd out towards the main road following the crowd. It had seemed like an insufficient goodbye, but then she questioned what exactly would be?

As with all of Eden's major facilities there was a tram stop right outside, and they lined up with several other grievers. Emily hadn't been to a funeral before, but the tone amongst the people seemed a little light. Perhaps it was the hot and sunny days that appeared to demand happier dispositions. She gave a mental shrug, Janet had seemed nice enough, and she'd had visions of forming a close friendship with her new neighbor, but Janet's matrimonial betrayal had effectively ended that plan. She had watched her mother eaten away by her father's constant wanderings and broken promises. If Janet was so unhappy, then she should have just left Chris. Her betrayal was unavoidable and unforgivable in her eyes. She knew that Michael would miss Chris if he didn't come back and she felt badly for him. Michael didn't make friends easily; she'd watched him struggle throughout their time together, failing to make any sort of meaningful connection with other human beings.

She suddenly hugged him fiercely and kissed him hard. He smiled back at her, the love between them was palpable, and the other queue members looked slyly at them with warm pleasure. Their family would have to be enough friends to go around; she and the new baby would suffice, judging by the events of the day, they were indeed truly blessed.

Michael cruised along the smooth, flat road. The day all stretched out before him, a welcome warm embrace full of cooling breeze and a little gentle exercise. There were large banners strung from telegraph poles beside the road proclaiming the approaching "Woodland Festival" near arrival. Throughout the town, the talk seemed to be all about the festival, Michael was unsure as to just why such an annual show would take such precedence in people's minds. There were massive posters and signs dotted around the town, and every store was abuzz with chatter.

The funeral yesterday had been a dark day, but it had not taken away from Emily's joy with their new home, and for that, he was eternally grateful. The morning had dawned beautiful and blue as always and Emily had woken him in the nicest possible manner. It was always said that death and sex were inextricably linked. He'd forgone his usual routine of sitting outside in the rear garden, Chris had still not returned, and the house next door was a sad, empty shell devoid of life. He thought that maybe he should attempt to track Chris down, but he'd tried his cell on numerous occasions to no avail. If anyone would know anything, then it would be Casper, but he felt a strange reluctance to contact the town manager. Everything in the town seemed to flow through

Casper and Michael felt the need for a little distance. Perhaps that was also what Chris would have wanted; a little distance, a little privacy, and who was Michael to intrude? He could only imagine how his own world would collapse if anything ever happened to Emily. When the car had smashed into her and taken their baby, he'd sat in an ICU ward not knowing the extent of his wife's injuries - it had been a two hour eternity. The subsequent police investigation had turned up nothing but an abandoned car about a half mile away. The car had been apparently reported stolen earlier that evening, and the police were eagerly writing the incident off as joy riding kids losing control of an unfamiliar vehicle. ***Joy riding***! Was there ever a more inappropriate phrase? Mindless thugs had stolen his unborn child and nearly taken his wife as well into the bargain. There was sure as hell no joy involved.

The mountain bike beneath him cushioned his increasing weight comfortably. The front shocks eased up and down, but were barely required due to the immaculate road. He had finally gotten around to purchasing the bike from a recommendation, as per usual, from Casper. Despite his reticence over the man, the town manager knew every corner of his small kingdom, and could always be relied upon to steer anyone in the right direction. Due to the nature of the town layout, bikes were always a useful addition to have. The roads were flat and perfect, and everywhere that you needed to get to was only ever a short pleasant ride away.

"Killians" was a small bike shop off of the square. The large display window held hanging bikes of all shapes and sizes on display. A purple awning that matched all the others in size, material, and shape hung outside. A cute black logo of a family cycling along with the store's name was embossed upon it.

Michael had entered the store with a soft jingling bell that announced his arrival. He'd stepped into the air-conditioning cooled interior and paused, smiling and waiting for an assistant to spring forward as they always did. This man was in fact the owner. He wore a long white apron over a short sleeved red checked shirt and stone colored shorts. His stocky boots looked fit for hiking and he wore long socks rolled down. He had long, bushy blond hair and a full heavy beard, and his face was tanned and lightly lined by the sun. Michael guessed his age at early thirties. He was fit and athletic looking with broad shoulders and toned legs, and obviously he was practiced what he preached.

"Jack Killian," the man announced with a broad smile and an outstretched hand.

"Michael Torrance."

"So what can I do for you today Mikey? We have the finest selection of bikes in Eden, of course it's the only selection in Eden," he laughed.

Over the next thirty minutes, Michael was taken through a rigorous matching process that he thought would never end. He was measured, weighed, and his legs were checked for muscle tone and strength. Jack paired him with several models, each time standing back and stroking his chin thoughtfully before retiring into the back of the store and trying another model. Eventually, as Michaels patience was wearing thin, Jack finally settled on an Airborne cross country Goblin in coolaid Green. It was a hardtail 29er with a hydroformed frame, RockShox Reba RL lockout fork, full SRAM X7 2x10 drivetrain, ELIXIR R hydraulics and a WTB wheelset. Michael had no idea what any of that meant, but the bike looked pretty damn cool. He forked over his credit card, his mood not even spoiled by the hefty, slightly over a thousand dollar price tag.

"That's the one my man," Jack pronounced as Michael sat aboard the bike, "That baby will get you around town or anywhere else that you want to go."

"Feels great," Michael said swaying from side to side, feeling the easy balance, and weight.

"So where are you thinking of heading for?" Jack asked.

The question sounded natural and friendly enough, but ever since the Sheriff outside of Janet's house the night that she died, Michael couldn't help but feel a little suspicious. Ever since they had moved to Eden, the welcome had been warm, and their new neighbors had been involving, but all of a sudden Michael found his imagination clocking in and starting work. He knew enough about himself to realise that his new novel-where a once welcoming town suddenly devolved into sinister overtones-was bound to influence his overworked mind. He knew this in a theoretical sense, but he could still not quite shake the feeling that all eyes were on him and Emily. The looks in some of the stores felt a little too long, and the questions seemed a little too intrusive. Michael was working hard so as not to spoil their new home. He was always looking for the other shoe to drop and he did desperately want to be happy, but he still didn't want to answer as many questions as he was getting, friendly or otherwise.

"Oh just around town you know," he patted his expanding middle, "Got to work some of your hospitality off," he laughed good-naturedly, if a little forced.

As Michael was leaving the store, he suddenly noticed faded green paint on the side of the bike shop. "Hey Jack, what's that?" He asked, pointing to the markings.

"Just a couple of kids with too much time on their hands I guess," Jack replied nonchalantly. "Sheriff Quinn will get them soon enough I'm sure."

Michael stared closer at the washed and faded paint, he could just about make out the fading words "Wake Up", a strange epitaph. Perhaps it was a new band or pop culture reference that he was unaware of.

He had soon been on his way with a wave and a smile. He'd woven his way a touch drunkenly down the main street. He had been a keen advocate of cycling in his youth, mainly down to the lack of any other transport, but it had been years since he had last owned a bike. He discovered that the old saying was true as he began to straighten his path and his momentum steadied. Soon he was cruising casually, not quite daring to take one hand off the bars to acknowledge the friendly catcalls as he passed people that he now knew. Ten minutes later he was out of the residential areas and headed back towards his home.

The view out of his writing room had long since tantalized him. The long, straight deserted road ploughed a path through lush green fields and stretched off to the forest horizon. He'd always planned to explore this picture perfect view, but for some reason he just didn't want to divulge those details to Jack Killian, or anyone else for that matter. Eden could be a touch smothering, he was beginning to find, and Janet's similar words returned to haunt him as she'd used that same word - smother. As great as he had found the town and its people, he was starting to desire a little quiet, a little freedom on his own terms and beyond friendly, but prying eyes.

He passed his neighborhood and continued out onto the main deserted road. The hedgerows swayed in the breeze as he left all houses behind. He was no farmer but the thriving fields looked pregnant with vitality and abundance.

He cranked up the volume on his MP3 player and the stinging chords of the Foo Fighters blasted his adrenaline levels as he charged the road. He could see the flat landscape stretching out in front of him like a luxurious carpet, and there were no farms in sight, no houses, no barns, or silos. Eden was surrounded by a large wooden wall on three sides, a great reassuring barrier that separated them from the outside world, a world where random cars mounted pavements and babies were lost. It had been the promise of protection, security, and safety that had brought them here in the first place and he could see the great walls from here, off in the distance. The fourth side of Eden was where he was heading. The wall seemed to be unnecessary there, as the natural thick forest barrier grew in its place, spreading out through the space where the manmade barrier ended.

The road in front of him began a gradual incline and he began sweating as his unpracticed legs pumped harder against the grain. Eventually he passed through the fields and shuddered slightly despite his effort. The temperature seemed to drop as he approached the woodland. He pulled up as he reached the edge of town; he rubbed the goosebumps on his arm wishing that he'd brought a long sleeve top, perhaps the weather was finally going to break. His heart sank a little with the thought of the glorious weather passing, he felt as many did, that moods and the weather were inextricably linked.

The woods seemed darker the closer he got, and a narrow pathway led from the now dirt track that he was riding along, as the tarmac gave way to a more natural base. The path wound its way up into the heavily canopied forest, a thin brown trail that disappeared into the darkness. As he'd approached the outskirts of the town he'd been eager to take his new toy off into the woods - now, however, he paused. He shut off the MP3 player and took out his earphones; he was met with an oppressive silence, the world was dead and cold around him. Despite the thick, dense forest, there were no sounds of animal life within the wooded area, there were no bird calls, and Michael looked up to the skies and saw no fluttering wings of any variety. Suddenly he felt scared, it was a panic that started in the soles of his feet and climbed with clutching bony fingers up his legs and into his gut. His hands trembled, and his primal mind flooded with flight or fight inclinations. Anger took hold, and he cursed himself for fearing a trail that stretched beyond some trees in a dusky light, like some modern day little red riding hood promise. He tucked his MP3 player into his pocket and lowered his head, his feet were unsteady as he placed them on the peddles. His throat was dry and the fear tasted bitter in his mouth. He took his not inconsiderable courage and plunged into the woods, his speed increasing as it was fuelled by fear. He brutally silenced off the thoughts that screamed in his head, telling him that this was a bad idea. The temperature dropped the further he rode hard onto the upward slope of the pathway. He disappeared from sight of the road and the world as the dark forest swallowed him whole.

Emily munched hard on the pastrami and Swiss sandwich. She was only a little over three months along but her energy levels were seriously flagging. It was only lunchtime but she was already exhausted. Teaching had always been a vocation rather than occupation to her, and she'd loved her job from the very first second that she'd stepped foot in a classroom and looked into the eager eyes of a room full of children.

She was sitting in the teachers' lounge; the room was bright and airy, the sofas long and luxurious, and on more than one occasion she had dropped off embarrassingly. The seating was a light orange and the room was painted a magnolia shade. There was a long table on the rear wall under a large sunny bay window. A top-of-the-line cappuccino maker hissed lightly with steamed milk, the coffee was easily as good as anything purchased in a store, and the cups were neither chipped nor stained. There was always a selection of fresh fruit and assorted pastries laid out each day. Emily had never felt so spoiled. Back in the UK the teachers' lounges were always a mad scrum of selfishness.

The door swung open and Sarah-Jane bounced in, Emily had yet to see her fellow educator in anything but a positive mood.

"Hey Ems," Sarah-Jane practically yelled, "What's good here today?" She asked as she made a beeline for the deli counter. "Oh I love Danish," she garbled through a mouthful.

"How are the monsters treating you SJ?" Emily asked jokingly.

"Oh they're not monsters," Sarah-Jane answered seriously.

Emily had found that Americans did tend to take everything that she said at face value. She stared at her friend with a raised eyebrow for a few seconds.

"Hey, you're joking," Sarah-Jane responded, pleased with her deduction,

"I'm getting good at this."

"If I tell you something, can you promise to keep it to yourself?" Emily asked.

"I suppose so."

"No SJ, not suppose, you have to promise, you have to mean it and keep it," Emily said earnestly. She stood and took her friend's hand for emphasis, "Promise?"

"Ok, I promise," Sarah-Jane used her free hand to cross her heart solemnly.

Emily looked SJ full in the face and considered. She was desperate to tell her friend, but she and Michael had decided to keep the pregnancy a secret, until at least after the first trimester. She took the plunge anyway, her desperation for a confidant overwhelming, "I'm pregnant," she whispered.

Sarah-Jane's face near exploded with joy. She grabbed Emily and hugged her tightly, jumping up and down, "That's so wonderful," she panted.

Emily's breath was squeezed out of her as she was bounced. "Easy, easy," she managed.

"Oh God I'm so sorry," Sarah-Jane stepped away, her hands raised to her face in horror. "Oh jeez, my mother always said that I was a klutz."

Emily laughed at her friend's worried and rapidly paling face, "It's ok, I'm not quite made of glass."

"Why is it a secret?" Sarah-Jane whispered, looking around nervously.

"I told Michael that we wouldn't tell anyone just yet, at least until the pregnancy is out of the red zone for potential problems, you know."

"I won't tell a soul, I swear," SJ nodded gravely.

Emily welled up at her friend's sincerity and then puzzled at the new and worried expression that SJ was suddenly wearing. She spun around to see the cause. Mrs. Thirlby the headmistress, framed the open doorway to the lounge. Her usual stern face was a stone mask. Her arms were folded across her spindly bony chest; her bird like fingers were clenched and her knuckles were white.

Emily watched as Mrs. Thirlby looked at her deeply, her pale blue eyes were piercing and defense defying. She looked back to Sarah-Jane whose face was desperately unhappy; she looked scared and nervous at the intrusion.

"Back to work ladies," the headmistress announced sternly, before marching rigidly past.

Michael checked his watch again, his eyes blurred and his vision swam. He felt dizzy and disorientated, and the world around him was full of vibrant colours and strange odors. He looked down at his feet, he was standing on the road some fifty feet from the woodlands and he felt that he was missing something. The bike! He looked around frantically, where was his bike? He'd cycled out here from the town, he'd reached the forest, and then..., his brow furrowed as his mind fogged. Had he gone into the woods? He thought that he had, but now he couldn't remember. He certainly didn't remember going in or coming out again. His watch told him that over two and a half hours had passed, but that surely wasn't possible, was it? He stared up at the woods; the trees loomed ominously across the horizon blocking the sunlight. The dark under the foliage was tangible, threatening, and strangely inviting. Giant spider egg sized goosebumps formed on his bare arms, and he shivered despite the day's warmth that was greater from this distance away from the forest. His breath stilled and the world stood silent. He felt sleepy and his limbs hung heavy - one foot lifted and took an involuntary small step back towards the forest.

"Mr. Torrance?"

Michael's heart felt like it actually stopped. His chest hitched violently, and an acidic lump caught in his throat, it was only shock that prevented him from opening his lungs and screaming.

"Mr. Torrance, are you alright?"

He turned slowly to face the enquiring voice, not knowing what to expect, but expecting the worst. An Eden Gardens' deputy stood before him. The man was wearing the uniform brown pants and tan canvas shirt with a star badge shining on his chest. He was a little shorter than Michael, and rather more slender than would be expected in a police officer; his face was gentle with a somewhat feminine grace. His features were delicate, and his hair looked a soft natural blond. His shoulders were narrow and his chest slim. The uniform must have been the smallest that the department had to offer, but it still billowed around him like a sheet.

"Mr. Torrance?" The deputy's voice took on a harder, more demanding edge.

"Yes, yes, sorry," Michael managed through a dry throat, "I was just, just miles away I guess."

"Yeah, you looked it," the deputy laughed, still watching carefully.

"Um, what are we doing here officer?" Michael asked, unsure of what exactly was going on in all senses.

"Well sir, I found you walking down the centre of the road about a mile away, you said that you'd gotten lost and left a new bike around here somewhere, so I drove you back."

Michael suddenly noticed the police car with the Eden crest on the side parked behind him, "Did we find my bike?" Was the burning question considering the price and his frugal nature.

"Yes sir, we found it here on the ground," the deputy said confused, "I was putting it in the trunk for you, when you suddenly went, well, a little bit weird to be honest sir. You were suddenly glued to the spot staring up at the woods, and I couldn't shake you out of it."

"Oh," was all Michael could contribute.

"Maybe I should call the doc out Mr. Torrance."

"No, no I'm fine, just a little spaced I guess," Michael managed, his voice stronger.

"Well, do you still want that lift home sir? I don't like the idea of leaving you alone out here."

"Yeah, maybe that'd be for the best."

Michael walked unsteadily following the deputy over to the car and made to get in the back seat.

"I think up front would be better Mr. Torrance, you don't really want to get a ride home in the back of a police car, people talk you know, especially here."

Despite their isolation Michael noticed that the deputy said the last part in a hushed nervous whisper. They both climbed into the car. Michael had only ridden in a police car once before, the night that an officer had knocked on his door to take him to the hospital where Emily lay unconscious and childless. The interior was typical of Eden, in that it was meticulously clean and spotless and the seats were soft tan leather, and smelt of fresh polish.

"How are you feeling Mr. Torrance?" The deputy asked again, his voice still loaded with concern.

"Fine, and its Michael, please."

"Michael it is then, at least in here. I'm afraid the Sheriff is rather a stickler for formalities in public."

"I can imagine," Michael paused. "I don't even know your name; I think I must have lost my manners along with my marbles."

"Stillson, Kurt Stillson, say that's a funny accent, where are you from, England?"

"Is it that obvious?"

"I've got an aunt who lives in Manchester, her name's Beverley Marsh, do you know her?"

Michael felt a genuine laugh rise and he caught it to avoid being rude. The UK had approximately sixty five million residents, but several Americans had already asked him if he personally knew some random citizen. The smile on his face felt real and natural, and it was a relief to sense a normal emotion. His brain still felt a little fried and his thoughts scattered, but the further they drove, the saner he felt.

"What were you doing out here? If you don't mind me asking," Kurt asked.

"Um, I'm not entirely sure to be honest; I was just looking for a little exercise."

"You know that no-one from town comes out here, they say that the woods are haunted you know."

Michael wanted to laugh, but his recent experience strangled that thought at birth. "Haunted, really, what's the story?"

"Oh hey, like you, I'm pretty new in town, I've only been here about three months, but even I know that those woods are not to be sniffed at. When one of the other deputies was ribbing me about it, I took a ride out here. I got to that trail that leads up into the trees, and that's about as far as I got. Nothing on earth could have made me go any further," he laughed unconvincingly.

"I guess that makes you smarter than me."

"Wait a minute, Michael Torrance, the writer?"

"Afraid so."

"Hey I read one of your books on a flight once, not bad, not bad at all."

"We aim to please."

"Hey, a real life celebrity."

Michael started to laugh before he realised that the deputy was being sincere. He had only been a moderately successful writer for a number of years now. He made a decent living doing a job that he enjoyed, but he had never even remotely thought of himself as being in any way famous. Simon Day, his agent, had his fan mail filtered, sparing him the attentions of the strange and desperate. His fan base seemed to be largely female, for whatever reason, and they were generally sane and thankfully loyal.

They rode the rest of the short distance back to his house in silence. He could feel that Deputy Stillson was burning with questions, but mercifully he was keeping them at bay.

They pulled up to the curb and both exited; Stillson hefted his bike from the trunk and held it for him on the sidewalk.

Michael was glad for the exaggerated show of friendliness that the deputy was putting on for the neighbors. He knew that the curtains would be twitching, and he didn't want his ride home to be misinterpreted. The bike looked relatively unscathed save for some scratching on the frame, "Thanks for the ride Kurt."

"You're very welcome sir, all part of the service," the deputy smiled.

"Say, if I wanted to know more about the haunted woods, who's the best man to ask?"

"Mr. Christian I suppose, he knows more about the town than anyone."

"And if I didn't want to go through Casper?"

Stillson paused, as he evaluated the question, "I sort of know what you mean," he whispered keeping his voice lower than ever, "He's a bit on the creepy side," he winked. "I suppose you could always talk to Darnell, Kevin Darnell."

"The handyman?"

"Yeah, you know him?"

"He helped us move in the first day, but I thought that he was close with Casper?"

"Strictly between you and me, he can't stand the guy, but you know Casper, nobody in this town makes a living without his say so."

Michael watched and waved the deputy off as he drove away; he pushed the bike around the side of the house and opened the large double garage door. He leant the bike up against the wall of the empty space and checked his watch again. Emily would be home any minute, and he was thankful that she had not been here to witness his return in a police car and the awkward questions that would have followed. He closed the door on the bike and headed into the house, tomorrow he would track down Darnell and start looking at the town with a serious eye. Perhaps it was just his imagination running away with him. He was writing a book about a town like Eden, where sinister intent lay behind friendly eyes. It didn't take a genius to surmise that parts of his story would filter into how he saw his surroundings, but today hadn't been a figment. The trip to the woods had been real, and his loss of time had been real. He was a writer without delusions of being a journalist, but tomorrow he would start to find out the who, the what, and the why.

Kurt Stillson drove back into town buzzing. He'd never met a celebrity before, and Michael Torrance had seemed pretty nice, not like some of the other jerks you read about.

Kurt had made the move to Eden after applying online. He'd been working as a security guard at the Woodfield mall in Schaumburg, Chicago. The days had been long and the pay lousy. The job had mainly consisted of chasing off poorly educated youths from hassling store owners, whilst they hurled insults over skinny shoulders. He was twenty six and the job had only ever meant to be temporary, but he had woken up one morning to discover to his horror that three years had scarily slipped by without him noticing. The weather seemed to be always cold and wet in Chicago, and he longed for action and excitement, but without the dangerous aspect that real police work would entail. It wasn't that he was cowardly; it was just that he was smart.

He'd been scanning the internet for police jobs in small, safe towns and it felt like he'd checked out every small town in America. He'd studied crime statistics, populations, and educational tables. Eventually, after about three months of painstaking research, an anonymous message had dropped into his email box from some small town out west called Eden Gardens. To his knowledge he had never contacted the town, or even come across it, but the advert had been small and classy. The text was minimal, but one phrase was hokey enough to catch his eye, "Heaven on earth and twice as nice".

He had replied to gain more information, not thinking too much about it, but around a week later he had received a clandestine package in the mail. He'd opened the large manila envelope after a day of being chastised for sipping from a bottle of water in order to swallow a couple of aspirin to keep a fever at bay as he sweated profusely at his post. He'd staggered home, his uniform a foul stench of a pungent flu inspired odour, and he'd ripped open the package half-heartedly, not really caring. About forty five minutes later he was sold; the town really appeared to be perfection in a hot climate. As he'd shivered under his virus, and the cold wind howled mercilessly at his crappy apartment, he'd made his decision. The next morning he'd quit his job, his apartment, and his Chicago life.

He leaned his arm out of the window as he drove. The warm air and hot sun caressed his skin and he couldn't picture ever being cold again. The town was indeed perfection for some, those with the financial resources to live in the mansions. For the rest of the townsfolk that had to work for a living, it was only close. The weather was wonderful and the people were friendly. His salary was fantastic, and even came with accommodation; a beautiful three bedroom house with a large garden and a small pool.

His position of deputy carried a certain level of respect around the town - the kids were well behaved, and the women were beautiful. However, the Sheriff's department and town regulations were explicitly clear on the fraternization permitted between town employees and residents. He'd had to endure a month long training program that seemed to mainly deal with his presentation and conduct, rather than his peacekeeping duties. He didn't mind the somewhat uptight attitudes, as he had moved here from a position of borderline desperation. Sheriff Quinn was a ball-breaker, and the town manager Casper Christian was more than a little weird, but overall it was a small price to pay for such as a cushy number.

He pulled into the Sheriff's office parking lot. There were two bikes hooked up to a stand and no other cars. One of the other joys about living here was that he didn't have to waste money on an expensive car. The trams crisscrossed the whole town making cars almost irrelevant. He also had no real desire to leave the town and travel to the world outside, when everything he wanted was here.

He pushed open the glass fronted door cringing at the overhead bell that jingled; every store in Eden seemed to have these quaint touches. The office was clean and organised as usual, the counters gleamed, and the chrome edges sparkled. There had yet to be a single crime since he had arrived and the paperwork was easily manageable. Most of the duties of the office seemed to consist of management systems for processing permits and alike. It was dictated that the officers were to be visible around town, and ever vigilant for town rule violations. Just lately there had been case of the graffiti artist that had been perplexing the Sheriff. Green slashing paint, spraying the words "Wake Up" had been found in various places around the town, which was driving the Sheriff and Casper to fits of purple rage. As far as Kurt was concerned, if a little paint was the extent of the troubles, then the town should thank its lucky stars for getting off so lightly.

Ellen Barlow was sitting behind the desk when he entered the office; she was twenty nine, and strawberry blonde, with green eyes and endless legs, and she was already the love of his life. He had yet to engage in any kind of meaningful conversation with her, but he already knew that she was perfect.

She glanced up and smiled at him as he entered, it was the briefest of looks, but he melted just the same. He had steeled himself in the car that this would be the day; this would be the day that he charmed and wooed her. Upon closer reflection, he discovered that actually, this wasn't the day after all.

He slunk past the desk and into the rear offices to change before he went off shift, cursing himself for his lack of courage as he crept past, head bowed, and cheeks blazing.

"Still not pulled the trigger Kurt?"

Tommy Ross grinned irritatingly at him. Tommy was the town's other deputy; he was broad, athletic, and handsome in every conventional way. Kurt thanked his lucky stars every day that Tommy was also gay. If they ever had to compete in the same market for dates, then his Friday nights would be long and lonely, well longer and lonelier than they were at present.

"I'm working on it," Kurt said sheepishly.

"Man you need to work faster," Tommy said, buttoning up his uniform over a bulging chest. His teeth sparkled, and his deep blue eyes shone brightly.

Kurt couldn't help but grin along with Tommy's infectious smile. Tommy had the sort of magnetism that Kurt could only dream of, and he was glad all over again that he faced no in-house competition for the fair Ellen's hand.

"Why don't you ask her to the carnival a week on Saturday? They set up on the square with rides and booths, the games aren't rigged and the food's great. I know that she goes every year with friends, I'm sure that she'd like to go with you."

"Why?" Kurt asked suddenly with the pinched pained face of a love struck teenager, "Did she say something?"

"Oh for..." Tommy strode past him with an exasperated expression, "Hey Ellen," he shouted, "You wanna go to the carnival with Kurt on Saturday?"

"Sure," drifted the shy response.

Kurt's heart skipped more than just the one beat. He peered out around the changing room door and Ellen's face smiled back at him as he blushed furiously, "Pick you up at seven?" He squeaked.

"Sure," she blushed back.

"Love's young dream," Tommy said smiling and shaking his head.

Emily tramped grumpily to the tram. She was closer on the scale to exhaustion than tired, and she hadn't even started the day yet. She cursed Michael under her breath, *lucky sod*, she thought, *bugger can sleep in all day if he feels like it*. She didn't like this new morning voice, and she cut it off at the knees. She knew that the only reason that they could ever afford a life like this was from his talent. His writing had made this all possible; the new country, the house, the fresh start. Even the sun that shone warmly down on her face was because of him. Her moods had begun to swing wildly and were rather disconcerting. She made a mental note to contact Dr Creed to schedule an appointment ahead of their next, just to set her mind at ease. The last thing that she wanted was to start flying off the handle at work. Young children were less understanding than adults she wagered.

The morning tram rattled around the corner, ice picks stabbed at her head with painful knives digging into her brain. Every noise seemed amplified tenfold, and she ground her teeth in annoyance.

"Morning you two," Eddie greeted her softly with a wink.

"Morning Eddie," she mumbled eager to sit down. Only as she entered the tram, did she think about what he'd said and puzzle over it. As she passed the usual crowd, packed into their usual seats, she caught sight of the excited faces that beamed at her. She had used the service enough to be on smiling nodding terms with the regular passengers, but now some touched her arm with love as she passed. She sat in her customary rear seat, her head thumped and she gave serious thought to calling in sick and heading straight home. But her work ethic ran deep, and besides she wasn't about to drop Sarah-Jane in it at the last minute. Surely people couldn't know about the pregnancy, could they? She and

Michael had made a pact not to tell anyone, and after Chris had left, who would Michael tell? She had told Sarah-Jane, but the sweet girl had promised not to tell anyone, and despite her unbridled excitement she was sure that it was a promise kept. Thirlby, she suddenly thought. Mrs. Olivia Thirlby had been spying on them in the teachers' lounge. Had she overheard? The Headmistress hadn't mentioned anything to Emily during the rest of the day, but suddenly it made sense. That twisted, miserable, dried up old bitch, she..., Emily suddenly recoiled at the black, angry thoughts that had scuttled through her mind like hairy spider legs. Even if Mrs. Thirlby had overheard and mentioned it to someone, was it really such a big deal? Maybe after losing their first child she was a little overly sensitive. Her thumping head slowed, and the oppressive pressure that had been building gently eased. She rubbed her temples gently, breathed deeply, and forced a smile at the worried faces around her.

Darnell's yard was the neatest of its kind that Michael had ever seen before. It defied every stereotypical thought that he had approached the address with. There were no rusting cars up on blocks, there were no corroded chain link fences hanging loose and broken, and there was no snarling, drooling, matted coat Cujo to greet him. The yard was tarmacked and clean and there were three cars all lined up neatly awaiting treatment in front of a large brick built workshop. The sign reading "Darnell's" looked fresh and shone in the sunshine - gold letters curled on a deep red background. The yard was right on the far side of town and he'd passed through the privileged neighborhood mansions, through the expensive houses and passed the town employee homes that were still ten times the home that he had ever lived in. Darnell lived out past the residential and commercial areas, so far out that the rear of his property actually backed onto the town's huge wooden walls. His house was compact and neat, the wooden structure was painted a pristine white as was every other house in town, and his front lawn was clipped and glowed a healthy green. The house stood to the left of the hefty sized yard that contained the bulky workshop which stood proudly, its corrugated red roof shining beneath the hot sun.

Michael heard machinery whirling behind the closed double workshop doors. A radio played echoing music that rolled around the air and drifted on the breeze. Michael picked up the strains of Springsteen hoarsely trumpeting just what he and baby were born to do.

Michael walked up to the large wooden doors expecting to have to hammer loudly, but the smaller door within a door suddenly swung open and Darnell stood before him, his eyes blazing with naked suspicion. Darnell was a man in his early sixties. He was white haired with a handlebar moustache, he wore stained grubby blue canvas overalls, and for all the world, he reminded Michael of the actor Wilford Brimley. Darnell shuffled forward with the gait of a long term arthritis sufferer; his left leg dragged with a limp. His left hand was slightly hooked, and his right held a shiny claw hammer. Michael took an involuntary step backwards from the naked aggression of Darnell's face. All he had done was to walk up to his door, and the man looked worryingly ready for a fight.

"Whatdaya want?" The handyman growled menacingly, hefting the hammer.

"Hey, easy there Mr. Darnell, it's me Michael Torrance, you helped us move in a while back, up on Fairfax."

"Torrance?" Darnell stared suspiciously.

"Yes, Michael and Emily."

"You the English?" Darnell lowered the hammer to a safe level as he considered the information.

"Yes, that's us," Michael smiled his friendliest smile.

"Oh yeah, right," Darnell said through an embarrassed expression, "Sorry," he said looking at the hammer that he still clutched, "Get some troublesome kids round here from time to time."

Michael nodded knowingly, but inside he couldn't believe that Eden had rowdy kids of any description, let alone all the way out here. He had ridden his scuffed, nearly new bike out here this morning after Emily had left for work. It was starting to take her longer and longer to drag herself up in the mornings and get her engine cranking and he was now rising with her early, in order to give her a push out the door.

"What is it that you want?" Darnell asked, "Problem with the house?"

"Not exactly."

Darnell's eyes narrowed, and the suspicion was back on his face in an instant, "What do you want then?" He asked apprehensively.

"The woods."

"What about them?"

"I understand that they have a history, a story, a legend?"

Darnell stared for what seemed like an age, "Why come to me, aren't you better off taking to Casper?"

Michael stared back at him, sensing that this was some kind of test. He was being evaluated by Darnell for some reason, and so he took a shot. "I don't like the guy," he said truthfully, "I don't know what it is about him, but something's off with that guy. Way off."

Darnell stared harder at him, his eyes boring in and his forehead furrowed. His body stood rock still, and Michael could almost hear his mind ticking over. "Well then," he said, seemingly making a decision, "Why don't you come on in? Oh and Mr. Torrance," he said lifting the hammer again and waggling it, "Just be warned, if you're the next person to tell me that I look like Wilford Brimley, I'm liable to use this."

The mess inside Darnell's workshop was somehow reassuring to Michael, he suddenly realised that he was lacking a little chaos in his own life. Every corner of Eden had seemed like heaven to begin with, every building, every street, every blade of grass looked perfect, but perfection was starting to seem a little plastic. He was beginning to feel that there was cellophane wrapping over the town and its inhabitants - a wipe easy surface that preventable spoilage. The only trouble was that he was starting to wonder what exactly lay beneath the protective cover.

He could immediately relate to Darnell's lack of organisation. There were large boards up on the wall with tool outlines in white to identify where everything went. Almost all of the hooks were empty, and the chalk outlines looked lost and lonely. The tools themselves were scattered around a large table graveyard of discard and neglect. Despite his best intentions, Emily was always chastising him for leaving things out; books, tools, ingredients - he seemed pathologically destined to leave a mess wherever he went.

The workshop was long and busy. A car ramp and pit dominated the centre. Various machinery sat on benches all along the walls on three sides. A table saw and several drills were in various states of age and battering. This felt like the first piece of reality that he had found within the town walls, and he realised that he'd missed that kind of anchor.

"So what is it that you want to know Mr. Torrance?" Darnell asked gruffly.

"Please, it's Michael, and it's about the woods at the back of town."

"That's not somewhere that a nice man such as yourself wants to be going Michael."

"What's wrong there?"

"Now that's the question, isn't it?" Darnell smiled grimly.

Michael watched as Darnell walked over to a wall cabinet and pulled out a corroded and battered old coffee tin. He looked around furtively despite them being alone and pulled out a small metal flask. He unscrewed the cap and took a long drink from it, his face grimacing. He looked back at Michael and with a look of slight regret, he offered the flask. Michael accepted the hospitality and took a small sip. and immediately began coughing and spluttering as the harsh liquid exploded in his throat. "What the hell is that?" He stammered.

"Old family recipe," Darnell laughed as he pounded Michael on the back.

Initiation passed, Michael pressed on, once he'd regained his breath, "**Is** there something wrong with this town?" He asked deliberately abruptly.

Darnell stared at him, his face hard and impossible to read. "Eden is perfect, heaven on earth and twice as nice," he recited in a neutral tone, his eyes flint but watchful.

Michael stared hard back at him, "I'm just looking for some answers here, I'm not looking to make any waves, honest I'm not."

Darnell suddenly grabbed him hard by the thin polo shirt that he wore. The old hands augmented by years of manual labor pinched the skin painfully, as Michael was driven backwards, his arms cart wheeling wildly against the sudden, violent movement.

"Who sent you?" Darnell snarled, his face inches away, "You tell Casper that I've done nothing wrong, you tell that fat pig Quinn as well."

"Easy, easy," Michael panted against the older man's surprising strength, "Nobody sent me, certainly not Casper or the Sheriff."

Darnell's grip didn't loosen, "So why are you out here testing me boy? Why the questions about the woods, of all places?"

"Alright, two things," Michael snapped, his anger rising fast after his initial shock. "Firstly nobody, I repeat nobody sent me, and secondly, get your fucking hands off me." His own eyes were hard now; his temper was typical of those slow to rise. He was mainly a mild mannered man and most things simply washed over him whilst Emily fretted, but once his slow burning temper cranked up, you would be wise to get off the runway.

Darnell released him warily, he stepped backwards without ever breaking the eye contact that crackled between them, "Ok," he said slowly, "OK then."

"Back in the early 1800's," Darnell began, as they sat in his kitchen across the stained and marked wooden table some ten minutes later. A six pack of beer bottles was opened for Michael, whilst Darnell stuck to his flask, "the Christian family came to this neck of the woods, so the story goes."

"Story?"

"Aye, in my opinion the legend and the truth often get tangled over time. You ask Casper and he will tell you of a noble family that ploughed their way west looking for a brighter future. A righteous brood that found fertile woodland and built a town. Saviors to man, the whole damn family, but the truth is never quite so poetic I've found." Darnell paused and took another long drag from his flask. "You can never tell anyone what I'm telling you," his face suddenly looked older and sadder as the worry lines deepened.

"What is this fear that Casper seems to hold over everyone here?" Michael asked as he leant forward.

Darnell smiled at his eager face, "Don't get excited Mr. Writer, there's nothing supernatural about the man. He's just an egotistical prick, and nobody works on a town contract without his say-so. If he knew that I was talking to you about his family, then I would be out of work like that," he clicked his fingers for emphasis. "He also frowns upon..." he waggled the homebrew flask, "Libations of a, personal nature, shall we say."

Michael relaxed, disappointed and relieved in equal measures, "So what about the woods then?"

"Ah, now therein lies a rather spookier tale altogether," Darnell continued, the strong alcohol greasing the gears. "The Christians founded their own town alright, but it wasn't the workers' paradise that Casper would have you believe. The conditions were appalling, dozens of good men died both building, and working in the mill, and many more through illness as the Christians refused to pay for a doctor. Casper's family grew fat and wealthy off of the backs of the workers. Casper's distant relative, Tolan Christian, was a religious tyrant of the Old Testament persuasion, a real fire and brimstoner. From what I've heard of the rumors back when I was a boy, before Casper took an iron fist hold over the town, Tolan Christian was nothing short of a monster. It is even said that..." he looked around the small kitchen and then rose and pushed the window curtains aside to check the yard, "He would carry a wicked sharp axe that he would use at random on the workers whenever he heard God's voice. Eventually, it's said that towards the end, it wasn't God's voice that he began hearing."

"How the hell would he get away with that?" Michael asked incredulously.

Darnell snorted bitterly, "This town was a speck on the landscape. Hundreds of miles from anywhere, the Christians ran the town, and Tolan ran the Christians. There was no law here, other than the one that he laid down." Darnell sat down wearily, "Before they all died out, some of the other old timers around town would tell stories about how Tolan grew more and more disturbed, more and more fanatical. He closed the church in town and began holding services out deep in the woods. The town priest soon disappeared, and Tolan conducted the ceremonies himself. Soon he had recruited several of the largest workers in town to his cause, their job being to keep the others in line. Punishments were swift and brutal, and the town lived in fear. It's said that he literally crucified men in the woods when he'd adjudged them to have angered his God by their blasphemous ways."

"Jesus," Michael sighed.

"Not exactly," Darnell smiled back humorlessly.

"How the hell is Eden still here today?"

"Therein lays the mystery my young friend," Darnell slurred, "For some reason, there is a very small gap between the madness and the prosperity, and it's a mystery that I'd wager Casper and no other descendant would want opened."

"That'd make one a hell of an addition to my book," Michael mused.

"WHAT?" Darnell roared, his arm swept the beer bottles off of the table and several shattered on the floor. "You can never write about what I've told you," his tone suddenly dropping from anger to pleading. "You can never open up those wounds, he'd never let you," he reached out and took Michael's arm gently. "You've got a beautiful wife and home and a baby on the way."

"How did you know about the baby?"

Darnell shrugged the question away, "You'll prosper here Michael, you people always do. Live your life and be happy. What more is there? Just be happy and leave old ghosts alone. Oh, and stay away from the Woodland Festival, it's not for you this year."

Michael stood outside in the sunlight again, his imagination was already running wild with thoughts of mad zealots and hauntings, and his research brain was ticking over fast. Should he really seek to uncover the dark secrets of Eden? He had spent his life writing tales such as this, but here was a real mystery. His intellect salivated at the thought; a book based in a reality stranger than any fiction that he had created in the past. But this was also his home now. Not just his, but Emily's, and soon to be their baby's as well. Emily had been horrified by his idea to write a fictitious account using Eden as inspiration. He shuddered to think just how she would react to him raking over the graves of the actual town. Real history, real deaths, and real horrors, perpetrated by ancestors of the current manager. Casper had obviously worked hard to bury the past beyond the sight of the living; the residents were growing younger and younger as the next generation moved in, and the stories faded with time.

He peddled slowly out of the yard and headed back towards town. His head was low, and his mind was crammed full of too many thoughts. As he cycled absently, his brain absorbed and processed. He did not see the car parked in the bushes as he passed. Whilst Michael wobbled his way attentively back towards home, the car pulled out carefully and drove towards Darnell's yard.

The car pulled up softly outside the workshop, and the driver hefted his bulk out into the day and flexed his stiff knee as he put his considerable weight on it. The man closed the door behind him, and the sticker on the door gleamed brightly in the dazzling sun. The decorative badge simply read Sheriff.

CHAPTER SIXTEEN
Interlude: A Brief Town History Part Two

Tolan Christian grew up broad and powerful, both in stature and physique. He was nineteen years old and could already hold sway over a crowd full of eager faces that were turned towards his sermons.

His mother, Chastity, was by now in a full embrace of her name, ever since the night that she had slain the demon inside her husband - the demon that had monstrously abused her innocent child. After that night, she had retreated into the shell of herself, and she became more and more strident about her religious views. She had always been a woman of faith, but now she was in the vice like grip of a spiritual mania. Tolan was raised within the confines of his mother's psychosis. They were bound together with chains of isolation, and they limped across the countryside relying on the kindness of others. They sought shelter in various churches and sects as they passed, seeking food and warmth against the cruelty of the outside world. Chastity had determined that they were touched by God's hand; a finger of fate had been laid upon them and had set their mission in progress. She only knew that God had a plan for them, she was not blessed with the specifics and did not ask during their nightly conversations. God had spoken to her on the first night of their fleeing as she and her son lay inside a neighboring village barn. They had huddled against the cold and the knowledge of her barbarous act. It was only a self serving delusion, as she could not face the truth over her son's defilement or her violent retribution. God had spoken to her and told her of his plans for them both. They were to head north and wait for his sign - he would show them the way - but only after they had first proved their worthiness. She was to take no provisions, no food, no money, no baggage, only the shirts on their backs and God's bible. Only then could they begin the long walk to his promised word.

Their days were arduous and tiring. They walked until their feet blistered, bled, and blistered again, until the skin eventually hardened like leather. They passed towns and villages, people and animals. Some greeted them with friendship, some viewed them with suspicion, and others with hostility. Chastity knew that they walked under the protection of God, that their path would be cleared, and they would only face the challenges that he saw fit. For five long years, they had traversed the country, relying on God's plan to show them the way. Every night without fail she would read from the Bible, bathing her son under the showering sermons. Under her preaching, God became a vision of power and retribution. He evolved and mutated into an omnipotent being of rage and fury. His love and compassion became lost to the growing Tolan.

During their five year marathon, Tolan would often deliver services to the towns and villages. He was an angelic at first, a child who captivated audiences with his grace and charm. Later as he grew and aged, he became a more vociferous and charismatic preacher. He was a powerful young man who carried God's word to the masses, and thrilled the young women of his congregations. Chastity succumbed to the sin of pride as she watched her son delivering powerful sermons in barns and fields. Amidst the mud and filth he rose above to be the voice of God. For five long years, they toured the country on foot, never deigning to take a horse or carriage. Theirs was a painful wandering on foot and empty stomachs, and they suffered as they must, and waited to be shown the sign.

Eventually, after the harshest of winters, Chastity watched as Tolan stealthily tracked a rabbit through the undergrowth, and they came across a clearing surrounded by thick and lush woodlands. The sun shone brightly and warmly on their upturned faces despite the season, and there was a fresh water stream that ran through the clearing. The earth looked rich and fertile and the forest teemed with bountiful and edible wildlife. Chastity knew that this was God's plan for them, and they were finally home. This was to be their future, their world, their Eden.

Chastity was still only thirty eight years old, but her body was eons older. The physical exertions had taken an irreparable toll on her fragile frame, and her mind was even more damaged. Since the night when she'd spliced her husband's head in two after discovering her son's abuse, her psyche had shattered, unable to deal with the guilt over Tolan's desecration and her own murder committal. Now all she heard or acknowledged was the word of God that ran through her thoughts and dreams, both waking and asleep.

After they had fashioned a rudimentary shelter, she had sent Tolan out to find converts to their cause. This would be a holy, sacred place that would require brothers and sisters to build a monument to the heavens.

Tolan was thirteen years old at this point. He was a handsome young man, blessed with his mother's looks, and his father's build. He turned heads amongst the girls, but had little interest in their bashful stares and doe eyes. Tolan's mind, much like his mothers, seemed to only exist from the dawn after the death of his father and he remembered practically nothing from that day spent in the woods. Only brief glimpses of humiliation and pain existed in the deepest of his dark dreams. Only some mornings when he woke, in those blurred lines between waking and asleep, did he suspect. His mother's will had been iron and absolute for over five years, but her unstable mind had leaked into his, poisoning his thoughts and stunting his emotional growth. He believed in the unconditional word and plan of God's will as relayed to him by his mother, and he preached the fire and brimstone of a dark and vengeful deity. His sermons were powerful and passionate; his audience were swayed by the booming voice that emanated from the chest of a child, his natural charm radiated outwards and over the assembled. He possessed a fluid, magnetic charisma that drew people towards him. Villagers gravitated to him, desperate to be closer, and they hung on his every word and gesture. Many of the towns and villages were in desperate straits; crops were failing, farms were collapsing, and sickness was prevalent in both townsfolk and livestock.

The people were fraught with worry and despair; they looked to the heavens for answers and were met only by silence and abandonment. In their fear, they turned to a thirteen year old preacher, a child of God sent to deliver his both word and their salvation.

Chastity waited patiently for seven months for Tolan to return, she grew weak despite the warm air and bountiful lakes that God had provided for her. Her right leg grew lame, and she had to fashion a crutch from a tree branch in order to hobble around. She sharpened the end of the crutch to a point, and used it to spear fish from the stream. She prayed all day and spoke to God in long conversations after dark when God showed her his vision for the town. God's influence was now drifting from her mind and thoughts. Instead his voice became a whisper in the trees, and the branches would rustle beneath the soft breeze as his voice sank into her. The voice showed her where the church would sit, where the mill would lay. It showed her the town square and the beautiful children that would run and play under the hot sun; it told her of Eden and all of its glory.

When Tolan returned he found his mother near death; she lay peacefully upon the lush grassland, her face burned by the sun, but a contented smile etched across her features. The large open field was crisscrossed with drawings that she had made by dragging the pointed end of her crutch through the earth. The rough sketches were a plan for the town, a layout of buildings and areas. All were labeled clearly and plainly for him to follow.

He had brought thirty three men, women and children with him. These were his disciples, the first of many brought by a hope of a new life. They had followed him as he had moved from town to town and village to village, collecting the lost and despondent. He'd accepted all before him and turned no-one away from the cause. He simply accepted it as God's plan that builders and farmers were among his party, another sign that God had now blessed him to carry on beyond his mother's tender fragile frame.

His mother passed away gently the first night that he returned. He had held her now almost emaciated body, her face was gaunt but happy, and she smiled at him and whispered her love before she died. Tolan buried her beneath the field where she had drawn her plans for the town. He had heard the voice in the rustle of the trees for the first time that night; it was the same voice that had spoken to his mother. Whilst his new disciples had slept, he'd opened the throat of an orphaned girl that he had selected for such purpose. The girl was not with any of the party that he had brought in and would not be missed. He'd shed her blood to bless Eden under the eyes of God, and she would not be the last.

CHAPTER SEVENTEEN

The bright lights twinkled and the Ferris wheel rumbled. Squeals of children's delight and wonder lit the warm summer evening's air, and joy radiated throughout the town. The carnival had arrived and taken over the square. Booths sparkled with vibrant colours, fairy lights hung low and danced amidst the night sky. There were antique looking attractions that glistened with gold trimmings. There was a carousel, bumper cars, a chair-o-planes ride, and an old fashioned ghost house. There were games of chance such as balloon and dart games, air rifle ducks, duck pond, ping pong fish bowl, basketball hoops, and baseball bottles. The mouth-watering aromas rose like tangible clouds from the food stands. Delectable fried fragrances and cotton candy tickled taste buds attracted the none too healthy appetites.

The D'Amour carnival had been operating for almost a hundred years. Preston D'Amour was the company's present chief operating officer and his family had founded and run the business ever since its inception. He was the incumbent charged with the running of the carnival; his was an iron fist forged in a thousand battles, in a sea of vipers who only understood discipline.

Preston took a slug of neat vodka from a chipped Spiderman glass tumbler that he grabbed from his bedside table. The trailer was large and spacious on the inside despite its antiquated exterior. Image was everything in his industry, and the crowds did not look kindly on luxurious Winnebagoes rolling into their towns. The carnival was all old, but immaculately maintained; the antique wagons glistened with care and the rides sparkled with love and attention. His was a travelling show of memories and longed-for childhoods, and his job was to bring an old, outdated demonstration of a better, happier time. They passed through many communities that had struggled in the present economic climate. Jobs were scarce and hope scarcer. They offered an evening away from worries and a brief hiatus from reality. Eden, however, was different; this was the one town where Preston felt like they were the ones taken back in time. This was a town isolated from the problems of the world. It was a community that bucked the trends and existed in its own isolation, the D'Amour Carnival was the intrusion of the modern world here. Eden was a lot further off the beaten track than Preston would have ever liked to normally travel, but the money that the town council offered more than made up for the inconvenience. The carnival planned its route every year to end in Eden, as after they played this town, they would split and retire for the winter. They always made five or six times their usual rate here, even without rigging the games or running scams. Casper Christian, the town manager, was always adamant about them running a clean ship here.

Preston shuddered and took another long, hard swallow, the neat alcohol exploded in his chest and warmed around the icy edges of his fear. Casper was a strange and scary man, despite his own formidable size and character, Preston always looked to avoid any situation that would place them alone together. Casper's rules were sacrosanct; no scams, no rip-offs, and no fraternizing out of hours. The carnival was allowed inside the great walls late Friday night and was to be gone before light on Sunday.

Preston considered himself a man of practical means, he had his family's legacy to uphold. He had forty seven workers to provide for, and rocking boats held no attractions for him. Every year they played the town with smiles and respect; they took their money and got the hell out according to Casper's schedule. Preston drained the glass, steeled himself, and stepped out into the arena.

Emily and Michael positively skipped their way towards the chiming music, laughter and bright lights of the carnival - their mood in tune with the evening. The dusk was warm, and they joined the throng of excited townsfolk bustling along the road towards the square. Back in the UK, fairs and carnivals tended to be grubby affairs - dilapidated machinery cranked by surly workers only interested in the contents of your wallet. The fairs rolled through towns creating mess, and drawing the worst in antisocial youths. Towns breathed collective sighs of relief when the diesel engines hauled off their fading carcasses once again.

Michael nodded and waved to those faces that he recognised. The deputy who'd given him a ride home, Kurt Stillson, was walking with a pretty blond woman; his face seemed to be in a constant state of blissful blush. He saw Justin, the large and gregarious butcher, Morgan from the deli, even Eddie the tram driver that ran their route was there with his wife. Michael had been hoping to spot Darnell, the handyman who'd told him tall tales of Casper Christian, as he was eager for more details or leads. He'd hoped to casually run into the man and uncover more facts than gossip. It had been two weeks since he had spoken to Darnell, and he appeared to be the one town regular who was absent for the evening. Perhaps this many smiling faces was not his scene.

Emily held Michael's hand as they walked briskly; she glanced down realizing that they partook in the public display of affection on most occasions now without thinking about it. She squeezed him gently, pleased by his happy face, their love was warm and currently her womb was filled in affirmation.

She looked as they rounded the corner; the whole square danced and sparkled with fairy lights. The Ferris wheel stood tall and proud over the town carrying smiling faces in its slow rotation. She was now around four months pregnant, and it was plain to see for anyone who cared to look. She had found that it was impractical to wear large and baggy clothes under the hot weather. She had taken to favoring classic smock maternity tops; tonight she wore a pink and white check one that allowed her frequently overheated frame to breathe.

She relaxed into the pleasant evening's entertainment ahead; the long day at school had been tiring and stressful. She had finally spoken to Sarah-Jane as soon as she had been able to get her alone. SJ had professed her innocence as to the unauthorized release of her pregnancy news. She had looked into her friend's warm and innocent face and been unable to believe that she would have broken her word. Mrs. Thirlby had hovered around her all day; every time that she turned, the stern Headmistress would be in the background, looking as though she desperately wanted to talk. Emily had begun to feel uneasy around the harsh woman; she hoped that it was only her increasingly unbalanced hormones that were colouring her emotions. She could easily picture Mrs. Thirlby spreading her news without care, far easier than she could picture Sarah-Jane doing the same. The Headmistress was a humorless woman; she was tight and contained, but now had taken on an air of disapproval towards Emily. Her usual reserved attitude was now verging on an almost hostile flavor. Emily did not know just what she had done to upset her boss, but she hoped that it would not sour the job which she loved. SJ had assured her over lunch that Thirlby could "just be like that" sometimes. She wished that if the Headmistress had something to say, then she would just come out and say it. She was growing increasingly irritated by the hard stares and disapproving looks. She shook her head to free such unhappy thoughts on such a beautiful night.

They crossed the road and into the carnival. Happy nods and welcoming smiles were passed around between residents, greetings were uttered between the better known.

"EMS!" a loud voice boomed in her ear as arms reached around and hugged her tightly.

She turned into Sarah-Jane, who, despite only seeing her a couple of hours ago, was greeting her like a long lost relative. She laughed and hugged her excitable friend back.

"Michael, this is Sarah-Jane, SJ, this is Michael," she introduced.

Sarah-Jane looked solemnly at Michael, for a moment Emily thought that she was going to curtsey, "Please to meet you Mr. Torrance," she said formally.

"And I'm pleased to meet you too," Michael said offering his hand that SJ shook shyly. "This is some carnival," he enthused.

"Oh this is nothing, just wait until you see the Woodland Festival, it'll be unreal this year, better than ever," Sarah-Jane beamed.

"Are you here alone?" Emily asked, looking around.

"No, I'm here with some friends," SJ answered disappointingly, she leant in forward and whispered, "They're all pretty lame to be honest."

"Why don't you join us then?" Michael asked.

Emily thought that SJ was having a stroke for a moment, her face turned the deepest darkest blush, and she stared at the floor unable to look him in the eye.

"I couldn't," she mumbled.

"Of course you could," he answered honestly.

"Really?" SJ looked up at Emily with desperation.

"Sure," Emily promised, stifling a giggle at the earnest face of her friend.

Emily watched as Sarah-Jane bounded over to her party of assorted friends, "That was very sweet of you," she said to Michael.

"Hey, I'm a sweet guy," he announced jokingly, "She seems nice, and I should get to know your friends."

Over the next two hours, two things happened; the three of them partook of every inch of the carnival, and Emily watched SJ slowly crawl out of her shell. She loved her husband all the more for his attention towards her shy friend. Normally he would only offer the bare minimum when it came to engaging in social offerings, but he seemed determined to draw the shy girl out into the world. Emily had watched SJ in private many times and in public; her boundless energy and enthusiasm seemed destined to be hidden behind closed doors. They would often walk to the square for ice-cream or coffee after work, Sarah-Jane's mood would slowly dampen as they approached the busy public area. She would be laughing and joking one minute, and then retreat violently back into her shell as soon as anyone else spoke to her. Emily had never met such a crushing case of dichotomy. SJ could be explosively extroverted in private when it was just the two of them, and painfully introverted as soon as anyone else spoke to her. She would often have to order for her friend as SJ became an aching twist of shyness before even the counter staff at the deli. She desperately wanted the rest of town to see the charming, happy bundle of energy that she saw. Sarah-Jane was a little heavy, but she was nowhere near what she imagined herself to be. She was pretty and fun, and would be a catch for any lucky man in town. Michael had spent the evening prying looks and words from her with painstaking care and attention. She did not know if Michael was aware of what he was doing, but he was doing it just the same. They played the games and Michael won a large pink bear shooting a water pistol into a clown's mouth that he gave to Sarah-Jane, Emily thought that her young friend was going to faint as she took the stuffed toy. They rode the ferris wheel and the carousel; Michael took SJ on the Bumper Cars and drove with a winner's attitude that drew several disapproving stares from their fellow drivers. They ate cotton candy, donuts, hotdogs and burgers until Emily thought she'd burst and all the while they laughed, by the end of their time SJ was unrecognizable. Her friend had gone from unable to look Michael in the eye, to teasing him about his inability to land a ping pong ball in a small fish bowl,

"It doesn't bloody fit," he grumbled.

"Use an arc," SJ offered unhelpfully.

"I'll bloody arc you," he mumbled grumpily.

They were now sitting on the blanket that Michael had unfurled from his backpack; Emily was often irritated by his foresight, even when it benefitted her the most. It was often annoying to see your own limitations illuminated by another. The three of them squeezed onto the tartan rug, and Emily smiled at SJ's gasp as Michael inadvertently brushed her leg. The fireworks were scheduled for ten thirty and her watch read ten twenty seven. If she'd learnt anything from their time here, it was that Eden ran to an unfailing timetable.

"Emily?"

She looked up to see Dr Samuel Creed's smiling face; his bushy beard was full of powdered sugar from an army of donuts that he'd obviously consumed ineffectively.

"Samuel," she greeted him warmly attempting to stand.

"Sit, sit," he ushered her.

"You too," she offered the large doctor. "This is my husband Michael and my good friend Sarah-Jane," she introduced.

Michael shook the bulky Dr's hand, "Pleased to meet you doc, I understand that my wife is in your hands," he held Samuel's hand for a second longer and held his gaze firmly.

"It's a position that I take very seriously Michael," came Dr Creed's sober response.

Emily watched as her husband relaxed, male sensibilities satisfied, she knew that Michael worried over the baby despite his protestations to the contrary. She had been eager for Michael to accompany her to the next appointment and was relieved to have avoided the maneuvering involved in getting him there.

"What brings you here Samuel?" She asked.

"I love the carnival, especially the food," he patted his stomach.

"So do I," came a quiet voice as Sarah-Jane utilized her new found confidence to speak to a stranger.

Emily glanced quickly at Michael and they shared a grin, "Help me stretch my legs for a minute Michael" she asked him. They wandered around the square leaving SJ and the doctor to talk, ignoring Sarah-Jane's frantic terrified glance as they left, figuring that sometimes, you really had to be cruel to be kind.

Michael walked his wife around, not quite understanding why she suddenly wanted to leave their comfy spot, but thinking that she often had motivations that were blind to him, so he often just followed. His mind was on hold for the evening, his talk with Darnell had raised many questions and piqued his writer's curiosity, and the idea of Casper having a blackened ancestral legacy was pretty juicy. His book was lacking a supernatural element - the idea of the haunted woodland that held sway over a town could be just the thing to spark his morbid intellect. It could be all the more interesting if some of the facts were actually true. The Christian's dark legacy wrapped in visions of demonic sacrifice would more than suffice to tantalize his audience. There were two wrinkles in this idea however; the first was Eden. The town had given him and his wife everything. They had been welcomed like family, and could he really trample over their lives? The second problem was the actual woods themselves. He'd suffered a blackout there; he'd cycled into the forest and emerged having lost a couple of hours. The more he probed, the more he'd likely uncover, and what if he didn't like what he found? Darnell had warned him to leave it alone, to just be happy here, but could he? Could he really just turn his instincts off like that? Could he be happy with his wife and child with such a mystery hanging over him? It was a crusty scab that he should ignore, but he was a picker.

Richie Duchamp looked around furtively; the street was deserted as the entire town seemed to be streaming into the carnival to watch the upcoming fireworks. He'd hung back deliberately as the stores emptied and closed, ignoring Gino's constant calls for him to take over on the bumper cars, ending the debate with one hard, icy stare. Richie was nineteen, and he was as hard as nails, and twice as mean. He'd hooked up with the carnival for the start of the season and had quickly discovered enough side enterprises to make it worth his while. The travelling nature of the business meant that he was never around for the morning enquiries when the local Sheriff came around calling for suspects. He had already stolen enough money for the season to be profitable - whether it was snatching handbags, muggings, short-changing, or rolling drunks, there was always money to be made. Preston D'Amour had taken all of the newbie's aside before they'd gotten to Eden; he'd made it abundantly clear that nothing untoward went on within these walls. The other carnies had toed the line, afraid of losing their additional income by getting not only fired from the carnival, but finding themselves dumped way out in the middle of nowhere, in one state of health or another. Richie, however, was not so easily dissuaded. He'd certainly made a valiant attempt to keep his fingers out of the cookie jar, but the store owner had made it far too tempting.

He had watched as the Starbucks did a roaring trade, the large fronted display window allowed him access to watch the tills being stuffed with lush green notes. The final straw had been when the last member of staff had left the building, turning off the lights, but not locking the doors in her haste. Richie had watched in disbelief as the unlocked door to a deserted store with fat stuffed tills teased him from across the street. He would be a fool to risk it, but he would be a bigger fool to ignore it.

With a last look around he crossed the road, walking casually, hands in pockets, and head down. He leant with his back against the door and reached behind to pull the handle down. The door swung open easily, and no alarms shattered the silence. He eased in quickly and shut the door behind him. He ducked down low beneath the sightline of the front window so as to remain invisible from the street. He efficiently emptied the three tills, grabbing fistfuls of abundant green notes and stuffing them deep into his pockets, leaving the coins despite the value. He turned to leave when he spotted the rear office door; he stood and considered. He had a few thousand dollars in his pockets already, it was the easiest score that he had ever made and yet, the back office. What if there was a safe? If the front door had been left open so invitingly, what about a safe?

Eventually his greed won out and he moved quickly beyond the large oak door marked private and stepped inside. The office was small, and he was about to search for more delicacies when the light in the doorway was blocked.

A large man with broad shoulders filled the gap. Richie panicked, his stomach rolled and dropped. *Preston*, he thought. Preston had the reputation for extracting his own form of justice when his rules weren't met. The large man raised a gun aimed at his chest, but a strange sense of relief flooded through him when he spotted the patchy light catch the gleam of the badge on the monster's chest.

"Hey officer," he started, when he suddenly saw that the weapon held aloft was longer than it should have been, the elongated barrel extension didn't belong on a 38 special.

The silenced gun spat venom and three fast blows collapsed Richie to the floor. He sank onto his knees, staring down disbelievingly at the small red holes that had formed on his shirt. His chest hitched and wheezed as he struggled for breath and a distant gurgle bubbled in his throat as the world turned black.

The fireworks were spectacular, the ooohs and aaahs radiated from mesmerized faces across the square and the black, clear night was illuminated in a million different rays and colours.

Emily sat with Michael as his childlike expression glowed with the display. She sat between his legs on the blanket, his arms wrapped around her, and occasionally she chanced a glance over to Sarah-Jane. SJ and the doctor sat beside them, huddled pleasantly without excessive intimacy, Sarah-Jane's beetroot face was fading as the evening passed. Dr Creed had an agreeable manner that seemed to set everyone at ease including, apparently, the world's shyest elementary school teacher. A sneaky gentle dig in the ribs from her husband caught her staring, his grin and a slight shake of the head spoke of his rebuke. She shrugged and smiled. If being a romantic was a crime then she was guilty, despite their age gap, she could see potential between her two new friends.

After the light show they made their respective ways home, Samuel offered to walk Sarah-Jane home, despite there being no need, given Eden's non-existent crime rate. Emily was flushed to see that she agreed in a warm manner that bordered on the charmingly bashful. As the doc and the teacher said their goodnights, Emily and Michael headed for home. The night was warm and the sky was clear. Their baby was healthy, and so were they, their finances were stronger than ever and life was good.

The carnival broke into its many pieces, steel skeletons were stripped bare of their decorative collage, and ugly machinery innards were exposed. The breaking operation was effective and efficient, a procedure that ran on autopilot during the silent night hours. Workers went about their business with precision born of experience; most did not need the light to unbolt and unplug, and the large flatbed trucks were soon laden with sections of the whole. Preston checked the head count again, still one missing - Richie Duchamp, his nephew no less. That punk had been nothing but trouble ever since he'd hitched his illicit wagon to the carnival. They often attracted the criminal element; he supposed that it was the travelling nature that drew those looking to keep on the move and away from recognizable addresses. A little thievery was always to be expected, he knew that many of the game operators ran crooked shows, and some of the female members of staff liked to offer shows of a more private and intimate nature after hours. Crime rates tended to rise whenever they rolled through town, and most local law enforcers tended to turn a blind eye as long as they were gone by morning and didn't leave a mess behind. For some reason, most town Sheriffs tended to be more concerned with litter than larceny - he paid a little contribution here and there to grease the wheels and expedite their way out of town. To date, he had yet to allow any of his staff to sully the carnival's reputation. He ran his business with an iron fist that allowed for no debate as to conduct, but Richie was a growing problem. He'd had to cover two muggings, a house burglary and a nasty sexual assault that had cost a small fortune to silence. He was sure that Richie was the culprit, but not sure enough to act decisively. He was already planning on dumping Richie off on one of his other businesses. Richie maybe his sister's son, but she was not his favourite sister.

"Hey Carlo," Preston called out as the Ferris wheel operator walked past wearily.

"What's up boss?"

"You seen Richie?"

"Your Richie?"

Preston cringed, was that how the staff saw the little fuckup, his Richie? "Duchamp," he snapped.

"Sorry boss, not tonight, Jesse said that he was supposed to be on trash around the Candy Hut, but he never showed."

Preston dismissed the underling with a contemptuous wave of the hand, *fucking Richie,* he thought angrily. His aging aching bones longed for his bunk and a sound sleep through the night as they left this weird place behind. Eden made his skin crawl more and more each year that they played here - he wanted nothing more than to crawl into his cabin and sleep as they put the town in their dust. Sighing he trooped off to find the errant pain his ass.

He headed through the now almost fully packed rides and stands; he stood opposite the darkened town hall wondering where to start.

"About time you were gone boy."

The voice startled him from the darkness, he turned uncharacteristically scared, it was an alien emotion to him, and one that did not sit well. He attempted to find his bluster as he stared at the large Sheriff before him. Quinn was a hard-ass of the old school variety, a six feet five and three hundred pound ball breaker. He moved with the slow grace of a man who had always been big, and greatly enjoyed the power that derived from his physical superiority. Preston drew his not inconsiderable confidence up to its full level, determined not to be intimidated by the bullying tactics of some hick Sheriff of Stepford.

"I haven't got all of my workers yet," he said.

"Really?" The Sheriff's tone was condescending; he looked over Preston's shoulder at the square and the breaking carnival. "I think that you've got all you're going to get," he turned his casual gaze from the square back fully onto Preston.

Preston stared back hard at the much larger man, attempting to take in the inference. "I'm missing one man," he attempted to speak with an angry tone, but it fell firmly into the pleading spectrum.

"Oh Casper wanted me to give you this," Quinn spoke as though Preston hadn't. "Here," he handed over a thick envelope, "Some sort of bonus for a good job well done I guess." Quinn hooked his thumbs in his belt and looked around nonchalantly as though they weren't dancing.

Preston hefted the weight of the envelope; he didn't have to open it to guess at the sort of amount contained. He weighed the contents and the Sheriff's intimidation, over the fact that Richie wasn't even his favourite sister's son. "Maybe everyone is here after all," he relented, self-preservation was a powerful ally after all.

"Well then, I guess we'll see you all again next year," Quinn offered magnanimously.

"Guess so," Preston said, thinking never in a million years, tonight when he put Eden in the dust, it would be for the last time, he'd never set foot in the town again.

Thom Bray viewed the house; it was empty and deserted, but in this town there was always someone listening. His mother worked for Christian Realty, showing homes in Eden. She made a good living and provided him with everything that he had never asked for. They were not on good terms since his dad had upped and left town last year. His mother seemed determined to avoid the subject at all costs, no matter how much he pleaded for his father's address so that he could write and find the truth.

Thom was fourteen, short and skinny for his age, but no-one seemed to care or mind, as the school had an effective zero tolerance policy when it came to bullying. Sometimes Thom felt that his life could use a little reality, maybe even a little dose of adversity. Since they'd moved here from LA almost two years ago, his world had become hermetically sealed. There was no crime here; no trouble, no poverty, and everyone seemed to smile all the time. His memories of LA were not particularly pleasant, his parents had fought a lot and life had been stressful and he remembered it as a world of rules and restrictions. His mother was constantly fretting over him and the city that they lived in. His father had spent most mornings scanning the newspaper for signs that the darkness was getting closer to their front door. He'd had a few close friends from the neighborhood, but none had stayed in contact after the move like they'd promised. He'd written a few times to Dominic, his closest friend, but had never received a reply.

At first Eden had been a paradise for him; the whole town was open to him, and his parents were no longer constantly peering over his shoulder terrified if he left their sight for even a moment. The school was clean and friendly, there were no cliques or gangs, no discriminations or segregations by race or religion. There was no bullying or tormenting like in his previous school, where it was a free-for-all jungle ruled by Darwin's theories. In Eden the classes were small and the teachers all had time. The activities and facilities at the school were fantastic, every interest that he had was catered for. He had joined many of the after school clubs and his life was supposedly wonderful. But just lately he was beginning to feel smothered by the encased world. Since his father had left, his mother had become more and more detached behind a wall of politeness, and her smiles were starting to look as plastic as the neighbor's.

The house that he now stood outside of was one of the large mansions over on Fairfax. Apparently some lady had killed herself in the bath, and her husband had just up and left without a word. He'd read all of this in his mom's files that she kept on the Christian's properties. She didn't know that he had access to her computer system, but he'd gained the address and the keys from her office. The large house was more luxurious than even their own; the rear garden backed on to open fields and he'd had little trouble in clambering over the short fence that looked designed more for style than substance. He'd wanted to go inside the house but now felt his feet drag. A woman had died in there, and he was excited and scared in equal measure of just what might await him. The feeling of being scared was delicious, it was a real emotion that pierced through the bubble of Eden and lit his senses. His mind tantalized itself with thoughts of ghosts and vengeful spirits. His was a secret love of horror that was frowned upon beneath his teacher and mother's disapproving stares. His father had shared his love of the genre, passing on book recommendations, showing him the quality that existed in the field. He'd read the likes of King, Campbell, Matheson, Straub and Barker. They'd watched movies huddled on the sofa, beneath blankets and face covering hands. He missed his father and did not even have an explanation as to his disappearance from his life. His mother had only once spoken of a betrayal, one so black as to threaten them all; from then on she point blank refused to so much as even discuss the matter further.

From his mother's records, he knew that the writer Michael Torrance had moved in next door to the now empty property in which he hovered outside. Torrance was not one of his favourite writers; his prose could be a touch flowery at times and he skirted the horror genre on the tails of thriller. He had read one book that he'd enjoyed about vampires and gangsters; it had been gruesome enough to satisfy, whilst still engaging him with intelligence. He had thought of approaching the writer, but his mother had been mortified at his ill advised public suggestion over breakfast, and he'd had to promise that he would not bother one of her more important clients.

He moved towards the rear patio doors. Even though the house was deserted, the glass still sparkled perfectly in the sunshine. Inexplicably he gleefully smeared a sweaty palm across the pristine surface. He used one of the smaller keys on the bunch that he had brought from his mother's office and unlocked the door. He slid them apart and stepped quickly inside. The kitchen felt cool; the counters were clean and polished, the furniture looked new and untouched, and the house lay empty waiting to be filled again.

He moved through the house checking the rooms one by one. The eerie silence felt oppressive and unwelcoming. His forearms prickled with goosebumps and he embraced his thumping heart and sweating forehead, his skin felt clammy with fear and trepidation. He placed one foot on the stairs. The bathroom lay at the top, the scene of a real death waited patiently for him, and he took another step. He ascended slowly, relishing the rushing adrenaline, the dread mixing with excitement.

Back in LA, late one night he had been awakened by loud shouts and flashing lights outside of his bedroom window. He had been ten and had crawled over to the window and peeked around the curtains. There were three police cars pulled up on the sidewalk, six officers stood hunched over the vehicles, guns drawn and pointed at a car that they had pulled over. Even through the window he had felt the air crackle with electric tension. He had felt the piercing nervous excitement as though he was watching a TV show parading on the world's largest plasma screen. Eventually as the occupant of the stopped car had staggered out into the night and thrown himself onto the floor unarmed, the tension had immediately fallen. Thom remembered a feeling of anticlimax, but he remembered the electricity of anticipation. He felt the same anticipation now as he moved slowly up the exotic staircase.

He reached the upper hallway, the soft cream carpet was thick and lush and it was also thankfully silent as he moved. He stood outside the bathroom door; his hand shook as he reached out slowly with a trembling hand. The metallic handle felt like ice under his grip and his breath stilled as he held it absently. His heart pounded hard against his chest, and he turned the handle. His imagination raced through a thousand scenarios of death and fear at what waited for him inside. The door eased open easily and smoothly; his eyes wouldn't blink, his limbs quivered and he couldn't catch his breath. One jelly leg moved forward and he stepped inside.

Michael punched the cancel button on the cell phone hard with frustration. He was still unable to contact Chris, and no matter how many messages he left, they were never returned. He was sitting out on his steamer chair in the garden, his face thoughtful and contemplative. It was a hot Sunday morning, but for once the weather offered little comfort. Emily had yet to rise and he was alone. He was normally a man of action and deed, but he felt impotent and confused. The more that he ran the facts around his head, the more they swirled into a continuous circle of uncertainty. He considered riding back out to Darnell's again; perhaps if the man was a little more sober or a little more drunk, he would have further thoughts to offer on the town and Casper's twisted family tree. He was stuck in limbo and he did not know just how to proceed. His book had stalled for the time being - did he pursue the story regardless of the possible damage? He wasn't naive enough to think that despite his best efforts, the town wouldn't see through any attempt to disguise the setting of the story. The residents of Eden would no doubt not appreciate his portrayal of them, no matter how fictionally he camouflaged them. Despite the undeniable juicy nature of Casper's family history, what else did he really have? His neighbor Janet had committed suicide, Chris had to all intents and purposes disappeared, and in the woodland beyond the town he'd lost some time. However, he didn't really know just what had lurked in Janet's heart; perhaps she and Chris had argued later that night, perhaps her infidelity wasn't a onetime deal. Perhaps Chris felt responsible, perhaps he left her that night, hell, perhaps he had even been complicit in her death, and that's why he'd disappeared.

The high pitched scream startled him; the noise appeared to have come from Chris's empty house next door. For a moment he was rooted to the spot as the sheer panic and terror rose from the scream. The shattering noise was halted as quickly as it had risen. He sat up on the steamer chair panicked. For a second he'd thought that something terrible had befallen Emily, but the noise had clearly come from next door. He stood on shaky legs, unsure as to what to do, and then he cursed himself for his cowardice and ran towards the fence. Someone was clearly in trouble, and this was now his neighborhood. He made a snap decision and clambered up and over the fence, landing in Chris' back garden in an ungainly lump.

The patio doors at the rear of the house were open and he moved towards them cautiously. The house smelled clean and sterile, and he was surprised to see the lack of personal touches. The photos and prints that had once hung on the walls and decorated the surfaces in silver frames were all conspicuously absent. If Chris hadn't been home since that night, then just who had been spring cleaning? Michael worked from home and would have undoubtedly noticed any unusual coming and goings, at least during daylight hours.

He moved slowly through the open plan lounge, here too, personal touches were missing; the furniture looked clean and new and the house stood empty, seemingly waiting patiently.

Michael moved towards the front of the house, suddenly the hallway was filled with two dark shadows, one huge and one small. The larger dragged the smaller down the stairs with ease. Sheriff Quinn held a small boy roughly by the throat, Michael watched as a cruel, sadistic smile perverted the huge man's face. The boy looked to weigh about eighty pounds soaking wet and the Sheriff's large meaty paw gripped the small boy by the collar as he dragged him, tearing the fabric of his shirt. His other hand reached back and pulled out something that glinted wickedly in the bright sunlight.

"P-P-Please" the boy begged.

Michael stared in horror as Quinn laughed; it was a disturbing rumble that seemed to shake the air. The Sheriff's face was alight with pleasure, seemingly at the child's now sobbing and trembling form. Whatever the glinting silver he held in his hand was now rising to the boy's face, Michael couldn't see what he held as his broad back was turned.

"And just how am I going to make sure that you learn a lesson?" Quinn whispered ominously.

"QUINN!" Michael shouted.

The Sheriff turned and in that split second Michael was afraid for his life. Quinn's face was a thunderous black mask of rage, his eyes squinted, and his whole body shook with fury. The intense vehemence suddenly melted away and the Sheriff smiled normally again, his giant shoulders relaxed, and calm exuded once more.

"Mr. Torrance," he greeted Michael, "You gave me such a fright," the huge man said in a friendly polite manner. "I'm afraid that we've had an intruder," he shook the boy to illustrate.

"And you were looking to hand out a little private justice?"

"You misunderstand Mr. Torrance, here in Eden we believe in preventative measures, a little scare works wonders, isn't that right Mr. Bray?" He said, addressing the trembling boy.

"Yes sir," Thom managed through his tears.

"Well now, I'll just be driving young Thom here home and having a little word with his mother," the Sheriff announced.

"Where is it that you live Thom?" Michael asked suddenly, feeling that it was important for the Sheriff to know that he'd taken an interest.

"Greenfields sir," Thom answered.

"Hey, your mom rented us the house didn't she, she works for Casper?" Michael never took his eyes off of the Sheriff as he spoke to the boy.

"Yes sir," Thom answered his voice growing stronger. "Hey aren't you the writer?"

"Yeah, Michael Torrance, I live next door, you know Sheriff Quinn, maybe I'll have a word with Mrs. Bray as well. I seem to remember that she was a single parent, I was raised the same way, and it can be tough," he said enjoying the large bully's uncomfortable silence.

"Whatever you think sir," Quinn said through a forced smile that never quite reached his eyes, "I'm sure that she'd appreciate the help."

"Jot down your number son and I'll be in touch," Michael said with a smile.

As Thom wrote his phone number down with a pen and paper that the Sheriff grudgingly produced, Michael looked at Quinn. The big man now knew that Michael would be checking up on Thom and that he would have to arrive home safely and untouched.

Michael watched as the Sheriff gently put Thom gently into the front of the police car parked outside. Quinn was all smiles and charm with the neighbors outside who had come out to watch the show, Quinn was nothing if not a reassuring presence to them. He was a huge bear of a man in a uniform that silently promised protection for the good citizens of Eden under a gleaming star badge. He seemingly offered a comforting blanket that proved why this town was different from the outside world.

The police department car pulled away from the curb amid the tuts and headshakes of the watching public audience, thankful for the swift legal intervention. Michael watched the car with an entirely different view of the Sheriff. Only he had seen the cruelty on Quinn's face as he manhandled a small and defenseless boy. Whatever had been about to happen, had only been stopped by his presence, and he shuddered as his thoughts ran wild with visions of just what the Sheriff might have intended.

"Let me get this straight," Emily said later, after Michael had relayed the events of next door to her, "What ***exactly*** did he do?"

"I told you," Michael replied.

"Yes but you didn't really say anything, did you?"

"You had to be there, if you'd seen the look on his face."

"Michael, he's the Sheriff, I'm sure that it was like he said, he was just trying to give the kid a scare."

"Jesus Em, the kid looked petrified, and Quinn looked positively evil. He had something in his hand that I couldn't see, but that kid was shaking like a shitting dog."

"Oh, lovely," Emily said in disgust.

"I know what I saw. That big ass son of a bitch was dragging that kid like a sack of meat. The kid was terrified, and Quinn was smiling like he was enjoying it."

"Hey aren't you the one who was always calling for tougher action on anti-social youths? During the riots back in London, you were the one who wanted water cannons and rubber bullets."

"This was different. This was just some bored kid nosing around an empty house looking for a ghost,"

"You spoke to him?"

"Yeah, I chased him up this afternoon. I just wanted to make sure that he got home alright."

"What did you think was going to happen to him in a police car?" She laughed, until she saw that he was deadly serious. "Jeez Michael, this isn't one of your novels you know, this is real life and that imagination of yours might be the money maker honey, but you've got to get a grip."

"This wasn't my imagination Em, I saw the look in Quinn's eyes, and it scared the shit out of me."

"Babe," she leant forward and touched his leg, "It's ok to be happy here you know, you do deserve to be happy. Stop picking at the corners and waiting for the other shoe to drop, it was never your fault, the accident, losing the baby."

"That's not what this is."

"Bullshit," she stated with finality, "I know that you carry the guilt. I know that you believe it was your fault. I asked you to go to the store that night, and you didn't, I could have waited but I didn't want to. I wanted the fresh air, I wanted to stretch my legs. I left the apartment and someone lost control of a car, they mounted a sidewalk and killed our baby. That's who we blame, not ourselves or each other."

"But!"

"No buts," she snapped viciously. "No buts babe," she added kindly as she stroked his face gently feeling the rough stubble coarse under her soft skin, "I think we've found a perfect little slice of happiness here and everything's going great guns. It's a new start for us and a chance to be a family. So what if the local law enforcement gets a little rough to keep things perfect, you are the last person I'd expect to have liberal, lefty leanings when it comes to crime."

"So what would you have me do?"

"Nothing, because there is nothing to be done, enjoy the sunshine, write if it still makes you happy, retire if it doesn't. Find a hobby, prepare for our baby, and be happy Michael, that's all I've ever wanted for you."

"Maybe you're right," he said rubbing his head, wanting to believe that it was all just rattles in his own musings. Knowing that he did have trouble in being happy and that he had a self-destructive streak a mile long. Maybe it was just his own vivid imagination that had witnessed the demonic glares of the large town Sheriff. Maybe he was overreacting again, and maybe he should just junk the book he was writing and go fishing.

"I've read your new book Michael."

Emily's voice suddenly interrupted his thoughts, he looked up guiltily.

"Don't worry," she said, "I'm not cross, I knew that you wouldn't be able to leave the idea alone once it had grown roots."

"What did you think?" He asked warily.

"I thought two things. One that it was good, and secondly that the town would shit a collective brick if they read it," she giggled disarmingly.

"You think that I should junk it?"

She looked at him seriously, "Yes I do. I think that if you finish and publish this book, then we couldn't live here anymore, it's that simple."

"Not if I changed…"

She raised a hand to stop him, "It doesn't matter what you change Michael, and you know that. We'd have to leave, even if they never asked us, I couldn't stand the shame of our betrayal."

"Did you read my notes?" He asked.

"Yes, yes I did and I've made an appointment for you with Dr Creed on Tuesday."

"What for?" He asked surprised.

"Michael, you said that you lost time when you cycled out to the woods, you don't think that might be a medical matter?" She scolded him.

"What about Darnell's story?"

"All that vague stuff about Casper's dim and distant relatives, tales of devil worship and human sacrifice?" She laughed, "It's not exactly Woodward and Bernstein style deep throat research is it?"

Michael could only shrug. His wife had always been his fiercest critic, and he was often irritated by her accurate questions and suggestions.

"Some lonely old guy, who by your own admission was half cut, telling old wives tales and gossiping. You're really going to take these as research facts Michael?"

Emily stood, hoisting her increasing weight up from the garden furniture, waving his helping hands away, "I'm going to take a swim my dear," she said grandly, smiling as she teased, "Why don't you join me, we'll make a little whoopee in the water."

Despite all of Michael's thoughts and doubts, he shut down the factory that ran in his mind, clocking the boys out and sending them home early for the night. He joined his wife in the pool. They loved each other in the water and dozed off after, happily holding hands as they lay on the grass beneath the hot sun.

CHAPTER EIGHTEEN

"So tell me about the woman who was here before me, Jessica I think you said her name was," Emily asked.

She was sitting in the outdoor seating area of Baskin-Robbins with Sarah-Jane; they were both indulging in a treat after a long day at work. The furniture was a wicker metallic blend and the chairs were soft and comfortable. There was no subtle seating designed to push customers on quickly and the parasols offered a welcome shade. Emily was manfully destroying a Chocolate Chip Cookie Dough Sundae whilst Sarah-Jane picked lightly at a Fat-Free frozen yogurt. Emily definitely felt that she was eating for two now. Her pregnancy was progressing without any problems. By now she had managed to relax into the term and had decided to go with the flow. She knew that her hormones were a little out of whack, but she figured that it was Michael's problem if she acted a little erratically from time to time. It was, however, the first time that she had seen her friend conscious about what she was eating.

Sarah-Jane was pleasantly curvy as far as Emily could tell, but she now appeared to be taking a closer look at herself. Emily wondered if the good Dr Creed had anything to do with SJ's sudden concerns over her appearance.

"What about her?" Sarah-Jane asked.

"I got the impression that Mrs. Thirlby didn't like her much."

Sarah-Jane shrugged in a noncommittal gesture, "I think that they used to get on well enough, and Jess certainly seemed happy here."

"Where did she come from?"

"Somewhere near Boston I think. Her husband David was some kind of investment banker I think. I didn't really know her all that well, she was quite private."

"And they lived in our house, out on Fairfax?"

"Yes, that I'm sure of. Jess was good friends with one of your neighbors, Janet."

"It seems a bit weird, don't you think? I take over her job and move into her old house?"

"Ah, you know Eden, everything and everyone are connected in one way or another. Just one of the traits of a small town I guess." Sarah-Jane pushed the half eaten yogurt away.

Emily noticed the movement, "So tell me some more about Dr Creed."

Michael waited patiently as Dr Creed reviewed the paperwork with genuine interest. The office was private and the door was closed. Michael didn't like the signs. "Damn it Doc, what's wrong with me?"

"Nothing that I can see Michael," Samuel replied casually.

Michael never knew how worried he had been until Dr Creed said those magical words. He had been poked and prodded for most of the day; he'd had bloods taken and tested and he'd been scanned in an iron coffin that they called an MRI machine.

Michael had met Creed in his office that morning expecting a precursory examination by the doctor, to be followed by some appointments at the small town hospital in a few weeks time. He'd been astounded to find himself whisked off to the hospital's full array of state of the art facilities within minutes. His natural pessimism told him that the doc had immediately spotted some terrible symptom as soon as he'd walked through the door. The battery of tests that he'd been subjected to was staggering, and it got to a point where he'd stopped asking questions about what they might be looking for.

"Nothing?" Michael asked incredulously.

"Nope, you could stand to drop your cholesterol a little, but even that doesn't require medication yet. Just throw some salad in with those steaks when you BBQ."

"Then what's with all the tests?"

"Hey, I'm like a kid in a candy store here. Look at all the shit they got." Creed leaned and whispered with a grin, "Besides, I wouldn't want to piss off your wife and she demanded that I made sure."

Michael smiled; he'd been on the end of more than a few of Emily's rants when he was in the doghouse, "So what about the blackout the day that I went out to the woods?"

"You got me," Creed stated succinctly.

"Is that your professional opinion?" Michael laughed.

"Hey this world can be a freaky place Mike. you know some guy fell 47 floors from a skyscraper in New York and lived. Some other dude was paralyzed in a motorbike accident and one day he was bitten by a brown recluse spider and walked again. Every day weird things happen in the medical world that baffles us all, and often we never get an answer. All I can tell you is that medically speaking there is nothing wrong with you." He leafed through the thick file of freshly prepared paperwork for emphasis, "Nothing that would explain a single, solitary episode of losing some time. Has it ever happened before?"

"No, never."

"Then I wouldn't worry too much about it to be honest. Stress is the mother of all killers. Just relax a little, find a hobby."

"Yeah, that's what Em keeps telling me."

"How are things at home?" Creed asked casually.

Michael waited for a flinch that never came. Normally just the idea of talking openly - especially with another man - would set his British sensibilities into overdrive. Men, especially British men, did not open up. But somehow Creed was easy to talk to. His manner was open and inviting and he gave off an aura of welcoming friendliness. He could see just why Emily had been so taken with the doctor. "Things are good, great even, as long as everything is alright with the baby," he suddenly looked up panicked.

Creed's face was relaxed and calm and he held up a settling hand, "Everything is fine with your wife and the baby. I always take good care of my best customers. I understand that Emily is a little out of kilter with her emotions." The look on Michael's face confirmed the fact.

"Yeah you could say that," Michael sighed, "She can go from out of control angry, to horny, to sad and back again before breakfast."

"Well that's the price that you have to pay my friend I'm afraid. You did the crime and now you've got to do the time. Emily's got to carry the load for nine months before the joy of childbirth. If you have to put up with a few mood swings then I'd suggest that you've got the better side of the deal."

"Is there anything wrong with Eden?" Michael suddenly asked deliberately off topic, wanting to see a genuine reaction.

Creed's expression changed to a creased and puzzled one. "What do you mean?"

"I mean this town, it's a little too Stepford don't you think? Everything's a little too perfect, a little too wonderful?"

"Let me get this right. You're concerned that everything is too good here. I gotta say Mike, that's kind of a strange thing to worry about."

Michael laughed aloud, "When you say it like that, I guess I do sound a little paranoid."

"Just a touch," Creed joined in with the laughter.

"How long have you been here doc?"

"About two years now, and I have to say that after paying my dues in the emergency rooms of county hospitals around LA, I was ready for a change of pace."

"Rough?"

"Man you have no idea." Creed's natural sunny disposition darkened, "There came a morning when I just couldn't face stitching up another gangbanger throwing his life away. The faces that came through the ER were just broken and soulless Mike, dead men walking. There's only so many times that a man can look into the eyes of that particular monster and stay sane."

"So how did you end up here?"

"A drop of fortune from the heavens that fell like a warm rain when I was at my lowest."

"Hey that's poetic, I might steal that," Michael smiled.

"I saw an advert for this town; it looked like everything that I'd ever dreamed of. Warm friendly people, no crime, no murders, no patch up jobs, just nice people and unheard of facilities to play with."

"Some people nicer than others?" Michael asked cryptically.

"What do you mean?"

"Hey you know the temper that my wife's got; she'll kill me if I don't bring home the juicy gossip on you and the fair Sarah-Jane."

Michael watched amusedly as Dr Creed's reddening cheeks told him everything that Emily wished to know.

Thom Bray dug through the box. The lighting in the attic wasn't the best and the box was fusty. Damp odors filled his nose with unpleasant wafts as he turned the books over looking for one in particular. He held a rubber handled torch in his mouth, using the thin beam to differentiate between titles. The taste was bitter and reminded him of the fear that the big Sheriff had put in him. His senses had been as taut as cranked wire when he'd pushed open that bathroom door.

He'd taken the keys from his mom's office as she worked for Casper Christians Real Estate Company and she often kept unwise items at home. The house had been the scene for Janet Beaumont's suicide and had been empty ever since. He was a fourteen year old with a borderline obsession with the macabre and it didn't take a genius to put those two facts together. His room was a shrine to horror; posters lined the walls with faces of death and his shelves were stuffed with books from contemporary authors. His DVD collection was filled with many volumes that his mother wrinkled her nose in displeasure over and a secret drawer that she would have blown a gasket over had she looked inside. He didn't consider his to be an unhealthy love for the genre. He didn't paint his face white and fanaticize about gunning down his fellow students in a rampage. His interest was simply born out of a connection to his father. It was a passion that they had shared, up until he had inexplicably walked out on them, and his mother still refused to even speak his name in the house.

When he discovered that his mom had the keys to the suicide house he had been overcome with a desire to step inside the room that had witnessed death's icy fingers. He had not expected to see anything until he had stood outside the bathroom in a dark and deserted house. He had driven his mind into a state of imaginative frenzy until he could stand it no longer. When he'd reached out and opened the door he had been fully expecting to see the bloated corpse in the bathtub, reaching out to drag him to hell. He had actually convinced himself that he was indeed seeing Mrs. Beaumont when the massive, powerful hand had clamped down hard on his shoulder from behind and he had screamed like a girl. He shuddered as he remembered the huge Sheriff bearing down on him,; the real life fear suddenly expunging the imagined terrors of his mind. He'd expected to receive a scolding of sorts and he wasn't unduly concerned as the people of Eden had been unwaveringly friendly and nice since his arrival in town. The Sheriff might look big and scary, but he was bound to be a pussycat. His view had rapidly altered when the huge paw had squeezed his narrow shoulder with painful and malicious strength. The big cop had damn near dragged him down the stairs faster than he could walk and all the while the big man had a frozen grin that scared Thom badly. He had watched and read enough fictitious scares to be scared in the real world. He had stumbled down the hallway trembling with fear and did not know just what the Sheriff had in store for him, but it did not look pleasant. His fear was expanding exponentially as the cop had yanked him into the open lounge of the house. He'd assumed that he'd be given a ride home and would have to sit through one of his mother's lectures. His opinion was rapidly changing as the Sheriff showed no signs of wishing to conclude their conversation in public, and manhandled him roughly. The Sheriff had reached into his back pocket and said something about teaching him a lesson. He'd only just won the battle of his bladder when the writer from next door had shown up. Mr. Torrance had yelled at the Sheriff and suddenly the cop was all politeness again; just the town welcome wagon mascot, all please and thank you. He had almost collapsed with relief at the opportune interruption. Thom was a boy blessed with a quick mind and he had realised that the writer was letting the Sheriff know that he would be checking up on Thom later that day. The cop still had hold of him at that point, and he'd felt the tension grip tighten as though the Sheriff was battling with his own temper. Eventually the grip had eased and he was indeed being given a ride home. The Sheriff was instructing him on the consequences of his actions but he'd stopped listening by then. Whatever the cop's intentions had been, they'd been cut off at the knees when he'd been interrupted by Mr. Michael Torrance.

He turned his attention back to dusty box of books. Suddenly he spotted what he was looking for; it was a copy of the one book of Torrance's that he owned. It was a novel called "Vengeance Has Fangs". He pulled the book from its hiding place and brushed the dust from the paperback cover. It had been a while since he'd read the novel and he wondered how it had aged.

For the rest of the afternoon and early evening he sat in the back garden engrossed in the novel, and after a while he even forgot to mentally curse the unbearable constant hot sunshine. Thom was a redhead like his father and not naturally predisposed for tanning. He would blister, peel, and then blister all over again. He knew that his mother loved the hot weather, but he found it a tiring drag. As he read, he realised that the last time he had read the book had been a few years ago. The story now ran deep and thoughtful whereas before he had grown a little bored at the lack of instant action. He began to feel for the characters, appreciating their three dimensional rounded edges. There was wit and charm to the story and he began to feel as though he was reading through the eyes of a young man rather than those of an impatient boy.

It was a little after 8pm when he was shaken from his literary world by his mother returning from some town duties to do with the Woodland Festival.

"Thom, for heaven's sake!" She shouted at him annoyed.

Thom looked up puzzled, "What?"

"I've been shouting you for hours," she said exasperated.

"What time is it?" He asked.

"Past dinner time, get in here."

Thom followed the enticing aroma of fresh steaks and baked potatoes into the house. He looked at the kitchen wall clock and was shocked at the time; the day had passed into dusk around him as he'd read. The book was certainly more engrossing than he remembered it and he made a mental note to seek out some of Torrance's other work.

"So how was your day?" His mother asked through a mouthful of sour creamed potato, "Anything exciting happen?"

Thom feigned boredom, surprised that the Sheriff hadn't been in instant contact with his mother as he'd assumed. He had been expecting a grilling from his mother and was not looking forward to it. Maybe the big cop had forgotten, maybe for once something demanding his attention had actually happened in Eden. Whatever the reason was, he was pleased. He loved his mother very much and did not want to see her in trouble because he'd taken the unsecured keys from her office and entered the empty house. He rose and walked around to the fridge; he grabbed the orange juice and poured two glasses out placing one on the table for her.

"Why thank you kind sir," she said teasingly, "And what have you done to feel the need to be so considerate?"

Thom shrugged, "Nothing, honest," he lied.

"Yeah, right" she viewed him suspiciously.

"I was thinking of having that writer who just moved into town autograph his book for me."

"I thought you said that it wasn't very good when I asked you before?"

"Well I'm much older and wiser now," he joked. "I am a man of more refined tastes these days."

His mother laughed, "Just don't go bothering anyone Thom. Seriously, the new folks are very important people to the town."

As he cleaned the table after dinner whilst his mother was going through some paperwork in her small office, it suddenly dawned on him that it was a very strange phrase to use. She'd said "important to the town", not "important in the town". He went to bed after kissing her goodnight later, still with the same thought rattling around his mind even as his eyes closed and sleep rolled in.

Kurt Stillson patrolled Eden. The night had drawn in around him and his shift, but the town was illuminated by the myriad of powerful streetlights that were run from their solar power sources. Eden had to be the greenest town in the country as far as he could tell. They had fully embraced the concept of solar energy and made full use of the constant sunshine. He had often wondered at how the greenery of the town maintained its lush condition despite the lack of rain. Tommy Ross - the other deputy on the town's payroll - had told him that there was a natural underground spring stream that was utilized for irrigation. He had wanted to question the effectiveness of this system but did not want to contradict Tommy; as far as he was concerned, Tommy now walked on water. It had been Tommy that had forced his hand into taking the delectable Ellen Barlow to the town carnival. In the following weeks their budding romance had begun to blossom slowly. They had been on several dates around town for ice-cream, drinks, and meals, and he was enjoying the almost innocent nature of the courtship. Ellen was strictly an old fashioned woman who believed in establishing a firm foundation before any funny business. As quaint and cute as the courtship was, the tension was getting unbearable. They had indulged in several, what could only be described in Eden as heavy petting sessions, but these left Kurt with a lapful of stressful lust. He was seriously beginning to wonder if they would have to get married before she would share breakfast with him. Although the idea was not unappealing, he was not sure if he could muster the sufficient self-control.

He wandered around slowly in the warm night; he really had no idea why the Sheriff bothered to send anyone out this late. The people of Eden were so used to the lack of crime that even his presence seemed unnecessary. Normally just the sight of a uniformed officer was enough to set the local minds at ease, but here his night shift was perfunctory. For whatever reason, the all powerful town council, under Casper Christians direction had deigned that the police department must operate a random and rotating rota. This meant that the three of them; himself, Tommy and Sheriff Quinn all worked 8 hour shifts that could be any time of the day or night. He had yet to uncover a single crime during any of his shifts, and that suited him just fine; he was all for the quiet life.

He strolled across the town square. His mind drifted back pleasantly to his first date with Ellen; one that had ended in their first feather-light brushed kiss. He checked his watch; it was a little after 2am and the town was sleeping quietly in their beds. Back in Chicago he would never have dreamt of drifting through the streets alone and after dark.

He was enjoying the peace and solitude, entertained by images of Ellen's lithe and coy body, when a flash of movement caught his attention. His shift ended at 2.15am but his interest was piqued and he went to investigate.

Whatever the movement had been, the square was now still. He walked across the immaculate lawns towards the sculpted bushes that bordered the town hall. The lighting was bright around the square but faded away behind the attractive town hall building as the street lights did not quite reach all the way into the shadows. Kurt did not carry a firearm, only a long metallic sturdy torch that he now hefted for comfort and support. He edged his way slowly and silently around the town hall. He ducked low and approached stealthily and he held his breath as he crept forward. Just then he heard a strange dim hissing sound; puzzled he slunk forward closer to the noise. In the dark he could just make out a figure hugging the shadows obscured in the dark corner. His heart pounded in the darkness, his lungs protested as he forgot to breathe and his forehead felt clammy despite the warm night air. His foot inadvertently landed on a branch lying on the ground. The snap sounded like a cannon going off and shattered the encasing silence. He switched the powerful torch on, shining the powerful beam into the blackness. Suddenly the shape snapped its head around in his direction, caught in the bright light.

The slender figure was dressed completely in black with its face concealed beneath a balaclava; only small, narrow eyes poked out. For what seemed like an eternity they stared at each other, eyes locked peering through the gloom. Whoever the person was, they had a backpack slung over their shoulder. Suddenly a metallic object spun through the air towards him and it smashed into his face with a precision aim and fuelled by adrenaline. The metal object exploded pain into his face as it crunched into his nose. Tears welled and flooded his eyesight as the figure sprinted past him.

He clutched at the runner; his fingers brushed woolen fabric, briefly snagging before losing his weak grip. He sank to his knees as blood flowed from his nose. He touched it gingerly; it was already swollen but didn't feel broken. He pulled a wad of tissues from his pocket that he carried due to a pollen allergy and he held the makeshift bandage to his wounded face as he attempted to stem the flow. He picked up the torch he had dropped when the object had hit him; the beam of light still shone brightly and caught the offending item still rolling on the floor. He bent and picked up the metallic cylinder. It was a can of spray paint. The green liquid was already congealing around the nozzle and smudged his fingers as he picked it up. He used the torch and illuminated the side of the town hall where the figure had been spraying; in large letters it spelled two words, "WAKE UP".

Emily grunted with displeasure in the morning heat. The boxes stared at her challengingly in defiance, daring her to continue; their dark forms wafting dust into the air as particles of allergy were illuminated by the torch light beam. She scanned the walls looking for the light switch; she knew that there was electricity pumped into the garage and did not fancy disturbing some unwelcome spiders in the dark. The crates had been sitting in the empty garage for just under the six months since they'd moved in. Michael had shifted the boxed belongings into the unused spacious double garage, claiming that they were her possessions and not his responsibility. They had argued extensively when they'd first moved. Michael was always one for fresh starts and all new property to go with it, whilst she had formed attachments to inanimate objects. Her irritation was further exacerbated when, after several months, she found that she had not required any of the items boxed in the garage and she had even forgotten that they were there.

She kicked a box viciously; her anger rose and rumbled uneasily in her stomach. She breathed deeply and tried to relax. She knew that it was the pregnancy talking, but it didn't make it any easier. She felt close to tears suddenly at the thought of poor Michael suffering her mood swings before that was quickly replaced by annoyance at his complaining as though he was actually in the room with her.

Their initial thoughts had been to purchase at least one vehicle when they'd arrived. However, the town's small circumference, the excellent public transport, and the weather made for perfect walking or cycling conditions. Making the car's acquisition redundant. As a result, the large and spacious double garage sat empty save for storage. The detached building was perfect for Michael's - workshop as soon as he found the time - as it was connected to the mains electricity and plumbing. There was a small apartment sized space upstairs accessible via a metallic staircase on the outside of the building leading to a door. She had dabbled with the idea of using the room for her own hobby area but the house itself was simply too large with too many rooms to require the extra space outside.

She began slicing the packing tape on the sealed boxes with a sharp pair of scissors and pulling through the contents. She started searching for anything of any use and wondering just why she had brought so many useless items. There were magazines that she did not want, books that she would not read again, and albums that she would not listen to again. There were items of clothing that she would never wear again and she was glad that Michael was not here to smile and tell her that he told her so.

She was around four and a half months pregnant at this time, and the large package that she carried internally was starting to grow a little uncomfortable. But she was determined not to be burdened any more than absolutely necessary. She knew that Michael would go mad if he saw her hefting boxes up staircases, but she also knew that she wasn't made of glass and wasn't about to act as if she was. The crates were relatively light and easy to lift and she made the decision to carry the boxes up into the room above. At least if they were out of sight, Michael was likely to forget about them and wouldn't have the opportunity to gloat.

She carried the first box on her shoulder up the outside stairs and was relieved to find the door unlocked; she dipped, pushed the handle down and stepped inside. The room was the same size as the garage level and without any dividing walls. The air was oppressive and hot and the two large windows on either side were firmly closed. She put the box down and opened the closest window, breathing a sigh of relief as the cool breeze floated in and began cooling the room. The large space was empty as far as she could see in the gloom. She plucked the small torch from her pocket and shone it around looking for a light switch; she found it and flicked it on. She tensed as the illumination instantly flooded the room and she listened intently for the telltale sounds of scampering claws on the hard floor as rent free tenants fled for cover. Luckily the room was silent.

She crossed the room to the second window to open that one as well. As she crossed the floor her foot suddenly dipped unexpectedly and she did well not to turn her ankle. She bent down to examine the uneven spot. The flooring was hardwood strips that were joined by tongue and groove. They were a dark oak color, and where it was uneven the piece sank slightly into the space between the floor and ceiling below. She knelt and carefully pried up the loose board, taking care not to damage the joint. She shone the torch into the dark gap; she could just make out that there was something secreted underneath. Growing impatient she yanked the board up hard. She grimaced as the wood splintered under her pressure. Figuring now that the damage was done, she pulled the board all the way out without finesse. A small book lay in the space; she pulled the paperback up and into the light. Her heart skipped with excitement; whatever the book was it had been hidden carefully away from prying eyes.

Michael was mowing the lawns; the large green expanse at the rear of the house seemed to grow beautifully all on its own. There were no intruding weed invasions; there was no discoloration and no fading. The grass was lush and green and smelled sweetly of summer as he mowed. Ever since Janet's dalliance with the imported gardener, the street was waiting for Casper to provide an alternative. Michael, however, felt uneasy at employing others to do the work that he was more than capable of undertaking. Besides, he had a new toy to play with; an MTD Gold riding lawn mower. He was driving up and down the lawns enjoying himself immensely and paying little attention to his cutting lines. He was wearing an MP3 player and the earphones were secreted under large cushioned ear protector muffs. The combination of the blaring Metallica under the muffs made him oblivious to the world around him; so much so that he very nearly ran right over a skinny kid who was waving his arms frantically to attract his attention. He only saw him at the last minute and it was close. He jerked the wheel violently to the left and the mower leant dangerously on two wheels for what seemed like an age. Michael's writer's imagination flashed visions of him falling and his legs disappearing under the vicious whirling blades as they sliced through flesh and shattered bone under a red mist. Fortunately this was real life and the mower merely lurched a little before responding and steadying. He switched off the ignition filing the murderous rage of a ride on mower in his mind for later professional retrieval.

The boy stood before him with a sheepish grin on his face. Michael immediately recognised Thom as the boy who'd escaped the dubious Sheriff's clutches. Thom wore camouflage combat shorts and a red checked shirt that despite its small size still hung from his bony shoulders. His grin was infectious and Michael noticed that he held a worn copy of his novel "Vengeance Has

Fangs" gripped nervously in his sweaty hand. Michael groaned internally; there was nothing that made him more uncomfortable than having to discuss his work with readers. Whether it was receiving praise or criticism, he was still British to his core and his natural instinct was to hide away from any kind of dissection of his work.

He held up a hand as Thom's mouth started to move, silencing him. He took off the ear protectors, plucked the MP3 player from his pocket, turned off the music and pulled the earphones out. His head rang with the sudden quiet. He massaged his ears as they recovered and he watched as Thom waited patiently and politely.

"Sorry Thom, couldn't hear a thing."

"What are you listening to?" Thom asked.

"Ride the Lightening," Michael said waiting for Thom to ask who the hell that was.

"Metallica, cool," Thom nodded.

Michael reappraised the kid; if he appreciated the classics then he undoubtedly deserved an autograph and a quick chat at the very least. "What have you got there?" he pointed to the book.

Thom dropped his gaze embarrassed, "I dug this out of the attic the other day and gave it another read."

"What did you think?"

"I liked it better this time around. The first time I read it I found it a little slow and a touch boring."

Michael smiled at the honesty, "How come?"

"I guess that I'm a little older now. I kind of like books to treat me like an adult."

"That's good. As a writer I always feel that writing a book is a kind of partnership, after all the work that I've put into a story it's only fair that the reader puts a little effort in too." He watched as Thom took in the theory and processed, nodding slowly. “So what can I do for you today Thom?”

“I just wanted to say thanks for the other day,” he jerked his head towards the Beaumont’s house, “You know, with the Sheriff.”

“You know that you shouldn’t have been in there Thom,” Michael said seriously, “What were you looking for?”

“I don’t know,” Thom said blushing.

“Yeah, I think you do.”

“I just wanted to see the scene, you know. I mean I read about death and horror all the time, I just thought that It’d be cool if I could see an actual site where it had happened.” Thom’s words grew faster as he spoke. “I mean nothing ever happens here you know, sometimes I feel kind of, kind of...”

“Smothered?” Michael said remembering Janet’s own words and his own thoughts.

“Yeah.”

“You know there are worse things in life than living in a boring town; you’ll find that as you get older.”

“I remember. We used to live in LA, and I thought that I’d never miss that kind of excitement, sirens and flashing lights, don’t get me wrong,” he added quickly, “I’d never want to go back there, but this is just so the other end of the scale.”

Michael laughed, “I know what you mean, when we first moved here I thought this place was perfect, now I’m starting to go a little stir crazy.” He viewed the boy a little differently now; he was obviously smart and capable. Whilst the Sheriff had scared him badly, he’d still returned to the scene of the crime, or at least next door to the scene. “So what did you see?”

“Sorry?”

“In the Beaumont’s bathroom,” Michael asked seriously, “Did you see anything, feel anything, a drop in temperature, strange lights, smells, or anything weird?”

"Afraid not," Thom said a little disappointed, "Nothing until that big ape grabbed me."

"Shame," Michael grinned. He leant towards Thom and whispered, just in case Emily was within earshot. "A little real life ghost hunting could have been interesting."

CHAPTER NINETEEN

Emily opened the diary and started to read; the day passed quickly around her as she quickly became engrossed in the scribbled contents.

SUNDAY 15th- the house is beautiful and the town is as well, Matthew keeps pinching me every time that I tell him I can't believe it's all ours, he's such a dork sometimes, but I love him just the same!

Emily read through the moving day thoughts. It was eerily reminiscent of her own first day in the house and their move in general. It was a time of wonder and nervous excitement. She skipped ahead through the pages, ignoring the growing heat, and the discomfort of her pregnancy temporarily forgotten as she delved further.

MONDAY 23rd – first day dawning, as I write this Matty is showering, if I wasn't so nervous I'd jump right in there with him ha, ha! School starts in a couple of hours, I walked past the building yesterday, looks nice, hope it is.

Just back home, school was good; kids are great, so much better behaved than back home. Met SJ today, what a bundle, I'm exhausted just thinking about her! The new boss is a little strange though, seems a bit creepy!

Emily smiled to herself; it would appear that she and Jessica had more than a little in common. If she'd kept a diary herself, it would read very similar to this one.

She scanned through several pages; it seemed very much the ordinary ramblings of a happy and contented woman settling into a new life. She was starting to grow a little bored with the diary now. When she'd pried the book loose from its secret hiding place, she'd been excited at the possibility of its contents. Now she found herself flipping through pages of picnics, gardening, and house arranging, the humidity of the hot day was beginning to bother her again as her interest waned. Suddenly a word leapt from the page in bold capitals.

MONDAY 27th- PREGNANT!!!!!!!

Emily found herself staring at the word; first the same house, then the same job and now a pregnancy thrown into the bargain. It all seemed a little too coincidental, but what it meant she could not tell.

She checked her watch absently; *crap,* she thought. She was running late for work. She jumped up as quickly as her enlarged frame could manage and waddled to the door.

"Who was it?" Sheriff Quinn demanded again, his voice rumbled low with menace and barely suppressed anger.

Deputy Kurt Stillson took a step back from the intimidation; the Sheriff was a huge man who seemed to enjoy his physical superiority over everyone in town. Kurt had just finished his written report into the graffiti vandalism and the escaped perpetrator, and his head still rang from the thrown paint can. He wore a large plaster over the cut and a bandage over the swelling. He'd been popping Excedrin all morning but they weren't making much of a dent and Quinn's yelling was only making it worse.

"I already told you sir," he tried again, "I couldn't see a face. Whoever it was, they were wearing black and had their face covered."

"You must have seen something for Christ's sake!" Quinn yelled even louder; his face purple and bloated with rage.

"Jesus it was just a little paint, what's the big deal?" Kurt flapped his arms in frustration.

Quinn was on him in a flash. Kurt found himself lifted by the collar and thrust painfully back against the wall. His head banged backwards on the venetian blinds and his wounded head sang out joyfully. Quinn's face was millimeters from his and the Sheriff's eyes blazed with a venomous fury that bored deep and Kurt's whole body was being lifted with incredible effortless power.

"I'll find out who did this you little shit. This is my town. My fucking town," Quinn spat in his face.

"Boss?"

Kurt looked over the Sheriff's massive shoulders and his knees went weak with relief. Tommy Ross, his fellow deputy stood in the office like a guardian angel. His voice brought Quinn back a little closer to his senses and the strength weakened from his painful grip. Kurt found his feet flush on the floor again and the Sheriff took a step backwards; the rage in his eyes ebbed away and returned to a state approaching normality. He smoothed out Kurt's shirt where it had been rucked up and pulled free of his pants.

"Sorry about that Kurt," Quinn said, sounding vaguely apologetic, "We just care passionately about this town is all. Zero tolerance means zero tolerance."

"S-S-Sure," Kurt stammered, "No problem." He was doubly grateful for Tommy's intervention and Ellen's absence from her office post this morning. He wasn't eager for her to see him manhandled like a rag doll.

"We'll get this bastard together, right boys? No-one is going to put a dampener on this year's festival," Quinn proclaimed.

"Sure boss," Tommy answered, his voice a little unsure.

"Yeah right," Kurt followed, regaining some composure.

Kurt watched thankfully as the Sheriff eased his large frame out of the office and off-duty. He looked at Tommy and they both waited until the purr of Quinn's car started up and pulled away.

"What the fuck was that Tommy?" Kurt asked somewhere between shock and anger.

"He just gets a little carried away with looking after the town Kurt, forget it," Tommy said turning away and busied himself conveniently.

"That's easy for you to say pal, it wasn't you that he just threw around the room. I thought he was going to kick the crap out of me."

"Ahh, don't get carried away Kurt you big girl. He just grabbed you a little, that's all, he wouldn't have really hurt you."

"I'm not so sure. He looked pretty serious to me."

"Nah, just the same though, we ought to catch this new scourge of Eden, just to be on the safe side," Tommy teased. "You know, before we find you buried out back in a dumpster," he grinned.

Although from Tommy's tone it was obvious that he was joking, Kurt couldn't have felt less like smiling.

Emily left her lunch largely untouched as she poured through the diary. The teacher's lounge faded into the background behind her as she read through the thoughts of Jessica Grady. The diary was thick and had begun in an optimistic fashion; the writing was clear and concise with the neat strokes of an ordered mind.

The Grady's had moved to Eden and had been delighted with the hospitality shown to them. Jessica spoke in glowing terms about the town and the people. Jessica had been the woman who had come to Eden much as Emily had. She had worked at the school as a teacher the same as Emily; she had lived in the house before Emily, and she had fallen pregnant as had Emily. The similarities were staggering and more than enough to make Emily feel a little uncomfortable. If she had read these facts in one of Michael's novels then she would have told him that the reader would immediately begin hoisting the red flag. She had read through the diary with increasing speed and was disturbed to find that Jessica was becoming more and more uneasy with her surroundings. Her writing was starting to unravel a little; the handwriting was growing scruffy and the spelling uneven. She skipped through long winded passages of abstract thoughts, searching for anything pertinent.

The lounge was empty this lunchtime. Sarah-Jane was in her classroom glued to her cell phone talking in hushed tones to Dr Creed; their budding relationship was gathering at a deepening pace. SJ positively glowed whenever the subject came up in conversation. Emily had gently probed around the edges but Sarah-Jane was charmingly coy at the very nature of their romance. Mrs. Thirlby was on recess duty today, leaving Emily alone, for which she was grateful. It seemed that every time that she turned around, the Headmistress was staring at her with a strange expression. Emily knew that her emotions were a little out of whack lately due to the pregnancy. Dr Creed had assured her that it was all perfectly natural, but that didn't make it any easier for her - or more so Michael - to live with. Travelling to work in the mornings on the tram had become an uncomfortable ordeal. She was sure that the gazes were all a little too intent and she thought that she could see hidden whispers on every face. Eddie, the regular tram driver, always seemed to linger his eyes over her swelling figure with an almost ravenous glazed glare. The other regular passengers also all seemed to covet her with envious, hungry eyes.

For the fourth time in the last ten minutes she checked the corridor to make sure that she was alone. She felt a deep instinct to keep the diary hidden; whatever lay inside the scribbled pages were for her eyes only. Once she was sure that she was unobserved she opened the book and continued reading. Jessica was becoming more paranoid and Emily was uncomfortable at the similarities that she began to see in herself.

THURSDAY 6th – Thirlby is all over me at the minute, every time that I turn around she's there, creepy-ass woman! School is becoming a real drag, just so damned tired all the time. Matty keeps nagging at me to go back to the doctors, but Dr Lempke seems as weird as the rest of them. You can't swing a cat for hitting some concerned neighbor, need a holiday!!!

MONDAY 10th – Casper came to the house today, spoke to Matty for what seemed like ages, took him aside so that I couldn't hear, Matty said that it was nothing, but he seemed strange afterwards, wouldn't talk about it.

FRIDAY 14th – Had a long talk with SJ today after school was out today, don't know what I would do without her, she's my rock, feel like I can tell her anything and she won't think I'm nuts!

Emily checked and reread. Sarah-Jane had told her that she did not know Jessica very well at all and yet Jessica was calling her "her rock". A little troubled, she read on.

SJ told me to be wary of Thirlby, I pressed her for details, but she just seemed scared of our boss, for one second I thought that she was going to tell me, but then Thirlby appeared like magic and SJ looked terrified. I always thought that Thirlby was a little creepy, but she scares the life out of poor SJ. What is it with this damned "Woodland Festival anyway? Everyone is going nuts over it.

TUESDAY 18th – Matty dragged me to Dr Lempke this morning, I hate that guy, he's always poking and prodding, doesn't seem to care about me at all, and he's only ever interested in the baby. I'm starting to feel like a delivery truck where everyone only wants the package inside, Matty thinks I'm paranoid.

THURSDAY 21st – Darnell, the handyman, kept looking at me strangely today when he came by to clear some hornet nests out of the garage. I'm a little over three months along now and showing, the freak kept staring at my bump the whole time.

MONDAY 24th – I AM NOT GOING CRAZY Matty keeps telling me to go back to Dr Lempke, but I'm not letting them pump me full of anything else, the pills that he keeps giving me make me feel just tired and foggy all the time. He says that they're only vitamins, but I don't believe him, I don't believe anyone at the minute.

SUNDAY 30th – SJ came by today, she said that she's worried, but I could see it in her eyes, she's one of them now, or maybe she always was, the whole town must be in on it. I told Matty that I'm leaving, with or without him. I have to get my baby away from here.

TUESDAY 2nd – It's Thirlby, I just know it. I caught her snooping around my bag at school. I'm sure that I've seen her following me around town, can't think straight sometimes, but I'm sure that I keep seeing her face around town.

WEDNESDAY 3rd – They want my baby, they want my child, I can feel them waiting, and I can feel their eyes everywhere. They're all in it together, I can hear them whispering as I walk past. Matt wants to have me committed, I fear they've got him too, I fear they've got everyone. They dragged me out of the school today when I started freaking out, I know that Thirlby has something to do with all of this, I'll get that bitch!!!

SATURDAY 7th – I can't stay awake, someone must have slipped me something, my head doesn't work too well, can't think straight, sleep now, sleep.

Emily struggled to understand the writing as it slurred and scribbled incoherently as Jessica's mind wandered.

SUNDAY 8th – Got To leave today, got to go now, got to escape, everyone will be at the Woodland Festival tonight, the whole town should be there, got to take this chance, it might be my only one.

The writing ended suddenly, Emily suddenly looked up from the book; she could feel her space being invaded and she spun around quickly from the sofa and looked up into the face of Sarah-Jane.

"What's that you're reading?" SJ asked a little too casually. Her eyes narrow and watchful.

Emily's first thought was to hide the diary and deny its existence. A stab of fear shot through her guts at Sarah-Jane's interest. She quickly scalded herself, this wasn't Thirlby, this was her friend.

"Can I ask you something SJ?" She said gently.

"Sure," Sarah-Jane smiled.

"How well did you know Jessica Grady?"

"I told you," Sarah-Jane said as she suddenly wouldn't meet her gaze, "I didn't know her really at all."

Emily passed her the diary and watched as Sarah-Jane's face fell and darkened with desperate unhappiness. SJ scanned through the pages quickly.

"Oh," she said sadly.

"Well?" Emily asked.

"Jess was a deeply troubled woman Em," Sarah-Jane's words were slow and awkward; her normally pleasant and cheerful face was creased with concern. "After she got pregnant, she started going a bit..., a bit strange."

"How do you mean?"

"She started getting paranoid. She was convinced that the whole town was staring at her. She thought that everyone was talking about her, it was downright weird. Did you ever see the Truman Show movie with Jim Carey?"

"The one where he lives on a reality show, only he's the only one who doesn't know it?"

"Yeah, she started to think that the whole town revolved around her. Like we were all standing and waiting for her to walk past before we'd move. It started to get pretty scary. She freaked here at school one day she thought that the kids were all robots with cameras for eyes. Mrs. Thirlby had to call the Sheriff in and Jess was taken to the hospital kicking and screaming. The poor kids were terrified."

"Who's Dr Lempke?"

"He was the doc here before Samuel," at the mention of Dr Creed's name Sarah-Jane's cheeks flushed a little in a way that Emily found endearing. "I think that Dr Lempke retired somewhere out near Maine. I think that he had a daughter out there."

"What about in the diary when Jessica says that you warned her about Thirlby? What did you mean?"

SJ leant in closer and lowered her voice, "Nothing sinister. Only that Mrs. Thirlby could be a bit of a cow sometimes, and Jess was starting to come into work later and later. I was worried that she might get fired."

Emily leant back into the sofa and processed; the impression that she got from the diary was of an increasingly disturbed woman. She was also concerned at her own somewhat paranoid feelings only this morning when travelling into work. On top of that she was also starting to feel that everyone was watching her in the same way that Jessica described. What did that mean? Was it a common side effect of pregnancy? Was there something in the water in Eden? Or had Jessica had genuine cause for concern? She suddenly realised that it had been an age since she had spoken and Sarah-Jane was staring at her with growing worry etched on her face.

"Emily?" SJ asked softly, "Are you ok?"

"Do you mean am I seeing my students replaced by camera eyed robots?" She had meant to speak lightly and with humor but she didn't feel that anything was funny here. "Don't worry SJ, I'm fine, just a little tired."

"Maybe you should take it a little easier. I'm guessing being pregnant can't be easy."

"You'll find out soon enough."

"Emily!" Sarah-Jane said shocked but smiling shyly.

"Oh come on Sarah-Jane, you and the good doctor will be married before you know it," Emily teased. "And you'll be squeezing out a classroom full of your own students before long."

Sarah-Jane turned embarrassedly and walked back towards her classroom, slowly gathering the children returning after lunch. "You're terrible," she said to Emily as she walked, her face alight with the thought.

Emily stuffed the diary deep into her shoulder bag and hefted it onto her shoulder as she walked slowly back to her own classroom. She stepped into the hallway outside the lounge and moved along the gloomy corridor. Suddenly she felt eyes upon her at the far end. Silhouetted in the shadows was the unmistakable form of Mrs. Thirlby. Emily shuddered under the distant gaze of the Headmistress. Her obscured features made her all the more intimidating. Emily had to walk several feet towards Thirlby and she positively ran the last few paces towards her classroom and the noise within. She wrenched the door open and jumped gratefully into the sunny room.

The clock crawled by slowly; the hands almost seemed to move backwards at times dragging the day interminably. Thom stared wistfully out of the window. The sun was bright and warm and the day was passing him by.

Eden High school was home to the town's teens aged between 14 and 18 and it was the sister school to the elementary school that was across town. The classroom held fifteen students; it was the limit in Eden, and it also meant that there were never any hiding places. Back in LA Thom had been able to drift to the back of the class and fly under the radar. The teachers at his old school had only seemed pleased to get out of the building unscathed at the end of the day; education had come a distant second to self-preservation. Here in Eden, however, it appeared to be deemed necessary for the educators to actually educate. Thom was an intelligent young man; he knew that he picked up subjects quickly and easily, and he had always performed on standardized tests with distinction. His attention problems seemed to derive from boredom. He could pick up the basics of any subject in a flash, but once his brain grasped the subject then it would switch off and search for the next injection.

"Mr. Bray?"

Thom looked up in surprise caught in his wanderings. Mr. Stark his biology teacher was staring at him awaiting a response. Thom had to actually stop and think in order to place the teacher and the subject.

"Sorry sir?" was the only response that he could muster.

"Have you been listening at all Mr. Bray?" The tone was more than a little condescending.

"Of course Mr. Stark," Thom smiled.

"Well?"

"Well what?" Thom asked politely.

Mr. Stark crossed his arms across his narrow chest; he was around fifty years old, balding with a retreating hairline that had long since abandoned the front lines. He wore a peppered white goatee and small round glasses. Stark favoured a wardrobe that had long since witnessed better days consisting of several brown and tan checked jackets, and grey slacks. He was the sort of teacher that Thom's previous school would have eaten alive. But this was not LA, this was Eden.

Thom glanced around the class at his colleagues; none were his friends. Since the move he had been unable to really connect with any of the other students in school. His tastes and interests just didn't seem to mesh with anyone else's. Where he had a voracious appetite for horror and metal, his fellow classmates seemed pasty faced replicated teenagers. The school didn't actively dissuade him from his tastes; no-one had ever dragged him aside to chastise him from his proclivities, and he was just simply left on the outside of all circles. In his experience of life and movies most schools had their various cliques and gangs, nerds, brains, jocks, Goths etc. But here everyone seemed content and happy. There were no divisions of race or color, no segregation of the popular and the not so. There seemed no in-house competition, as though Eden was all one team and they were all team players. In theory, it would seem an ideal environment and Thom certainly did not miss the constant violent threat that his old school had possessed. But in reality it was just simply dull.

"The question was, what is cell theory?"

"Oh right," Thom processed quickly and effortlessly. "Cell theory asserts that the cell is the constituent unit of living beings. Before the discovery of the cell it was not recognised that living beings were made of building blocks like cells. The cell theory is one of the basic theories of Biology," he recited as he watched the clock ticked closer to 3pm.

"Very good Mr. Bray," Mr. Stark sounded as though he was struggling to gain the upper hand again, "You see what happens when you listen to me in class," he announced, "Even Mr. Bray here can learn a thing or two."

Thom's smart mouth had often been his downfall but the school bell rang loudly saving him from himself for once. The class trooped out in its usual slow and considerate fashion . Not for the first time Thom thought of tripping up a classmate, or slapping the teacher just to get a real emotion even if it was anger. On the occasions that he had bumped into students in the halls - regardless of the fact that he was the accidental aggressor - he was always apologized to. He had been scared taking the keys from his mother's office and then fearful sneaking around the suicide woman's house. He had been terrified when he'd pushed open the bathroom door, only to then be painfully accosted by the giant Sheriff. As frightened as he'd been, at least it was a real emotion; his heart had pounded violently against his chest, but it was real. Since the move here there had been a dearth of reality in his world; his mother floated through the day with a smile tattooed onto her face as did most of the town it would seem. The sky was always blue and the sun always shone brightly. The only other person he had met that seemed real to him was the writer. He had spent the previous afternoon at Michael's house and they had talked about books and movies all within the horror genre. Michael's knowledge had been vastly superior to his own and he had gone away with a mountain of research to pursue. For an old guy Michael was alright; his taste in music and horror reminded Thom enormously of his absent father. He did of course recognise this fact and was aware of his own need for a figure to fill that void.

Thom moved along the hallway slowly. He didn't have anywhere in particular to go this afternoon. Michael had told him to call by anytime but he felt that he didn't want to outstay his welcome already. The hallway was by now deserted; the long rows of metallic lockers were all clean and graffiti free. The floor squeaked and sparkled as his lonely footsteps echoed off the abandoned walls. Thom always carried a small notebook in his backpack; he used the book to jot down his own story ideas. His imagination often ran at dizzying speeds, and without a notebook most would be lost to the ether. The dark hallway began the churning of tales within his mind as the gloom closed in around him and he felt the telltale increase of his heart rate as he delved into the recesses. He started to see long slithering tentacles sliding their way around the lockers; the metal boxes buckling under the power of the deep. Great suckers opened and closed hungrily with rows of flesh shredding razor teeth. The monstrous arms snaked their way ever closer to his juicy bones. The school was empty and no one would hear him scream in the dark. But the tentacles were only arms; somewhere hidden in the blackness was the body, a cavernous devouring monster that would send mortals into madness with only a glance at its hideous form.

Thom scribbled furiously, catching the prose before it fluttered away from his mind on distant wings. He could hear the wet slithers and he could feel the cold reptilian skin as it brushed his own. He could feel all of this as he wrote until sweating hands grabbed him for real and he screamed.

"Watch where you're going boy!"

Thom was jerked back into the here and now; the darkened corners of his imagination retreated reluctantly. He was standing face to face with a rather disappointing monster; his biology teacher.

"Sorry Mr. Stark," he muttered.

"Sorry doesn't cut it Mr. Bray, look at the mess you've made."

Thom followed Stark's pointing to the spreading brown stain on the front of his pants. The teacher had been carrying a large mug of coffee that was now half emptied in the most inconvenient of locations.

"Come with me Bray."

Thom noted the drop in Stark's angry tone; the biology teacher now had hold of his shoulder and was dragging him in his wake towards the teacher's lounge.

Stark barged open the door and pulled him inside; Thom was immediately struck by the lack of offending odors. Back in his old school the teacher's lounge had been a place of refuge, stale coffee, sweat, and fear aroma hung on the air whenever the door was cracked open and the sour waft ventured into the hallways. This lounge, however, looked like a plush apartment. There were several long and deep sofas, reclining armchairs, and large bookcases with both reference and fiction books. There were also excellent catering facilities. Two large vending machines stood tall and proud against the far wall; even from this distance Thom could see that the monetary facility was disabled. Fresh fruit and pastry crumbs sat happily on serving platters on long wooden tables as did two industrial coffee machines. Thom didn't eat this well at home.

"Sit Bray," Stark pointed to the furthest sofa from by the sink, grabbing some napkins and wetting them at the sink.

Thom obeyed the instruction and sat, enjoying the comfort, but less so when Stark sat down a little too close to him.

"Look at the mess you made Thom."

Thom tried to avoid staring directly at the slightly uplifted groin area that his biology teacher was indicating towards. Stark began dabbing at his trousers,

"You're a strange one Thom," Stark said pleasantly. "You've got brains, you've got intelligence, but no one seems to be able to, um, stimulate you."

Thom suddenly felt a little uncomfortable; the school around them was deserted of teachers and students, only his own dawdling had left him behind.

"I mean that you could go far, you could go as far as you wanted. You just have to give a little more effort," Stark said in a strange hushed voice as he continued cleaning his trousers.

Thom was not completely oblivious to the ways of the world; he'd had a couple of girlfriends back in LA, and he'd even brushed a tender breast over a thick jumper once before. It was not until Stark gently brushed a trembling hand across his cheek did alarm bells ring. Stark's other hand was still dabbing the coffee stain at his groin and his breathing deepened and hitched. For a moment Thom thought that the teacher was having a stroke of some kind - his breath was positively panting now. Thom's own mind suddenly exploded as he felt an unwanted hand brush his own thigh. He looked into the teacher's eyes and saw a strange blend of terror and excitement in Stark's expression.

The world stood still and Thom's body felt frozen like a deer in the headlights. He desperately wanted to scream and yell for help and tell the teacher to get the fuck off of him, but all he could do was sit and shiver.

Abruptly the poisoned silence was shattered by a ringing cell phone. Stark suddenly looked as though he was aware of his actions for the first time. The teacher's face reddened a crimson shade and he stood quickly and awkwardly. Stark took the phone from his inside pocket and flipped the ringing phone open. His expression turned from red to black as he saw the identity of the caller. Thom sat fixed to the sofa and he knew that this was his window, but something about the shaking biology teacher was fascinating to watch.

"H-H-H-Hello," Stark stammered, "I wasn't..." he spluttered nervously, "But I, I, I wouldn't, I resent the..."

Thom watched as Stark's face grew increasingly terrified; his expression was now a mask of terror. Whoever was on the other end of the phone was shaking the teacher to his very core.

"But..., but..." Stark was barely able to speak against the incoming tirade, "I will... of course... yes right away." He pressed the end call button with a shaking finger. "Thom, you'd better go home now son," he said in a strained robotic voice.

Thom managed to hoist himself up off of the sofa; Stark kept his back to him and wouldn't turn around and face him. As scared as he'd been, the slumped shoulders of the teacher now wobbling with the soft sound of crying brought forward an unwanted dreg of sympathy. He squashed it hard and left quickly and without a word.

Henry Stark was calculating the time that it would take for him to get home, get the ready-packed case and get out. His heart was pounding and not in the good way. He cursed his weakness; for so long it had been kept under control, locked and chained in the basement like the filthy animal that it was. He couldn't believe that one slip had already ruined everything. It was a roller coaster that had been set in motion; the car had climbed the steep incline slowly and steadily without him even noticing. He'd sat on the sofa staring into the eyes of the young, fresh virgin spoils, without even realizing that his mind was set in motion. Suddenly the rollercoaster had tipped over the top of the slow, steep incline and then pitched forward. The car had rolled with startling speed, careering forward and violently out of control. His primal instincts had taken over whilst his self-preservation had lain dormant and silent. All it had taken was one hand on one thigh and his world had collapsed around him.

His hands trembled with fear as he desperately tried to get his keys in the car ignition. He steadied himself with considerable care. If he didn't grasp onto the life preserver now, then he would never be found again. The phone call had shattered his fantasies into a million pieces and had dragged him back into the real world; a world that had now turned black and deadly.

Eventually he calmed himself enough to start the car. With forced control he pulled out of the parking lot slowly and nonchalantly drove the short distance to his house. He thumped the wheel in frustration; everything here had been perfect, so perfect. The money was fantastic; the classes were small and the students eager and manageable. The school board had even provided him with a house in town. It was a spectacular property far in excess than anything he had ever seen before.

Throughout his whole career he had been able to suppress his unnatural desires during work hours. There had been a number of select and discreet organisations that he had maintained a cautious membership to. This select band of merry men had provided him with enough data to enable him to function out in the real world; he had guarded his memberships with the utmost care and scrutiny. He had always been able to keep his desires under control through sheer force of will, and cowardice over his discovery and he had never laid a hand on any student. It was the most perverse of ironies that he had been suspended from his last job over an untrue allegation of abuse by a failing student with a grudge to bear. Alan Hatcher had been an academically underachieving thirteen year old. "Hatch" had been an all star performer on the field, the court, and the pool, but never in the classroom. He was popular with both sexes in the school. He had an easy, casual manner that drew people to him; boys wanted to be him, and girls wanted to be with him. His effortless charm had won him fans amongst the faculty, none more so than with the Principal who had come to Henry one day pleading with him to tutor the boy through his classes. Hatch's prowess in the sporting arena drew much wanted and needed attention to the school in an age of competition for funding. Henry had been the most effective teacher at the school, owing in no small part to his desire to be close to his children. At first Hatch had been willing and attentive but his interest had soon waned. His attention was difficult to hold; he would lose focus quickly and his temper became short and easy to blow. Henry noticed that Hatch would have mood swings and would become easily upset, and it soon became clear that a standardized test for ADD was in order. Hatch had been willing to try the test as the thought of becoming mellower and much more on an even keel was appealing to him as he was aware of his own troubles. The problem had been Hatch's father; a bear of a man determined to see his only son rise to the sporting heights that he had been unable to scale. Butch Hatcher had reacted severely and unexpectedly to the threat to his own dreams and Henry had soon found himself on the end of a particularly nasty smear campaign of sexual abuse. The irony being that Henry had often fantasized about that very subject and it had taken all of his iron will to keep his hands to himself. Fortunately - and surprisingly for Henry - the school had rallied around him; his students and fellow teachers had banded together and marched to his defense. It had been a rough few weeks but eventually Hatch himself, along with his mother had stepped forward and refuted the allegations. Henry had been lauded to the rafters for his dignity and calm in the face of such monstrous accusations. In reality, Henry had spent the weeks praying for a miracle, basking in the realisation that if he had ever acted on his impulses then this would be the reality of his fate. Once cleared, he had sought to leave the area and find another school far away from the inevitable distrusting eyes of those who would always wonder despite his clearing. He hadn't intended to take another teaching position, but the email from Eden had been a gift from the heavens; one promising a new and prosperous life. Once he'd visited the town he was sold. The school was a luxury for a teacher and the size of the town meant that he could never be tempted again. There would be no place to hide and no crowd to conceal himself amongst. Until today he had kept the promise to himself; it had been a mad slip, an insane fall from grace that had ruined everything.

He pulled into his driveway and ran to his front door; it was one of the few locked doors in the town he'd wager, but there were some dangerous publications that had been ever so carefully concealed within.

He flew up the stairs and into his spacious bedroom; his shoes scraping on the hardwood floor that normally would not have permitted such footwear. He quickly grabbed the ready packed suitcase from on top of the wardrobe. It was an old habit that had never died; an emergency door that he had never fully closed. The open bedroom door suddenly eased towards closing behind him and a vast dark shadow fell across his world, drowning him in terror. He turned slowly to face his reckoning, "Please," he wept, his hands up and out, "I can just leave, I'll go."

The shadow moved towards him slowly with black menace.

"I never even touched him," he sobbed.

The thick length of rope slipped effortlessly over his head and the massive man tightened the noose roughly. Suddenly he was being dragged forward with immense strength, his feet slipped on the hardwood flooring as he staggered. The man pulled him through the doorway and out onto the landing. Realizing what was happening, Henry began to struggle, but he was a feather caught in a hurricane. He was pulled to the thick oak banister that ran the length of the open landing. The bear pulled him in close and his feet were off the ground. He kicked backwards, scraping his heel uselessly down the bear's leg. He was held in one massive and powerful arm whilst the other end of the rope was wrapped around the banister. Suddenly he was hoisted up and over the rail; he was held out suspended in mid air and looked back into the soulless smiling eyes of his death. Then he was falling, the sharp snap did not break his neck completely and he was left to ponder the natural order of justice as he slowly choked and his world faded.

The barbeque was flowing along with the wine. As was customary the evening was warm and the company was pleasant. Michael turned the steaks several times pointlessly as was the want of men when cooking over an open flame. The smells drifted on the gentle breeze as did the occasional bout of laughter.

Emily sat with Sarah-Jane on the wooden garden furniture. The seating was comfortable and the conversation likewise. Sarah-Jane drank a little too much and a little too quickly. Emily watched with pleasure as her young friend's confidence grew and swelled before her eyes. She knew that the main source of SJ's happiness was standing with Michael griddling seasoned meats with beer fuelled expertise. Dr Samuel Creed held a chilled bottle in one hand and Emily guessed a very soft spot for a certain young teacher in the other.

"So have you, you know, yet?" Emily asked curiously.

Sarah-Jane blushed deeply, but for once she didn't drop her eyes from Emily's gaze, "Not quite," she confessed with a whisper. "We've done, you know, other stuff, just not that, not yet."

"Do you think he's big all over?" Emily giggled.

"EM!" SJ shrieked unable to contain her explosive laughter, "I certainly hope so," she whispered again leaning in closer, her cheeks burning.

"What are you two laughing about?" Michael called from the grill smiling.

"Oh you know, just girly stuff. Clothes and shoes," Emily teased, smiling back poking her tongue out.

The evening had passed happily despite Michael's concerns over Sarah-Jane and the doctor's fledgling relationship. He had expressed his concerns to Emily that they would all spend the evening sitting in awkward silence. His fears had been fast laid to rest. The doctor was a comfortable companion; he didn't garble away aimlessly and he didn't look to dominate the conversation, he only spoke when he had something to say. They had quietly discussed Emily's pregnancy; Michael knew that his anxieties were normally unfounded but they persisted all the same. His nagging fears crept around the corners of his mind in the small dark hours, exclusively at first, but they soon grew tired of the unsociable hours and began making their presence felt during the bright day. Michael knew that until the day he died he would carry the responsibility of Emily's accident and their baby's loss, no matter how much Emily protested. It wasn't a case of not believing that she had wanted to venture out on that fateful winter evening, it just simply didn't matter. His actions - or lack thereof - had directly contributed to Emily being struck by the car that had changed their lives. Unbeknownst to Emily, Michael had held several informal appointments with Dr Creed; the purpose being to talk through his guilty conscience. Michael had slowly come to accept that his guilt was perhaps not quite as fulsome and complete as he had once believed, but it would always exist and he would have to make peace with that.

Michael was drooling over the BBQ's melting meat when Thom Bray's face appeared around the house. Michael immediately raised a hand in welcome, but stopped when he saw the boy's face. Despite their conversations and Thom's obvious brightness and maturity, he was still really a child. Michael saw that child's worried face, illuminated with fear and something else; shame, embarrassment, he couldn't quite tell.

"Thom!" Emily yelled an enthusiastic greeting as she spotted him, her words carrying across the large garden, "Come in, come in, you hungry?"

Michael saw a reticence on the young man's face. He handed the tongs to Creed, "Take over for a minute doc, use your steady surgeon's hands."

"Perhaps I should have told you before Mike, I actually flunked medical school," he taunted, "I did get my vet's license though."

"Funny man," Michael laughed, "I'll remember that next time I have to write you a check."

He left the party and headed over to the waiting boy. "Thom," he said as he got closer, "Everything okay?" He could see from this distance that everything was most certainly not. "What is it, what's happened?" Thom's trembling face threatened to collapse into tears and Michael felt a strong and not unpleasant paternal tug. "Here, come into the house." He led Thom in through the patio doors and into the kitchen. The light was dimming inside but an instinct made him not turn on the lights. Whatever had happened, perhaps Thom would prefer a little dim lighting.

Thom ran through the afternoon's events and Michael fought to control his rising temper. Thom spoke slowly and stutteringly. He told Michael that his mother was out at work for the day and wouldn't be home for another couple of hours. Michael noticed several times that Thom's thumb rose towards his mouth in an unconscious childhood mannerism.

Primal instincts run deep in man and Michael's first thoughts were of retribution. He would hunt and he would kill. Violent thoughts were augmented every time that he looked into the deeply scared and embarrassed face of a skinny fourteen year old boy. He was saved, however, by a soft hand on his shoulder. He turned and looked into the knowing face of his wife and her gaze was steady and her eyes were clear. Reason returned and sane rationale took hold. Storming castles with pitchforks and lit torches would benefit nobody at this point - least of all Thom.

"Tell me from the beginning Thom," she instructed rather than asked in an authoritative voice born from years of teaching and experience of children.

After telling the story for a second time Michael watched as Emily's manner calmed and settled Thom. His voice grew stronger and more assured and Michael knew that in the boy's place, he would already be thanking his lucky stars that he had gotten off this lightly. Thom had suffered an almighty scare;

the thought of what might have happened without the intervention of the fortuitous phone call was truly horrifying. Just who had been on the other end of the line that had scared the teacher back to his senses was a matter for consideration, but their priority now had to be Thom and Mr. Stark.

Sarah-Jane appeared in the kitchen behind them. Michael turned to see her face filled with sadness seemingly directed at Thom.

"I've called the Sheriff's office and told them about what happened," she said gently "They're going to pick up Stark now and someone will be by for Thom."

Michael and Thom shared a private look; the last thing that either of them wanted was for the big Sheriff to come rolling in again, as Quinn's motives were still a cause for concern.

Deputies Kurt Stillson and Tommy Ross pulled up to Stark's house and found the teacher's car was still in the driveway. They exited the squad car quickly and carefully; neither man was armed as was the way in Eden.

Kurt placed a hand on Stark's car bonnet. A maneuver that he had seen on television countless times; he was pleased to feel that the engine was still warm. "He hasn't been back long," Kurt said with authority. He led the way to the front door. Tommy moved behind him with a smile.

"You see that on TV?" Tommy whispered as they reached the door.

"No," Kurt bristled, "Standard police work."

"Yeah right," Tommy laughed.

Kurt took a pair of disposable gloves out of his back pocket and began struggling to pull them on.

"What are you doing?" Tommy giggled.

"Fingerprints," Kurt hissed annoyed.

"Whose exactly? Stark lives here alone and you're opening the door."

Kurt gave up the job of trying to pull the tricky gloves on and his mood darkened. For the first time since his move here he had envisioned a real crime and a real arrest, hopefully with resistance. Tommy was spoiling his daydream with boring reality.

Kurt pushed the door open not bothering to knock, "Mr. Stark," he called out loudly, "Stark!"

The front door opened into a large open plan lounge area. The bay windows let in plenty of natural light and Kurt was admiring the tasteful decoration when Tommy elbowed him painfully in the ribs.

"What?" He turned to his partner. Tommy's attention was located upwards; Kurt followed his eye line. Swinging from the landing banister was the teacher in question. Stark's face was swollen and puffy, and his eyes had rolled back in his head. The noose ended rope swayed gently under the soft breeze of the air conditioning and Kurt moved closer to the body. Stark's tongue lolled grotesquely from his open mouth and the closer Kurt got to the body the more his nose wrinkled in disgust at the voided odour emanating from the dead man. Despite his initial terror, Kurt found himself morbidly fascinated by the corpse.

"Kurt," Tommy's urgent voice shocked him back, "Don't touch anything, not a damn thing, oh, and it might actually be an idea to put those gloves on after all."

CHAPTER TWENTY

"So let's just get everything out on the table" Michael announced to the room.

Michael, Emily, Thom, Sarah-Jane, and Dr Creed were all sitting in the doctor's office. The door was closed, his secretary was out to lunch and the blinds were drawn. The five of them were squashed in cozily. The A/C was pumping out on full but the room was small and packed fit to burst with hot bodies.

"I'm kind of lost here," Dr Creed said.

"Yeah, me too," Sarah-Jane added nervously. "What is it that you're saying?"

"That something very odd is going on in this town," Michael stated. "Our neighbor Janet supposedly committed suicide after a fling with the gardener. She confessed all to her husband Chris and to cut a long story short, they made up and were going to move away."

"Then why would she kill herself?" Sarah-Jane asked puzzled.

"That is the very question," Michael answered. "Janet and Chris were round at ours the night in question. Chris seemed happy with the idea of them moving away and making a fresh start. Next thing I know I'm waking up to flashing blue lights and the Sheriff is telling me that Chris left Janet and she's dead at her own hands. Now, apart from the fact that only a couple of hours earlier they were still together and planning for the future, just what the hell is the town Sheriff doing divulging confidential details about a death to me out on the sidewalk? Now add to those facts that I haven't been able to contact or locate Chris since that night and the whole thing seems pretty damn peculiar."

"Forgive me Mike, but don't you write peculiar for a living?" Dr Creed asked analytically, "I mean doesn't it stand to reason that you might see weirdness everywhere when it might not exist?"

"Sure, that's what I, we, thought," Michael said indicating towards Emily. "But here's another one; I cycled out to the woods and basically after I went in I lost a whole bunch of time. After that, I went out to see Darnell."

"Kevin Darnell?" Sarah-Jane asked.

"Yes, you know him?" Michael responded.

"Well, he's kind of known as the town drunk to be honest," she replied embarrassed.

"Well that's as maybe, but I haven't been able to find him since our little conversation either. And another thing, what is with this town and the Woodland Festival? It seems to be the only thing on anyone's mind lately. Darnell even told me to stay away from it, but wouldn't say why."

"It's just an annual festival. A small town tradition really. I've never seen anything untoward going on," Sarah-Jane answered.

"So how many people are we talking about having disappeared?" Thom asked intrigued, his sense of self was returning quickly after his scare. His mind may be imaginative, but it was also resistant.

"Well that's Chris and Darnell that I know of," Michael said.

"There's also this," Emily held up Jessica's diary. "This belonged to Jessica Grady. She had my job before me and our house before us. Oh and she was also pregnant as well. She speaks of growing more and more paranoid about the town; up until the point when she says that they are going to escape - and that is the word she uses, escape. She talks of them wanting her baby. She doesn't say who **they** are, but she seems terrified. She says that her doctor was Dr Lempke. Samuel did you know him?"

"Yeah sure, Dr Lempke was here before I took over. I can probably dig out his old notes on Jessica, just as long as none of you leak that fact," he said seriously.

"But Em, I told you all about Jessica. She was unstable and acting weird, She had to be dragged out of school and carted away," Sarah-Jane interjected.

"But she also says here that someone was drugging her. She talks about suspecting Thirlby."

"Oh God," Sarah-Jane suddenly said unhappily, "She tried telling me, and I wouldn't listen. It was me that called the Sheriff when she started going nuts at the school."

Samuel put a large arm around the now crying teacher, "What do you mean going nuts?"

Sarah-Jane trembled as she spoke; her shoulders hitched with low sobs, "She attacked Mrs. Thirlby with a pair of scissors right in front of her class. The children were screaming hysterically when I came in to see what was going on. Luckily Jess just seemed to suddenly go weak as though she just suddenly lost her strength, and I was able to calm her enough until the Sheriff turned up."

"So what happened to Jessica Grady and her husband?" Thom asked pertinently.

The room looked at each other, "SJ?" Emily asked.

"Sorry but I don't know, Thirlby just told me that they'd left town suddenly. I asked if anyone knew where, but no-one did. I wanted to make sure that they were OK and that the baby was as well, but I couldn't," she sniffed.

"Anything else?" Dr Creed asked.

"What about the graffiti that keeps springing up around town?" Michael said.

"The Wake Up signs?" Sarah-Jane asked, "What does that even mean?"

"I've seen them, the town's cleanup crew get there quickly enough, but I thought that was just kids?" Creed said.

"Maybe, maybe not. We saw the first one on the day that we moved into town," Michael answered "And I remember thinking that it was a little weird, but at this point, we're in danger of perhaps reading too much into everything."

"Well, I've got to be honest, Thirlby always freaks me out a little," Emily said.

"Likewise the Sheriff," Thom added, "When he caught me in the Beaumont's house, I didn't know what he had planned but it wasn't an after school special."

"Oh I'm sure that he just wanted to scare you straight young man," Samuel said with a slight reproach.

"Oh hey, I'm not denying that I deserved a little spook, but you didn't see his eyes; the way he was dragging me out the door he looked like he only had evil intentions. It was only when Michael surprised him that he stopped, and boy did he look pissed. Then there's Mr. Stark," Thom said in a small, quiet voice; the whole room dropped their eyes and looked down at the floor.

"So what are we saying here?" Sarah-Jane asked a little testily, "I've lived here all my life and up until this morning I thought that it was a pretty perfect place to live, and now all of you," she paused and blushed furiously, but pressed on regardless, "I'm sorry, but outsiders move in and start tearing the place down."

Samuel held her hand gently and looked deeply at her. "No-one is saying anything, other than perhaps we should take a closer look. The last thing that I want to do is upset you SJ, but I worry about you more than anyone else here, no offence," he smiled at the room. "If people here are in danger then I want you to be safe more than anyone."

Sarah-Jane looked up lovingly at Creed, "So what can we do?"

"Well, when I want to find out anything when I'm working, it all comes down to the writer's least favourite word in the dictionary research," Michael said.

"Where do we start?" Emily asked.

"Well Darnell told me quite a tale about the history of the town and of Casper's twisted family tree. It probably doesn't have anything to with today, but you never know. We should pull some skeletons out of some dark closets and take a look at the moldy bones. Doc see what you can drag up on Jessica's medical history; what she was taking, what Lempke diagnosed her with etc? Let's also take a look at modern Eden; how many others have died mysteriously in accidents or unlikely suicides or just plain disappeared?"

"My father!" Thom suddenly blurted, "My father just upped and left one day. My mother won't talk about where or why, do you think...?" He looked to Michael with tears in his eyes for comfort, but Michael had none to offer.

Casper called the meeting to order, the faces that greeted him were filled with eagerness and anticipation. They were waiting to be fed and led. The room positively crackled with hope and eagerness and Casper held the news that they were all dying to hear within the yellow folder. The pages held the very prosperity of the town and all of their futures and presents within the printed word; so much rested on so little and all rested upon his shoulders.

Deputy Kurt Stillson hung his uniform inside the plastic body bag ready for cleaning; the shirt and pants stared at him from across the room. The festival was only days away and his attendance in full uniform was apparently mandatory. He had given serious thought to burning the clothes as soon as he had taken them off; it was only his stubbornness that prevented him. He knew that it was only his imagination that fed him odors of death clinging to the fabric. The teacher had been hanging from the banister and although he had never actually touched him, he could feel the very presence of fatality buried in the cloth.

Kurt bristled at his own shortcomings; Tommy Ross had taken over with a natural leadership, shaping the situation into one of order amidst the chaos. Kurt, however, had stumbled around like a tourist. He had dreamt of a real crime falling across his lap for months and when one finally had, he had been found wanting. Tommy had presented the Sheriff with a full rundown when he'd appeared on the scene and Quinn had taken over; quickly dismissing both of them outside to look for witnesses. For reasons that Kurt was still unsure of, Eden seemed to operate almost entirely on its own authority. There had been no state cops arriving on the scene taking over the investigation as you might expect - no outside interference ever seemed to breach the town walls. Quinn had quickly announced that Mr. Henry Stark, biology teacher and apparent pedophile, had taken his own life. Quinn had not deigned to furnish them with any further details. Kurt had spoken to the surrounding neighbors - surreptitiously of course - after all, this was Eden and maintaining the balance was always the priority. No-one had seen or heard anything; no-one coming or going from the house. Apparently Mr. Stark was a quiet, well-mannered man, pleasant to his neighbors and all round nice guy. Apart, of course, for the large stack of grotesque and highly illegal child porn material that the Sheriff had pulled from the house, carefully concealed in a brown paper bag. Kurt knew that Quinn had only been searching the house for a matter of minutes before he'd emerged with the exceedingly guilty material along with a more troubling suicide note. Kurt had stepped closer to the body than Tommy had, although he had not admitted such to the Sheriff. Kurt had not seen any note, either on or near the body. Normally Kurt was very much in favor of going with the flow as a life philosophy, and the apparent suicide of a teacher with monstrous tendencies should not alter that. But somehow it still itched inside, somewhere deep.

Michael was rolling his bike out onto the road when the Sheriff's car pulled up alongside him.

"Good morning Mr. Torrance," the Sheriff's tone was friendly and open, but his deep voice boomed with authority.

"Sheriff," Michael said, fighting the impulse to tip an imaginary cowboy hat. "What can I do for you?"

"Perhaps we should talk inside sir?" the question was posed, but never really existed.

Michael led the hulking man back inside the empty house and into the kitchen, "Coffee?" He asked.

"Why not."

Michael poured two cups from the machine; despite his usual preference for tea he was gaining a taste for the bitter caffeine rush. He laid the cups on the counter and sat one side on a stool facing the Sheriff. Quinn eased his massive bulk onto a metal stool on the other side of the counter and used it to support his knee off of the floor with a wince.

"Old football injury," he said catching Michael staring, "Plays up from time to time."

"Must be tough, you know, in your line of work."

"Well it's not really like the TV; we're rarely called upon to chase killers through the streets of Eden."

"Just graffiti artists," Michael joked.

Quinn's face darkened, "Crime is crime Mr. Torrance, and we take all kinds extremely seriously here in Eden."

"Hey, me too," Michael said in an appeasing tone, "Hang 'em all for all I care."

Quinn stared for a long time and Michael was glad for once that Americans seemed to have trouble telling when he was joking or not. "Well, I wouldn't quite go that far sir," he smiled.

"So what can I do for you today Sheriff, only..." Michael looked down at his watch.

"It's about young Mr. Bray."

"Thom?"

"Exactly, I am aware that young Thom has spoken to you and your wife about, um, his experience at school."

"You mean when he was nearly molested or worse?" Michael snapped, annoyed at the Sheriff's tactful manner.

"Exactly."

"Have you arrested the teacher, this Stark?"

"There was no need."

"NO NEED!"" Michael exploded, "After what he tried to do, there's no fucking need?"

Quinn's plastic smile faded, "I would appreciate it if you would refrain from using that kind of language sir."

"Are you kidding me?" Michael near shouted incredulously, "There's a pedophile teacher on the loose and you're worried about my language?"

"He's not on the loose, he's dead," Quinn stated.

Michael was suddenly shocked into silence as he processed the information, "Dead, how?"

"Suicide, he hung himself."

"Did he leave a note?"

"That must be the writer in you Mr. Torrance, asking such pertinent questions."

Michael could feel the barely suppressed anger that bubbled under the Sheriff's surface. The large man was all smiles and politeness, but it all seemed a little too forced; a little too perfect, a little too Eden. "**Was** there a note?"

"Yes, yes there was," Quinn stated.

The Sheriff's face was granite. His expression impassive and impenetrable, only his eyes seemed full of life.

"What did it say?" Michael asked snappily, growing tired of the dance.

"I'm afraid that's confidential, suffice to say that the note was, shall we say, appropriate."

"What happens now, what happens to Thom?"

"Nothing."

"Nothing?"

"Well, I think that it would be best for the boy if he didn't have to go through a long drawn out investigation. From what Thom says there was only the suggestion that something might have happened. This is a small town Mr. Torrance and word would soon spread about the embarrassing details, and that surely cannot be good for the boy."

Michael wanted to argue, if only for the sake of it. Something about Quinn just rubbed him the wrong way. But there was no doubt that with Stark dead it would only bring about humiliation for Thom, however unfairly. "What about the school board, the Principle? Surely someone must be responsible for employing Stark. Someone didn't do their homework."

Quinn's eyes suddenly blazed as though Michael's accusations were directed at him and Michael felt extremely nervous. The house suddenly felt very empty and deserted and his closest neighbors were gone. No-one would hear his shouts if the bear opposite him reached over and snapped his neck like a chicken bone.

"Well that is something that we will be looking into sir, rest assured."

Michael did not feel assured, "What exactly is it that you want from me Sheriff?"

"Only your utmost discretion Mr. Torrance. We've spoken to the boy and his mother and I have personally guaranteed them that all of the details will remain strictly confidential. I only ask that both you and your wife would honour the family's wishes as well."

"Then you have it."

"Marvelous, then I will be on my way. See you at the festival Mr. Torrance," Quinn said as he heaved his vastness up and out.

Michael walked him to the door; the Sheriff walked a little too closely, seemingly enjoying his immense size and the natural intimidation that it brought. The Sheriff walked with a slight limp and paused in the doorway. The sun streamed in through the gap and Michael raised his hand to shield his eyes.

"We've got ourselves a nice town here Mr. Torrance. We aim to keep it that way," the Sheriff said with a friendly tone that Michael didn't quite buy, before adding, "No matter what," in such a tone that he did.

Dr Samuel Creed sat thoughtfully at his desk. The office was quiet today and appointments were scarce. His receptionist had taken a half day with his blessing as he'd wanted the place to himself. This town was an enigma to him, much as Michael had stated to him. The whole *"Heaven on earth and twice as nice"* motto was wearing a little thin by now. He had been seduced by the thoughts of a town free from the horrors of the outside world. The first year or so had been a whirlwind of pleasures; calm and peace reigned over his world and he'd bathed under its warm glow. The depression of his time drowning under the yoke of the various but always similar emergency rooms of LA had slowly drained from his thoughts and mind. His LA days had become mired in hopelessness and self-medication. Each day had dawned darker than the last and no matter how much he slept he was always tired. Eden had indeed been true to her name; she had offered him a way out, a chance to become a doctor again rather than a pit stop mechanic. In this small, pretty town, he had found his calling once again; he was a helper and a healer. Polite and friendly people called into his office during civilized business hours and they chatted over coffee calmly and with social graces. His finances had grown along with his peace of mind and he'd made acquaintances rather than friends, but that suited him fine. His life was so full of people during the day that he often longed for solitude after hours. That was until he'd met Sarah-Jane. She was a bubble of happy joy, one that was far more infectious than any disease he'd ever encountered. Their dates had progressed charmingly slowly. For all of his growing desire, slowly was just fine with him. His life had been a closed book for so long now that he knew it would take time to open the pages again.

With a final look around outside the office to make sure he was alone, Creed headed downstairs to the basement. The doctor's office was on two levels with the lower floor given over to storage for all of the town's hard copy files. He thought back to his early days in town when he had taken over from Dr Lempke. The old man had been a strange one to be sure. Lempke was a small, skinny man who did not project an aura of health and vitality. He was around five feet four with a slightly hunched stance; he had a crooked hawk nose and deep set eyes that had made Creed uneasy just to be looked at. Lempke was close to seventy when they'd met and had insisted on staying on for an additional six months that grew to eight in order to ensure a smooth transitional handover. Creed's initial interview had been before a town council that had consisted of Casper Christian as town manager, Malcolm Lempke as the towns outgoing doctor and Sheriff Quinn, for reasons that he was never entirely sure. The interview had been intense and all encompassing. His life had been pulled apart; his records, education and his private life. Every corner had been examined under the brightest of spotlights. It had actually been a relief to find that the town took his appointment so seriously. If it was indicative of their interview techniques and acceptance standards then he would fit in here just fine.

Despite the town's reputation he had never felt able to leave the records room unlocked. He opened the large padlock that he had personally installed and swung open the basement door. The fusty smell radiated from the room;

cardboard boxes sat upon large metal filing cabinets that lined the walls encasing the entire room. The metallic sentries stood guard holding the entire town's medical history. He knew that he was breaking all kinds of rules - both personal and professional - by planning to share any information that he found on Jessica Grady. He knew that Casper would fire him on the spot for such a breach, but his job no longer seemed as important to him as the truth. He knew deep down, in the places that we don't like to visit very often, that something was rotten here. Eden was perfect, but that very perfection must come at price somewhere along the line, and what worried him the most was just who was footing the bill.

Unbeknownst to his new friends and even Sarah-Jane he held his own secrets, as several times he had patched up mysterious injuries to townsfolk that the Sheriff brought in. A broken arm here, a bloody face to be stitched there, and to his shame he had never asked the origins of these wounds. It was an unspoken rule that he was merely to perform his duty in silence and without question. The strange thing was that the injured parties had always seemed more ashamed than injured. Heads were bowed and gazes averted and the Sheriff had stood tall in the examination room. His massive frame dissuading all conversation; his powerful arms folded across his broad chest and his eyes were dark and cruel. Creed knew that something was wrong and he should be more troubled than he'd acted. His intentions had been eroded by time, the sun always shone and his days were happy. His life was far removed from the days of crushing depression in LA and he had found that a man would do almost anything for a sound night's sleep. So he splinted the occasional arm and stitched the occasional wound. He didn't know just what these occasions had meant, but he knew that he should have asked and his shame was intensified by his new friends' concerns. Michael and Emily were new to town and Thom was just a boy, but they were all unwilling to turn a blind eye to whatever was going on here. Creed knew that it was about time he stood up and asked a few questions of his own; starting with Mrs. Jessica Grady.

He began scanning the cabinets, checking for surnames. He ran his finger along the cool metallic surfaces; the room was gloomy and despite his being alone he felt a strange aversion to turning on the lights. His ears were constantly attuned to the building around him, listening for any telltale creak of a floorboard announcing unwanted arrivals.

The filing system appeared to be alphabetical, but when he got to the G's there was no Grady to be found. He checked and double checked. He scanned the files all around the room; only one cabinet was bereft of labeling and he pulled the top drawer open. It was resistant at first and the drawer moved with a soft, tight squeak and Creed had to jiggle it all the way open. The files were of various ages; some were yellowed with time and the dust irritated his nostrils, whilst others were newer and brighter. His fingers flicked over the paperwork until his eyes caught on the name Grady. He plucked the folder from the cabinet and pulled it out into the low light.

A sudden noise from above him made him pause; a creak on the floor. The door to the basement room swayed gently as a soft breeze brushed against it. Creed knew that the breeze must have come from the outside door being opened.

Inexplicably panicking he wrestled with the thick folder, attempting to bend it and force it into his pants in order to hide it. He ran for the door and up the stairs, struggling to conceal the Grady file as he stumbled. His heart pounded violently against his ribs as his breath caught and his chest hitched painfully. His hands shook as he sprung into the main waiting area outside his office; his eyes scanning desperately around the room. He could feel another's presence. Someone was here, or had just left. The hidden folder suddenly felt important. It was suddenly the most important thing in his life, whatever lay within its pages had to be seen and had to be told.

Despite his own size he was not a man capable of violent thought or deed, regardless of the situation. He had the tools; he was strong and powerful but he lacked the will. His was a nature of flight rather than fight. He moved slowly, hoping that his bulk would not give him away. He moved gently towards the main exit; the outside world and its many witnesses were suddenly terrifically appealing. He stepped as lightly as he could. There were no obvious sounds behind him as he tiptoed. His hand brushed the cold brass door handle and he eased it down. His lips pulled as he willed it silent. He pushed the door softly open. The warm breeze caressed his face and invited his yearning to be gone; he had one foot in safety when the hand grabbed his shoulder and he screamed.

Emily got off the tram with Sarah-Jane helping her down somewhat awkwardly. She was finding that as she got bigger with the pregnancy, she was lacking the natural coordination and the grace of the larger woman. Emily had always been slim as a matter of fortunate genes and a healthy lifestyle, but now she felt like an oil tanker needing about a week to change direction. For the first time since their arrival in Eden she was beginning to despise the weather. No matter what she wore she could never feel cool enough. It was only at home sitting in the pool that she was able to feel comfortable.

Sarah-Jane took her arm in a subconscious act of protection and Emily was glad of the company and the comfort of her friend. She was still not convinced just exactly what they were doing, any of them. Michael had asked Dr Creed to break his oath and reveal confidential details about a prior patient. As well as involving a teenage boy who had narrowly avoided a potentially serious assault, but had surely suffered some psychological damage. Michael had always had a tendency towards an occasionally destructive imagination; it was a curse of his profession and talent. He could be right in his suspicions, or he could just be seeing tigers around every corner.

They were on their way to meet with Alice Garfield. Alice was the oldest resident in Eden at officially 105 years old. Emily had done a double take when Eddie the tram driver had suggested her and revealed her age. They had told Eddie that the school was looking to do a project on town history with the children, and did he know of the best resident to approach?

Alice lived out on Livingston. It was the oldest part of town and the houses were all original, as the town council had decreed that the buildings had to be maintained in their original design. All alterations to any house in town had to be approved and there was nowhere that this was more stringently regulated than in Livingston.

As they walked slowly around the area Emily was charmed by the colonial style properties. All were beautifully preserved; the whites gleamed under the bright sun, the wooden fences and the decking were sanded and smooth. Most had quaint swing seats swaying in the breeze and it made Emily ponder whether they had chosen the right area to live in. Their house was a beautiful mansion, and as lovely as it was, it was new. The home was perfect but perhaps a little soulless. Both she and Michael were used to having history surround them; back in the UK buildings held centuries of life and experience within the very bricks and mortar.

Eddie had given them an address for Alice and they found the house easily as the streets were clearly marked with pretty signs. Alice was sitting on the porch swing seemingly waiting for them as they approached. She stood with greater ease than Emily was currently managing.

"Hello," Alice cried with a spry voice, her arm waving healthily, "Come in, come in."

Emily climbed the five steps up to the house with Sarah-Jane's welcome support. The wooden decking was planed and painted white and there were no worrying creaks as she hefted her ever growing expanse upwards.

"Sit my dear, sit," Alice said, "My, you are positively glowing child, may I?"

Emily didn't know what "may I" meant, but she was glad to get off her feet and onto the padded cushioned porch swing, "Sure," she said.

Alice leant over with one crooked claw stretched out towards her pregnancy swell, and for one terrible moment, Emily thought of the witch in Hansel and Gretel. Alice's kindly face was twisted into a mask of monstrous hunger; a hideous snarling façade of ravenous drooling. Emily must have turned green and looked faint.

"My dear, are you quite all right?" Alice asked with kindness.

Emily almost laughed at her silliness; one vivid imagination in the family was already quite enough. "I'm sorry," she apologized, it must be the heat."

"Let me get you a drink dear, perhaps your friend can help me carry a tray. I'm not used to serving guests I'm afraid," Alice laughed with a tinkle.

Emily watched as SJ flicked her a concerned look; she squeezed her friend's hand briefly, just to show that she was ok and then she was alone as Alice and SJ disappeared into the house. The closer that they'd gotten to the house, the older Alice had looked. She still moved with a spryness that belied her years but her face was crinkled and lined with a century of experience woven into every crease. As Emily sat on the swing she could just about glance in through the lounge window. The house was orderly and clean and there were about a million ornaments sitting proudly on display. Emily's own grandmother had been a hoarder and collector and her house was a cavern of glass and china oddities; strange and useless delicates sent from relatives without a clue as to just what annual presents an elderly woman could possibly want. She could hear the gentle clinking of crockery from inside the house towards what must be the kitchen. Sarah-Jane's high pitched voice sang on the breeze but did not carry coherency far enough to reach her outside.

The street was quiet and the houses were typically well swept and kept. The lawns were lush, green and well mowed, but the neighbors were absent from the hot sun's full glare. Emily suspected that most residents would be somewhat elderly in this area, a fact confirmed by Sarah-Jane on the trip over. Eddie had told them that everything was history in Livingston; houses and people alike. Emily had figured that the best place to start looking into the Casper Christian family tree would be amongst the town's oldest residents, and apparently Alice Garfield was the oldest.

"Sarah-Jane has been filling me in on what you are after Mrs. Torrance," Alice's voice surprised her from behind; the old lady had crept up without a whisper, a soft slipper shuffle.

"Please, it's Emily Mrs. Garfield."

"Then I'm Alice, and we're just three gals gabbing," Alice said smiling as she sat down with barely a joint creak onto the porch swing next to her.

Sarah-Jane pulled up a lovingly kept rocking chair and sat facing them. She placed a tray of two ice cold homemade lemonade jugs on a small table that she pulled over and placed between them. "I was telling Alice about the school project. You know, bringing history alive for the children."

"It sounds like a lovely idea," Alice said, "Sometimes I feel that all this knowledge is just going to rattle here forever," she said tapping her head.

"Well we just thought that nobody could know the town better than you Alice, and I know that the children would love to hear all about the interesting history of Eden and her founding fathers," Emily said as she reached for one of the lemonade jugs to pour a glass.

"Not that one dear," Alice said quickly, "Take the other one, it's unleaded," she said smiling, "In your condition I wouldn't advise drinking one of my personal concoctions. An old lady's prerogative," she said with a cheeky grin.

Emily drew gratefully on her non-alcoholic lemonade glass; the cold liquid was sweet and refreshing in the heat.

"Well dears," Alice said looking as though she was settling in for a long story. "The founding of Eden goes back a long way indeed, perhaps not quite as long a history as you might be used to," she said nudging Emily, "But for us over here it's terribly old indeed," she winked. "The Woodland Festival is coming up and the whole town comes out to celebrate our founding, although you can be assured that none of what I am going to tell you will be included in the festival," she cackled.

"Were the Christians the original founding family?" Emily asked unwilling to get sidetracked so early on. She had the feeling that Alice could wander if she wasn't directed.

"Oh yes, and they were quite the fearsome bunch as well," Alice said quietly looking around the street to make sure that they were alone. "Tolan Christian is Casper's great, great, many times great, grandfather. It is said that Tolan built the town around a logging company. Mind you this was back before companies were thought of in today's parlance. Tolan merely brought together a congregation to Eden and his people were converts to his word. I think that he was around his early teens and a lay preacher, as he and his mother were moving around from village to village giving sermons. If you think that Casper has a certain aura about him, you can only imagine what Tolan must have been like. For a teenage boy to draw a crowd to a new land I bet he'd give those television evangelists a run for their money," Alice cackled.

"Why did they follow him here?" Sarah-Jane asked.

"Times were hard, crops were failing, and hungry people will seek sustenance wherever they can find it when they're starving dear," Alice continued. "From what I remember of the stories that my grandmother told me, from what her grandmother told her etc, pretty much all of the villages within a few days walking distance of here were dying. Tolan had the ability to hold a crowd of desperate people in the palm of his hand, and he brought them with him towards a promised land. A town that they would build and prosper from."

"They felt that their God had deserted them and so they left their homes and followed a teenage boy out into the forest?" Emily asked incredulously.

"You must remember dear, this was a time of superstitions and omens. People were fraught with the idea of being abandoned. No matter how much they prayed, they were never answered. I'm afraid that they didn't have the chance to check the interweb highway or whatever it's called. If they found a black snake it was considered a sign of a good harvest and seeds planted by a pregnant woman should flourish."

"How many did he bring with him?" SJ asked.

"Not too many to begin with I don't think. I know that there were enough hands to begin building the town. Apparently it was taken as a sign from God that only the right people showed up. Builders began building and farmers began farming. As word spread throughout the area, more and more people began showing up. They were drawn by the tales of a chosen boy who had the ear of God himself. Tolan was treated as a prophet, a holy vessel through which God spoke and Tolan directed his will. As the crops thrived and grew strong and healthy, Tolan's legend swelled. Soon Eden flourished and prospered and her reputation became a draw for the best and brightest. The woodland was laden thick with quality trees fresh for the harvesting and the ground was rich and fertile. Soon the mill was constructed and they began the logging process. Timber was used first to build the town and then for exporting beyond her borders. The town grew rich, and Tolan, powerful; his word was the law and all followed it if they wished to stay within Eden. Word around the campfire was that Tolan kept an inner circle of five members and they were responsible for enforcing the law," Alice said with a gin infused, lemonade loosened tongue and a chuckle.

"I heard that Tolan's teachings took a rather dark turn," Emily said delicately.

"Oh, you've heard that have you?" Alice said between slurps, "I bet that was old Darnell. He always had a loose way about him," she winked conspiratorially. "I know that there were whispers of black magic, about deals with shadowy woodland forces that kept the town prosperous. Kevin Darnell will no doubt tell you about sacrifices and crucifixions committed by those disciples of Tolan who did not ask questions. I remember hearing as a child, stories of monsters and murder. Tolan became a bogeyman for the kids of Eden; eat your vegetables or Tolan Christian will come for you in the night and snatch you into the dark woods."

"Surely this can't all be fact," Sarah-Jane said, "All due respect Alice, but surely these are just stories. I mean I'm sure that Casper wouldn't appreciate us teaching a class that spoke so horrifically about his ancestor?"

"I think there was even a song. Now how did it go?" Alice spoke as though Sarah-Jane hadn't.

"While Eden sleeps in the cold, black night,
Boys and girls pray for the early morning light,
For something stirs in the deep, dark forest,
Tolan's ghost and the axe that he cherished,
Are rising from the grave in search of fresh chopping,
For naughty children's heads are ripe for the lopping"

"Lovely," Emily said under her breath casting an eye towards SJ.

"Well it was just a rhyme for children. We used to skip to it if I remember rightly," Alice said, her eyes were drooping and her voice was suddenly heavy with tiredness. "I remember when the mill still employed everyone in town, before the money men took over and all the rich people moved in," she slurred slightly and a little bitterly. "This used to be our town, before Casper and all of his great schemes. We used to be a town of the right faces and color."

Emily felt Sarah-Jane's foot nudging her. She looked over and her friend was nodding her head away from the house indicating that it might be time to leave. Emily agreed. Alice was beginning to drift away on a tide of gin infused lemonade.

"Now we've got blacks and browns..." Alice murmured under her breath.

"Ok, time to go," Emily announced not liking the direction that Alice's thoughts were going in, "Thank you for your time Mrs. Garfield," she said primly as Sarah-Jane helped her up to her feet.

"So I'll hear from you about talking to the children?" Alice said slumped in the porch swing.

"Yes, sure," Emily said, thinking that there was no way she would place a racist old woman in front of impressionable children.

"Take care Alice," Sarah-Jane said pleasantly.

"Whoa, she took an ugly road pretty damn quickly," Emily said when they were out of earshot.

"Well, that's now two old people with gossip and stories; her and the handyman Darnell that Michael spoke with. Not exactly credible witnesses, as they would say on TV," Sarah-Jane replied.

"No I guess not," Emily couldn't help but agree.

As they walked back to the tram stop, she couldn't help but keep the childish song rattling around her head. Suddenly she felt as though she was being watched and she turned back around sharply towards Alice's house. She could still see the old woman now sleeping on the porch and she could hear the faint sound of snoring floating on the air. For just a second she thought that she saw a large dark shadow at the side of the house. She squinted and it was gone, but her skin crawled as though something evil had just walked across her grave.

"What is it?" Sarah-Jane asked worriedly.

"Uh, nothing, I guess, nothing. Come on I'm starving, let's go eat something decadent," she said grabbing SJ's arm.

"You know you're terrible for my diet," Sarah-Jane giggled.

"Oh I'm sure that the good doctor prefers a little meat on his bones," Emily teased.

"Why what did he say? How much meat?" SJ asked seriously, looking down and pinching her sides.

Alice watched the young girls heading away. When you got to her age, she thought, pretty much everyone was a young girl. Her head swam from the gin. She knew that she shouldn't drink so much, but she figured at her age what else was there to put a smile on her face? Visitors were so rare these days; she had some grand children and great grand children scattered around the country, but she paid them little attention these days. About as little as they paid her. Her daughter had run off and married a man of questionable color much against her wishes. She had warned Maggie against diluting her race but her daughter had paid her no mind. Even the photos in the beginning of cute children wrapped in oversized comedic outfits had not warmed her frosty heart. Everyone knew that even **they** were cute at that age.

She hefted herself out of the porch swing with reluctance and the usual creaking bones. She knew that once she passed the one hundred year old milestone she really couldn't complain, but that hadn't stopped her. The gin infused lemonade sloshed in her hand and the ratio of alcohol to soda had long since slipped to the wrong side. Her head swayed and her vision clouded as she stood up too quickly. The hot sun was always welcomed on her old bones, but now it only made her feel queasy. She put a hand on the banister railing to steady herself. Her legs felt weak and her hands trembled. The glass suddenly fell from her grasp and shattered on the porch floor; the yellow liquid spraying the wooden floor darkening as it spread.

"Let me give you a hand there ma'am."

A rumbling voice suddenly appeared at her shoulder and a powerful hand clamped onto her arm steadying her instantly. The touch was insistent and she soon found herself being led through her front door and into the house. Her assistant had to dip his head slightly and turn sideways to navigate in through the opening.

She craned her head up for what seemed like an awful long way to see the man's face, "Sheriff," she said gratefully, "Thank you for your help young man, I guess the sun was just too hot today."

"All part of the service Mrs. Garfield," Quinn replied pleasantly. "Let me help you into the lounge, maybe you'd like to sit for a spell."

"I think that might be a good idea," Alice said finding herself moving into the lounge as though the choice was ever really hers to begin with.

"Here we are Mrs. Garfield," the Sheriff said as he placed her into the old but comfy sofa. The springs sank with familiarity as it took her weight. She watched as the huge man eased himself gently into the armchair facing her, and for a moment she worried the chair would not take his bulk. She envisaged the chair collapsing under his sheer size and it brought a tipsy smile to her lips; even as inebriated as she was, she instinctively knew that laughing at the man mountain would not be a good idea. As pleasant as he came across, the Sheriff was one of those men who had a smile that never quite touched his eyes; eyes that were distant and cruel. Her thankfully long dead husband had been such a man. He could smile and laugh but he had a quick temper and a quicker fist. One minute they would be sharing a joke and the next she would be laying on the floor with a bleeding mouth for some imagined slight that only David had seen.

She watched the Sheriff now. His large round face was smiling but his eyes were watchful. The dark orbs darted around the room and back to her time and again.

"I saw that you had some visitors leaving, just as I was passing," the Sheriff said casually.

For some reason, an alarm bell rang loudly enough to pierce her gin soaked fuzz and it slapped her in the face like a bucket of cold water, waking her senses fully. As relaxed as Quinn's voice was - and as seemingly casual as the question was - she felt panicked, trapped in an empty house and suddenly free from the view of her neighbors. Her eyes darted around the room which had never seemed smaller or darker.

"What did they want?" The Sheriff leant forward unfurling his colossal arms from across his broad chest and placing his massive paws on his knees.

"Oh it was just a couple of teachers from the elementary school. They wanted an old fart to talk to the children about the town's history," Alice attempted a tone of levity, but knew that she was falling some way short. Her voice trembled and the air was thick with menace.

"Really, and that was all they wanted?" Sheriff Quinn stood and stretched, he was a huge man, and his mass was overpowering.

From her seated position Alice sank further into her seat. The disparity in their sizes was never greater and she trembled as the Sheriff towered over her.

"Now I don't believe that you are being entirely truthful here Alice, are you?" He smiled with shark's teeth as he placed a hand under her chin.

Alice trembled; even the Sheriff's lightest touch was painful as she guessed it was meant to be. He tilted her face upwards, his rough fingers stroking her cheek with a sandpaper caress.

"I think that I would like to hear everything that you told them Alice my dear, and I think that I would like to hear it right now."

Alice whimpered as the powerful hand squeezed her chin, soft tears spilled out and ran down her face. "I didn't say anything, I swear," she sobbed.

"Now why don't I believe you?" Quinn whispered his voice low and hoarse.

"I promise," Alice cried.

"You do?"

"Yes, yes, I promise, I didn't say anything, nothing."

"Well, if you promise."

Alice grabbed at the lifeboat, "I promise," she said repeated earnestly.

The Sheriff released her face from his painful grip. He eased backwards away from her. Alice sighed, trembling with relief, her mind racing and confused.

The blow was loud and the pain monstrous. Alice fell from the sofa propelled by the Sheriff's powerful fist; her nose was crushed and her throat filling with the coppery taste of her own blood as it flooded downwards. She dizzily raised a hand to her face; the nose was shattered and spread across her cheek and the skin was split open by the large class ring that Quinn wore. Her vision blurred with tears on the onset of a concussion. Both eyes felt swollen and her breath hitched dangerously in her thin chest. She tried to crawl but her senses betrayed her.

The huge shadow of the Sheriff fell across her as he watched her feeble escape attempt. A thick, heavy work boot kicked her side absently and she felt the rib crack instantly and curled into a ball.

A hand suddenly gripped her neck and she was airborne, her feet jerking wildly above the floor. Her weight was meaningless to the powerful Sheriff as he brought his face in close to hers. His breath was fresh and minty, but his teeth were ivory and sharp. Despite her drifting consciousness she screamed when he bit her. His teeth sank into her cheek and ripped a chunk of bloody flesh away. She stared through blurry vision as he smiled and swallowed.

"You're going to tell me," he said through insane eyes.

"I don't know what you want," Alice panted painfully. "I don't know what you want me to tell you," she sobbed hysterically.

"Oh, I think that you're going to tell me all sorts of things you bitch," Quinn spat, "All sorts of things."

As it turned out, before she died - broken and bloody - he was right.

CHAPTER TWENTY ONE
Interlude: A Brief Town History Part Three

Eden grew tall and proud during the first few years. Tolan's flock were garnered by his strength and fuelled by his will. Their ears burned with the word of God as preached by their founding father. Tolan drew a metaphorical border around the town long before a physical one was constructed. The thick woodland to the rear offered a solid wall of privacy; one that was unbreakable.

Tolan was by now a man of broad shoulders capable of carrying a town's burden. He gave powerful sermons that sang to the heavens from the building skeleton that would become his church. At this point, Tolan was now hearing the voice of God on a regular basis. The voice came to him in his dreams, sometimes dressed as his mother in the bright day, and sometimes dressed in the dark as his father. The voice was always clear and always demanding and Tolan never failed to listen.

The town construction was steady progress; he took it as a divine sign that those followers who found their way to this holy place were always of the most welcome use. Builders and farmers were put to task utilizing their expert skills. The forest provided an endless supply of first rate timber that was used in the construction, and was also traded for other essentials.

Tolan's own home was the first to be built and he oversaw the project personally. His cabin was on the outskirts of what would be the town; far removed from the centre and secluded up in the woodlands that would become their lifeblood. The home was functional and spacious, and as per Tolan's own instructions, a small cellar was dug out at the rear. The builder who carried out the secretive work met with an unfortunate accident at the end of Tolan's axe - forever ensuring his silence. The cellar was to be a surreptitious place of worship as instructed to him by God in the voice and face of his father. It would be here that the will of God would be carried out in blood and sacrifice. The cellar's existence would require secrecy from the masses as they could not comprehend the mysterious ways in which God would sometimes move. The necessary removal of the builder was unfortunate, but Tolan was assured that the man would be grateful upon his embrace into heaven.

As the years passed Eden grew. Cabins sprung up around the town with regularity, housing the disciples who had travelled many miles to join their community. A substantial wooden barrier had been constructed around the town's borders and potential new residents would be vetted by Tolan himself. There was a smaller room inside the town hall where Tolan would hold the interviews, accompanied only by his right hand man Gabriel Quinn. Quinn was by far the largest man in Eden; he stood at over six and a half feet tall with a barrel chest and huge, powerful arms that could crush the life from a bear. Quinn was as devout as they came; his devotion to Tolan was absolute and he followed his orders without question. Gabriel believed that God himself spoke through Tolan, and that the words were pure. Eden was to be shaped into the new garden on earth, and its inhabitants had to be as untainted as the virgin snow.

Tolan watched as his vision developed. He knew that his mother would be sitting at God's shoulder proud of the beginning of his work. He would spend his days walking in the forest, the voices of the leaves blowing beneath the soft breeze would whisper in his ear. His dreams had begun to fade and now he only heard God's voice in the woods.

He had come to realise that God was a vengeful and harsh deity and there should be no other word than his. He had learned that the New Testament was only an incorrect human interpretation, as God was not a blissful figure of grace and love. God in fact was a being of wrath and furious anger who demanded complete submission and payment in blood, and it was Tolan's place on earth to cover the bill. Whilst Eden could prosper it would come at a price; a price that was paid in Tolan's cellar where it was met with screams of pain and whimpers of death.

The thick woodland that backed onto the rear of his cabin soon became a burial ground for small, lonely shallow graves. When interviewing families for entry into his haven, Tolan would often turn away those with young children perfect for his purposes. He would then send Quinn out into the wilds to follow the spurned families and return with the children, after first disposing of the parents. Quinn would deliver unto him just what God demanded.

Tolan took a perverse pleasure from his work, but saw this only as a justifiable reward for his service. His cellar would be awash with young blood on the eve of the full moon, and he would indulge only his darkest desires in order to purge the town from suffering from them. He would inflict the most monstrous damage imaginable on the young innocent flesh, as the tiny bodies were subjected to the sort of long suppressed abuse that he himself had once endured at the hands of his father.

The corpses were unrecognizable as Tolan emerged from the darkness out into the light of the moon; his body blackened by their blood. Once his savagery was cleansed, the town would be as well, and God was satisfied. The trees parted, allowing him access to the heart of the forest where he would bury the sacrificed children. He knew that God was indeed pleased with his work, as the harsh winters grew faint and distant. Their icy fingers retreating further and further until the season was but a memory. The warm caress of summer became a constant companion. The ground grew ever more fertile under the hot sun, and the streams ran flush with fish and the woodland thick with game.

After a time, Tolan's sermons became more and more intense and he began to preach about the darkness of God's will and the merciless adherence to his word. Soon Tolan took an inner circle, including himself there were five that sat on the council, and they were tasked with the running of Eden. Tolan received his instructions from the forest and it was the council's job to enforce them. Quinn was designated as the town Marshal; his was a fist of steel that suffered no discussion. As close as he was to the inner council, only Quinn was aware of the cellar sacrifices. The other members were only too willing to accept God's generosity without having to foot the bill.

As the town grew and thrived, word soon spread about Eden and the town was becoming inundated with prospective residents. There were more bodies that Tolan could ever hope to spend in sacrifice. They began to concentrate their efforts on the strengthening the town's borders, turning them from markers into a defensive line of protection and seclusion from the outside world. It soon became necessary for the walls to become defended as more and more outsiders sought to benefit from the prosperity that Tolan had earned for his people. Makeshift campsites sprung up outside the town walls as the desperate came and waited for their acceptance. The hungry and the poor, the lame and the crippled all came to bathe beneath the promised sky and live amongst the privileged. Tolan watched the camps from his position atop the great walls and he saw the unfortunates that had nothing to offer his town or his people. Eden was indeed a promised land, one blessed by the touch of God himself. His lands were bountiful and flush, but Eden was not infinite; her land had borders and she could only feed so many. Her population was already full and her people were all deserving; all contributors, there were no passengers here. No drains on the resources, only the faithful and the worthy. Tolan sequestered himself deep into the forest for guidance and he slept beneath the huge dark trees and dreamt of his purpose. He was told of what had to be done, and steeled himself for the days ahead. When he returned, he informed the inner council of God's will and what needed to be done in his name. Most of them had baulked at the idea, but all followed Tolan into the darkness.

It was Quinn who led the assault on the camps. He took those men in town that he could trust; only the most devout disciples with iron wills and stomachs to match. They opened the town gates and walked to meet the campers and they were greeted with kneeling prayers as saviors. The desperate prospects wept with joy as they believed that their long suffering was to be finally rewarded.

Quinn and his men tore through the camp with sharp blades and cold hearts. The earth ran red with the blood of the weak and the hungry; the men were slaughtered and the women and children violated in grotesque fashion. The bodies were strung up towards the entrance to the valley as a warning to any who would seek entry to the town, and they successfully dissuaded all from approaching. The legend of Eden soon became known throughout the surrounding lands and it became a town known of horrors and nightmares. A bedtime story for children who would misbehave and shame their parents; *eat your vegetables or I'll drop you at the gates of Eden, where they eat naughty boys and girls after dark.*

Tolan knew that after the massacre there would be members of his own congregation that would voice their disapproval and he knew that in the days and weeks following he would need to be strong. He would have to offer iron leadership and suffer no challenge to his voice. Quinn was designated to handle the repercussions and relished the task. Tolan retreated to his forest and the voices within and waited as Quinn brought him those tainted with a lack of faith. Tolan gathered the town into the forest as the church became empty and obsolete. His preaching's were now being taught under the shadow of the huge dark trees as the wind whispered through the lush leaves and around the kneeling congregation. Faces were upturned and bathed under the soothing words that flowed through Tolan and over them. Disbelievers were not tolerated, and the worst were crucified on the largest branches; hung to die as a reminder to the town of just who they all answered to. Tolan was the word and his was the voice that guided them all.

Eden prospered in her seclusion as the outside world went about its business. The days were hot and sunny, the sky was blue and the lands lush and bountiful, and all for a relatively small price that had to be paid from time to time.

CHAPTER TWENTY TWO

The town library was as old and as quaint as all of the other colonial style buildings in Eden. Michael and Thom crossed the town square and Michael felt an inexplicable need to walk nonchalantly as though they were under constant surveillance. He looked over all too casually to see Thom smiling at him, barely suppressing a laugh.

"What are you doing?" The young man asked.

"Trying not to draw attention to ourselves," Michael replied quietly.

"Walking like that?"

"Like what?"

"Like you're in a bad movie. Just relax, no one's looking at us, no-one cares what we're doing."

"Cheeky sod," Michael murmured under his breath.

"What?"

"Nothing," Michael said sulkily.

The library building was a smaller, similar version of the town hall. As always the outside was pristine white. A protruding pitched roof porch had four large columns and smooth wooden banister railings.

They passed under the entrance porch and into the building's foyer, finding that the air was blissfully cool compared to the perfect weather outside. The foyer was decorated with posters and banners, all advertising the upcoming Woodland Festival - Michael was already sick of those two words. The foyer walls were also lined with cute pictures drawn by what would appear to be elementary aged children. Colorful swirls depicted buildings and figures, homes, and people. There were images of the school; the square, the town hall, and carnival, but Michael's eye was pulled to the pictures of the woods beyond the town. The trees were drawn with traditional colours; waves of green circles atop long brown stems, but there was also a lot of black. Dark black scrawls beneath the foliage canopies. Some of the pictures also had drawings of stick figures, small figures obviously meaning to represent the children, most disturbingly for Michael, some of the figures were vertical, but some were horizontal with crosses for eyes.

"What do you make of these?" He asked Thom in a hushed whisper that seemed appropriate for the setting.

"Not really my taste, I'd prefer a Pollack," Thom smiled.

"No, I mean the..., hey what do you know about Jackson Pollock?"

"Born in Cody, Wyoming in 1912, youngest of five sons, a major figure in the abstract expressionist movement."

Michael stared at the fourteen year old, more and more impressed with the young man's attitude and intelligence. The child that they had lost in the accident back in the UK had been a boy and Michael couldn't help but wonder what his son would have turned out like. He hoped that he would have been strong and smart like Thom.

"You mean the woodlands, the dead looking children?" Thom said seriously, "Pretty creepy right."

"There's a lot of darkness here," Michael said half to himself, "Under the surface, and beneath the night, there are buried corners in Eden where people don't want to look Thom."

"Until now," Thom said gravely. "Something happened to my father here, one day he just up and left us," soft tears began to fall as he spoke. "My mother told me that he left us and wouldn't say any more than that. Every damn time that I've asked her since she just won't talk about him."

"What do you think happened?" Michael asked gently.

"I think that the same thing happened to him that happened to the others. I know that he wouldn't have left me, not without saying anything first. But I got sucked in here like everyone else. The perfect weather, the perfect life, facilities and activities all under the hot sun. I should have asked more questions, I should have looked deeper for him." Thom was openly sobbing now, "I should have looked," he punched his clenched fist down onto his skinny leg.

Michael put an awkward arm around skinny shoulders. Thom suddenly seemed like a small, lost boy again, all pretence of adulthood and maturity melted away. They stood like that for a few minutes until concerned glances from townsfolk entering and leaving became uncomfortable. "So let's go do something about it," Michael said, firmly releasing Thom from his embrace.

"Fuck yeah," Thom said wiping the tears from his eyes and smiling through with bravado.

Emily and Sarah-Jane hopped off of the tram at their next stop. Emily found it difficult to ignore the glances and stares of the tram's passengers. It seemed that everywhere they went at the minute, someone was watching.

"Take it easy ladies," Eddie said as they alighted.

Emily smiled pleasantly in return, but for some reason, she could not bring herself to completely trust Eddie's agreeable face. His smile seemed a little too forced and his eyes a little too watchful. She took Sarah-Jane's arm for support and they headed across the road towards their destination.

The churchyard was deserted as they entered through the impeccable black iron gates. No creepy creaking graveyard entrance for Eden.

"What is it that we're doing here again?" Sarah-Jane asked quietly.

"When we were here for Janet's funeral I caught a glimpse of the graves. The dates all seemed to be a little unbelievable," Emily replied in equally hushed tones. "I wanted a closer, slower look at the tombstones. Here look," she said leaning towards the nearest one and reading aloud. "Jacob Hawksbee, born 1907, died 2010. That's 103 years old," she said quickly doing the maths. "Here another one, Melissa Lupton, born 1898, died 2003, that's 105. Look they're everywhere," she swung her arms around pointing to the headstones. "Check out the ages, 110, 108, 100, 99,111, 103, how is that possible?"

"Everyone seems to live to ripe old ages here," Sarah-Jane shrugged. "Good living, good weather, low illness, it doesn't seem like a bad thing does it?"

"It depends,"

"On what?"

"On what the price is," Emily said ominously. "Maybe we should try and talk to the deacon,"

"About what my dear?"

Both Emily and SJ positively jumped into the air. Both women gasped loudly at the sudden arrival and the voice from behind them. Emily turned to face Landon Sheldon-Wilkes, the deacon. His smiling face was suddenly contorted in concern at their upset at his hand, more so when his eyes dropped to the swell of Emily's pregnancy.

"Oh my dears," he said with genuine distress, "Oh I'm so sorry Mrs. Torrance, please come inside and sit down, I didn't mean to startle you both."

Emily let herself be led into the church with Landon and Sarah-Jane taking an arm each. In truth she felt fine but figured that it would perhaps be best to play faint in order to poke around and ask a few questions.

Landon helped her to a pew and sat down beside her, with SJ on the other side. "How are you feeling Mrs. Torrance?" He asked warmly, "Can I get you anything?"

"Perhaps a glass of water?" She replied.

"Oh I can get that for you," Sarah-Jane piped up sensing the cue to make herself scarce and poke around. "Through here is it?" She said standing and moving quickly towards the rear of the church and the door that led through the private quarters.

"Uh yes," the deacon said a little unsure. "Through the door and there's a small kitchen to the left."

Emily watched as SJ disappeared, "Is it always this quiet?" She asked, looking around.

"We do weddings and unfortunately funerals mainly here," Landon said in a slightly strained tone. "At my last posting there was always too brisk a trade in sorrowful tales and hopeful advice. But it would seem here that folks tend to be happier, and less in need of spiritual guidance. I suppose it must be the weather," he laughed hollowly.

Emily glanced around the surroundings; the church interior was spotless, the pews were gleaming and well polished, and the kneeling cushions were unmarked and looked pristine as though never used. "What about services?"

"Oh yes of course, we are always here for those who need us," Landon said a little too quickly.

Emily watched the deacon surreptitiously; his manner seemed confusing. He appeared nervous and awkward, but not sinister, as though he held a dark secret; a secret that was his to know but not to own. His eyes darted around towards to the inner sanctum door where Sarah-Jane had walked through some minutes before, and his fingers wrestled fretfully on his lap. "I couldn't help but notice the gravestones outside; the ages seem disproportionately high don't they?"

"Oh a little I suppose," Landon chuckled nervously, his hands still fidgeting. "I guess God must smile on this little corner of the globe."

Sarah-Jane suddenly appeared from the back and hurried up the aisle clutching a glass of water which Emily took and gratefully drank from.

"And when are we going to see you and your beau the good doctor gracing our doors with a wedding Miss Mears?" Landon asked, addressing Sarah-Jane.

Emily smiled as SJ's face blushed furiously. She dropped her eyes, and for an instant, Emily thought that she looked desperately unhappy.

"We'd better be on our way," Sarah-Jane said quickly, tugging at Emily's sleeve.

Emily found herself being ushered swiftly out of the church entrance, leaving behind a bemused deacon waving them away merrily. "What's the hurry, did you find something?"

"What, no sorry," Sarah-Jane replied.

Emily was concerned to see that her friend was suddenly close to tears, "Hey, what is it?

"Oh, I'm just being silly; it was Landon talking about marriage."

"What about it?"

"It's just never going to happen."

"Oh come on, the doc's a smart man, he'll see sense at some point," Emily commiserated, "You my girl are way too big of a catch to not have a ring put on your finger."

Sarah-Jane looked off sadly into the distance, "No it'll never happen," she said firmly "Not anymore."

Emily let the words hang on the air; maybe SJ and Samuel had had some kind of fight, a falling out. Michael hadn't said anything from the doc's side, whatever the problem, she was sure that her friend would tell her in due course.

Michael and Thom had been plowing their way through the history of Eden via the library's computerized system. There was only one newspaper in town, "The Eden Times". Stories were mainly vapid pieces of a perfect small town, carnivals and public events, summer evenings on the square, dog shows, and bake sales. As he searched Michael began to notice a chilling pattern through the decades. There were disappearances, suicides, and fatal accidents; seemingly far in excess of what should have been expected for a town of this size. The newspaper articles went back as far as the 1940's, as this seemed to be the extent of the converting process to transcribe the newspapers onto microfilm. There were similar pieces throughout the years. Michael's eyes began to tire and pinch painfully as he read article after article, all of which carried a timetable of fatality. As well as the myriad of deaths, there was also another fact that jumped out from the pages. It would appear that there had been a Sheriff Quinn serving as the town law for as far back as the newspapers went. Nepotism was apparently another tradition that was alive and well in Eden.

THE EDEN TIMES

ILLUSTRATED WEEKLY NEWSPAPER

Member of the Associated Press

Est. 1869 | Wednesday, November 24, 1946 | Price 6d

COMMUNITY SHOCKED BY SUICIDE

The Fairfax property (above) where Mr Dorian's body was discovered

The area of Fairfax was shocked late last night when the body of popular local electrician Donald Dorian, was discovered.

Police were called after suspicions were raised when Mr Dorian had not been seen for several days. Local sources suggested that Mr Dorian was depressed lately due to a high level of gambling debts that he had accumulated.

Deputy Thomas Ross affected entry into the Fairfax premise where the body was discovered. Police have said that there were no suspicious circumstances.

THE EDEN TIMES

no.203.078 | April 17th 1968 | Since 1869

TRAGIC DISAPPEARANCE OF LOCAL COUPLE

Sheriff David Quinn has issued a notice to the town concerning the hiking trails around Eden after the tragic disappearance of Alan and Deborah Jacobs. The couple had taken to the surrounding hills for an afternoon hike last Tuesday; the alarm was raised when they did not return by nightfall.

The Sheriff said, "Hikers should always be aware of the potential for danger, and they should always carry sufficient supplies. The Sheriff went on to say that it would appear that neither of the Jacobs took sufficient precautions, describing the incident as a "Tragic and unnecessary waste"

The River Point Trail (above) where Alan and Deborah Jacobs were believed to be heading

Date today 11/01/86

NEWS

GRISTLY DISCOVERY MADE IN HUNT FOR MISSING TEEN

Miss Hart, pictured here at last years Woodland Festival

Sheriff Quinn confirmed the discovery last night of the body of local missing teen Amy Hart. Miss Hart, 16, was reported missing two weeks ago by her mother when she failed to return from school. A large search was organised at the time by the Eden Sheriff's Department, but to no avail. Local sources have suggested that Miss Hart had been deeply upset over a domestic situation with her boyfriend. Police are now convinced that Miss Hart may have run away from home, possibly due to an unwanted pregnancy. The body was found in the heavy woodland, sources say that Miss Hart was found hanging from a tree. Police say that there are presently no suspicious circumstances.

LOCAL ELECTIONS LOOM

This years election for town Sheriff will once again be a formality for Sheriff Ellis Quinn, as he is due to run unopposed again.

Sheriff Quinn said "It is always my great honour to serve our wonderful town at the will of the people"

This will be Sheriff Quinn's forth and final term in office. Deputy Gerry Quinn is expected to continue in his fathers footsteps, and maintain the legacy of a Quinn holding the office and responsibility of Sheriff.

THE EDEN TIMES

www.edentimes.com — SERVING OUR COMMUNITY — Since 1869

TRAGIC ACCIDENT SPELLS OUT DRINK AND DRIVE DANGERS FOR MOTORISTS

The scene out on Highway 5, early Friday morning

The Eden Sheriff's Department confirmed that the accident late last night that claimed the lives of Eden town residents Adele and Robert Bunton was the result of an intoxicated driver.

Sheriff Quinn gave a statement that spoke of the grave dangers of driving under the influence.

"This was an avoidable accident that should have never happened"* the Sheriff said, he continued *"We have witnessed the tragic loss of two valuable members of our community; I can only hope that their misfortune will serve as a reminder of the hazards of drinking and driving"

Michael found many more similar instances dotted over the decades. "Notice anything strange?" he whispered to Thom who was trawling through his own research.

"Yeah, I never read a report that had so many facts presented so quickly before," Thom said.

Michael was impressed yet again with Thom's quick mind; he'd always assumed that everyone under the age of about twenty five should be spoken to at an automatic level of derision. "Exactly, you've got newspaper reports here stating gossip as fact; teenage pregnancies, intoxication, gambling debts, all giving the impression that everything is explainable."

"But why doesn't anyone ever ask the same questions?" Thom asked puzzled.

"I honestly don't know. Perhaps if you are born here, or lived here for a long time then you just don't ask questions full stop. There seems to be a fog that falls over most eyes in town. People lead blissful lives and don't want to look beneath the surface."

"Yeah, it's like loving hotdogs but not wanting to know how they're made," Thom added succinctly.

"Hey Mr. Torrance?"

Michael looked around the library nervously before locating the source; Deputy Kurt Stillson came bounding over between the large imposing bookcases. He was wearing civilian clothes and a tight expression.

"Deputy," Michael responded suddenly feeling guilty. He noted that Thom was desperately trying to shut the computers down before Kurt could get a good look.

"Easy kid," Kurt said grinning, "I'm here to help."

"How?" Thom asked

"With what?" Michael asked, casting a disapproving eye towards his young companion.

"With whatever the hell's going on around here," Kurt said.

Michael took a furtive look around their immediate surroundings; the library was a two story building but only the ground floor was open to the public. The long open space was well lit and airy. Large bay windows ran the length of the room, flooding the area with natural light filtered through special glass to avoid damaging the books. The bookcases were built from the same timber that most things in Eden were constructed with; dark wood shorn from the thick trunks of the forest. Michael found that there was a welcome absence of the usual overhanging fluorescent lights that burrowed into your brain with a painful throbbing hum. There was a brisk trade in residents coming and going, armed with texts and laden with hope. It was somewhat difficult for Michael to find a quiet secluded corner in which to converse. He and Thom were secreted on the furthest table that contained the state of the art computers. He had limited technical knowledge, but even he could appreciate the standards set in the public library.

He motioned for the deputy to sit in the empty chair opposite, "What exactly is it that you think is going on here deputy?" He flashed a "be still" look towards Thom; he wanted the cop's thoughts unfiltered.

"Something pretty damn odd actually," Kurt replied, his voice conspiratorially low. "I haven't been here that long, but it's long enough to get a weird vibe. I know about the teacher," he looked gently towards Thom, "I also know that the story is already all over town that Stark committed suicide."

"Do you know differently?" Michael asked.

"Well I do know that Tommy and I were first on the scene, and that I got real up close and personal with the body. Then not more than an hour or so later, the Sheriff is telling everyone about the suicide note, but there was no note on the body, I'd have seen it."

"What else?" Thom asked.

"Well, have you seen any of the graffiti around town?" Kurt answered.

"Yeah, sure, the Wake Up signs," Michael said, "What about them? I figured that it was just kids, some new band or movement that they got caught up in."

"Can you see any of the kids in this town spraying graffiti?" Thom said incredulously.

Michael opened his mouth to say of course, but shut it with a firm snap. Could he really see these kids being antisocial? He had never seen such politeness around the town. There was no litter, no scrawling, and no defacement of any kind. "Well what is it then?" He asked Kurt.

"All I know is that the Sheriff has been going nuts since no-one has been able to stop them. And I do mean nuts," Kurt said taking a look around over his shoulder to make sure that they weren't being observed. "And then there are the locals," he whispered.

"What about them?" Michael asked.

"Stepford?" Thom answered.

"Yeah, major league Stepford," Kurt nodded, "You know I've been seeing this girl from the Sheriff's Department and I can't even get my hand up her jumper without her speaking about marriage. It was kind of quaint at first, but now it's just kind of creepy."

"You know what I could never figure out," Thom said, "Why in every horror movie, every character has never seen a horror movie."

The three of them pondered, whilst they did, they were being observed.

Marina McFadden was keeping a close eye on the two men and the young boy sitting and scheming together - in broad daylight no less. Marina had run the library for the last twenty seven years. She was a vigorous woman, one who had never married and was childless. Now at seventy-four she was happy in her self- imposed exile from most modern conventions. Her duties lay squarely within the four walls of the town's history. She was the keeper of truths and hider of lies. Every corner of the library ran to her explicit will; every display, every shelf, every book lived under her roof. Her position brought with it a certain level of respect within the town and she was revered by those around her and indulged in her desire for control. She was a tall woman, handsome if not attractive. She walked with a straight back and her shoulders were not stooped by the common afflictions of age. She wore her blonde white hair in a short bob cut and she favoured loose skirts and floral blouses. The library was expertly air-conditioned and the temperature was moderate. She recognised the new writer, the Bray boy and the new deputy. Of course everyone that wasn't born in town would always be new to her, no matter how long they had lived here.

She picked up the phone and carefully dialed under the counter. She raised the handset to her ear and waited for the pickup. "Library, far end, computers," she said succinctly down the line before hanging up. Her smile was cold.

"Look here," Michael said pointing Kurt's attention to the screen, "Does this seem like normal police procedure to you?"

Kurt's eyes ran over the newspaper reports quickly and efficiently, "Not even close," he stated. "I'm not exactly a fully trained detective, but even I know that you don't report gossip as fact to reporters and allow it to be printed."

"So what do we do now?" Thom asked.

"Well for starters you're going home," Michael said to Thom's disappointed expression.

"You can't be serious," Thom hissed through clenched teeth.

"Deadly," Michael said his eyes not flinching, "Look Thom, whatever is going on here I don't want you caught in the middle of it."

"Oh really, you mean like when a teacher tries to jump me and then ends up dead? You mean not in the middle like that?"

Despite Thom's anger Michael was still impressed that the young boy kept enough cool to keep his voice low and quiet.

"Look maybe the kid can help?" Kurt offered, "His mom works for Casper's realty company right. I bet that she keeps office files, keys and stuff at home. Whatever is going on around here you can be damn sure that Casper Christian will be at the bottom of it."

"A look around Casper's personals might be just the ticket," Michael agreed reluctantly. "Alright Thom, do you think that you can get hold of a set of keys to Casper's office?"

"Easily," Thom smiled.

"Alright then, do it carefully and don't get caught. Phone me when you've got them," Michael said as he placed a warm hand on Thom's bony shoulders, "Carefully" he reiterated sternly.

Emily hugged Sarah-Jane deeply as they said their goodbyes and she promised to head straight home. Sarah-Jane was anxious to find Samuel as she had not heard from him all day and she said that he was normally a rapacious texter. Their destinations took them in opposite directions and they caught different trams. She watched as Sarah-Jane left her behind at the stop. She knew that SJ was an avid worrier and despite her promise to head home, she actually had another location in mind.

She lifted herself up off of the waiting bench; her increased bulk was becoming more difficult to maneuver effectively. Her worries were growing by the day and she caressed her swell gently; it seemed that perhaps this paradise was not so great after all. She knew that she was late getting to the party, but perhaps it would not be too late. The diary of Jessica Grady had shaken her greatly. Their lives were running along parallel lines and Jessica and her husband had both seemingly disappeared. Same job, same house and most worryingly, same pregnancy; whatever fate had befallen Jessica she was determined not to follow on the same path. The Grady's had disappeared without a trace and the best place that she could think of for answers was the one woman that Jessica had suspected - the Headmistress Mrs. Olivia Thirlby. Emily boarded the tram and headed for the school.

CHAPTER TWENTY THREE

The room was small and windowless; the air was clean and artificially freshened but the smell of citrus hung oppressively on the air, irritating the throat of the watcher. The man sat in a tall-backed and comfortable chair of luxurious leather. The seating was maximized for viewing the huge bank of plasma screens that lined the walls. A long control panel ran the length of the dark oak counter. Lights and buttons blinked in futuristic fashion, dancing with precision and grace.

The man hung up the phone and typed furiously into the keyboard with nimble fingers. The largest screen sat in the middle of the display, orbited by smaller televisions and displayed the current selection.

He peered forward, not bothering to reach for his glasses that lay discarded in his backpack, for this was the first time on his watch that he had actually been called into action. His heart raced feverishly as he sought to maintain his composure. The thought of reporting in without all of the facts terrified him. Quinn had once reamed him out royally for leaving an empty cup behind and unwashed; he shuddered to think of the consequences for missing crucial details off of a report of this potential magnitude.

The man slapped his head in horror and quickly reached over to press the record button. In his haste he'd almost forgotten; he shuddered again, only more violently. A mistake like that could lead him to having to take the walk out into the woods. His hands felt clammy and his forehead beaded with sweat at the very thought.

He leaned in and hit the un-mute button. He could see the three figures in the library huddled around a table in the computer area. He immediately recognised the writer. He'd tried a couple of his books when he heard that he was moving to town, but hadn't really been able to connect. He'd watched the home of the writer before; every new town member was immediately put under close surveillance when they first moved in. The broadband installer had gained access to the Torrance's house and installed a little more than internet access. He also recognised the boy who'd had the run in with the teacher at the school recently. He hadn't been on duty that day, but someone was, and the system once again had functioned perfectly. The third figure annoyed him and he unconsciously gripped the desk with whitened knuckles. A deputy no less;

the new man Stillson. He could only guess that Stillson had yet to be inoculated into the program.

His face tightened and his anger rose further when he caught their conversation. He pounded a fist down hard on the desk and violently grabbed the phone. The call was answered immediately as the caller id notified the recipient just who was calling, and any call from this number was never less than essential. The man gave a brief report, efficiently and succinctly as he'd been trained. He nodded slowly as he listened to the reply and thanked his God that he was not in another man's shoes today.

Michael got out of the deputy's car and walked up towards his front door, motioning for Kurt to follow him. He could feel the stares of his neighbors behind twitching curtains and their curiosity was palpable. Michael unlocked the large front door and they slipped inside, grateful to be out of sight.

"You want a beer?" Michael asked.

"No thanks, but I'll take something soft if you've got it," Kurt replied, looking around the plush house that dwarfed his own modest home.

"In here," Michael motioned towards the kitchen.

"Man, this is some place," Kurt said in awe, "I thought that my place was something."

"Ah, it ain't nothing but bricks and mortar," Michael said awkwardly with the typical shyness of a Brit.

They walked into the sunny kitchen. Michael's attention was on their next move and his concern that Emily was not already home. His first instinct was to just pack a bag and leave; they could be gone by morning and not look back. This wasn't his fight and it didn't have to be his home, but now there was Thom to consider. Could he really just walk away and leave a young boy behind helpless? Could he face himself in the mirror every morning knowing just who and what he had abandoned? He knew that Thom would keep looking and eventually he knew that Thom would find something; something that would get him hurt or worse. His thoughts were torn when he suddenly realised that they weren't alone; a very large shadow loomed across the patio doors with menace.

"Sheriff," Michael said, his mind racing fighting for an exit.

Sheriff Quinn smiled unpleasantly; his perfect teeth were white and vicious. His uniform was pressed and spotless; his silver badge gleamed beneath the bright sun and his arm moved quickly. The gun was large but still barely registered in his huge paw. The barrel was black and oiled and the grip wooden. The explosion within the confines of the kitchen was monstrous.

Michael closed his eyes and waited for the pain; he stood rock still and feared the oncoming death. His life didn't flash before his eyes and there was only the deep regret that he would never hold his child. The next sound he heard was the heaving falling behind him. He cracked his eyes open and felt his chest. There was no hole and no pain. Confused he turned around.

Kurt was lying on the floor, his chest was splattered across the wooden surface and Michael went to him. He travelled in slow motion and he knelt; his knees sinking in the red gore. Kurt took his hand weakly. His eyes were puzzled and perplexed. His mouth bubbled with a fine crimson mist as the life ebbed slowly away. Michael spoke without turning back to face the Sheriff, "You, you killed him," he said incomprehensively.

The Sheriff moved into the gap between them, "No," he said swinging the handgun and bringing it down hard on Michael's head rendering him unconscious, "You did."

Emily pushed open the school doors after unlocking them with her own key. Due to the weekend there were no classes, but she knew that Mrs. Thirlby would be in attendance as always.

She eased her way down the long darkened corridor. The building seemed infinitely more eerie when empty, and even the cheerful pictures that adorned the walls etched by young hands and fertile imaginations seemed creepy in this gloomy light. She walked as slowly and as quietly as she could manage. Her hands instinctively cradling her bump. She knew that she should not be here for her child's sake, but she also knew that she had to - for her child's sake. She walked on tiptoes to alleviate her early announcement as she approached the

Headmistress's office. Beyond the door she could hear the faint clacking of a typewriter thumping out noisily. For some reason Mrs. Thirlby favoured using the antiquated machine over a computer and her office was small and removed from the main walkways of the school. Emily paused outside of the frosted glass finding her courage and steeling her mind. She was not a woman who enjoyed confrontation in any form, but this was necessary; this was her family's future.

"Come in Emily dear," the voice rang out from within.

Emily reached out and turned the door handle with a shaking hand. She pushed the door open and stepped inside, "I think that it's time we talked," she mustered.

"Yes dear, I think that you're probably right," came the reply.

Michael's head swam and his vision blurred. He tried to sit up slowly but the dizziness only increased. His memory was confused and spotty; he leant forward and found his legs hanging over a small metallic bed. He looked down and saw that his knees were wet and darkly stained. He touched them confused when suddenly the images flooded back through the redness. *Kurt*, he thought. He saw the body again now fresh in his mind; the deputy dying before his eyes.

"Well now, look who's up," a cheerful voice startled him.

Michael turned to face the low rumbling voice through the bars; the Sheriff stood tall and broad cradling a mug of coffee; his face relaxed and calm, almost pleasant.

"You murdered him," Michael spat.

"Oh I'm afraid not," Quinn leant forward and whispered into the cell, "I fear that was you Mr. Torrance. You've committed quite the crime. The cold blooded murder of a police officer," he shook his head theatrically. "I only wish that I was in time to stop you, instead of just subduing you," he frowned.

"You really think that anyone's going to believe that?" Michael laughed incredulously, "This isn't the movies you dumb hick, I'll have the best lawyers that money can buy flown in and they'll tear you apart on the stand."

"Ah maybe so Mr. Big shot, only something tells me that this'll never come to trial." he smiled menacingly, "In fact, you look positively suicidal to me Mr. Torrance."

"Who the fuck is going to believe that? I'd love to see Dr Creed signing off on that little medical marvel."

"Oh I'm afraid that the town is currently seeking a new town physician. It would appear that Dr Creed just isn't going to work out. In fact, it wouldn't surprise me if he isn't already gone. Just upped and disappeared into the night."

Michael sat back with the worst feeling crawling in his guts, "You killed Samuel," he stated rhetorically.

"Why Mr. Torrance that's a terrible accusation," the Sheriff said walking away laughing quietly to himself.

"Why don't you have a seat Mrs. Torrance," the Headmistress said, pointing to the chair opposite.

Emily eased herself down with as much dignity as she could muster; her eyes darting around the small office. Thirlby sat behind a metallic desk. Her furniture all seemed oddly matched and without coordination. The shelving was plastic and the chairs were metal. The flooring - which was a lovely hardwood everywhere else in the school - was covered with a thick carpet. A metal cabinet stood behind the desk; the door was slightly ajar and Emily's eyes caught on a green crusted puddle that had spilled out onto the carpet. The Headmistress's eyes followed Emily's to the green stain. She reached behind and pushed the door quickly shut, but not before Emily saw the spray paint cans.

"I want to know what's going on in this town Mrs. Thirlby," Emily announced primly, "I also want to know just what the hell happened to Jessica Grady," she leant forward, "And her baby."

Emily was prepared for indignation, denial, anger, accusations; what she wasn't prepared for was when the stone face of the Headmistress broke into sorrowful sobs that seemed to wrench from her very soul. She could only watch as the ramrod woman opposite her broke down until her cheeks were soaked with tears.

"Oh that poor child," Olivia wept. "That poor family, I tried, I really tried Emily, you have to believe me, but there's only so much one person can do in this town."

"Wait a minute," Emily snapped, "The graffiti sprayed across town, the Wake Up signs, that was you?" She said skeptically thinking of the paint cans hidden in the cabinet behind the sobbing Headmistress. She had a hard job picturing the elderly widow creeping around like a hooded teen tagging the pristine town walls.

Olivia nodded, "Yes," she admitted. "It was all I could think of."

"WAKE UP, what does that even mean?" Emily asked.

"I was just trying to get the town to look around them. Too much goes on here under the radar. I firmly believe that most people in town are good, decent people Emily; they just tend not to ask too many questions. There's a state of fog that settles over us here, the sun shines and investments grow, people get fat and lazy like cats on the asphalt."

"So what is happening here, what about Jessica?"

"Oh Jess," Olivia began to softly weep again, "She was such a sweet girl, so happy and full of life. When she got pregnant I think that she was probably the happiest girl in the whole wide world. I knew that they were watching her, so I tried to make her leave. I tried to make things unpleasant for her here so that she would just go before it was too late, but she wouldn't," Olivia said with tearful respect, "She was too stubborn for that, but I couldn't tell her, she wouldn't have listened, nobody would have."

"Listen to what? Who was watching her?"

"It's all so confusing Emily. After all these years I don't even remember what's truth and what's myth anymore."

"How many years?" Emily asked suspiciously.

"How old would you say I am Emily? And don't pander to a woman's vanity."

Emily studied the headmistress; her hair was streaked with silver, her face was lined and creased if not wholly wrinkled, and her frame was healthy and lean. "I don't know, maybe fifty three, fifty five, something around there."

"You're very kind," Olivia said gratefully, "But you're a little out, I'm ninety eight years old."

Emily paused as she processed, trying to decide if the woman sat opposite her was mad or actually pushing a hundred years old. She opened her mouth to speak, before finding that she had nothing to say. Her lips clamped together and plopped like a goldfish's.

"Don't look too bad do I?" Olivia said sadly. Her voice was heavy with weariness.

"Is everyone...?" Emily left the question hanging.

"No, not everyone, some folks here are as old as me, a few are older and others moved into town like you and your husband."

"How is this possible?"

"The town is old, but the woods are older, older than perhaps time itself. Ever since Eden was founded we have been isolated from the outside world. Only every now and then are newcomers selected and invited in. The Woodland Festival is an annual event that is somehow linked to the prosperity here as far as I can tell."

"What is it?"

"The town partakes in an ancient tradition. On the surface it is just a fun carnival, the town celebrates the founding of Eden, just like a kind of Fourth of July. But that's just the window dressing; over the years I've often suspected that there is another, more private tradition that takes place away from prying eyes. Although I've never been able to establish just what, and people in town just don't care to ask or even think."

"But how has this never gotten out?" Emily asked skeptically.

"Because no-one ever leaves, I mean who would want to? This is a paradise protected from all of the horrors of the rest of the planet and people live very long, very happy lives, and who wouldn't want that?"

"But tell me this Olivia," Emily demanded, "You may have perfect weather, perfect neighbors, perfect lives, but just what exactly is the cost?"

Thom crept lightly into Casper's office; the room was empty as the staff had left for the day. The Woodland Festival was nearly upon them and apparently the event was a big deal for the town. Most of the council employees had been drafted in to help with the event and it seemed to take everyone's attention. There had been weeks of talk at school about the festival; there would be floats and parades. The school teams would all be represented and most of the other kids were desperately looking forward to it.

He had taken his mother's office keys from her home desk and headed for the Christian Realty Office where she worked for Casper. He knew that he should have looked closer at his father's leaving a long time ago. A knot of guilt was tied tightly in his gut and no rational arguments against validity would loosen the bind. He was stirred into action now. Michael and Emily were newer to Eden than him; perhaps if they had been here longer then they would have slid into the hazy fog that seemed to overcome suspicions. But they were fresh, with minds still intact and brains that still asked questions. He liked Michael a lot and hoped that he wouldn't let him down.

He slipped the stolen key into the lock and eased open the office door. The interior was dark and the shutters were down; light barely permeated the gloom. The offices were deserted today because of the festival as everyone was preparing for tomorrow. As far as Thom was concerned, the sooner that it was over the better. He dared not use the overhead light and instead took a small torch from his pocket that he had brought from home. The light beam illuminated his way. The office was lined with metallic filing cabinets that stood guard, and padlocks glinted under his torch. The fact that the office was locked from the outside was both surprising and suspicious. In Eden no-one locked their doors even at night. If the office was locked and the files padlocked, then there must be something worth seeing and worth protecting.

He recognised his mother's desk from the framed photograph of himself perched on the top; he did a quick scan of the contents. The drawers were unlocked and there was nothing of any great interest inside, just an assortment of papers and stationery supplies. He woke the hibernating computer and the screen opened with a picture of the woodlands as a screensaver. Thom's eyes were drawn to the dark trees and he felt himself sink sleepily into the picture. His mind rebelled against the alien invasion; the black thoughts washed over him, drowning his mind in their seduction. *Perhaps he should just go home. He could lounge by the pool or eat burgers and fries in front of the TV and sleep; sleep beneath the hot sun's caress and the shade of the trees.* He shook his head violently to clear the invading thoughts. He felt tired and sleepy and his body felt weighed down by expectation. He was just a kid after all and it wasn't fair to put all of this pressure on his narrow bony shoulders.

Sighing, he clicked the mouse to open the password box. His mother tended to use the same password for everything and his fingers quickly typed his birth date and the system woke. The screen was filled with files, headers, properties, dates, times, appointments, locations, and contracts. Nothing seemed to jump off the screen as meaningful. He checked the system settings and found that all the computers were linked on the same network. He sat forward, suddenly interested. One of the computers on the network must belong to Casper himself. The security in the office was practically non-existent and thankfully none of the employees would appear to be particularly computer literate. He accessed the system and searched for a sign to direct him towards Casper's computer. He was engrossed in his search and did not hear the man approach and his heart nearly stopped when a hand fell onto his shoulder. He turned around slowly with apprehension and fear, and his eyes fell upon the smiling face of Casper Christian.

Michael sat on the surprisingly comfortable cot. The cell was clean and well kept, and even the bars looked polished and gleamed. His mind was spinning with worry, and not just for himself; Emily was out there with only Sarah-Jane for protection. There was also Thom to worry about now. If the Sheriff had plans for him, then surely the others would all be in danger of the gravest kind.

The cell was around eleven feet squared; the metal cot was covered with a thick mattress and non-itchy blankets. There was a toilet in the corner that was odour free and a small window about two feet wide by one foot high. The window wasn't barred, but the space was obviously too small for anyone to fit through. Michael looked up through the glass to the day outside; a day that had begun in the realms of theoretical mysteries and ended in crushing reality. The sun was setting and he knew that Emily would be getting worried about him soon. Tomorrow was the dawn of the Woodland Festival, and all eyes would be directed towards the annual event, and away from one small writer locked in a jail cell at the mercy of the Sheriff.

He looked out through the cell bars into the Sheriff's Department; the room beyond was open and empty. There were several wooden desks that sat hunkered to the ground beneath sleeping computer screens that hibernated softly Cheerful open windows let the sunny rays and gentle breezes through.

The glass fronted door suddenly opened and a large athletic blond man walked through. The man wore a deputy's uniform and his eyes were fixed and hard. His expression was undiluted rage and he walked menacingly towards Michael's cell.

Michael took a step away from the bars. He had been intending to shout loudly at his outrageous treatment, but his mouth closed as he saw the pure hatred in the deputy's cruel smile.

"You," the deputy said. His voice barely audible.

"Hey, easy now," Michael said, suddenly glad to be behind bars and out of harm's reach.

Deputy Tommy Ross walked slowly to the cell; he drew a large set of silver keys from a hook on the side of a desk and gripped them with white knuckles. His face was drained and flint. He reached the cell door and inserted the key slowly and deliberately.

Up close Michael could see the tendons straining in the man's powerful forearms. The deputy was taller and broader than Michael; his frame was toned and dominant, and his shirt bulged over gym honed muscles. Michael felt waves of fury emanating from the deputy as the key turned and the door pulled open slowly.

"Easy officer, I don't know what the Sheriff told you," Michael said walking backwards until his back was halted by the rear cell wall. His heart pounded with fear and he glanced anxiously around the outer office desperate for an interruption. He opened his mouth to offer a civilized explanation when a bone hard fist shattered the notion. Blows rained down from high angles with venomous anger. Michael attempted to cover himself with fruitless protective arm, as he was pummeled in the enclosed space. A punch hooked hard from the right and his vision blurred with pain and blood sending him crashing to the floor. He sank to his knees as heavy work boots thudded into his crouching body. Suddenly the attack was over; he coughed violently and his insides felt like jelly. He spat a glob of worryingly dark blood onto the cell floor and rolled onto his back. He stared up into the hateful eyes of the deputy - eyes that were now weeping softly.

"So this is how it ends," Michael managed through a swollen mouth of loose teeth and an acidic copper taste, "You finish me off and dump my body in a shallow grave for the animals to pull apart,"

"You killed him, you'd deserve it," Tommy said softly and distantly.

"I didn't kill anyone you dumb prick. Do you really not have brains in this town, are you all that fucking stupid?" Michael laughed painfully.

"You murdered him, and that's the truth."

"The truth, the fucking truth! According to whom exactly? Oh let me guess, good old Sheriff Quinn no less, did he send you here?"

"You killed my friend," Tommy's voice now a little confused and unsure.

"Did he send you here? Did Quinn simply wind you up and turn you loose?" Michael said sensing the faltering, "He did, didn't he, he just led you by the nose and sent you here to finish me off you moron. Did you ever stop to think? Did you ever ask yourself why the hell I would gun down a town deputy in cold blood? In my own house no less. Don't you care about motives or is that just for the TV shows?" Michael's voice rose in anger despite the pain. He dragged himself up onto the cot holding his sides as though it was the only thing keeping them together. His own fury was building; he was just a man living his own life and looking to care for his family, and now he sat in a jail cell with the crap beaten out of him and his life in grave jeopardy. "Just what the fuck is wrong with you people?" He spat "How is it that you just turn your rational thoughts on and off like a goddamn radio?"

"Sheriff Quinn said..."

"I don't give a shit just what Quinn said, I'm asking you what you think."

"Yes Tommy, what exactly do you think?"

Michael spun around to the new voice as quickly as his battered body would allow, Sheriff Quinn's towering frame filled the room and his face was lined with a smug grin. Michael would have launched himself at the Sheriff if he was able, if only to wipe the arrogance from his face.

"You know Tommy," Quinn continued, "I should have known that you wouldn't have the balls to do what needed to be done. I guess that's the price we pay for employing one of you," he said dismissively. He turned to Michael as though Tommy wasn't there, "Did you know that he was a faggot?" He jerked a thumb disgustedly towards the deputy, "Can you believe that we had to let him wear a uniform." He shook his head sadly, "You can keep your modern world Mr. Torrance, you really can."

"What happened to Kurt?" Tommy said addressing Quinn; his voice was low and hard.

"Oh I put a large hole in him," Quinn said casually.

Suddenly Tommy threw himself at Quinn. Michael watched as the athletic deputy smashed into the larger man; Tommy was strong, but Quinn was a force of nature. Tommy's fists were a blur of swings and connections; Michael saw his chance and limped past the brawling figures and out of the cell. Michael's thoughts were now completely of self-preservation. He had a life and a pregnant wife to consider; the two cops struggled and rolled as he stepped past the mayhem. He had reached the door when he chanced a look backwards; he had hoped for a deputy upset victory, but as he looked back Quinn was now sat on Tommy's back. His massive paws had hold of the deputy's ears; again and again he slammed the head into the stone floor. With every sickening wet thud the deputy became more and more unrecognizable. His face disintegrated and his features became obliterated into a bloody pulp as chunks of flesh splattered across the unforgiving floor. Michael limped out of the door as quickly as he could manage. His sides burned and congealed blood crusted over his nose and mouth making breathing difficult. He heard the Sheriff's roar as his absence became noticed. He passed through the frosted double doors and out into the world beyond. He staggered down the stone steps and onto the street, barely able to keep his balance. Suddenly a car weaved its way drunkenly towards him accompanied by the screech of metal on metal as the vehicle hit the police vehicles in the parking bays. The car staggered to an uneven stop opposite him and the passenger door flung open. Michael stared in horror as Casper's face loomed at him from the backseat, his hands beckoning wildly.

"Get in" Thom yelled.

Michael turned in surprise towards the young boy sitting in the driver seat; he stared at Casper in the back of the car, thinking of the devils that you know, and then he stumbled into the car. Just then the crash of the Sheriff exploded through the double doors behind him; the sound drove him forward through the pain. Before he'd even managed to close the car doo the vehicle lurched off down the road, peeling away from the curb drawing hard disapproving stares from passer-bys.

"What the hell is he doing here?" Michael shouted indicating angrily towards Casper in the backseat.

"You want to have a long conversation about that now?" Thom yelled back as the Sheriff hit the sidewalk and raised a cannon of a handgun.

"Just go!" Casper yelled from the back.

"Watch out!" Michael shouted as they nearly mounted the curb and hit an elderly man as he waited to cross the road.

"Don't yell at me," Thom yelled, "I've never driven a car before."

"Jesus kid, pull over before you get us killed," Michael laughed with borderline hysteria.

"Hey, I'm starting to get the hang of it now," Thom said through gritted teeth of concentration, "Where are we heading to?"

"I've got to find Emily and then we get the hell out of here."

"No-one knows just what goes on behind the scenes here Emily," Mrs.

Thirlby said, "We all follow the rules and keep our heads down and the town keeps ticking, and so do we."

"Don't you care?" Emily said.

"More and more," Olivia sighed heavily, "As you get older, you find that you have more time to think. When the night comes and you can't sleep, you sit in the window waiting for the sun to rise again and your stomach sinks with fear and anxiety. I don't know just what greases the wheels and keeps this town turning, but it can't be anything good."

"So who runs the town? Whose hand is on the crank, is it Casper?"

"I would assume so, but whenever anything bad needs to happen, it's the Sheriff that shows up."

"That guy gives me the creeps," Emily shuddered.

"You're not alone there my dear."

"What do you think happened to Jessica?" Emily asked softly, her voice strained with worry, as her hands cradled her swell.

"They wanted her for something."

"For what?"

"I honestly don't know," Olivia's eyes dropped, "I wish that I did, so that I could have warned you, but it is one of the closest guarded secrets here."

"Well I'm getting my husband, and we're getting the hell out of here," Emily said rising.

"Where will you go, they're everywhere, they know everything, and you'll never get out," Olivia said with sorrow.

"Come with us, you can help. You don't have to be a part of Eden anymore," Emily said hopefully, "Help me Olivia," she said cradling her unborn child, "Help us."

Olivia stood up firmly with a broken heart, "Ok, I'll do what I can, but we have to be quiet about it."

Emily took the Headmistress's hand and they walked to the door. She squeezed the hand gently to express her thanks. Olivia gave a brief squeeze back before letting go to open the door and step out into the hallway.

"First things first..." Olivia began.

Emily had just enough time to scream as the loggers axe swung through the air whistling with murderous intent. The razor sharp blade struck Olivia between her breasts, and blood exploded out of the gaping wound as the honed metal edge struck bone with a clang before being wrenched free. Olivia turned to Emily, her face confused, startled, and waning by the second. Her eyes clouded and faded as she fell to the floor face down. A dark puddle began spreading out from beneath the body on the hardwood floor as Olivia jerked once, twice, before being still.

Emily looked up into the assailant's eyes; Sarah-Jane's once pleasant face was splattered with blood and gore; she hefted the axe expertly in her hands, and her expression was ice.

"Time to go Emily," Sarah-Jane said gently, "Time to go."

CHAPTER TWENTY FOUR

Thom pulled the car over and reluctantly switched places with Michael, he felt like he was finally starting to get the hand of driving and Michael looked in no fit shape to be doing anything, other than sitting. He glanced over at the writer; Michael's face was still a puffy mess. They had cleaned him up as best as they could by squirting the windscreen washing liquid onto a top belonging to his mother that they had found on the back seat. He quaked at the thought of just what his mother was going to do to him when she saw the damage that he had inflicted on her car. Working for Casper she often had cause to leave beyond Eden's walls and she was one of the few people in town who bothered to own a car. He had taken the keys from his mother's purse at Casper's suggestion; apparently Casper did not drive. Thom had damn near soiled himself when the town manager had crept up on him at the realty office. He had turned expecting to find a knife at his throat only to be greeted with a worried and concerned adult. Thom had immediately gone into denial mode, but Casper had waved away his protestations,

"Michael's in trouble," Casper had simply stated.

"What's going on?" Thom had asked.

"I'm not quite aware of all the facts yet, but suffice to say that Sheriff Quinn's finally gone off the deep end."

The mere mention of Sheriff Quinn had been enough to get Thom moving. He had first-hand experience of looking into the giant cop's eyes.

They had taken his mother's car and headed straight for the Sheriff's Department. They had just turned the corner when Michael had staggered out of the building seconds before the Sheriff charged through the doors. Thom had just enough time to see the darkening spread across the Sheriff's broad chest, it looked like blood, but more than would have come from Michael's wounds. They'd barely managed to pull away from the curb in time; Thom had risked a glance back in the rear-view mirror only to see the Sheriff pulling his gun. It was the act of drawing his weapon in broad daylight that worried Thom more than anything. Every dark deed in Eden was normally committed exclusively under the cover of darkness. Yet if the Sheriff had lost his own self-control then just what would that spell for the rest of them?

With the car stopped and pulled over on the outskirts of town and carefully secreted behind a large hedgerow, Michael whipped around furiously towards Casper. His face was swollen and painful and his top lip was split open and raw, "What the fuck is going on in your town Casper?" He growled.

Casper looked as though he wilted under Michael's anger; he held his hands up in surrender, "Mr. Torrance, Michael, please, we don't have time for this."

"Bullshit," Michael spat, "I just watched the Sheriff, **YOUR** Sheriff, murder two people right in front of me. He shot one in cold blood and smashed the other's face into the ground until there was nothing left. I've got a neighbor who is one minute making plans for the rest of her life, and the next she's committing suicide. And then her husband disappears off of the face of the earth. I spoke to a man who told me all kinds of juicy shit about you and your freaky ancestors and the next he disappears. We've got a psycho Sheriff on a killing rampage, we've got a very disturbing diary from a woman who apparently led our very lives before Emily and I moved here. We've got creepy graffiti sprayed all over town from someone who apparently doesn't agree with the town's philosophies. Thom's teacher conveniently commits another suicide, oh and a whole back catalogue of town deaths and disappearances stretching back decades," Michael stopped exhausted. His chest still ached from the heavy work boot kicking that he'd received earlier and his head still spun worryingly.

"We were supposed to be a perfect haven," Casper said in a small voice, "A true Eden, secluded away from the outside world and all of their problems. We wanted to keep everything perfect," he said, longingly staring out of the car window and off into the distance. "We set up an inner council in order to maintain the town, to keep undesirables out, through discouragement," he added quickly. "We're not monsters Michael," he paused, "At least most of us aren't."

"Quinn?" Thom interjected.

"Quinn," Casper said heavily, "Quinn was always one to take things too literally, I have long suspected that his methods were..., questionable, to say the least."

"Questionable!" Michael shouted, "He's fucking killing people you idiot, are you really going to tell me that you didn't know?" He asked incredulously.

"Not at first," Casper said; his gaze dropped low and ashamed, "I started to suspect that he might be going too far, but by then he ruled this town. I mean come on, you've seen him in action, how exactly did your standing up to him work out for you Michael? Have you looked in the mirror lately?"

"But you could have told someone, surely?" Thom pleaded.

"Who, precisely boy? We're stuck out here, miles from anywhere, you really think that Quinn wouldn't notice if anyone tried to speak against him."

"Hasn't anyone ever tried to stand up against him?" Michael asked, fearing the answer and not liking how Casper was looking towards Thom.

"Of course, but they are the ones who ended up in accidents or suicides, or just plain disappearing."

"My father?" Thom asked tearfully.

"I'm sorry," was all Casper could say without meeting the young boy's eyes.

"Where's my wife Casper? Where's Emily?"

"He has her."

Michael leant in towards the back seat, "And what exactly is he going to do with her?"

"Oh Michael, I'm so sorry," Casper said sadly, his voice breaking.

"WHAT!" Michael roared grabbing hold of the town manager's jacket roughly, tearing the soft fabric.

"He's going to take her to the square during the festival. He believes that the town's fortune and prosperity are tied to the ancient rituals of the past, according to the scriptures. I'm ashamed to say of my own family's writing, the land is made fertile by..."

"By what Casper, what?" Michael said releasing his grip and feeling his own heart sink.

"By sacrifice, sacrifice to the trees and the land, the blood of a mother and unborn child, the most pure of all surrenders."

"When?" Michael asked.

"During the Woodland Festival."

"You mean the whole town's in on it?" Thom asked disbelievingly.

"Heavens no," Casper replied, "As far as most are concerned the festival is nothing more than a celebration of our founding. Whoever Quinn has on his own inner circle will be present."

"Where?"

"You can't stop him Michael. Take the boy and run because he will come after you next."

"Where?" Michael snarled, "You tell me where Casper or so help me God I'll bury you at the side of this fucking road. You're going to tell me and you're going to come with me..."

"With us," Thom interrupted softly but with a hard edge to his voice.

"With us," Michael agreed, hating to but knowing that he needed all the help that he could get, even if it was from a skinny youth, "Now you're going to show us where they've got my wife and child."

Emily watched the town pass by deserted. There seemed to be a veil of mist that had descended over the resident's minds. The town square was decorated with large banners strung from the tree branches promoting the "Woodland Festival". The scene should have been one of typical town perfection but she was scared. Scared, not just at her abduction at the axe wielding hands of her supposed best friend, but also at the sudden desertion of the town; it was as though everyone had received a hidden signal to simply go home and sleep.

"Sarah-Jane, SJ," she tried again. Her friend had been silent since loading her into the back of the waiting car outside the school. The bloody axe sat slowly dripping on the front passenger seat besides its mistress. Her mind whirled and twirled in shock and she had to fight hard against the rising tide of emotions; her horror at seeing Mrs. Thirlby brutally slain in front of her and the betrayal of the one woman that she thought she could trust. She feared for Michael as well - where was he? Was he still alive? Her hands formed across her swell; most of all she was afraid for their unborn child.

They drove slowly as they headed through the residential homes and out towards the commercial downtown area, and all the while Sarah-Jane was silent. Emily could just see her friend's face; her eyes were glassy and distant, blood spots were crusted on her cheeks and she made no effort to wipe them away. Emily suddenly recalled a conversation from earlier when Sarah-Jane had spoken so surely about the fact that she would never marry the doctor, "Not now", she had stated firmly.

"SJ," she tried again, "Where's Dr Creed, where's Samuel?"

At the mention of his name Emily saw a soft tear trickle its lonely way down Sarah-Jane's cheek, turning the red stains a watery pink. But still she would not speak.

"Where's Michael Sarah-Jane, is he ok?" Emily strove to keep her voice steady at the mention of her husband's name, "Is he alive?" She choked.

"Everything's going to be fine Emily," Sarah-Jane's voice was robotic and toneless, her eyes never faltering from the road ahead.

"Where are we going?" Emily tried, hoping that if Sarah-Jane would engage then maybe she could talk to her friend who must be in there somewhere.

"To your destiny," came the enigmatic reply.

The houses soon passed. Emily had been desperately searching to find someone out in public whose attention she could have attracted, but there was no-one in sight. She thought frantically for a plan of some kind; she could attack Sarah-Jane, perhaps make her crash the car, but what about the baby? Until she knew for sure that they were in mortal danger she couldn't take the risk.

She watched out of the window and the view reminded her very much of their first day in Eden. That glorious day had been full of hope; their whole lives had stretched out before them rich with promise. She had wandered through the town square, pausing to cast her eyes over the window displays. The people had been so warm and welcoming; both Michael and her had been almost smothered by affection from virtual strangers.

"Nearly there," Sarah-Jane said pleasantly, "Not much further."

"Nearly where, SJ?" Emily kicked the back of the driver's seat, "Nearly fucking where?" She screamed losing her control. "Where are you taking me, you bitch?" She punctuated with more thudding kicks.

"Nearly there," Sarah-Jane said oblivious, "Nearly time."

Emily began sobbing gently. She couldn't help it, she wanted to be strong; she wanted to be a heroine in one of Michael's novels, but this was real life. She had witnessed a bloody murder right in front of her eyes and now she was kidnapped by a betraying best friend, and being dragged towards a destiny not of her own making. She wanted to fight. She wanted to scratch the eyes from Sarah-Jane's face, to pull the hair from her head in bloody handfuls, but all she could do was softly cry.

The car pulled gently into one of the few parking bays opposite the town square. The day had turned to dusk and the streetlights cast a warm glow across the lush green lawns. She could see people through the gloomy light. There seemed to be hundreds circling the square; dark silhouettes gathering ominously.

Sarah-Jane got out of the driver's door and Emily felt the car's suspension lift. She watched as her ex-friend walked around the front of the car to the passenger door, reached in and retrieved the bloody axe. Emily felt her heart race as Sarah-Jane opened the rear door and motioned her out.

"Please," she begged, "Please Sarah-Jane, don't hurt me."

SJ looked at her like she was mad, "Hurt you? Don't be silly Emily dear, why on earth would I ever hurt you?"

Emily looked at the blood crusted axe and the stains of Mrs. Thirlby that hung splattered across Sarah-Jane's chest.

"I would never harm you Emily, I love you. You're the most special person in this town," she said seriously, "We all need you, so very much."

She allowed herself to be helped out of the car and waddled her way towards the town square as Sarah-Jane held her arm with one hand and the axe in the other. They wandered slowly across the deserted road. All of the pretty store fronts were dark and empty; their quaintness now replaced by an air of sinister watching and waiting. The glass fronts were all laden with early closing signs due to the Woodland Festival. Emily had expected the town square to be teeming with activity and life, but there was only a hushed silence. Whatever the Festival was it was apparently a quiet and somber affair.

"Everyone's here," Sarah-Jane said happily, "They are going to be so glad that you came."

"Who's here Sarah-Jane? Who's waiting?" She pointed towards the ominous dark audience.

"Everyone that's anyone," she replied

Eventually they came to the centre of the throng, they passed through almost everyone that Emily recognised from the town, and the friendliest faces were suddenly glazed and distant. The wooden, hand carved bandstand that had held such family friendly events throughout their short time in town now looked imposing and threatening. Emily could see several figures standing patiently around a wooden table under the structure. The table was carved from tree trunks and adorned with thistles and brambles. Twisted branches curled around the sides like serpents and blood red roses sparkled in amongst the dark thorns.

There were three men standing with their arms behind their backs and welcoming smiles on their faces; she recognised all three. Sheriff Quinn stood proud in a fresh and pressed uniform. Eddie the tram driver wore a long white robe with gold braided trim that was matched by Morgan, the deli owner.

"Mrs. Torrance," Sheriff Quinn boomed warmly, "Welcome, it's almost time."

"Almost time, almost time, almost time," the other three chanted as a whisper. The words soon became leaves on the wind as the gathered crowd took up the chant. Emily felt hysteria rise and threaten to consume her whole. No-one would look her in the eye and every expression was vacant.

"Help me," Emily sobbed "Please, please," she looked around desperately for aid, but none was forthcoming.

Sarah-Jane prodded her forward with the axe handle and Emily stumbled. She looked at the hand crafted wooden table; it was long enough for someone to lie on and there were leather straps connected, one on each of the four corners. She looked in terror as she got closer and saw that the table top was stained with dark maroon colours. It also had several ferocious grooves dug deep into the wood, grooves that looked about the size of an axe head. She began to scream.

Michael drove back into town carefully; his battered face was painful and felt huge and swollen. His right eye was puffy and almost closed and his lip was grotesquely engorged making talking an arduous task. Despite his injuries he still felt safer driving the car; Thom had about ten minutes worth of experience and Casper had apparently never driven before in his life. Michael felt that crashing into a tree was perhaps not the greatest way to begin a rescue attempt. His stomach churned with an acidic torrent; his wife and unborn child were out there somewhere having God knows what done to them, and it had been his Nancy Drew investigation plans that had led to this. His guilt was overpowering. He'd put them all in peril by leading them down a road of real dangers whilst caught up in his literary world. All the while when they had been discussing ways in which to find the truth about Eden he had been thinking about the book - he book that would flow from all of this; the true story bestseller that would land with a statement. But look at them now. He was busted to shit, Thom was on the run for his life, Sarah-Jane and the doc were God knows where and poor sweet Emily carrying their child was in mortal danger; of that he was sure.

"Are you sure that this is the right way?" He asked Casper angrily.

"Yes, the town square is where they will gather, beneath the wooden bandstand. Haven't you learnt that by now Michael? It's all connected to the forest and their dark bounty. They own us. Every myth, every legend. It all dates back to those damn trees."

"What are they going to do with Mrs. Torrance?" Thom asked nervously.

"I'm scared to think child," Casper replied in a small voice "At this point I just don't know what Quinn is capable of anymore."

Michael pulled the car over; they would have to approach the town square on foot. Due to the severe lack of cars in town, any car approaching would shatter the silence and notify everyone of their intentions.

As they all began to walk stealthily his heart wept for Kurt the poor deputy; another that had suffered because of his arrogance. He had watched Quinn shoot the man down in cold blood, blowing his innards all over Michael's kitchen floor and all because Michael had gotten the man involved. All he could hope for now is that he might have the chance to live to regret his own actions.

The town seemed deserted. Every house window was black, curtains were drawn against the night and prying eyes; sleeping minds and sleeping thoughts, distant from the events outside. They edged their way through the darkened neighborhood. Michael had been prepared for the masses to be out in force but the streets were bare and dark.

Through the darkening night they crept. Michael felt Thom's apprehension but was relived for the company. Casper's presence was a surprise but Michael knew that his cavalry charge was severely depleted but nevertheless, he needed all the help that he get.

They eased into Main Street and past the row of stores that surrounded the square. Michael could just make out the silhouettes spread out across the lawns. Dark figures stood huddled and motionless, illuminated only slightly by the gentle glow of the streetlamps and strung fairy lights, hoisted especially for the festival.

"Jesus, there's hundreds of them," Michael whispered nervously.

Casper dipped into his pocket, "Maybe this will help," he drew out a smallish silver revolver and handed it to Michael.

Michael took the gun. Despite being relatively small, it was still surprisingly heavy. Michael had never handled a gun before, but there was something reassuring about the weapon. "So where do we go?" He asked Casper, still testing the gun's weight in his hand.

"We go towards them I suppose," Casper said pointing at the gathering.

Michael looked across at Thom; the young man was firm and steady, his eyes were focused and devoid of the sort of panic that Michael himself fought against. Casper looked pale and nervous and Michael couldn't blame him. Whatever the purpose of the Festival was, it was surely something to be feared.

Michael paused and looked long and hard at the large gathered crowd, his feet refusing to move forward despite the urgent need.

"I know that you must be scared Michael, I understand, I truly do, but Emily is there with your child," Casper said moving closer to Michael and whispering in a strangely seductive tone in his ear. "After already losing a child once, I don't think that you would want to go through that again. That car coming out of the darkness when poor Emily was all alone in the darkness. All of that pain and guilt that you carry, knowing that you could have saved your child once before, can you really afford to make the same mistake again?"

Michael felt his feet move forward. Casper was right, he couldn't lose another child, he couldn't be responsible a second time.

He began to drift forward and the trees loomed up to greet him. He crossed the road, the asphalt giving way to the wet grass. His mind was drifting and his focus was waning. An unwelcome hand tugged at his arm. He shook off the annoying interruption.

"Michael?"

A soft voice permeated the gloom around his thoughts; he ignored it and began to cross the open grass.

"MICHAEL!"

The voice insisted again, the tugging harder, *leave me alone*, he thought, Emily needs me, my baby needs me.

"MICHAEL!"

This time the shout was punctuated with a loud slap and a cry of pain. Michael suddenly looked back. Something was wrong, something was off, but he couldn't think; his mind was a foggy haze. Something someone said was wrong. Suddenly the seas parted and the sky cleared, and all of a sudden he could think again. "Casper," he said raising the gun up to shoulder level "How did you know about the accident? How did you know about us losing the baby back in the UK?"

"You must have mentioned it in passing I suppose," Casper answered, his voice a little shaky.

"No, I don't think so; I rarely talk about that to anyone. It's the guilt you see; I have always blamed myself for the accident. It's a twisted, knotted, rotten secret that I keep hidden, buried in my basement festering in the dark."

"Emily must have told me then. What is this Michael? Time is wasting here whilst you play twenty questions, we need to move."

"It's possible I suppose," Michael said standing rock still, the gun still leveled, "It's possible, but I don't think that she did. It's in your eyes, you're lying to me Casper and lying badly," Michael cocked the revolver; he had seen enough movies to know that such a weapon had a safety on the side and that you had to pull back the hammer.

Casper stared back at him for seemed like an eternity, his face creased as he sought an answer, "Well I guess that she didn't then, you really are proving most problematic Michael, you and your merry band."

Michael glanced over at Thom; the young man's face was showing a red handprint on his cheek from where it had been struck violently.

"I suppose that it has been such a long time that I've forgotten what it is like to have to expend any sort of energy. Even with all of my experience, I suppose that I need a little reminder about the sins of pride and sloth. I thank you for that Michael, I truly do."

"Why did you bring us here Casper? Why the charade?" Michael asked.

"Just a little housekeeping my dear boy, we've got to keep things neat and tidy. Everything and everyone in their place. You see this town has grown complacent, the people here have forgotten just who it is that keeps the lights on. I thought that it is time for a little public exhibition; it's been so long since I have preached to a crowd. All of this cloak and dagger stuff does grow so very tiresome."

Michael tensed as Casper took a step towards him; he gripped the gun tightly and aimed with great care, "Stay where you are Casper."

Casper took another step.

"I'm warning you, stay back," Michael said again, his fingers tensing on the trigger.

Casper took another step smiling broadly with his hands linked behind his back, "Are you really going to shoot me down in cold blood Michael? Do you really have that in you?"

The hammer snapped down loudly in answer, Michael tensed himself for the explosion that never came as the hammer hit an empty chamber. He pulled the trigger again over and over as Casper walked towards him, but every chamber was empty.

"Did you really think that I would give you a loaded gun?" Casper laughed loudly.

Michael hated himself for his judgment. Everyone in town had told him in one way or another that nothing happened in Eden without Casper's knowledge or consent.

"THOM, RUN!" He yelled before throwing the gun and launching himself at the town manager. The silver revolver glinted beneath the soft streetlights as it flipped end over end. With a primal growl somewhere deep in his throat Michael followed the weapon's path. Casper was older and looked healthy but frailer, and Michael flung his full weight into the white haired man. It was like hitting a redwood trunk. Michael bounced off of the man like a rubber ball thrown against a building, his already severely damaged ribs howled in pain and protest as he hit the ground. He looked up at Thom who was still rooted to the spot, "Run," he whispered to the youth, "Please."

Suddenly he was lifted off the ground with ease. Michael looked down into the eyes of Casper; they were eyes full of power and madness, and then he was flying through the air. The last thing that his conscious mind saw, before he smashed through the large delicatessen front window, was gratefully the sight of Thom running away as fast as his skinny legs could carry him.

Thom ran fast; his under-muscled legs pumping hard as he charged back into the anonymity of the dark streets. He cursed his lack of natural athletic ability. The last thing in the world that he wanted to do was to run away, but he saw no other option. He had watched as Casper had put Michael under some kind of spell. He had shouted and pulled at the writer's shirt to no avail; all that had bought him was a resounding slap across the face. Casper's hand had been smooth but hard; the blow was strong and undeniable, but suddenly Michael had found himself and returned just in time. Whatever Casper had overlooked had come back to haunt him big time. Thom had rooted for the gun to fire, only to be sorely disappointed. Casper's true face had been revealed ever so slightly when Michael had denied him his will and Thom had furtively peeked around the corners of Casper's mask. His face had briefly looked drained and gaunt; a face full of age and fury. Michael was a good deal younger and looked like he could handle himself, but Casper had flung him aside with inhuman strength and contempt. For the time being Thom could only pray the he was so far down on the relevance list that he had a little time on his side. He had to come up with some kind of a plan. Was there really anyone in town that he could actually trust anymore? His mother, a teacher, a town official? He instinctively knew that if he told the wrong person, then they would all pay the price.

Emily sat still and quiet on the altar; her tears and fear were beginning to subside. There was only so much panic that one person could emit before tiring. She wondered that if a person fell from a tall building, would they scream all the way down, or would there come a point when screaming suddenly seemed pointless?

Her mind searched desperately for a plan, any plan. Morgan the kindly deli owner who had often spoken to her warmly and with affection; Eddie the tram driver who always had a smile on his face and a friendly greeting and her supposed best friend now all standing guard over her. Their faces were slick with a sheen of insanity and there was a pungent, ripe, acidic odour that flowed from them. Their eyes were all glassy and distant and no-one would respond to her attempts to engage. The huge Sheriff Quinn leant against the side of the bandstand, his bulk a test for the wooden structure. The white robes that the three incumbents wore would have been laughable if it wasn't for her dire predicament and that of her child. She had seen enough movies to know that long robes and altars with restraints could only ever mean bad news.

The three men suddenly jerked to attention and a few seconds later the thronged and strangely silent audience parted and another tall man appeared. Emily gasped in anguish as she recognised the hopefully only unconscious Michael, being carried effortlessly over Casper's shoulder. Casper's eyes lit with delight when they met hers.

"Mrs. Torrance," he greeted her as though they were meeting under the most pleasant of circumstances, "So good of you to join us, I must apologies for the unpleasantness, a necessary evil I'm afraid." Casper placed Michael down gently upon the bandstand floor.

Emily could only stare daggers back, infuriated by the politeness almost as much as the situation. "What do you want with us Casper?" She said low and angry.

"Is that not clear?" He said smiling and looking towards the altar, "I would have thought that the more pertinent question would have been why."

"Alright," she said playing the game and praying for time, "Why?"

"Because you will be our savior Mrs. Torrance, or may I call you Emily?" He smiled.

"You can go fuck yourself," Emily spat, enjoying the recoil that the profanity produced.

"Really Mrs. Torrance, there is no need for such language," Casper aimed a powerful kick at the slightly stirring Michael who curled under the blow, "Why is it that we always hurt the ones we love?"

"No, please," Emily immediately pleaded.

"You will allow our little town to continue to thrive and prosper Mrs. Torrance. I'm sure that you have come to appreciate the sheer delights of Eden. Unfortunately such privileges for the many must come at a cost for the few," he bowed his head sadly. "We have created a utopia here, a heavenly haven for those disciples pure of heart and deed."

The crowd chanted in unison, "Pure of heart and deed."

"This is a place where we will tolerate no dissention to the word," Casper preached. "This is a place free of sin, free from the horrors of the outside world; let them wallow in their filth and decadence." He spoke with fervor and passion to the crowd beyond. "We denounce them as unbelievers; they are the forsaken, the lost, and the discarded. Our faith is rewarded in a fertile land under God's hand. We rise above the tides of man's blasphemy and they will be punished accordingly."

"We rise above," the crowd chanted in unison.

"Bullshit," Michael's soft and steady voice rose from his prone position on the bandstand floor, "What happened to my neighbor Janet?"

"An adulterous whore," Casper dismissed.

"And her husband, Chris, what was his richly deserved fate?"

"Mr. Beaumont proved to be a disbeliever, one who sought to usurp our authority, the authority of God Michael. You know, omelettes and eggs and all that."

"And Darnell?" Michael countered.

"A drunkard, an abuser of alcohol, hardly a pillar of the community," Casper answered.

"How many others Casper?" Michael said struggling to his feet, "How many others have you judged to fall short of your standards? How many shallow graves would we find in the forest?"

Casper waved a staying hand towards Quinn who had taken a menacing step towards Michael. "Ours is a community of God Michael" he explained as though speaking to small child, "We will not suffer the sins of the fallen; a pedophile teacher, a racist old woman, betrayers, adulterers, thieves, swindlers, addicts, abusers, BLASPHEMERS!" Casper yelled, his voice reaching strident preaching tones that echoed through across the square.

"Blasphemers," the crowd's joined voice rose softly.

"And what does that make you Casper, what can possibly be gained from killing us?" Michael yelled back his voice gaining strength.

"You misunderstand Michael, we are not here to kill you, this is not murder."

"Then what is it?" Michael said incredulously.

"Sacrifice," Emily answered.

"Exactly my dear," Casper said happily, "The earth must be renewed, the sky reborn and God must be worshipped."

"How the hell is this worshipping God?" Emily threw her hands in the air.

"Oh don't be confused by the teachings of your Sunday schools Mrs. Torrance. God is not a being of divinity and love. His is a desire for servitude and bowing; his is a demand for blood and sacrifice."

"Blood and sacrifice, blood and sacrifice," the crowd chanted.

"Blood and sacrifice," Quinn agreed.

"Then just take me, let Michael go," Emily implored.

"Not a chance you bitch," Quinn snapped much to Casper's obvious disgust. "I'm going to take my time peeling the skin off of that bastard, and then the little boy too." Quinn's eyes sparkled with sadistic glee.

"Sheriff, please," Casper cast a warning look towards the much larger man, "We will have none of that here, this is a holy place, a sacred place of worship."

"Sacred place," the crowd agreed.

"You are all out of your fucking minds," Michael shouted to the bowed heads of the gathered. "What's wrong with you people? Can't you see that this murder?" Michael scanned the audience for signs of recognition and life. "Wake up damn you, WAKE UP!" He screamed, "For fuck's sake, you must have your own minds, you can't agree with this madness."

Emily could see Casper flinch at the bad language and wished that Michael would be quiet.

"The lot of you are fucking certifiable. There is no God here, God is hell and gone from this place," Michael continued.

"Michael," Casper warned in a low angry tone.

"This place is damned Casper, Goddamned," Michael laughed.

"Sheriff," Casper instructed.

Shut up Michael, just shut up, Emily thought desperately as Quinn marched threateningly towards him.

Michael watched as Quinn walked closer, it wasn't much of a plan, but at least it was something. He'd staggered and swayed in an exaggerated fashion, and he was somewhat more recovered than he was letting on. He could never understand why in movies people would submit to digging their own graves; if you're going to die, then the only thing that you had left was how you went out. Quinn moved in closer, his confidence in his own massive bulk was overwhelming and entirely justified.

"You're going to eat those words little man," Quinn said with a cruel grin.

Michael was never one for the Marquis of Queensbury's rules and stepped forward swinging his boot as hard as he could possibly muster. His foot struck Quinn between the legs and the huge Sheriff's face crumpled in pain as he sank to his knees. Michael closed the space between them and lifted his knee stiffly into Quinn's face. He grunted in satisfaction as he felt the Sheriff's nose shatter under the impact, but the collision also sent shockwaves painfully up his leg. Quinn rolled onto his back clutching his face and Michael launched himself on top of the Sheriff. He landed hard, knocking the remnants of breath out of the bigger man. Michael grabbed for the large revolver on Quinn's belt and pulled it free, he rolled off and stood rather drunkenly, his head still feeling the after effects from his unconscious spell. He staggered towards Casper who had remained unmoving and unmoved during the brief struggle. He raised the heavy gun with difficulty. "Want to bet that this one's loaded Casper?"

"Oh my dear boy, bravo, such spirit, well done, well done indeed," Casper clapped sincerely.

Michael stared back at Casper. Despite the large and loaded handgun that he was currently pointing, Casper merely looked amused. Movement to his side caught his attention and he turned to see Eddie, the once friendly tram driver whose face was now a snarling mask of hatred charging towards him. Michael swung the gun towards Eddie. He thought briefly of his pregnant wife and their current situation and then he pulled the trigger. The explosion was deafening, even in the clearing of the town square. Eddie staggered backwards and fell to the floor. The bullet had struck him in the centre of the chest more through luck than any judgment and the coppery smell of gun smoke filled Michael's nostrils. He spun around to face Morgan, the welcoming deli owner who had fed them during the first few weeks of their arrival in town. Morgan took a step backwards under Michael's glare. Michael fired a second time, telling himself that these men had sought to murder not only him and his wife, but also their unborn baby and a cold reptilian rage filled him. The once friendly deli owner was flung backwards off of the bandstand and into the silent audience. The vacant eyed masses merely cleared a space for the body that now lacked a face. Michael looked over at Sarah-Jane the biggest betrayer of them all; she was huddled on the floor cowering before the violence, and she seemed to be no threat, at least for the time being. Michael looked out across the crowd; their faces were expressionless and the gazes were distant and far removed from the reality and gravity of the unfolding death that surrounded them. They seemed transfixed by a voice that only they could hear. Michael thought of the graffiti that had been sprayed around town, "Wake Up". If only they would, or could.

With Casper still making no attempt to physically intervene, he walked slowly back towards the downed Sheriff, the gun still raised.

"Casper?" Quinn said in a blood choked voice as he struggled to sit up and face the wrath.

"Oh yes Michael, by all means, we can never have too much bloodshed in his name," Casper said delightedly rubbing his hands with glee.

"Casper what are you doing?" Quinn pleaded as Michael loomed over him, "You can't let this happen, not after everything that I've done for you."

"Sadly Mr. Quinn, I'm afraid that we no longer have a position for you. You have grown sloppy and dangerously prominent in our town. Your little escapades are rather too messy for my tastes these days and I'm afraid that you draw a little too much attention to us. Look where we are now; some amateur detectives have pieced enough information together to put us all at risk. Driving women off the road, beating poor old ladies to death, all rather distasteful I'm afraid. But I do wish you luck with all of your future endeavors," Casper smiled gently.

"You can't be serious, stop him, stop him, you bastard, stop him, I've given everything for this town," Quinn begged.

"Not quite," Casper replied.

Michael pulled the trigger, at such close range the Sheriff's head disappeared in a red cloud. Michael kept the thought of his family close as he carried out the impossible. His nature repelled against his revolting actions, but he locked that sense away and thought of his family. With a final deep breath he turned back towards Casper. He risked a look at Emily; her sweet face was strong and she nodded through her horror, imbuing him with the knowledge of what had to be done. Michael lifted the heavy weapon one last time and walked back past the still motionless Sarah-Jane towards the ever smiling Casper. The gun seemed to weigh a thousand tones and his shoulder protested at the torturous effort.

"Tell me something Michael, would..."

Casper's voice was silenced by the gunshot; Michael had no more patience left for the ramblings of madmen. Casper's body fell to the ground with a large hole punched through the middle of it. Michael dropped the gun and went to his wife, "Emily, Em, are you OK?" He asked, worried as much by her health as how she might feel towards him after his actions.

Still sitting on the altar she grabbed him and pulled him desperately close; her vice- like hug almost crushed the life out of him and ground his damaged ribs together. It was still the greatest sensation that he had ever felt.

"Well now, wasn't that interesting."

Michael and Emily turned slowly back towards the rising Casper in terror; the hole through his chest was already closed; only the blood-stained mess of his clothing gave testament that it had ever existed.

"You know I've never been shot by one of these modern weapons," Casper said, retrieving the revolver from the ground where Michael had dropped it and turning it over in his hands. "It isn't all that pleasant to be perfectly honest."

"What the hell are you Casper?" Michael asked shocked and stunned.

"Oh please, call me Tolan; it's been such a long time since anyone used my real name."

CHAPTER TWENTY FIVE

Thom moved reluctantly back towards the open space and away from the safety of the dark abandoned streets. The only bright spot of the evening had been that his mother had answered her phone from the road. He had been calling her on and off for most of the day to no avail. She had purchased him a cell phone for emergency use only; although Eden had always been a safe haven, after the incident with Mr. Stark his teacher she had wanted him to be able to reach her at any time. When he'd finally reached her, he was relieved beyond measure to find that she was on the road. Apparently Casper had sent her away in his own luxurious car on important business to Hanton. He desperately hoped that she wouldn't return until after this whole mess was resolved one way or the other.

Whilst it seemed like most of the town were in attendance on the square, he knew that many others were turning in for an early night; inexplicably tired and sleeping the sleep of those with blind eyes turned. It was this dereliction of duty that had enabled him to creep unobserved through the unlocked stores.

He could feel the waves of crazy washing over him even at this distance and there was a large part of him that wanted to join them. He wanted to be saved, to worship. He wanted to belong and be loved. He angrily shook the invading feelings away with thoughts of his father. His father had been taken from him, stolen by the town and by Casper and he felt a very reasonable stab of anger and frustration. He was just a kid, just a skinny fourteen year old that had never gotten past second base and now he was expected to save the world.

The bottles chinked together worryingly and noisily in the backpack that he now carried. The liquids sloshed around in their containers he tried to carry carefully. The smell was unpleasant, as several spilled their contents into the bag, but he could only hope that it would work. He heard the four gunshots as he approached the square; whatever was going on there was clearly taking the full attention of the town. He could only hope that if there had been four shots, then hopefully that would not mean that they were meant for Michael and Emily. He found it hard to believe that so much trouble would have been taken to involve Michael and Emily in such an elaborate and theatrical setting, only to shoot them.

He had headed for the closest restaurant on Main Street, one that he knew carried a liquor license. The "Seafarer" was a popular eatery for many of the residents. It was one of the more formal restaurants in town, operating exclusively in the evening hours. As such it was one of the few places where people would regularly drink alcohol and one of their specialties was the extensive range of liquor coffees.

A thought had dawned on Thom; the entire town was dominated by the woodland, both literally and metaphorically. The town was founded by loggers; the original finances had all derived from the timber mill and the town revolved around those damn dark trees. Every building in Eden was a timber construction and the roots of the forest sank deeply beneath the town. Their twisted, rotting limbs took a crushing grip on the thoughts and minds of the people here and their influence was dark and unmistakable. This "Woodland Festival" was proving yet another indicator of the reach of the forest. The trees were worshiped, and Casper led the congregation. The forest was far reaching; it stretched to the heavens and was deep, dark and dangerous. But a forest was made of trees, and trees can burn.

He had found a large backpack in the staff changing rooms of the "Seafarer"; it was left in an unsurprisingly open locker. The bag was blue and held the logo of some football team printed on the side that Thom did not recognise. He had quickly scanned the bar area of the restaurant; he had pretty much zero experience with alcohol, but he knew that only some would be highly flammable. Once - what seemed like a million years ago - his father had taken them all to a restaurant back in LA for his tenth birthday. The evening had been a pleasant one; his parents had been happy and content in each other's company and the food had been his first attempt at an adult sized portion. The evening stuck out in his memory now, because at the next table the couple had ordered a flaming dessert. The Crepes Suzette had arrived amidst the oohs and ahhs of the surrounding tables and his father had explained to him that the orange smelling liquid was a Grand Marnier based sauce. He had watched in awe as the flames danced and swirled before the couple had eaten the sizzling crepes. He had searched the shelves of the "Seafarer" for a bottle of Grand Marnier. A single tear spilled onto his cheek as he thought of his father and he hoped to watch the flames dance again.

He now eased his way through the trees that grew thickly on one side of the square behind the bandstand, meaning to approach in a clandestine manner.

He peered through the thick foliage and saw the dead bodies lying strewn around a creepy looking table sitting beneath the bandstand. He could see two bodies dead on the floor and dressed in weird white robes, whilst a fourth female figure was moving ever so slightly, still alive. He could see the Sheriff or what was left of him; the head was largely missing, but the size of the body was unmistakable. Michael and Emily were close together by the altar and Casper was standing before them. Casper's white suit was massively stained and shredded down the front with what looked like blood, but he appeared unharmed and even jovial.

Thom reached behind him into the backpack that he had found at the restaurant; on closer inspection it was a faded Georgetown Hoya's logo on the bag. He had seven bottles in the bag. He had only been able to find two bottles of Grand Marnier, but he had spread the contents as far as he could. He'd mixed any other strong smelling liquid that he had been able to find - vodka, whisky, bourbon - had all been sloshed around together. He wasn't sure just what was the most flammable, but he figured what the hell, hopefully they would all burn. He watched enough television to have seen Molotov cocktails being hurled flaming through the air, whether during movies or riots. He had taken a large handful of paper napkins from the restaurant. He twisted the first one and dipped one end into an opened bottle, pulled it out and inserted the other end leaving enough sticking out to light. He repeated the process until he had seven deadly missiles.

He watched Casper through the trees and hatred filled his young mind, his father was gone, presumably buried in some shallow grave, unmarked and unvisited, all at the hands of Casper or one of his underlings. His mind was full of his father and rage; in that moment he no longer cared about anything but revenge. It was a childish notion, but he was still a child after all.

Emily stared at the man calling himself Tolan, "That's not possible," she stated, "You can't be Tolan, that would make you over two hundred years old."

"And then some," Tolan agreed with a smile.

"It's not possible," Michael added defiantly.

"Oh really," Tolan answered, "You can believe your eyes but not your ears?"

"How can you be Tolan?" Emily said.

"I told you Mrs. Torrance, this place is blessed by the hand of God himself, and I am his emissary. He speaks through me and I carry out his will on earth. Everything is possible here in Eden. I am afforded little luxuries in order to facilitate my work. Every true member of our little congregation ages slower, but I age but much slower than others. It is a gift. It is a sign that our town is protected by his hand, but we must refresh from time to time."

"Why me, why us?" Emily demanded.

"Oh you were selected specially Mrs. Torrance, we take great care here. Only the best and brightest are chosen and called."

"But we only came here after, after..." Emily began already fearing the worst, "You, you were responsible for the accident back in the UK, you took our baby," she spat.

"Well not me personally," Tolan laughed, "I'm not about to go globe-trotting joy riding random cars."

"But it was your hand wasn't it?" Emily stared daggers, "The accident, our baby. Why me?"

"Have you never done a family tree Mrs. Torrance? They really are most fascinating. I'm sure that if you go back far enough you will find that yours is a bloodline that intersects through our very first sacrifice. I was always fond of tradition. It only seems fitting. All that was required was for you to sign a contract of willingness; it's a pesky little clause that all sacrifices must be made willingly."

"But I never signed anything," Emily said defiantly.

"Ah, yes, a little subterfuge I'm afraid. Over the years it has become more and more difficult to find willing recruits," Tolan explained regretfully.

"Go figure," Emily said sarcastically.

"I know,," Tolan replied seriously. "Well I've found that a willing signature is all that's really required. As long as the intention is pure and the participant is agreeable, then it doesn't really matter whether or not people know what they are signing."

"The lease," Emily said suddenly understanding, "You had me sign a second copy of the lease on the day that we moved in, but it wasn't really a house lease was it?

"I'm afraid not," Tolan smiled.

"You signed a document without reading it?" Michael said incredulously, "Why the hell wouldn't you have checked it first?"

"I thought it was the house lease," Emily shrugged.

"Well guess what, it wasn't," Michael said testily.

"Is this really the time?" Emily snapped, nodding towards Tolan.

Tolan turned his attention to Michael. "You Michael are just the sort of man we need," he looked over at the near headless Sheriff, "We appear to have an opening," he smirked.

"And why exactly would I want to live here and work for you?" Michael asked in disbelief.

"Think about what I can offer you Michael; an endless lifetime of pleasures beneath a perfect sky, prosperity and luxury forever - well almost forever," he smiled, "Members of my inner circle can live a hundred lifetimes Michael."

"And all I have to do is commit the occasional sacrifice, starting with my own wife?"

"Exactly," Tolan beamed.

"Go fuck yourself, all the way to hell and back again, whatever the hell your name is."

"Well, you can't say that I didn't ask," Tolan said, his good nature unaffected. "Sarah-Jane, why don't you be a good girl and pass me that axe and we can get started? Time's-a-wasting I'm afraid."

Emily turned towards her former friend who stood slowly and doubtfully, the axe still hanging from her grasp. "SJ, what happened to Samuel? What did he make you do to him?" Emily watched as the doctor's name struck home and SJ began to cry softly, gentle tears falling onto to her puffy cheeks.

"I had to," Sarah-Jane mumbled softly, "You don't understand Ems, he gets in your head, he gets in there until it's the only thing that you can hear any more. The whole world stops turning and there's only him," she sobbed, "Only him," she turned to Tolan.

"Come come dear, let's have no more of this silliness," Tolan said motioning Sarah-Jane forward impatiently, "Give me the axe."

"Think SJ," Emily pleaded, "Think about Samuel, think about everything that you wanted with him. Think about everything that you dreamt of; a life, a marriage, children. Think about everything that they took from you. What **HE** stole from you!" She pointed at Tolan accusingly.

Sarah-Jane faltered as she stepped to Tolan. She looked down at the axe swinging in her hand as though she was actually seeing it for the very first time. Her mind caught glimpses of memory flattened and repressed. She had gone to the doctor's and found Samuel in the basement. She had startled him and he had screamed an inappropriately high pitched scream. He had laughed at his embarrassment, and then he had seen the axe that she was holding. His expression had turned to puzzlement before she had swung it, and his expression then became one of terror. Her mind filled with images of him falling; of the blood and death, all at her hands. For the first time in a long time her thoughts were her own, and she knew exactly what had been stolen from her, and by whom.

Emily watched as Tolan's face changed to bewilderment at this unexpected treachery. His forehead crinkled and his eyes lowered, "Give it to me, you silly girl," he commanded.

And Sarah-Jane did, the axe swung hard with the power of hurt, loss, love and betrayal. The sharp weapon struck Tolan powerfully in the neck; the honed edge buried itself into flesh and blood spouted like a fountain. Tolan collapsed to his knees, his voice gurgling and struggling as his throat was torn open. His hands clasping helplessly at the wound as it sprayed a red mist into the air.

Michael saw the chance for escape; he had no doubt that the creature before them would soon heal himself and rise again. After blowing a hole right through the centre of Tolan and watching it close before his eyes, all they had was to run. He was about to drag Emily away when a sudden explosion of movement from the trees caught his attention, he turned towards Thom as he burst forth.

Thom had watched in horror as the chubby teacher buried the axe in Tolan's neck. The blade sank itself deep and nearly severed the man's head. Thom had heard Casper's pronouncements about his true identity; he was claiming to actually be Tolan himself. He would have laughed at the absurdity of the situation if it wasn't for the gathered hypnotized masses; the bodies lying in strange robes and a man resurrected from a fatal gunshot wound. Thom's head was already too full of fictional nightmares brought to life. His mind narrowed his vision and selected only the path ahead and what had to be done. He struck a match from the pack that wore the "Seafarer" logo that he had taken from the restaurant. The napkin burst into flames instantly and he threw the bottle in a drunken arc with a panicked burst of adrenaline. The Molotov smashed into the wooden bandstand spraying flaming liquid across the roof. The flames jumped angrily and began great greedy licks up the pillars. The dark wood was suddenly ablaze and the bodies of Eddie, Morgan, and the Sheriff were soon being consumed. Thom lit more bottles and threw them towards the surrounding trees. Before long the whole town square was encased in hungry flames and choking smoke fumes. The effect on the crowd was sudden and violent as people began stampeding away from the spreading fire. Thom could hear moans and screams as the less athletic were trampled underfoot.

"Michael!" Thom yelled, waving towards him.

Michael caught sight of Thom waving frantically across the grass; he grabbed Emily and pulled her with him and away from the flaming bandstand. He looked back as Tolan was already struggling to his feet and trying to wrench the axe from his neck with a crimson burst.

"MOVE!" he snapped at his wife, dragging her painfully. Incomprehensively,

Tolan was already starting to look as though he was healing; the reason returned to his eyes which were now full of a feral rage. "QUICKLY! QUICKLY!" Michael screamed panicked.

They ran across the wet grass. The sky was now filled with thick black smoke and the heat was unbearable as the fire jumped from tree to tree, aided by an unusually helpful wind that had sprung from nowhere. Emily staggered behind him, running as fast as her heavily swelled bulk would allow. They reached Thom and Michael could see that the young man's face was shaken and scared, but he was still there. Michael grabbed him in a clumsy embrace and Thom buried his face in his chest. The stench of alcohol was overpowering but there was another odour mixed in; something familiar.

"Thom," Michael asked, "Is that gas I can smell?"

The night was suddenly shattered in an explosion that dwarfed the small town. Every face turned towards Main Street as the sky turned red. The fleeing crowd were suddenly driven into a mad frenzy as they bolted like wild cattle, scattering in all directions. Familiar faces were wild-eyed with terror and confusion. They clawed and kicked their way free from the flames and smoke, and free from the sudden intruding thoughts that threatened to awaken them from their slumber.

Thom had left the Seafarer restaurant with his bounty of flammable missiles; he'd also left behind a gift for the town - a gift from his father. He'd spotted that the large commercial ovens were on the gas mains and he had dragged the smallest one forward. He'd struggled with the weight but he had refused to be denied, finally managing to pull the oven a few inches away from the wall. He could then see that behind the oven was a metal flexible hose poking out. He had tried unscrewing the hose but the metallic cylinder hadn't given an inch. Growing frustrated he'd began kicking the connection frantically, knowing that time was already growing short. Suddenly the hose had given way and the unmistakable hiss and smell of the gas had assaulted his nostrils. He'd left the kitchen of the restaurant and paused by the bar. Taking one of the bottles of brandy, he'd spilled the contents over the wooden bar and left a trail towards the front door. He'd lit the liquid path and watched as the flames raced along the trail, engulfing the wooden bar counter. A stab of vicious anger filled him as he'd left; the wood behind him burned and waited for the gas to reach the flames.

Michael could only stare at the spectacle before him; the large building along Main Street was overwhelmed by the flames as they touched the sky. He could see the fire leap from one building to another, consuming ravenously as it danced. The buildings were all wooden in town and he could already see that the whole street would soon be ablaze and he felt the same vicious stab of cold anger that Thom had felt earlier.

The three of them began backing away from the figure of Tolan as he moved menacingly towards them under the smoky sky. Michael suddenly became aware that Tolan's healing had somewhat stalled. It seemed that the more the town burned, the more energy he lost.

"You got any more of those cocktails?" he shouted towards Thom who was staring at the slowly approaching town manager. Tolan's face was contorted with pain and anguish; his eyes were full of rage and maybe just a little fear. The gaping hole in his neck caused by the axe had stopped healing altogether and the skin flaps hung loosely and bloodily.

"Huh?" Thom said from seemingly a great distance.

Michael didn't bother to explain and roughly snatched the backpack away from the young man. The bag clinked joyously and he reached in and checked for ammunition.

"THOM!" He yelled again, "THOM!" He slapped the boy hard across the face, regretting the action but doing it anyway. After several murders what was a little slap after all? "We have to burn the town, the wood, the trees. It's what feeds him."

The trees that had so lovingly framed the picturesque town square, offering gentle welcoming shade from the sun were now all screaming with fire; the wind blowing the flames from branch to branch.

"Give me a bottle," Emily shouted as dark silhouettes ran around them beneath the canopy of thick smoke. The townsfolk who had greeted them so warmly now ran for their lives as the town burned for its sins.

Michael looked to his wife and loved her more than ever. Despite everything she was still fighting for them all. He handed her a bottle and a matchbook as another explosion ripped through the air. Michael looked back to see Morgan's Deli being swallowed by the fire. The flames had now spread alarmingly quickly and almost all of the store fronts were now being slowly devoured, as the wooden frames were quick to burn.

Finally Thom returned to the world. Emily grabbed his hand and Michael thrust the backpack back into his small arms. Michael pointed to the surrounding quaint colonial buildings on the square. "Burn them Thom," he snarled, "For your father Thom, burn them all."

Michael watched as Emily and Thom ran across the square towards the Town Hall. If nothing else, at least they were away from Tolan. Emily suddenly stopped and turned back towards him; he could see her clearly through the stampeding townsfolk and her eyes were bright, clear, and brave. She carried their child within her and he knew that she must survive this night no matter what. He raised a fist to his chest and pounded it hard twice. My heart beats twice now, he had told her years before; once for me and now once for you.

He turned away from her quickly before he succumbed to his instincts and ran to join her; instead he gave his full attention back to Tolan. The town manager was a revolting mess. His head leant drunkenly to the right as the axe that Sarah-Jane had buried had severed the tendons that should have kept his head upright. Blood no longer spurted, but now softly leaked from the open wound. White bone poked through red torn flesh and Michael's stomach lurched at the sight. Tolan's eyes were still alert and still burned with fervor. His mouth flopped like a fish on the floor and his words formed but could not exit due to the damage. Michael could see the axe still hanging limply in Tolan's grasp from when he had wrenched it free of his own neck. Michael felt tired; his whole body ached from the physical and mental assaults that his senses had suffered. His head was still dizzy and his breath rasped worryingly through possibly broken ribs. He had no strength left to talk, and none to process and understand the unfolding events. He had brought his family here; he had brought them to be safe, to begin a new life under the sun, and to live in happiness and safety. But all he had brought them was misery and near destruction. The blood of others was on his hands; just how many he would thankfully never know. All he had left was to fight, so he put his head down and charged. His last attack on Tolan had ended as swiftly as it had begun, as he had been thrown aside with contemptuous ease through a store window. But at least he could buy Emily enough time to get away.

He hit Tolan with his shoulder as hard as he could muster. To his surprise Tolan gave ground and staggered backwards. A clumsy swing of the axe narrowly missed Michael's head as he ducked more through luck than judgment. Tolan tottered around him in an awkward circle, holding the axe in his right hand, and his left gripped his own hair in an attempt to straighten his own loose head. To Michael's horror the wounds seemed to be closing slowly; the gaping hole in Tolan's neck no longer gaped quite as widely as the flesh knitted. The axe swung again, only this time the swing was more controlled and accurate as though more of Tolan's senses were returning. Tolan opened his mouth to speak again, but whatever words came out were drowned out by the noise of exploding glass as another Main Street store exploded. Michael took the opportunity as Tolan visibly sagged and he ran at the town manager launching a clumsy dropkick. He connected awkwardly and they both fell to the muddy floor. Michael scrambled in the darkness for the fallen axe; the flaming trees immediately around them had now burnt to the ground and the light had faded with them. His hands searched desperately for the weapon as a sudden powerful kick caught him in the shoulder and he rolled away from the painful blow. He could just see through the smoky gloom that Tolan had already regained his feet. He scrambled around on his knees, still searching for the missing axe. Another, more carefully coordinated kick caught him in his damaged ribs. This time it was much harder and he was punted a few feet away. He rolled onto his back and stared up at the blackened heavens clutching his tormenting sides. *Just a little help* he thought bitterly towards the heavens, *just a little*. He could see Tolan making for him again with murderous intent when the Town Hall suddenly went up; the explosion was smaller than the others but it seemed to have a larger impact on Tolan.

"No," Tolan rasped through his slightly repaired throat.

Michael stood on shaky legs and staggered forward; he didn't thank the heavens for the assistance as it had been provided by his wife, a skinny 14 year old, and a bottle of flammable liquor. He stumbled and his foot hit a heavy wooden stick on the floor. He bent down through the thick plumes of smoke and grasped the axe - *alright*, he thought, looking up, *that one's all you*. He looked back at Tolan who was now limping slowly towards him; the rage in the town manager's eyes was now replaced with a pleading pity. Michael hefted the axe; the weight was balanced and comforting and the sharp blade glinted in the flame light.

"Please," Tolan whispered through parched lips,

"I heard what you told Emily," Michael said in a tired voice. "You arranged the accident back in the UK. You had Emily struck with a car. You nearly killed her and you took our child, our baby, our son."

"It's not too late, you can still stop this Michael," he pleaded. "I can give you anything, anything."

Michael loomed over the staggering preacher. He raised the axe high and his arms shook with power fuelled by retribution. "Then give me back my son," he roared, bringing the axe down again and again and again.

Emily grabbed Michael's arm and pulled him violently; he was standing over a pulpy mess that had once been the town manager. His eyes were vacant and distant and his mind was finally shutting down. She had thrown the Molotovs until they were all gone and redundant. The whole night sky was now a thick fume colored blanket and the smoke burned her eyes and throat. The whole town around them seemed to be on fire and her feet repeatedly stumbled over bodies lying crushed in the mud; she was glad of the thick fog that obscured her vision.

She felt fuelled by a sense of power. There was a light that suddenly illuminated the now fume filled clearing showing a path to safety. A hand suddenly grasped her elbow and she swung around in the dark ready to claw the eyes of her attacker, only to recognise Sarah-Jane's desperately miserable sob-filled face. Whatever malevolence that had filled her friend was now gone, leaving only a crushing weight of guilt. Despite Sarah-Jane's striking down of Tolan when all seemed lost, she still felt a stab of hatred towards her, no matter what influence she had been under. Her friend had almost taken her life and that of her unborn child; it was an unforgivable betrayal and one that she could not forget. But along with the stab of anger there was also a slither of pity; Sarah-Jane had taken the life of Samuel Creed, the one hope for love that she had ever found.

"Thom!" She shouted desperately looking for the boy. She spotted him through the hazy light, "Grab SJ," she pointed. He grabbed the teacher and Emily was relieved to see that he was thinking clearly.

With her dragging Michael and Thom pulling SJ she led the way. She followed the shaft of light that showed her the way. She was not sure why she trusted this sense, but she did. Something good was guiding her now; it may have been largely absent through their struggles, but it was helping them now. She knew that they were blind in the fire; the smoky air engulfed them, and they had to get out from under the choking fumes. She led the way strongly as her legs burnt with muscle and potency. She pulled Michael as he coughed and spluttered, but her throat was clear and her mind sharp.

"Do you know where you're going?" Thom yelled through the darkness.

"I'm following the light," she called back.

"What light?" SJ mumbled her voice distant and confused.

"The light, the light in front of us," Emily said irritably.

"I don't see any light," Thom yelled.

Emily pushed on regardless; she could see the light and she knew instinctively that it was there, and it was there for them.

Eventually they passed out into the fields beyond the town. Emily turned back and looked at the rising inferno; the sky was black with smoke as the night was choked by the fire. As far as she could see the flames rose and touched the sky; it seemed like every building was burning and the heat even at this distance was unbearable. She turned to Michael. His face was bewildered and blackened and she looked deeply into his eyes and saw him slowly return. "Are you ok?" she asked, knowing that the question was questionable, to say the least.

"I think so," he said, before he began coughing violently and spat out a black mucus lump onto the floor.

She thumped him on the back until he got himself under control, "Are you ok?" She asked again.

"I'll be bloody better if you stop thumping me," he sat laughing on the outskirts of hysteria until he began coughing again.

"Thom?" She asked, "How about you?"

"I'll live," he said bravely.

"Sarah-Jane?" She asked reluctantly.

"I'm alright," came the shamed response.

"You saved us," she said to Thom. "We wouldn't have gotten out of there if it wasn't for you, either of you," she added looking towards Sarah-Jane

Thom looked tired, but proud; SJ merely looked at the ground.

"I don't know what you have done over the years Sarah-Jane and I don't want to. But somehow you are going to have to live with your actions. I only pray that Tolan took your memories to the grave with him," Emily said. "But there is a town down there that is going to need you and a lot of good honest people. Not everyone was under a murderous spell; I think that most people were just living under a fog that meant that they just couldn't see the woods for the trees, so to speak. We can only hope that Tolan's spell is broken and that the power died with him."

"What about the others still there?" Michael asked, "What if someone else wants to take over from Tolan or Casper, or whatever the hell his name was."

"If Sarah-Jane has her faculties back again, I'm guessing that hopefully others will too," Emily answered.

"You guess? That's not exactly very comforting," Michael replied.

"I have faith, faith that this town can rise from the ashes and live again," Emily replied looking out over the fire.

"Faith?" Michael asked inquisitively.

"It's all any of us can ever have," Emily said, turning and looking deeply into his eyes.

"Is that enough?" He asked placing his hand on their unborn child.

"Yes," she said smiling.

"What'll happen now?" Thom asked them both curiously.

Michael looked to him; his imagination shaking off the cobwebs and ticking again. "Are all the old folks going to drop dead? Will they revert to their real ages and crumble to dust on the town square without the protection of Tolan and the forest?" He asked Emily.

Emily looked at him with a well worn grin, "How am I supposed to know?"

"You're the one that led us out of there somehow. How exactly was that by the way?" Michael asked.

"Honestly, I've no idea," Emily said sitting down heavily on the ground; her strength that had been bestowed upon her during the escape was now waning fast. "Something just came to me. One minute I was feeling about ready to lay down and die, and the next I could see a bright shaft of light that I just knew we had to follow."

"You don't think," Thom said pointing up at the sky.

"Honestly I don't know," Emily replied, "It does seem a little convoluted that we were all brought here, all together at the same time. Maybe someone up there was tired of Tolan and fancied a change of management."

Michael and Emily looked at other, "There's only one thing that I know for sure," Emily said "We're moving."

The fires raged throughout the town. They leapt from building to building, destroying as they went. Raging infernos burned through the night aided by the fortuitous wind that carried the flames to the wooden structures built with blood sacrifice timber. Main Street was decimated; the pretty trees that lined the streets only served to carry the fire with effective and efficient ease. The fire was insatiable and burned with an intensity that seemed to act with an intelligent design. Town council buildings were destroyed, the commercial district was gone, as was the older residential areas. All of the areas that had been constructed solely with timber taken from the surrounding woods were ravaged and eaten by the fire.

By the time that the dawn light arrived, the flashing blue and red lights of emergency vehicles had finally arrived from the towns within driving distance. The first responders encountered a town gutted by the fire, and the surviving residents staggering around dazed and confused. There were over a hundred bodies on the town square, and many others were dragged from burnt out-buildings. Over the next few weeks the fire investigators were shocked to find that some buildings had been left untouched. Somehow the fire had just simply bypassed some houses. The flames had spread along whole streets, but had left odd houses untouched, but destroying neighbors on either side. One fire-fighter from nearby Hanton commented that the devastation could have been much worse if not for the downpour of rain that suddenly materialised out of nowhere. He remarked that he could not ever remember the weather in Eden being anything other than perfect sunshine; the rain, he'd said, had seemed heaven sent.

Eventually word spread nationally and the press coverage grew. The locusts descended and every corner of the town was illuminated. A picture emerged of a wonderfully quaint American town; picture box buildings and small town sensibilities untouched by, and untainted by the modern world. As is the way of the modern world, jealously soon turned covetous voices into cynical ones; Eden began to be viewed with suspicion and derision, and they became a subject for snide jokes and sneering. They became known as a real life Stepford, inhabited by inbred hicks and stuck out in the middle of nowhere. Rumors of everything from cults, to right wing extremists, survival nuts and everything in between permeated the national culture as many sought to justify their own lifestyles.

As the national spotlight beamed brightly, answers were firstly sought and then demanded, but none were ever satisfactorily found. Eventually the attention dwindled as the modern day attention waned and Eden began to pick up the pieces again, but the town was never the same again. The weather suddenly seemed changeable and seasons returned as did the cold and the damp. The economy began to take on the aspects of the outside world as investments fluctuated for the first time and the town found itself having to adjust to life in the real world. They were no longer the protected and the blessed; they were no longer the chosen and the righteous. Soon the unimaginable exodus came, as families moved out of Eden for the first time that anyone could remember; normally they were the desired and the sought after.

One June after the fire, a small skinny fourteen year old ran for class president. He lost in a landslide to the captain of the football team. He was derided and scorned for the defeat and found himself on the unpopular side of school. But strangely he was able to smile about his humiliation and subsequent mocking. It was almost as though he relished the everyday politics and genuine emotions of an everyday school.

EPILOGUE

Are you looking for a new start in an old style

ARE YOU TIRED OF THE RAT RACE, TIRED OF RISING CRIME AND FALLING HOUSE PRICES?

WE CAN PROMISE YOU A WORLD OF THE PAST,
A SAFE HAVEN FOR YOUR FAMILY.

A WORLD OF YESTERDAY, WHEN YOU COULD LEAVE YOUR DOORS UNLOCKED, AND YOUR CHILDREN PLAYING.

HERE AT SERENITY FALLS WE CAN TAKE YOU BACK TO THAT SMALL TOWN PERFECTION, ONE THAT YOU THOUGHT WAS ONLY A DREAM.

WHY NOT LET US MAKE YOUR DREAMS A REALITY.

Malcolm Pegg looked in disbelief at the images on screen; the mansion homes, the crystal blue lakes, the laughing smiling faces of happy families parading for the cameras, and all beneath the hot sunshine. Malcolm looked away from the computer and stared out of the window, depressed as the rain lashed against it regardless of the summer season.

His wife wandered into the room. She had her hands placed in the small of her back. Her stomach was already swollen with the pregnancy and she walked awkwardly with obvious discomfort.

"Take a look at this email," he asked her excitedly, "It just came through, and it looks almost too good to be true."

GATED II: Ravenhill Academy

It has been 10 years since the events in the small picturesque town of Eden. Lives were forever altered as two newcomers found the courage to peek behind the curtain and bring Tolan Christian's reign to a violent end as the town burned around them.

No-one was more affected than Sarah-Jane Mears. The once bubbly ball of good nature is now a shadow of the former woman she used to be. After travelling to try and find a new home she has eventually settled in Northern England. She has taken a teaching position at Ravenhill Academy, an exclusive private school.

But now there is a new student who has just transferred. A young American boy who is strangely familiar and oddly charismatic. As the school breaks for the Christmas holidays the harsh winter weather has cut them off from the outside world. Sarah is starting to learn that Ravenhill is an old building seemingly with a life and an energy of its own, one that is slowly stirring.

She is going to realise that not all lessons are learnt in the classroom and that some secrets won't stay buried.

"*Gated II: Ravenhill Academy is as good a suspense thriller as any written by the big name authors. Indeed, it could serve as the Indie Publishing Poster Child*" **READERS' FAVORITE**

"*If you read Gated & loved it, then I know you will enjoy this book. The ending leaves us with an opening for a third book which I'm sure is what you want!*" **HORROR NOVEL REVIEWS**

ABRA-CADAVER

*Winner of a prestigious **Indie Book of the Day** Award*

Tommy, Dixon, McEwen, PJ, and Alison were always a close knit group until Tommy's 12th birthday party. Tragedy strikes when a magic trick goes horribly wrong and a woman lays dead.

A local magician Albert Trotter is railroaded during a rigged trial and locked away. Forever protesting his innocence and after a vicious assault in prison, he is eventually sent to a mental institution in a catatonic state.

Now Tommy is 36 and heading home for the first time in over two decades, but he's not alone. Someone is slaughtering the residents of Denver Mills with magic trick themed murders and holding those involved with the Trotter trial in a steely grip of fear.

Tommy will have to find the strength to bring his old friends together as secrets and lies are exposed throughout the small town of Denver Mills.

Something evil is coming home, and they're bringing a whole new bag of tricks.

"The perfect slasher novel, someone make the movie! 10/10"
SCARYMINDS.COM

"This will serve to excite and thrill gore fans"
THE BRITISH FANTASY SOCIETY

"A suspenseful, on the edge of your sit, thrill ride. A great read that will leave you sleeping with the light one!"
FAERIETALEBOOKS.ORG

ASYLUM – 13 TALES OF TERROR

A Horror/Anthology Chart #1 best seller
& voted #5 on The Horror Novel Review's Top 10 Books of 2013

Blackwater Heights is a building with a long dark history, some of it is well known but more is shrouded in myth and legend. None more so than that of its founding father Horace Whisker.

Martin Parcell is an ex-journalist with shattered dreams of an author's career. Sidelined through a car crash's injuries, he finds himself forced through governmental austerity measures having to take a custodians position at a private mental health hospital. A writer with undoubted talent, but an author without a story.

He begins his new job deep in depression and drowning under waves of his lost dreams. On his first night he meets Jimmy, his elderly supervisor who has spent most of his life within the hospital walls. Jimmy is nearing retirement age and desperate to rest his weary bones. Jimmy offers Martin a way out for both of them, access to the background histories and stories of the hospital's patients.

A collection of 13 tales from the darkly disturbed minds of the residents of Blackwater Heights.

As the long night unwinds, Martin finds himself deeply troubled as the tales unfold before him and threaten to drag him down into their insanity.

"*Matt Drabble is nothing short of a genius when it comes to painting a picture of his characters. This novel was sensational! I started reading and couldn't stop*" **LITTLE BLOG OF HORROR**

"*Consistently very, very strong like Stephen King, or Clive Barker, there's simply no telling what the man will deliver in a package of this nature*" **HORROR NOVEL REVIEWS**

"*It takes skill to make the short story format work and Matt Drabble has mastered it as he is able to establish both character and story in a matter of pages while conveying a sense of horror and terror*" **REELYBORED.COM**

"*Turn down the lights, turn off the TV and cuddle up with these stories tonight - talk about being afraid of the dark!*" **BOOK FIDELITY**

AFTER DARKNESS FALLS VARIOUS VOLUMES

10 tales of terror & the macabre

A new horror anthology collection,
look out for future volumes

"Matt Drabble has come out with another winner. Ten terrifying tales guaranteed to make you shudder 5/5"
HORROR NOVEL REVIEWS

"Guaranteed to keep you awake at night, while fully entertaining you during daylight hours. 5 Stars"
READERS' FAVORITE

"MATT DRABBLE DELIVERS THE MUST HAVE UK COLLECTION OF 2013" **SCARY MINDS**

For more information check out my author page on Amazon

My website: **www.mattdrabble.com**

Look for me on Facebook: **mattdrabble.3**

Twitter: **MattDrabble01**

Printed in Great Britain
by Amazon

40347362R00159